FUR COAT NO KNICKERS

FUR COAT SERIES:
BOOK 1

C.B. Martin

POOLBEG

Published 2018
by Poolbeg Press Ltd.
123 Grange Hill, Baldoyle,
Dublin 13, Ireland
Email: poolbeg@poolbeg.com

1

A catalogue record for this book is available from the British Library.

ISBN 978178199-3170

www.poolbeg.com

About the Author

C. B. Martin was born in London in 1967 to Irish parents. She worked in the Hair and Beauty industry for over 30 years (where she gained much inspiration for her characters and anecdotes) before finally pursuing her ambition of becoming an author.

Currently residing in Hertfordshire, England, Caroline has three adult children (who are the lights of her life) and a wonderful long-term partner.

Caroline's debut novel, *Fur Coat No Knickers*, became a #1 Bestseller in Romantic Comedy and Fictional Humour, shortly after being released on the Amazon Kindle UK market.

Acknowledgements

It was my medicine when I got sick, my friend when I got lonely. My precious *Fur Coat No Knickers* couldn't have come this far without:

Editors: Teena Lyons and Domenico Marsala. Thank you both for believing in me.

Proofreaders/Copy Editors: Sandra Martin, Domenico Marsala, Christiano Marsala, Francesca Marsala and Martin Ouvry.

Cover Illustrator: Alex Furley of AF Designs.

I'd like to thank Mum, Dad and my beautiful sisters, whom I love very much.

To my sisters: you both mean the world to me. I couldn't have got through this without your continuous love, support and daily encouragement.

To my partner, S.I.: thank you for your patience and for still loving me while I lived in an atrocious fluffy red dressing gown for years when writing this, my first novel. And thanks for your patience when I screamed in frustration if things didn't go my way.

To my utterly bonkers best friends: don't ever change – I love you all. You know who you are.

To my dear friend, J.M.: without you, Franc (pronounced "Fronk") would have never existed. I miss you.

Lastly, to my three perfect children: I'm so glad you got

the beauty and the intelligence genes. Thank you for wiping my tears when my short-term memory blew its fuse. I couldn't be more proud of you all.

If I have missed anyone out here, my apologies, but I fully intend to blame my (bastard of an) underactive thyroid.

And finally ...

I would like to dedicate this work to Mum: the kindest and bravest woman I have ever known.

The following story is based on true events.

Chapter 1

I glanced up at the tinsel-covered clock; it was nearly closing time at the Glamma-Puss salon.

Just Siobhan's hair to blow-dry, a quick change of clothes, and I'd be off to the airport to spend, no doubt, another crazy Christmas with my family in Dublin. I couldn't wait. This break had been a long time coming.

As I counted down the hours to my big getaway, I could hardly believe that my London-based hair and beauty salon was about to go into its second year of business.

I had loved setting the salon up – although every aspect of it had been hard work. With a microscopic approach, I had thought carefully about every decorative detail, mixing contemporary with boudoir – soft mushroom accessories, cream walls and dark oak floors. I went to town with all the fixtures, mixing rich French curtains in shimmering taffeta with dramatic, swooping tails in a mix of silver and pale gold. The walls were covered in large baroque mirrors, with matching workstations – and, for the complete *wow* factor, flanked on either side by gold Bourgie table lamps was a gold leather chaise longue that took pride of place at reception.

I'd also been lucky enough to find a great team who complemented the feel of the salon perfectly. Jackie, my beauty therapist, was in her early fifties, quite tiny in height, with sharp, short, copper-coloured hairstyles. She was bubbly, bright, eager, and was forever upping her game, enrolling herself on the latest beauty courses. Her beauty room proudly housed framed certificates that climbed her walls like a beanstalk. She was great for business and was constantly stacked out with clients from opening to closing time.

As for my drama-queen nail technician, James, aged 23, he'd simply minced in like he owned the place.

"I am your right-hand man," he declared with a dramatic curtsey when he first came in for an interview. I instantly loved him; although, to this day I still don't recall actually advertising for a nail technician. He had arrived on opening day, white-blond hair waxed a mile high, clad head to toe in a neon-pink boiler-suit, and fluttered around like Miss World. He simply set up a portable nail bar with every colour of polish and acrylic you could think of and promptly hired himself. I hadn't been able to say no.

Then there was Jayde. Aged 20, she was short, curvy, blue-eyed and blonde. The definition of a rough diamond. A pure out-and-out Londoner. Despite this, from the moment I met her I could see she was passionate about hairdressing; she just needed those rough edges smoothing down a little. She needed someone to believe in her. So whilst she came across as a bit crass, I nonetheless felt compelled to nurture her and give her a chance.

I remember the day of her interview: Jayde had arrived an hour early, wide-eyed and eager to show me what she was made of. Clutching crumpled shopping bags, she asked if she could use the staff toilets to change. She emerged in a jacket and trousers combo that in no way formed a matching suit. Worse still, the price tags were dangling for all to see.

"If I don't get the job, let me know, cos I've still got the receipt for the outfit, see. Otherwise I'll just take it straight back to New Look," she'd said, unashamedly fiddling with one of her many gold-hooped earrings.

Inquisitive and unable to help myself during the interview, I delved deeper into Jayde's background.

Her mum had died of cancer when she was just three years old, and she never knew her dad. As a result, Jayde spent most of her life being fostered out. Luckily, her last set of foster parents had generously put her through college to learn the art of hairdressing.

Astounded by her resilience, happy-go-lucky attitude without a trace of *woe is me* in sight, despite having such a harsh start in life, I could see that she considered herself to be one of the lucky ones. Humbled, I felt compelled to tuck her under my wing; I went on to offer her a few trial days and made her permanent on day two. When I took her to one side and gave her the good news, she promptly burst into tears and squeezed me so tight I thought my silicones were going to rupture.

I was on a roll and was thrilled to be hiring another valuable member of staff. Sheila, an aesthetic nurse practitioner, joined us one day a month to perform a range of cosmetic skin treatments and non-surgical procedures. She was a 1940s screen goddess if ever there was one. Her signature retro hairstyles, siren-red lipstick and hourglass figure were admired by all who met her. She was the perfect candidate for my expanding business, adding another exciting string to my fledgling enterprise.

Of course, this diverse mix of staff meant there was never a dull moment at Glamma-Puss, and once you threw my best friend Siobhan into the mix, you'd never know what might happen.

As if on cue, a glass of red wine in hand, tinsel wrapped round her neck, Siobhan stumbled through the salon door. "Howerya, everyone. Meeeeerrrrrryyyy Christmas!" She loved an entrance.

"Hi Siobhan! On the sauce already, I see? You lucky thing, you. I'll be with you in five. James, take Siobhan's coat. Jayde, shampoo her for me, please?"

As I crossed the salon floor to have a word with Jackie, who would be managing Glamma-Puss while I was away, I could hear the usual rapid-fire banter begin.

"Hi James, howerya?" said Siobhan.

"Oh my! That's a rather gorgeous coat. Is it from the new Dior collection?" James asked. He stroked it as he hung it up, then stepped back, a hand planted firmly on each of his slim hips, and gave it a fuller inspection.

"What? That old thing?" Siobhan said with a dismissive swipe of her hand. "No, it's a Primani special, twelve quid outta the bargain bin! Does it look like a Dior coat?"

"*Actually,* on closer inspection, it certainly does not," said James. Repulsed, he turned on his neatly polished slip-ons and pointedly distanced himself from the offending garment.

Jayde was bent over laughing, slapping her thigh in hysterics. "I fort you gays were meant to know your designer labels?"

"Get on and do your job, you filthy little scrubber," James shot back.

Siobhan pulled an awkward face as Jayde gowned her up. "James seems a bit grumpy today."

"Ignore him, he's been a whiny bitch all day," said Jayde, without an ounce of discretion.

"Jayde!" said James. "Had *you* not made such a catastrophe of my crowning glory, I wouldn't be so upset!" He pawed at his peroxide hair in the mirror. "You've completely annihilated my asymmetrical fringe for the party season!"

"Ah, come on now, James, your hair is – well – it's lovely." Siobhan knocked back the last dregs from her glass of wine and smacked her lips together before leaning her head back into the washbasin.

James tisked in protest. "Siobhan, you of all people should know me better than that! I don't do *lovely* – I do *fabuliscious* or *magnificent!* How can I do my blond-with-strategically-placed-violet-tips hair flick now my fringe no longer rests on my high cheekbones? That is *sooo* the point of asymmetrical-ness," he ranted. "It's simple; it *all* has to be perfect – something you don't know the meaning of, Jayde. It's all about tight-arsed glory!" He barely paused to breathe as he swung around, wiggled his tush and threw his tall but tiny frame into a *slut drop* (this being one of his best party tricks. The clients loved it).

I watched with raised eyebrows as James went full *performance-mode*. "*This* has to resemble a piece of *art*." He swept his hand theatrically down his body. "Do you think this all comes naturally? *No*, no – it does not! For example – *if* I may continue?" He glared as Jayde began to mimic him. "These freckles, or, as I prefer to call them, *clustered beauty spots*, have been cleverly blended by one of my bestest friends. *No*, not you, Jayde - the sunbed! Artfully amalgamating them through years of baking and frying oneself has giveth *moi* a sexy tan, and *violà!*" James lifted his Jean Paul Gaultier floral shirt, revealing a toned, tanned and boyish body. His freckles had indeed joined together to give the illusion of an even tan.

It had to be said: he was such a pretty boy. His feline features accentuated his continual purr of pride as he performed to his captive audience. In fact, I'm sure some clients booked in just to watch *The James Show* rather than for a particular treatment. The James Show nearly always included dramas about his latest love conquest; or the highs and lows of whichever *rubber-arsed bastard* had broken his heart this time. The gossip of his constant sexual onslaughts was complicated, dramatic and thoroughly entertaining, to say the least.

Having such strong personalities in our den of madness inevitably meant there were frequent clashes in the ranks. With everyone else, James had a carefully crafted diva-type personality, but when it came Jayde, he was different. Cut-throat. It hadn't gone unnoticed that when *he* felt the scales of my attention tipping in Jayde's favour, out came the claws. He was brutally vocal about her, claiming that I'd been blindsided by her pity story and that there was something dark and untrustworthy about her. *Which of course there wasn't,* but James was having none of it and he most certainly wasn't swayed by pity for her tough upbringing.

Jayde, for her part, was used to fighting her own battles. She made it clear from the start she wasn't going to tolerate any flak and so gave back as good as she got.

The resulting confrontations were highly entertaining, as long as you didn't listen too closely. Now and again, though, I had to catch my breath in wonder at how they could speak to each other in such a spiteful manner.

Of course Siobhan loved to disturb the peace, so she lobbed in the odd verbal grenade if she ever sensed hostilities between the pair were flagging.

"So, James, have you been in receipt of any *swollen* goods lately," she asked, her voice full of innuendo.

"Hmmm ... it's a sore subject," said James. "I'd rather not talk about it now. Well, certainly not in front of *her*." He narrowed his stare in Jayde's direction.

"Might dat subject be your arse, you dirty fecker?" chuckled Siobhan, while Jayde massaged shampoo into her hair.

"Keep your 'ed back, Siobhan. I can't wash your locks wiv all your moving around!" said Jayde.

"Sorry, but this is even better than the *The Jerry* feckin' *Springer Show!*" Siobhan leant forward mid-hairwash, retrieved a bottle of red wine from her handbag and took a generous glug. Belching, soapsuds dripping down her face, she settled herself back while me, James and Jayde stared at her open-mouthed.

Watching her banter with Jayde and James, I was reminded of the day we first met. Effervescent as ever, Siobhan had burst into the salon wearing a tacky peach bridesmaid dress, her face covered with a bouquet of plastic flowers, demanding a pot of wax. I had a hard time understanding her through the foliage, but in a broad Irish accent she was mumbling something about being *mortified*, with a few *feckers* and *gobshites* thrown in. Detecting my bewilderment, she'd whisked the bouquet from her face and gave a fuller explanation.

"I didn't want to go to the poxy wedding anyway. I was only going for the free bar!" she ranted, as though I should know what the hell she was talking about. [Sobbing] "There we were, me and this fella, all ready to go to his cousin's *stupid* wedding, when the gobshite started eyeballing me – all strange, like. He turns round to me and says, 'You've a moustache when the sunlight hits your face.' Then he says, 'I don't know whether to fight you or fuck you.' He thought it was hilarious!"

At the time, I had to turn round as I couldn't suppress the grin on my face. I managed to say that Jackie would be able to sort her out, but when I saw Siobhan pawing her top lip and imitating a male voice, I couldn't hold back any longer and burst out laughing. Luckily, she cracked too, and soon enough the tears were rolling down our faces. And that was it; our friendship was made from that single moment of madness.

With the racket everyone was making, I couldn't think straight.

"James, Jayde – c'mon, you guys, it's Christmas Eve! Where's your sense of forgiveness?" I signalled Siobhan to come take a seat so I could blow-dry her hair. "Why can't the pair of you call a truce?"

I watched them eyeball each other. James's jaw tightened. Jayde's eyes hardened.

Jayde was the first to offer an olive branch. "I dunno, James, you'd nearly be alright if you stopped snorting that nail acrylic stuff."

"You uneducated bitch!" James responded. And in an instant, hostilities had resumed. "I'm a designer nail technician, getting high off the fumes is part of my job!" he snapped.

"It's gone to your 'ed," said Jayde. "I'm telling ya! I mean, you could totally do with sorting out that fake tan of yours. You look like a malnourished Oompa Loompa."

James's eyes flared. "Much as I'd like to thank you for that compliment, Jayde, I'd like to point out that your pores are so diabolically huge they should be paying council tax!"

"Ho-Ho-Ho!" said Siobhan, like a referee Santa Claus. "Round two, ding-ding-ding!"

"James, Jayde," I pleaded, "stop. And Siobhan, stop encouraging them!"

"Ah, c'mon now," she responded, "there's no customers in, and we're only playing."

I rolled my eyes to the heavens and switched the hairdryer on to drown out the lot of them.

Is this what I've really signed up for? A life of keeping this lot in place?

I began to daydream …

I should have a rock-solid, gob-smackingly gorgeous husband by now, who dotes on me and our perfectly behaved children. We'd name them Hugo, Tommy and Mercedes. They'd attend the finest schools. Hubby would be here, with me, right now, keeping this lot in order, but only after he'd finished preparing a three-course Michelin meal that would be waiting for me when I got home. Yes, he'd be a top chef, I mused to myself. *Not one who screams and shouts and loses his temper, although Gordon Ramsey telling me to "get my fucking head down" on him would be nothing other than an absolute pleasure.*

I digress, where was I? *Ah yes, my husband would be so*

successful he didn't have to work over Christmas. He could even have retired, very young. Actually, scrap that, idle minds equal idle hands, we don't want them wandering ... No, wait ... we'd have a nanny! A live-in nanny. A butt-ugly one, that's very important. She'd have warts – not genital warts or anything like that, but decent sized facial warts – with sprigs of pubic-like hair darting around. A Nanny McPhee type. Yes, that would be perfect.

We'd remain in London – live a posh mansion – in Hampstead. Our home would have to be huge because it would need to house, amongst our brood of children, a humongous Christmas tree – a real one. It would be decorated traditional-style, with fairy lights, all white and twinkly, and huge red-velvet bows.

We'd decorate the tree together as a family. I could see my gorgeous husband lifting our eldest, Tommy, to place the angel on top ... No, wait, Hugo would be our eldest; Tommy could turn the lights on. But then Mercedes might feel left out. Gosh, being a parent is difficult. Perhaps I should just have two children? I've got it! Even better: I'm pregnant with Mercedes! I'd be a vision of fertile loveliness for the festive season.

"*Ouch* – that's hot!" said Siobhan. "You're scalding the head off me, woman!"

"Oh – sorry! I was miles away."

As I was adding the final touches to Siobhan's hair, Jackie was effing and blinding in the staffroom.

Switching the hairdryer off, I called out to her.

She looked wretched as she stormed over. With red blotchy patches creeping up her neck and onto her thunderous face, she pulled me to one side and passed me her phone.

[Text from Pete]

Hi sexy, can't wait to see u tonight. Wear that new underwear I got u :-) xxxxxx

"Oowh, lucky you." Unsure of where this was going, I handed Jackie back her phone. "Sounds like you're on a promise with hubby tonight!"

"Pete said he was working late tonight!" Her face contorted as angry words spat from her mouth. "And, he hasn't bought *me* any new underwear!"

My heart sank. *Working late on Christmas Eve?* I deliberately tried to avoid eye contact with Siobhan because I knew she'd been eavesdropping and this didn't sound good.

"I'm sure there's a reasonable explanation," I said, as brightly as I could. "It'll be one of his work colleagues messing about with his phone or something."

With jerky, angry movements, Jackie wound her scarf tight round her neck and did the buttons of her coat up, before furiously fumbling in her bag in search of her gloves.

I didn't know what to say, so I tried to give her hope.

"I bet Pete's phone has been hacked. It happens all the time. Try not to worry until you have the facts." I rubbed her arm. "They'll be a logical explanation. Promise."

"For our children's sake and our twenty-five-year marriage, I hope you're right."

With my arm around her shoulder, I walked Jackie to reception, reached into a drawer, pulled out the salon's spare keys and handed them over, along with her Christmas bonus.

"Thanks for all your hard work this year."

She was miles away. Unresponsive. Her expression riddled with shock.

"Get yourself home and call me if you need anything. *Anything*, okay? Day or night."

I gave her a hug. I could tell she was desperately trying to hold it together - and get outside, so she could unleash the huge volley of sobs.

She nodded, forced a smile. "Enjoy your family Christmas, Tara. Bye, everybody, Merry Christmas."

Opening the door with what looked like the weight of the world on her shoulders, she stepped out into the cold Christmas Eve night and disappeared into the darkness.

I made my way back to Siobhan and started spraying her hair into place. "There's no way Pete would play away. He wouldn't do that to her, *would he*?"

"Well," she said, "Pete *is* in his fifties, and didn't you tell me he recently bought himself a mid-life-crisis penis-extending set of wheels?"

"Siobhan!" I chided, tapping her on the head with a tail comb. "It's just a car." Quietly, though, I conceded to myself: she did have a point. But I shook my head. "They were childhood sweethearts. They've been married for forever." I removed Siobhan's gown. "They were the perfect couple, *weren't they*?" What hope did the rest of us have if those two couldn't make it!

"Ah Tara, c'mon now," said Siobhan, "Jackie has five kids! She must have a fanjita like a clown's pocket!"

"She hasn't got five kids, she's got three. And do you have to be so crude?" Tutting, I handed over her coat.

I was just about to launch into a lecture on the sanctity of family life when James and Jayde flew over.

"We couldn't help overhearing – what's going on with

Jackie?" Jayde asked.

"*Nothing* is going on."

"Pete's cheating on Jackie, fucked her over good and proper," said Siobhan.

I whirled round and snapped at her. "Shoooosh!"

After a collective gasp, the salon momentarily fell silent.

James shooed a shocked Jayde away and in true narcissistic style, turned the conversation to himself. "Pete's a naughty bugger! And talking of naughty buggers, my new hot piece of man-candy has fallen off the *gaydar* system and gone icy-cold on my little behind. It's put me in such a foul mood! I keep texting him and he's not replying. It could have something to do with what he said about being *confused* – but I've told him, his undercarriage is for men only! It's just ridiculous!"

Forgetting about poor Jackie, Siobhan was all ears.

"I mean, how could *anybody* be confused after a night like that with *moi?*" James continued, raising his manicured hand to his chest. "I might need to give *him* the silent treatment so he realises what he's missing."

James readjusted the fluffy halo he'd been resolutely wearing in the salon throughout the run-up to Christmas. "But how do you give a man the silent treatment when he's the one being silent? It's *so* hard."

"How *hard?*" Siobhan asked, one eyebrow suggestively raised.

"He's so sexical, you know. Sex on a stick. And don't get me started on what he keeps in those tighty-whities. I could ride his disco-stick *all-night-long.*" With that, James threw back his head and laughed uproariously while treating us to a little wiggle of his leather-clad bum.

"So wait, back the feck up. You said he was confused?" queried Siobhan.

"Well, he's only recently discovered that *gay is the way* after I showed him the night of his life! But he has since *wrongly* decided that he isn't so sure!"

"NO! So he goes both ways …? He's bisexual?" questioned Siobhan.

"I'm talking five foot ten of toned perfection," James continued, ignoring Siobhan's hopeful conclusion.

"How many marks out of ten would you give him?" she pressed. "Oh feck it, I'm getting myself all worked up now!"

"Off the Richter scale," said James with a long, loved-up sigh.

"James, because I love you sooo much, I'll do you a favour and test-drive him with me fanjita for you, just to see what genitalia he likes best. That way you'll know for sure," said Siobhan conspiratorially. "I can't be any fairer than that, now can I?"

"Thank you for offering the use of your lady-garden, Siobhan, but I plan to keep him on the dark side," said James. "But happy Christmas, darling."

James and Siobhan were both clearly pleased with the exchange and finished the performance with an elaborate display of air-kissing on one another's cheeks.

"Happy Christmas to my best friend," said Siobhan. She threw her arms round me, locking me into a bear hug. "Don't be worryin' about Jackie, she'll be fine!"

My heart missed a beat thinking about what Jackie was going home to.

"I'll miss you so much when you're in Dublin," said Siobhan. "Be good, now. And if you can't be good, be damn good *at* it!"

"Happy Christmas to you too," I replied, squeezing her tight.

"See you on New Year's Eve! And James ... if you change your mind and want me to take lover-boy round the block for you, do let me know," she said with a wink.

With that, she sailed out of the salon, grabbing her fanjita and thrusting her hips as she left.

The salon fell silent again. It was always like that with Siobhan. She was such a blizzard of wit and wisecracks and energy that when she vacated it felt like a vacuum.

I was desperate to recover the festive feeling, so I retrieved James and Jayde's Christmas-bonus envelopes.

"James, where's Jayde?" I hid their gifts behind my back.

He shrugged nonchalantly, examining each of his nails. "*Umm* ... hopefully flushing herself down the lavatoire?"

"It's present time."

Motivated by money, James flew off to get Jayde like Speedy Gonzales.

"Thanks, Tara!" they both chorused, shoving their envelopes in their pockets while shooting each other evil stares after they'd realized they'd chanted in unison.

Jayde broke the tension. "I weren't gonna give you a Crimbo pressie, James; but it is the season of giving to the unfortunate."

"Well, well well, I got you one too." James passed her a beautifully gift-wrapped box complete with tag, bow and curled ribbon. Jayde then passed James an Aldi carrier bag, before unceremoniously ripping her gift open.

"Err ... so kind," he said, with a downward curl of his mouth. He was holding the bag with his fingertips as though it contained toxic waste. "I'll take mine home and put it under the tree *outside*."

"Wow, James! Ya got me a tracksuit! An' it's all chequered an' shit," shrieked Jayde. She held up a brown and white outfit and smoothed it out with one hand.

"It's called Burberry," you uncouth beast!

"Wow, what a generous gift, James," I said. It seemed there was hope for these two being friends after all – that was until James whispered in my ear, "Don't get your hopes up, darling ... the tracksuit is fake. I acquired it from ChavLand.com."

Having said our goodbyes, I switched off the never-ending looped Christmas CD, blew out the mulled wine-scented candles and pulled out the plug from the Christmas tree lights.

I went into the staffroom, which was still littered with mince pies and plastic cups containing the remnants of a bottle of Cava, got changed and ordered a taxi to take me to the airport. As I made a half-hearted attempt to tidy up, I mused on what lay ahead for the New Year.

In what seemed to be an increasingly common habit of mine, I circled and rubbed my tummy longingly. The desire to have a baby was growing ever stronger. I'd become obsessed, wishing I could go back to my younger self. However hard I tried, I'd *still* not found my Mr Right. *Perhaps I should settle on a Mr Nearly Right?* Who was I kidding? I'd have leapt at a *Mr Slightly Right* given half the chance!

Even though I joked about my hopeless situation with my friends, I felt despondent that another year had passed and I still had no husband - and no baby.

It's true what they say: youth is wasted on the young. I stared at my thirty-eight-and-a-quarter-year-old reflection in the staffroom mirror. The extended platinum-blonde hair, my blue eyes heavily made up, my face frozen with Botox - and all the other cosmetic enhancements - but I couldn't stop my biological clock. Each minute, each hour, each day, youth was slipping from my fingertips and there wasn't a thing I could do about it.

I didn't want to go down the road of having my eggs frozen and stored like frozen petit pois. My baby would get frostbite and if he/she was anything like me they would hate being cold. And what if something happened to me whilst it was in the freezer? Would it be left there for eternity? And might they accidentally defrost my petit pois and plant it in some other mummy by mistake? It wasn't that I had anything against those who took this route. In fact, I was almost envious that they had the courage to do it. I just wanted a fresh one, straight from Mr Right: planted in my own lady-garden where I'd keep it warm and safe.

No, the answer was definitely to continue my search for Mr Right. Surely this coming year would bring me the happiness I deserved?

I was stirred from my daydream with a text from Jackie. A guy at work *had* been mucking around with Pete's phone. It was all a misunderstanding. Pete had managed to get himself out of work early – and he *had* bought Jackie new underwear. He'd bought the wrong size (at least three sizes too big) but it was the thought that counted. They'd ordered a take-out and were now snuggled up on the couch together watching a Christmas movie.

Just as I fired a quick text back to Jackie (and my staff and Siobhan) saying I knew Pete was as straight as an arrow – my taxi for the airport beeped outside.

I lugged my suitcase from the staffroom, locked the salon door behind me and breathed a huge sigh of relief.

Chapter 2

Feeling exhausted, I scooted over to my window seat and flopped down. I couldn't help but notice a gorgeous ride coming down the aisle. *Phwar!* I thought, *Please let him be sitting next to me*. He could most definitely be a candidate. My heart sank a little as I watched him slink past. He didn't even give me a second glance, the gobshite.

It was then I noticed a commotion further up the plane. I could hear, then see a man wearing a Father Christmas outfit singing "Fairy Tale Of New York" by The Pogues (off key) at the top of his voice. He was tall as a giraffe, limbs flying everywhere, ruddy cheeks, a drinker's nose and spangled drunk: evidently unable to walk in a straight line. Everyone had to clear a path for him as he randomly selected a seat and fell into it (with a passenger already in it), only to be told that wasn't his seat and would he kindly find his own. *Sweet Jesus*, I thought, as he pitched up to soprano level and began murdering the song again. *Can he not keep a lid on it till he gets to the other side?*

I shot him a disapproving look and breathed a sigh of relief as he swayed his way passed me. Then, all of a sudden, he stopped and began to perform a three-point-turn in order to manoeuvre himself round into the seat next to me. *Oh, for the love of God,* I thought, trying to shuffle as far over as possible whilst grabbing my possessions at the speed of light. I couldn't help but watch his dithering arse coming towards me.

I snapped my eyes closed. *Why do I always get the weirdos?*

With the help of other passengers, he finally managed to align himself and headed for landing, but in a matter of seconds his body started to spread, his elbow and leg already launching a full-scale invasion of what was left of my personal space, despite the fact that I was leaning so far the other way. All I was left with was a few centimetres – leaving me precariously balanced on one bum cheek.

He gave me a cheery smile. "Howerya there, missus?"

Recoiling further, I gave a dismissive nod, the fumes from his breath nearly knocking me out.

"Bad Santa's the name," he winked, through a playful, bloodshot eye. "Sorry there now, I'm not the best flyer. Have to have a few jars first."

With a tight expression I glanced at his red, shiny, neglected face. He looked and sounded just like my dad. Any excuse for a drink.

He fumbled round for his seat belt, and, unable to locate it, he clambered back up so his arse was right back in my face again. Swinging my gaze, I pointed out the two ends of his belt and quickly turned away.

"If I chat, it helps pass the time," he said, landing with an almighty thud and buckling himself in.

I knew exactly what was coming next. The compulsory boring aeroplane chat, which of course my spangled new seatmate followed to a tee.

"So, you heading off home for the holidays?" he began as the plane taxied down the runway.

I nodded through gritted teeth. "Christmas with the family." *A pound to a penny he's going to ask where my family are from next.*

"So, where in Ireland are your family from?"

Bingo! I just wanted him to shut the feck up and let me close my eyes so I could snooze during the flight.

"Rathmines in Dublin." He would of course know the area well and his uncle and three-times-removed cousins would be living there. He'd be asking the family name next.

"Ah sure, I know those parts very well – what's the family name?"

"Ryan," I answered shortly.

"Ah sure, I know the Ryans well. Fine upstanding members of the community."

That's when I knew he definitely had the wrong set of Ryans. Even though my family's story had started romantically, the middle and end of that story was far from a fairytale.

My parents had met and married in Mills & Boon-like circumstances back in the sixties. My dad, Michael (a fine young whippersnapper), had had his heart stolen by my mum, Josephine. He'd first spotted her sunbathing on Greystones Beach in County Wicklow.

"A thunderbolt," Dad had said, eyes brimming with tears. "'Twas love at first sight. There was your mother, in her polka-dot swimsuit, kicking the sand about without a care in the world and shrieking with laughter as she dipped in and out of the sea. I could've watched her for hours - her long, dark, glossy hair catching in the summer breeze, floating across her lightly tanned skin. She was a vision."

Mum, however, having had a very strict upbringing (yet with a playful edge to her personality), declined my dad's incessant offers of courtship.

"You'll have to ask me daddy," she teased. "But he'll probably have you hung, drawn and quartered for even daring to ask." Unwittingly, Mum set a challenge that dad would never refuse.

Undeterred, Dad indeed sought permission to take my mum out. At first, my grandfather had roared laughing in his face. Then he turned deadly serious. "Not in your wildest dreams would I allow you to date my daughter. Sure what would the likes of you have to offer her?"

"I'm a qualified bricklayer, Mr. O'Leary," Dad added with pride, offering his chapped hands up as proof.

"No scaffer's dating any daughter of mine, I can tell you that for nothing!" shot back my grandfather. "Goodbye, on your way so. Good luck, son, but the answer is *no*."

"I play the guitar and sing as well, sir, sure, I may become a professional musician – *even a rock star*," my dad stammered in a last-ditch attempt before the door was slammed in his face.

"Not in a million! Go-way with you, *shoo* – a rock star indeed. Never have I heard anything so ridiculous in all my life. You stay away from my daughter!"

For weeks that summer, Mum secretly revisited Greystones Beach every day at the same time in the hope of bumping into Dad. Unbeknown to her, Dad was still brooding over his encounter with her dad. Forbidden to talk with her, he poured his heart out on paper and wrote Mum a love song. Instead of going to Greystones to swim or sunbathe, after he'd finished work on the building site he would head down to another part of Greystones called the *The Men's*. Back then, females and children were forbidden by law to enter this part of the beach. It was for *men only*.

The Men's had dangerously high, ragged rocks covered in slimy algae where only the bravest would perform acrobatic dives into the sea, risking life and limb. Many were injured, even met their death as they attempted to out-do each other, performing twists and turns as the ante was raised to execute the perfect dive.

Dad was a great sportsman and swam like a dolphin, effortlessly performing complex dives with ease and grace. No one knew that when he climbed high on the rocks in preparation for his dive, he was secretly stealing glances at mum.

On one particular afternoon, the clear blue skies began changing and a storm formed from nowhere. Mum, unaware, was swimming out of her depth. Dad could see she was getting dragged out to sea. Without a second thought, he dived from the rocks and began swimming in her direction. Fighting currents and crashing waves, he managed to get her to safety. They lay together on the beach, exhausted. Entwined in each other, they kissed for the first time.

"Son," said my relieved grandfather, "I'll be forever in your debt. You have my blessing to date my daughter."

My parents were soon married and, in search of a better life, crossed the waters to England, where they'd heard the streets were paved with gold.

Dad immediately got work as a bricklayer and Mum fell pregnant with my eldest sister, Laura, with me soon to follow. Dad had to work harder than ever to keep a roof over our heads; times were good, but *tough*. He was building by day and singing in a band at night, gigging round London.

But the dream came crashing down.

The catalyst – Dad's beloved love song. He'd taken it to a music producer who said it was *extremely marketable*. This producer made all the right noises about him becoming a star and vividly described how he would be playing gigs to thousands of adoring fans. Earning a fortune. Then, inexplicably, the producer went cold and stopped answering his calls. It could have been the perfect story. My parents could have made their fortune and returned to their native land happy and prosperous in later life. Having had a taste of potential success cruelly whipped away, Dad began to change.

He started skipping odd days at work, and then as time went on, weeks at a time, claiming he was too exhausted to get up. It left poor Mum struggling with me and Laura, and she was pregnant with her third (Katie). She had to take every odd job she could to support us all.

A year after Dad had met the music producer, a new rock group hit the scene. They were an overnight success with their slick outfits, perfect good looks and romantic melodies. And their first number one hit? My dad's love song.

The betrayal destroyed him. He was devastated and, heartbreakingly, never recovered. Sure, he consulted lawyers about the theft, but they said it would cost thousands to sue and the chances were he'd never win against the powerful music moguls.

By then my parents didn't have a penny to rub together. Any money Dad did get went on booze. He had two moods, one anger the other despair. Often they came together. Try as she might, Mum couldn't pull Dad out of his spiralling despondency.

Recognising her husband had reached an all time low, to save Dad's mental health *and her own* she marched him down to the doctor's. He was diagnosed with depression. The doctor insisted Dad would get better and prescribed him antidepressants – which he point-blank refused to take. All he wanted was his song back, and there wasn't a tablet in the world that could do that.

"Please, Michael," Mum would beg, "take your medication. We love you. We need you. When you're better you can write another song!"

Dad disappeared for days on a drunken bender, and that night, when he stumbled back in, eyes bloodshot, reeking of booze, his voice loaded with poisonous words and accusations, we knew he was rapidly declining.

With the booze slept off and a temporary plateau of calm, *with Dad on his knees, head bowed, eyes closed, hands together, reciting the rosary* – and him back to the mild-mannered man we knew and *loved*, we forgave him.

We knew he was ill, though.

As a family, weekly, sometimes daily, we would draw a line in the sand and start again. It was exhausting.

Only Dad's mental health got worse.

Much, much worse.

One night, haunted by voices in his head, I overheard him having a conversation *with God*. Then Jesus's disciples. To some this would be fine, normal even. We are encouraged to seek out a higher being in times of crisis – but not when you're being prompted to throw yourself off a multi-storey car park, being promised by God that no harm would come to you because you would be caught at the other end – because you was the *chosen one*.

His disordered thinking disabled our entire family. His once genius mind had turned on itself, his behaviour escalating to such psychotic levels that he could no longer be trusted not to harm himself, so Mum, Laura and I took it in turns to suicide-watch him on a rota. Trying to anticipate what he might use to hurt himself, even end his life, we confiscated his razor, belts, painkillers and electrical appliances – we even removed the strings off his precious guitar. He took this out on Mum, accusing her of plotting against him. That's when we, heartbroken and resigned, knew his ability to discern between reality and delusion was now non-existent.

This cycling torrent of abuse and paranoid, catatonic behaviour went on for over a decade.

Mum had to make a decision.

The biggest decision of her life.

She had no choice.

Her once beloved husband had changed beyond recognition. With her marriage in tatters, she informed me, Laura and Katie that we were going to flee England – *without Dad* – and move back to Ireland. Of course, as the middle child, that automatically entitled me to (self-diagnosed) stroppy middle-child syndrome. And strop I did. There was no way I was leaving London having already started a hairdressing apprenticeship. So I opted (*pleaded*, clinging to the walls and any other bit of furniture I could cling to) to stay in England, promising Mum that I would personally attend Dad's Alcoholics

Anonymous meetings with him, and would speak with his mental health team about his terrifying schizophrenic behaviour and get him on better medication. As frightened as I was, I couldn't leave him all alone. I convinced Mum that I'd finish my hairdressing apprenticeship and by then Dad would be better. Without me budging an inch, Mum, Laura and Katie left – and that's when it became solely my responsibility to look after Dad.

Back in Dublin, the years passed by and my eldest sister, Lickarse Laura (as she was known to me and Katie), the *Einstein* of the family, became a career girl and studied for a doctorate in Psychology. When she graduated, it was one of Mum's proudest moments. She was Mum's pride and joy – *but this was short-lived*, as that very same evening Laura announced that she was twelve weeks pregnant. With a shotgun wedding swiftly organised, a wedding band barely on her finger, Laura left her husband just three short weeks later and filed for a divorce. In my secret opinion, Laura shared one too many of our dad's traits: the life and soul of any party, everyone's best friend, but get one too many drinks inside her and she would revert to a female version of Dad – wild, intimidating and erratic.

Then there was Katie, my youngest sister, who was currently residing in rehab. She was, however, allowed home for a few days for the Christmas holidays. Her stint in rehab was due to her newfound hobby: shoving every which substance she could get her hands on up her nose. To top it off, her home-grown cannabis plant had been lovingly tended and watered by none other than our poor, unsuspecting mum. Bless her; Mum was as clueless as she was penniless.

"I ought to get shares in Kleenex!" Mum would sob

on our weekly phone calls. "Katie goes trew a box of tissues in a day. I can't keep up with the child. And she has a constant sinus infection. Her poor nose is collapsin' with all the congestion!"

Katie and her tree-hugging weirdo mates had gone too far one night. She had been found wandering the streets, totally out of her hippy-dippy trolley, sobbing, claiming that she had committed a murder and would never forgive herself.

She was picked up by the local priest and confessed all. The account was a bit garbled by the time the poor man of the cloth got hold of Mum. He was clearly suffering from some sort of post-traumatic stress, but this is pretty much what Katie confessed to him (in her unstoppable motor-mouth style):

"See, I had a few friends around, Father – while Mammy was at mass. We had a few jars, and, you know yourself – *well, on second thoughts, maybe you don't.* Anyways, I looked at poor Moses (that's Mammy's budgie) and felt sorry for him. Sure, he's always locked up, so I thought I'd give him a little treat. I only put a little bit of me lager in his cage – but then I accidentally left his door open and before I knew it Moses was whizzing around and around Mammy's lounge at a hundred miles an hour like a fighter pilot. It was just sooo cool to watch him. He looked so happy. So free. But then Moses kinda crashed into the patio door. That was it, Father – he dropped to the floor like a bomb, flat on his back, his little bird legs bolt upright up and stiff. I had to do something, and fast – so I panicked and ran up to Mammy's bedroom. She has one of those ceiling fans, so I kept throwing Moses up into it, you know, just to try and get some wind beneath his wings. I begged him to start flapping his little bird arms, but his feathers just dropped off all over Mammy's bed. He was ice cold, so I wrapped him in cling film – *not over his face, now, Father* – I'm not that stupid! Anyway, I popped him in the microwave to warm him up a bit – but instead I accidently nuked him. I mean, there were a few of us alright that had polluted the air with, ummm ... let's say, *plant fumes* ... but sure, I'm confessing and you don't need to know every single detail of the murder, do you, Father?"

With that, Katie held out her wrists to be cuffed. And that was it for her: off to rehab she went. I don't think Father Murphy was ever the same after that.

I jolted awake to find Bad Santa's dithering arse back in my face.

We'd touched down.

I must have dozed off.

Feeling drowsy, I collected my luggage. With Laura's daughter Jemi away travelling, Laura was spending Christmas at Mum's with Katie and me. She was picking me up from the airport, and as I stepped through Arrivals there she was, waiting to give me a lift.

On Christmas morning in Rathmines, Dublin, I woke up to my phone beeping from my handbag.

[Text from (Unrecognised)]

Ur not gunna feckin believe this. Danny #2 found out about Danny #1 and tried 2 go thru me phone ... so I swallowed my SIM card! My throat is feckin' killin me! Siobhan Xxxx (PS this my new number).

[Text to Siobhan]

Omg! I've only been gone 1 day and you're in trouble already! I'll call you later. But if you were able to swallow it, you'll be able to pass it. Just keep your eyes peeled for a shiny shite coming down your chimney! Merry Xmas Xx

I shook my head. Siobhan was crazy. Only *she* would do something like swallow a SIM card!

I stretched out in my cosy bed, basking in the feeling of having nothing to do; no bickering to break up (well, apart from my sisters), just a few days of resting, eating and drinking in front of me.

Mum's house was so warm and inviting. I loved being there. You could lose yourself in the big, soft, brown velour sofas whilst your feet sank deep into the shag-pile carpet. The house was a medley of beiges, browns and oranges. Nothing matched, but it all worked somehow. There were little multicoloured trinkets dotted around the place, but the one that tickled me the most was in the bathroom: a legless plastic doll whose meringue-esque pale blue frilly skirt concealed the toilet roll beneath it.

At this time of year, Mum had her usual plethora of gaudy Christmas decorations up. And of course there was always a real Christmas tree, overloaded to the point of collapsing, with ill-matched yet strangely aesthetically pleasing bits and bobs. Mum had hung Katie's embroidered stocking on the mantel above the roaring log fire and surrounded it with tinsel. I always had to duck here and there whilst walking round the house, in fear of being strangled by Mum's paper chains. And, of course, there was the wave of two thousand or so Christmas cards, supported by cotton string and thumbtacks. Santa's grotto had nothing on our over-illuminated beacon of Christmas trash.

By the time I wandered downstairs at the blissful hour of 11 a.m., most of the hard work had already been done. The table was beautifully set for Christmas lunch, wineglasses placed accordingly. There was a carafe filled with red wine on the table; Laura saw me and poured us both a glass.

"*Sláinte*," we both chorused, and took a gulp.

"Eww ... what the hell is *that*? Is that – *RIBENA?!*" Laura and I spluttered at the same time.

Mum waltzed in from the kitchen, rollers in her hair. "The doctor said Katie wasn't allowed to be near anythin' *mind-altering* while she's on release from rehab. She could end up with one of those corse-diction things."

Laura spat out the remains of the offending Ribena back into her glass. "You mean *cross-addiction,* Mum," she corrected, wiping her mouth.

"She's the best child in the house. Got up and set the table with the good linen an all. She's a pet," said Mum, ignoring Laura and wrinkling her nose at Katie with pride and affection.

I wanted to remind Mum that neither Laura nor I lived there, so Katie was the *only* child in the house. And she wasn't a child. She was an adult and needed to act like one.

I watched Katie smirk behind Mum's back and stick her pierced tongue out at me. I did love my youngest sister, but it was infuriating that, even when she'd done something horrendously bad, like not attend college, get addicted to drugs, nuke poor Moses, traumatize a priest, she still got praise.

"My arse she's a pet," I growled under my breath as I straightened out the Christmas crackers. "Katie's had more chemicals in her than a lab rat!" I threw her a look that could kill.

"Well, *you'd* know about chemicals more than anyone else, Tara," Katie countered. "You have your road-mapped face injected every week!"

I gasped out loud. "I most certainly do not! I only have Botox every once in a while!"

Annoyed, I enviously looked at the olive, wrinkle-free complexion of both my sisters. They'd both been lucky enough to inherit mum's beautiful skin. I was the only one in the family that had milky, winter-white skin. My artificial glow came courtesy of St. Tropez's finest spray-tan and the tanning booth. Even more unfairly, that was the case in the breast department as well. The memory still smarted from when I'd spent hours as a teenager gently picking out the stitching from Mum's *Dynasty*-style jacket and borrowing the shoulder pads for my bra fillers without her knowing. Of course, I got caught putting them back while Katie was *apparently* on guard. I was grounded for a month. It was back to stuffing socks down my 28AA bra for me. A few years later, with help from a plastic surgeon, I got the coveted chin-hitting breasts I so desperately wanted. I deliberately went twice as big as my sisters.

At full volume, Mum started screeching from the kitchen.

We all rushed in.

"Lord preserve us, where's the feckin' turkey gone? I

couldn't close the door when it first went into the oven! Sweet Jesus ... May God forgive my blasphemy – but I know I cooked it as it said on the instructions!"

The cooked bird was pathetic in size. Like something a cat would bring in. By now Mum was sobbing, flapping her apron up and down, blessing herself all at the same time.

"Oh, Mum, don't get upset," Laura hushed reassuringly, "there's enough veg, stuffing and Yorkshire puddings to feed a small army. Plenty to go round."

It took Mum a few minutes to calm down, but she was a trooper. With her daughters rallying around her, she soon recovered her composure and resolved the show must go on.

"Right, girls, that's it - my New Year's resolution is to attend a cooking class," she said, pulling it back together in an instant. "It's never too late. I'll be purchasing a brand-new oven - one of those ones that them celebrity chefs have." She kicked the oven door closed with her Santa-slippered foot, "I want a new kitchen altogether. *I'll have to get saving*. Right! Lunch - or should I say *rations* in five minutes."

While we were waiting for Mum to put the finishing touches to the Christmas lunch, I scuttled over to the sofa where *Saint Katie* was lying. I handed her a Christmas cracker as a sort of olive branch because I hadn't shown her much support over our temperance drink of poxy Ribena. If I was honest, though, I really *really* wanted what was inside it, whatever plastic shite it turned out to be. I guess you never really get over that competitive sibling rivalry thing. Plus, now I think about it, I had never quite forgiven Katie for poking out the eyes of my much-loved Tiny Tears doll when I was young. Okay, I didn't play with it anymore, but that wasn't the point, I didn't want her to have my things. Being the younger sibling, she ruined everything. And now I thought about it, she'd also cut the doll's hair, too, the little bitch! I only allowed her to play with it because Mum had forced me!

Katie and I heaved and pulled at the shiny cracker, my hand carefully placed near the middle to try and guarantee me victory. But, as it went *bang*, I felt the body of the cracker slip from my hand. I had lost. Katie had won the prize. It was a novelty keyring in the form of mini-handcuffs.

"That's a sign from the Big Man Upstairs," I said malevolently. I couldn't help it, I had to throw *something* in. "He's reminding you to stay on the right side of the law." Inexplicably, the usually robust Katie seemed to crumble at my words. Her face dropped and she looked tearful. Maybe I *had* gone a little too far this time?

Feeling a rush of guilt and sisterly love (and relief that it was only a pair of poxy plastic handcuffs, which were of no use to me anyway), I sat down beside her.

"We all just want the best for you," I said. "You've got enough talent to complete your Music diploma – *if* you start applying yourself. Dad would've been so proud." I rubbed her shoulder. "And who knows, maybe a year or so down the line, when you've cleaned your act up and proven yourself, you could get yourself a nice, steady boyfriend. You've got so much going for you … and you are a looker." I forced a smile. As much as I admired her floral hair garlands, tie-dye gypsy skirts and hand-made Aztec jewellery, I hated to say it. It really smarted that it was all so natural and effortless for her. She never wore make-up – she didn't need to.

With twinkly eyes and a beaming smile she said, "I've got a secret –"

"Lunch!" interrupted Mum. "I thought that butcher had a shifty-looking face." She was still muttering under her breath about the shrinking-bird problem. "He couldn't even look me in the eye when he sold me that dodgy bird, so he couldn't. Mind you, he had only one eye, so he did. Strange looking fella all the same."

With a firm shake of her head, indicating she didn't want Mum to hear, Katie whispered, "I'll fill you in after lunch."

We both shot up and ran for the dinner table, both trying to get the closest seat to Mum.

"Who wants to carve the bird then?" Mum looked at me, then directly either side of her, to Laura and Katie. The budgie-sized turkey was on a platter that took up half the table, dwarfing it even further.

"Umm ..." we all stammered, avoiding eye contact with her.

"You're the head of the family, Mum. *You* carve the budg – *er* – turkey," said Laura.

She always was (and *still* is) such a complete lickarse.

"Right so." Our mother, armed and dangerous with an electric carving knife the size of a hedge trimmer, proceeded to try and carve. But as soon as the enormous blade made contact with the minuscule turkey, it flew off the platter, hitting the wall at breakneck speed. Then it fell to the floor with a soggy thud.

We all gasped in horror.

"Fookin' hell!" Katie shot up out of her chair. "The bird is only after tryin' to fly away!"

"Saints preserve us!" said Mum, in shock. Getting to

her feet, she shook her head, staring at the mess it had made.

After exchanging glances, we all burst out laughing. We continued to dish up the rest of the (now turkey-free) Christmas lunch, and fortunately even Mum started to see the funny side.

With the atmosphere settling down, we toasted with our Ribena and pulled the rest of the Christmas crackers. By the time we were finished, I was full to bursting, but couldn't help enquiring about dessert. Mum always made *the* best Christmas pudding.

I rubbed my bloated tummy. "I've left a little room for dessert. You know how much I love your Christmas pudding. Are we going to set it alight?"

Mum began briskly tidying the plates away. "Sure they're laced with alcohol, so no, there's no Christmas pudding. I've gone for something else this year."

"Oooh," I said, "what is it? Trifle?" I loved Mum's trifle.

She shook her head once again.

"Sure, that's full of sherry." She nodded in Katie's direction.

"Tiramisu?" I asked hopefully, my mouth salivating at the thought. It slowly dawned on me that that also contained alcohol. I felt an all too familiar surge of resentment towards Katie. "I take it there's no chocolate liqueurs for after either?"

"Well, I thought I'd go with something a little more modern, given our *fragile* family situation."

I waited with bated breath.

"We're havin' angel fairy cakes and toffee-filled Rolos with coffee!"

I shot my eyes in Laura's direction, but she was

deliberately avoiding my gaze. I looked back at Katie, who was sitting all prim and proper, like butter wouldn't melt.

"How thoughtful of you to think of Katie *again*, Mum," I said, unable to keep the sarcasm out of my voice. I continued to shoot death stares in Katie's direction. Katie (rightly so) put her head down and started fiddling with her Christmas paper hat.

"Oh, I forgot," Mum added, blissfully unaware of my scorn, "I've made mince pies!"

"But I don't like mince pies!" I moaned. Of course I was just playing up, but then I looked at Mum's crestfallen face. I was being a moanyhole and I shouldn't be, not towards Mum. Once in front of me, I shoved a whole mince pie in my mouth, placing two more by my side so Katie couldn't have more than me. They were yummy, generously sprinkled with copious amounts of icing sugar.

At the speed of lightning Katie said, "I bagsy licking the plate!"

"Ugh! I was going to bagsy that!" I said. Annoyed that I hadn't been quick enough I deliberately sprayed some spit on it while passing it down to her.

"Ha! You're getting a bit *slooooow* in your old age, Tara," teased Katie, unaware of the germs I'd just bestowed upon her. "Maybe Santa should've put some TENA-ladies in your stocking."

"Ha, come on now!" I said, "There's no need for that kind of talk. I could throw one in about needing extra large nappies and how long you wet the bed for, but I won't – because it's Christmas!"

With Katie guarding the mince pie plate with her life, we moved to the lounge to watch the Queen's speech. It was the same every year (our routine, not the speech).

We'd all wait for Mum to fall asleep (which didn't take long, usually 30 seconds) then the silent but deadly fight for the remote control would start between the three of us.

This time, as Katie and I fought (perhaps not for the remote, but more probably because we just wanted to knock the shite out of each other), Lickarse Laura dived in and took charge of what we were about to watch. A boring documentary about penguins. I mean, *really*? *REALLY?*

Not in the mood for penguins (unless they were of the chocolate variety), I remembered that I had some unfinished gossip to unearth from Katie.

"So, what was the secret you were going to share with me before lunch?" I probed. I resolved to put Katie's last TENA-ladies, cutting comment behind me, and exhausted from our scrap, flopped down beside her.

She cupped her hand around her mouth, leant forward and whispered in my ear. "I've met this fine, fit thing and think I might be in lurv –"

"Hang on! How could you have possibly met somebody and fallen in love while you've been in rehab – while you're meant to be *recovering from alcohol and drug abuse*?!" I was still out of breath from our scuffle and pissed off because Katie had pulled one of my hair extensions out. Angrily, I shoved it back in.

"Listen till I tell you," she said, speaking quietly, yet rapidly. "Big John was visiting his little brother – who is also called John – at rehab and we got chatting about caravans – don't ask me how *but we did*. It may have something to do with Little John living in one –"

"WHAT?!" I screeched. "Don't tell me you're seeing a PIKEY?"

Katie shoved her hand over my mouth. "Shhhh!" she implored. "Don't be sayin' that in front of Mam!"

Slapping her hand away, I struggled to keep my voice down. "Jesus, Katie! Will you *ever* learn? They're not allowed to date outside of their community. They have to stick to their own; and so should you! Surely you've watched *My Big Fat Gypsy Wedding*?"

I shook my head in disgust and then set upon her again (well, I was on a roll. Why stop now?).

"You, young lady, were told *no relationships* for a *year*! And you start one up the *minute* you go into *rehab*? You are *not* to have anything to do with Big John or Little John ever again. And I *mean it*. Or I will tell Mum and Laura!"

Katie started fidgeting and fingering the icing sugar around the mince pie plate.

"I'm better now, and Big John is up for a laugh ... *and* he's offered to do Mammy's front drive at a knock-down price."

I rubbed my face in despair.

Katie's enthusiasm melted into nervousness. "You've no idea what it's like at rehab, Tara. I thought I was gonna die of boredom ..."

"Not another word!"

I was bitterly disappointed. Despite our differences and arguments, I genuinely wanted my sister to get past her addictions. Disgusted, I turned away. When I turned back to give her another mouthful, my eyes nearly popped out of my head. Katie had arranged the icing sugar on the plate into - lines. *Oh my God. White lines. Oh my God! AND* SHE'D ROLLED HER CHRISTMAS PAPER HAT INTO A SUSPICIOUS-LOOKING STRAW-LIKE SHAPE.

"*Katie!*" I shouted, nearly taking the roof off the house. "You *stupid* crackhead! *Mum!*" I grassed, shaking her awake. "Look what Katie has done with the icing sugar! And she's moving into a caravan with her new *PIKEY* boyfriend!"

"What? Aww, bless her ... she'll have a grand holiday in a caravan when she's better," Mum said, her eyes fluttering closed, not taking a blind bit of notice of my outcry.

"The plate, Mum. Look at what your eejit daughter has done to the plate!"

Mum managed to peel half an eye open. "Ahh, would you look, she's made some snowy roads with the icing sugar. They're *lovely*, pet."

I turned to appeal to Laura, who was now nowhere to be seen. *Typical!*

I was overwhelmed by an immense surge of anger, catalysed by Mum's blind ignorance. Heaving myself off the sofa, I snatched the plate off Katie and marched into the kitchen. In desperation, I started raiding the cupboards, looking for alcohol, but not a drop was to be found. This enraged me even more.

Despite this, I was terrified of ending up like our dad. Moderation of alcohol being key, reserved for high days and holidays. Celebrations. Christmas, weddings and birthdays. There was no way any of my children (if I ever managed to have any) would have to get on their knees and beg me to stop drinking.

The dark days of my youth clung to me like a rash that never quite went away. It was always there, lurking beneath the surface.

I was of tender years, in my usual hiding place, crouched

down at the bottom of the stairs, in between the coats. I was peering between the banisters through to the lounge, my nightdress over my legs to keep warm. I always took Panda (my teddy bear) with me. I could cry into him and no one would hear me. Sometimes I would put him over my eyes so I couldn't see Dad hurting Mum. Father Brian was here again. Mum was run ragged, trying to conjure up food we didn't have, then afterwards, the visitor biscuit tin was presented and emptied. Dad and Father Brian would drink till all hours - till they could barely stand. With the drinks cabinet dry and the priest now on the wobbly road home due to an early mass to prepare, and with the front door now closed, Dad began ranting at Mum. He said she was keeping bad company - accusing her friend of being dishonest to her husband, that Mum was covering for her, and that they'd both go to hell for their sins.

I didn't like the word hell. It was a bad, bad place where devils burnt you slowly then ate you alive. I wanted to go in and stop Dad shouting at Mum, but it went quiet, very quiet. I inched forward just so I could see through the crack of the door. I could see my parents praying. Mum was sobbing. I raced upstairs to Laura's bedroom, tried to wake her. She always pretended to be asleep, but I knew she wasn't. Back downstairs I went, listening till my burning face was wet with tears. Till my body shook. Till my nails were bitten down to the cuticles. Till Mum's bloodied face and trembling body carried me up the stairs reassuring me that everything was okay, even though I knew it wasn't.

Mass was a regular occurrence in our household. We went as a family to repent our sins. This, I never understood.

Until one day, I did. The Big Man in the sky would help my dad stop drinking, *if I asked him nicely*. If I was good. Only, even though I'd asked him a zillion times, he never heard me.

With poor Mum juggling everything while screaming, attention-seeking Katie was joined to her hip, and with Laura shut in her bedroom, her nose buried in a book, I realised it was up to me to make him better.

As I got older, braver, I'd get down on my knees, take Dad's nicotine-stained hand in mine and beg him to stop drinking.

"If it's good enough for God's disciples to drink wine, then it's good enough for me," he said. This was his favourite saying.

One day, after my mum and sisters had left for Ireland, I'd been out celebrating my 21st birthday with friends; sneaking home late, I'd selfishly gone straight to bed without checking in on Dad.

Late the next morning I found him slumped on the living-room floor. Eerily still, he was clutching our family photograph and the lyrics of the stolen love song he'd written for Mum so many years ago.

Frantically, I waded through the debris of empty cans and bottles, and fell to my knees beside him.

"Dad?" I called in alarm, looking at his expressionless face. "Talk to me!" I cupped and pulled at his ice-cold hands. "You've had too much to drink. You've passed out."

I shook him for some kind of response. "Come on … up we get! Wake up! Please. *Please …* " I cried. "I'm sorry I didn't check in on you. It was selfish of me to go out. Come on, Dad!" With all my might, I heaved him into recovery position.

Everything was happening in excruciating slow-motion as I ran to call an ambulance. My fingers, like elastic bands, struggled to dial the number. I begged the operator to make the paramedics come quickly. She instructed me to stay calm and check his breathing. Dropping the phone, I dived down to where he lay. Tilting his head, I placed my ear to his mouth. Nothing. The only sound was my own rapid breathing. I checked his pulse. There wasn't one.

At that moment my worst fears were confirmed. *I* wasn't going to be able to save him. But I'd promised Mum. Unable to accept he was gone, I tried to resuscitate him.

"It's you and me – we made a promise to each other," I pleaded. "Wake up!"

Adrenaline-fuelled hysteria set in as I attempted to perform CPR. I sealed his lips and tried with panic-stricken breaths to bring him back. "Please don't go ... don't leave me all alone."

His tortured soul was departing this world. I could feel what little warmth was left fading from his crumpled body, disappearing into my arms. I grabbed a blanket, lay on the floor beside him and wrapped us up together. I held him tight, my body trembling in disbelief, my eyes drowning in tears.

I don't know how long I lay there before the ambulance arrived, but eventually I drifted off to happier times. I saw flashes of Dad teaching Laura, Katie and me to play guitar, encouraging us to sing. Laura sounded like an angel. Even Katie showed signs of great talent, with her young yet undeveloped voice. Sounding myself like an alley cat being strangled, I ran off and got my recorder, and even though everyone stuck their fingers in their ears as I played, it was a happy, magical moment.

I wanted to hold Dad for as long as possible, but the weight of his body was gradually slipping beyond my grasp. I knew I had to let him go. But I wasn't ready, not yet. I needed more time with him before he was permanently taken away from me.

Supporting his head with a cushion, I reached over, grabbed his guitar, plucked a few strings and, with my heart broken, sang to him for the last time - remembering the wonderful dad and husband he was before the poison entered his veins and stripped him of his life.

A torrent of pain and regret turned me inside out as I called Mum with the news. It all seemed so long ago, but the spirit of our dad still hung strongly about us, even now. Christmas never felt quite right again, even though for so many years the 25th of December only meant an extended day of drinking and arguing for my parents.

Wanting to escape the Christmas family drama, and in bemusement over Siobhan swallowing her SIM card, I gave her a call.

"*Merry Christmas!*"

"Merry Christmas from England!" she yelled.

"So, what on earth was *that* all about?" Mug of tea in hand, I made myself comfortable. "Are you okay?"

"You'll not feckin' believe it when I tell you!" Siobhan relished an opportunity to tell the next crazy instalment of her chaotic love life.

"Oh, I *will* believe it, tell me!"

"Well ... you know that ol' tosspot I was kinda seein' for a while?"

"Which one?" There'd been a few.

"Danny!" she exclaimed.

"*Danny?*"

"You know: *Danny.*"

"Oh yeah – Danny!" I bluffed. "I didn't know that you and Danny had split up. When did that happen?"

"I'm not talkin' about Danny #*2* now, Tara, because I'm still riding that one! I mean Danny #*1*, the gobshite that was looking to drag me arse up the aisle. You know who I mean, the eejit who got sacked for stealing funds – went to court and all that malarkey, had to downgrade from a top-end BMW to a clapped-out Skoda."

It all came flooding back.

"Ah yes, I remember him. The poor guy who lost everything," I said.

"Poor guy, me arse! He knows I'm with the Danny #2 and the stupid fecker only went and texted me out of the blue wanting to hook up, and Danny #2 only went an' feckin' read it! Really, the gobshite should never have been goin' through me phone, but he did, then had the cheek to go all confrontational on me, so, I grabbed me phone and feckin' *ran*, I tell you, and locked myself in the bathroom. Danny's on the other side of the door, trying to kick it down. He hurt his foot, and he's there, whining like a baby that his toe is the size of a tennis racquet - which served him right. But then ... he starts to jemmy the lock with a fookin' two-pence piece, trying to get me phone back off me! I was like, fook that for a laugh! He would've seen the texts from all the others as well! So I took me phone apart and got the SIM out. The second he comes through the door, he sees me shoving it down my gob to get rid of the evidence."

"Couldn't you have flushed it down the toilet?"

"He would've feckin' dived in an' got it. He had his fingers down me throat trying to get it back, he's such a loon. So anyways - I bit the bastard. It's the only way I was gonna get him to stop!"

I burst out laughing, as did Siobhan.

"I was *shittin'* myself, I tell you, Tara."

I had to ask: "Why do you keep going for the bad boys, Siobhan?"

"*Duh,* cos I *love* a bastard. I love them wild, moody and unpredictable. Turns me on, even if it does scare the living bejayas out of me. Should probably go and see someone about that really." She was off again howling with laughter. "Anyway, I've got to go, I'm meeting Danny #1 for a drink."

"Okay," I said, even more baffled. "I'll call you when I'm home. Merry Christmas, bestie!"

"Send your mam and sisters my love!"

I'm sure she meant to say Danny #2 ...

Heading back into the lounge, I immediately began to regale them with Siobhan's story. I was desperate to share the craziness of it.

"Sounds like she could do with a bit of help if you ask me," said Laura, in her everyone's-dysfunctional-apart-from-me voice.

"I'd love to go and stay with her for a weekend," added Katie, wide-eyed.

"You're not going *anywhere*, you brazen hussy!" I barked.

"Right, who fancies a game of Trivial Pursuit?" asked Laura, diverting the conversation in another direction to prevent a row.

"Not me," I protested. "You're a boffin, Laura. You only want to play because you know you'll win!"

"Well, you might learn something," she said, all teacher-like and patronising.

"Why don't we all have a nice game of Snap?" suggested Mum.

Now *that* was a game I could play.

It had been a typical Christmas day (minus the turkey and alcohol, of course). We had eaten, we had bickered and we had laughed. Mum then went to bed whilst Laura, Katie and I stayed up chatting and squabbling until the early hours of the morning.

Chapter 3

My final night in Ireland had arrived. After a few alcohol-free days and nights of staying holed up at Mum's to show solidarity for Katie, cabin fever had begun to set in. The rehab doctor had given Mum strict instructions that Katie was not to go anywhere she might be tempted to look for drink and drugs and was to be kept in a controlled environment. Long story short: Katie couldn't set foot outside the house.

Laura and I had more than done our fair share of going without; it was *our* time now. So we felt obliged to go out and get respectably rat-arsed.

I couldn't help but feel anxious about Laura's temperament for the evening. Sometimes she was a wise, intellectual type with patience akin to a Buddhist monk. However, get one too many drinks in her and she would revert to a party animal that never wanted to go home. As I said before, she showed traits of our dad in more ways than one. However, needs must: I wasn't going to let anything stop me from going out and having some much needed fun.

Laura and I made our way to our favourite cocktail bar in Dublin city centre with a *lock up your husbands, we're on a mission* attitude. Upon arriving (skipping the long queue) Laura confidently approached the doorman, legs first. I stood back awkwardly and wondered what the frig she was doing. I watched her provocatively allow the side-splits of her pencil skirt to flap open as she wrapped her tanned, toned leg around his waist, using his body like a pole - shimmying up and down him in a sultry, risqué manner. She was such a show-off! *God, I wish I had a quarter of her carefree attitude.*

I looked down at myself, feeling suddenly butt-ugly. *I knew I shouldn't have worn this outfit!* I'd agonised what to wear all day. I'd wanted to look sexy yet stylish with a carefree edge. But now I felt none of these things. I'd stupidly opted for my metallic silver skinny jeans and silver sparkly off-the-shoulder jumper, with huge matching silver bangles and four-inch open-toe silver-encrusted sandals. Even Mum - who never noticed anything important - said I looked like an inflated roll of tinfoil (although I think she was trying to be encouraging).

Laura, on the other hand, had just thrown on a tight black pencil skirt and crisp white shirt and pulled it together with a wide black-buckled leather belt, which gave her the sexiest hourglass figure. *Me?* Well, there was no strategy whatsoever. I mean, for the love of God, I hadn't even put my best assets on show. And I had paid enough for them! What was I thinking?

I jumped from one foot to the other on the gravel to keep warm. The wind was so biting it could shave a goat. I should've worn my fur coat. I thought Laura was never going to stop flirting with the doorman; I just wanted to get inside - I could hear the band doing a fantastic rendition of "Valerie" by Amy Winehouse. Becoming impatient and trying to keep warm, I put my best foot forward and attempted to shimmy sexily to the beat when suddenly a stone flicked back, ricocheting off my ankle bone. "Awww!" I huffed, puffed and hopped around in sheer agony. I thought I was going to throw up. I reached out for Laura, holding up my foot, desperate for sympathy, but instead of rubbing it better she used it as her handbag holder so she was freed up to finish her bribery of the doorman.

There she was, Ms Lickarse Laura, caressing the mountainous bulk, running her hands seductively down his round face, snapping into what looked like some kind of Argentinean tango, her short black bob flicking right to left, left to right. The show finally ended (thank God) with the doorman cupping the base of Laura's spine and throwing her down into a dramatic, exotic dip. Everyone in the queue applauded.

Her eyes were wild. "Tara!" she shouted, her face upside down.

"Yep?" I winced, wondering if I needed to get to Accident & Emergency.

"Bar!" she announced, with an authoritative point.

As the doorman swung the doors open, I hobbled in, rubbing my swollen ankle, while Laura waltzed through the crowd like she owned the place, oblivious to my practically broken ankle. To our joint pleasure, we found the bar heaving, noticing pickings were far from slim. The local rugby team were out on a Christmas jaunt and it just so happened that both Laura and I were very partial to a bit of muscle. We stood at the bar, scanning the crowd.

I nudged Laura. "We can afford to be picky tonight."

"That'll make a change for you!" she jibed.

Ignoring her comment, I raked my fingers up through my long platinum-blonde hair, trying to give it extra height. Pulling the curled length around my shoulders, I applied another coat of sticky lip-gloss.

As Laura ordered our drinks, the shortest player on the rugby team immediately approached her. He was what she would later dismissively call a "typical Irish leprechaun". However, despite his lack of height, Laura seized the opportunity and flirted unashamedly with him in order to get an introduction to the rest of the team.

He must be the one who ends up on the bottom of the scrum pile, I mused to myself as I watched Laura fluttering her eyelashes. This guy definitely had a face only a mother could love.

Laura's flirting had done the trick, and before I knew it we were whisked over and introduced to the rest of the team. Thank you, God! Miraculously, the pain in my ankle subsided, my focus turning to the bulking frames of pure muscle around me.

I was going to play it super-cool, noticing one of the rugby players was staring, giving me a cheeky, megawatt smile. I slyly scanned him head to toe. He was perfection personified. Like he'd been made in a lab. He was tall, definitely over six feet, which meant I wouldn't have to shrink in my heels. His jeans were skin-tight, his black T-shirt even tighter. Complexion tanned, arms strong, legs meaty, sturdy. Good head of dark floppy hair, enough to tug and wrap round my fingers ... *Hmmm* ... absolutely *the best-looking ride I had ever seen.*

I checked myself, cleared my throat and, taking a deep

stabilising breath, pretended I hadn't noticed him. No way was I going to make eye contact - which made him stare even more to get my attention. I did my *I haven't even noticed you* routine, simply exaggerating my body language, oozing femininity to stir him up, while nonchalantly scanning the rest of the team.

Trying to find confidence from somewhere, I hatched a little plan. With my heart pounding, I swaggered in front of him towards the toilets. The prime objective of this killer strategy was to give him a whiff of my new *take-me-now* perfume, which perfectly complemented my *take-me-now* glittery eyes. As I got within a few feet of him, I opened my mouth as if about to blow a bubble, rounding my lips into the perfect "O" shape, in the hope of the perfect pout. As I drew up beside him, I paused, seductively placing my hand on his torso, and in the slowest, sexiest voice I could conjure up, said, "*Excuuuusse me.*"

Unable to contain myself, I kept moving on while sensually trailing my fingertips across his muscular torso. I could feel adrenaline coursing through my veins, my breathing short and sharp as I battled to keep my composure. That's no walk in the park while wearing four-inch heels, vacuuming your stomach in, sticking your chest out, keeping your shoulders back, pouting your lips and wiggling your backside all at the same time.

As I slithered across the floor, I could feel his eyes burning into the back of me. And knowing how visual a man is, I thought I'd go one step further - emphasise my womanly sensuality a tad more by exaggerating my bum-wiggle, while sticking my chest out a few inches further for ultimate sex-bomb effect. I was nearly at the toilet door when I felt my (severely battered) ankle give way.

The next few seconds were like a scene from *Bambi*. My knees banged together while my flailing arms grabbed some poor, unsuspecting woman, knocking a drink clean out of her hand. God love her, she managed to steady me but I hardly had time to apologise to her (apart from shoving some euros in her hand) because, in trying to regain my prowess, I turned to find Laura standing right beside *my* prey.

"Feck – arse – shite!" I scolded myself. Mortified, I limped through to the toilets. *What if he saw me?* I waved furiously at Laura from behind the toilet door, beckoning her over. Once I got my sister within arm's reach, I yanked her in. "Oh my God, I'm *so* embarrassed. It could *only* happen to me!"

"What's up?" she asked, ignorant of my near fatal mishap.

"Did *he* see? Did *you* see? Did *anyone* see?"

"What *are* you talking about? See what?" Laura looked confused.

"Me falling off my shagging heels on the way to the toilets!"

"No. I've been way too busy checking out the wall-to-wall cock-a-locka."

"I'm sure I've broken my ankle. It's karma; I always get punished when I think naughty thoughts," I sulked. "I was acting like a brazen hussy and now I'm paying the consequences."

"Oh stop with all that Catholic-guilt nonsense." Laura picked up my foot, twisted my ankle in every conceivable direction (while I screamed the roof off the building) and informed me it wasn't broken. Well, I thought, if it wasn't broken before, it certainly is now!

Laura swung the door open. "C'mon," she encouraged. "We're wasting time. I didn't come out to spend the night in the bogs, let's go have us some fun!"

"I'll be out in a bit," I sulked. I really needed to undo my jeans so I could at least make some use of my embarrassing *trip* to the toilets. Back at Mum's, I'd eaten the remains of an old box of rejected chocolate liqueurs that I'd found at the back of a cupboard (well, all the rum-flavour ones, anyway), and they were now terrorising my insides and giving me gas. Added to this was the small issue with Siobhan's Christmas present (*small* being the key word here). She had bought me a thong, which was at least two sizes too small. To be honest, after my chocolate-gobbling session, it was maybe three sizes too small. It had felt okay as I was leaving Mum's, but the minute I got into the taxi I felt like my arse was sitting on a cheese wire. The offending garment had developed an intimate appetite for my nether regions. I squeezed my hand down the back of my jeans and tried to release the torment of the string, but within seconds it was back, slicing me in half again.

Realising there was little I could do about the thong issue (perhaps another vodka would act as a painkiller), I reapplied lip-gloss and ruffled my hair, making sure my extensions were all in place. Swallowing my pride, I nervously held open the door, willing myself to step out.

I'd been single for way too long. It's not like I couldn't find a man or anything. I had a graveyard full of failed relationships all suffering the same fate: *him* getting too close, *me* running for dear life. I couldn't help myself. When I found a man I liked, I'd sit down with a notepad and analyse him to death. By the time I'd finished, my finger was always pressing the panic button on my emotional ejector seat.

I wasn't about to make that same mistake again. No sir-ee! I was far too aware of the time I'd wasted, which is why I was in my late-thirties with no husband, no babies and a bleak, lonely future ahead of me. Besides which, I didn't need a notebook to know for certain that Mr Gorgeous Rugby Mán was absolutely, without a doubt, prime husband and father material.

Taking a little more care this time, I strutted my stuff back out to the bar. While trying to see where the object of my desire was, I was stopped by a "yokel". A yokel is Laura's code word for a farmer who needs a wife, who only knows how to speak to the animals and has no female contact in his life except that of the female heifer variety.

"Sure you're a fine-looking woman," said the yokel.

I smiled sweetly, thanked him and tried to get back to the gang of hotties. I was just pulling my arm back when he came right out with it and asked me if I was looking for a husband.

"No!" I replied, trying not to sound rude. *Well, yes, actually*, I thought, *but it's not gonna be you in a million years, chum!*

"Can ya milek cows?" he inquired. He had the strongest Irish accent I had ever heard. It was then I noticed he had a tooth missing - as if there weren't enough nails in his coffin.

I was beginning to lose patience.

"No, I can't milk cows!" I said petulantly, putting on a cut-glass English accent. "Why on earth would I want to fondle a cow's udder when I could pick up a carton of semi-skimmed from Marks & Spencer?"

Is he mad? Clearly he was. Whilst trying to get away from the eejit, I spotted the ride from earlier staring straight at me, so I quickly switched tactics and pretended to enjoy the painstaking conversation with the yokel. I turned back to him and smiled sweetly, slamming on the flirtation switch.

"Actually, on second thoughts, maybe I *would* play with a cow's udder," I added deviously.

The slobbering yokel looked delighted. "Sure that's grand news, so it is. Can you cook? I'm a meat and two veg man meself, so I am."

"*Hahaha!* You're *so* funny. Me, cook? I can't cook for toffee!" I gave him a playful shove, accidently knocking the featherweight off balance. "Oh, I'm *so* sorry!" As I grabbed him by his gangly arm I stole an opportunity to see if my hunk was still watching me. He was.

"Ah, never mind sure, you're me dream woman, so ye are," said the yokel, straightening himself upright. "I likes a bit of rough and tumble myself." He shuffled his way closer. Then closer still. I stepped back, horrified. I didn't care for his *meat and two veg*. I wanted the gorgeous ride's meat and two veg - that was far more appetising!

"Can I catch you for a dance later?" leered the indefatigable yokel.

Mum had strict views on this. She'd brought us girls up to know that if ever a man plucked up the courage to ask us to dance, we were never to say no. She'd really drummed it in. So of course, my answer was *yes*. However, I drew comfort in my get-out clause – my would-be dance partner would have to try and find me first.

I turned on my heel ready to dart away. "I'll be back for that dance later." He picked up my hand and slobbered a kiss on it. Yuck! Smiling through gritted teeth, I weaved through the crowds - but the man of my dreams had vanished! Bitterly disappointed, I stomped over to Laura.

She was on her third pint of Carlsberg already. I'd never been able comprehend how she was able to drink beer at the same rate as men and remain upright at the end of the night. She seemed to be having a ball, flirting outrageously with a six-foot, broad, blond Adonis. She was in her element. The Adonis pulled her out to dance and I was left self-consciously alone.

With a beady eye I scanned every inch of the place in the hope of spotting *my* ride from earlier. Nothing. *That bloody farmer!* My heart sank further. Giving up hope, in a very unladylike manner I threw back my vodka and Coke, when out of nowhere all six foot-plus of my hunk emerged from the darkness and was striding directly towards me. My heart rate instantly accelerated, my instincts screaming: *Pout! Pout! Pout! Look cool! Act like you don't care. Don't look at him, Tara! I said don't feckin' look at him, you silly cow!*

My stomach flipped and our eyes locked. I tried to look away but was mesmerized. I managed to pull myself out of my stupor for a split second to check out his left hand to make sure there was no Mrs Beautiful - *there wasn't.* After that, I was lost again.

"Are you okay? Your friend said you fell over."

Laura was a bitch! If he hadn't seen me falling off my heels, *why the hell did she have to go tell him? Sometimes she stoops lower than a centipede's arse!*

"I'm fine, thank you." I quickly exchanged my thunderous expression to one of sugary sweetness.

"I haven't seen you around here before."

He had an English accent. I was thrown. I'd presumed he'd be Irish.

"Can I buy you and your friend a drink?"

Nodding, I fluttered my eyelashes, "But she's no *friend* of mine." I was still raging with her. "That's my *much* older, big-mouthed sister." I couldn't help myself, adding with a mischievous grin, "We call her Lickarse Laura."

He laughed, his chocolate-brown eyes twinkling. "What are the pair of you drinking?"

Oh, great, now I'd have to ask for a pint for my boozy sister. I was so embarrassed that Laura drank pints, it was so unfeminine.

"I'd say she'll have a *small* glass of Carlsberg, and may I have a vodka and cock ... *errr* ... I mean vodka and *Coke*, please."

For the love of God! Did I really just ask him for some cock? Cringing with embarrassment, I prayed he hadn't heard me.

I watched nearly every woman (and man) check out his powerfully built body, whispering to each other as he headed to the bar. Two waif-like girls who looked to be all of thirteen years old broke free from their circle, their skinny little legs and firm little bottoms going ten to the dozen in order to get over to him. Pen at the ready, one of the girls proceeded to hang herself seductively over the bar - wearing a red micro-skirt. She drew her stilettoed heel up to her bum and grabbed some napkins.

In alarm, I flicked my eyes away, and then, unable to help myself, flicked them back again. The neck of those man-stealing girls, would they take my grave as quick!?

I cast the pair of them venomous stares.

Wiping lipstick off his face and with a smile as wide as a tunnel while both girls squealed, napkin autographs held up like a victorious flags, he picked up his tray of drinks and headed back to me.

"There's your vodka," he winked, "I'll see what I can do about getting you that cock later."

My face went crimson.

Trying to steady my breathing, I changed the subject.

"Oh, *umm*, that's a rather big glass for a lady." I was desperately hoping the flame-red of my cheeks would disappear, so I pointed out what I presumed to be Laura's drink.

"Well, I couldn't help but notice you earlier, and that your sister was drinking out of a pint glass."

Colour crept back up my face.

"Don't worry, it's acceptable for ladies to drink pints in Ireland."

I involuntarily laughed as he swept away my anxieties in one fell swoop. Our eyes locked for a moment.

"By the way, my name is Travis Coleman."

"*Travis*. That's a cool name. Mine's Tara. Tara Ryan. Nice to meet you." We chinked glasses. "Where are you from?"

"Manchester," he replied, proudly.

Hmmm, a northern ride, I thought, suddenly developing a thing for northern men. I then explained that I too lived in England and was over visiting my lunatic family for Christmas.

We quickly became engrossed in deep conversation. It turned out he'd had a very successful career playing rugby for England and had toured the world. In his late-thirties he retired from playing professionally and was headhunted to become a manager/fitness coach for Dublin for the coming season. He was living between the two countries, but flew home to see his parents as often as he could. He shared digs with other players in Dublin, but planned eventually to move to Ireland on a permanent basis. *Really?* I thought, disappointed with the latter information. I'd soon put a stop to that!

By now, the bar was rocking, the dance floor overflowing, with the giant-sized rugby team taking up most of the space. I kept hearing shrieks of laughter coming from them all. Glancing over at Laura, I could see she was in the thick of the dancing crowd, trying to teach the rugby lads salsa.

Travis and I smiled indulgently at them; despite the noise and wild atmosphere, it was as though we were in our own personal bubble. I liked him. I liked him a lot, and was certainly getting some high-definition flirty signals back. It took me a little while to pluck up the confidence ask him the question I really, really wanted to know the answer to – despite the absent wedding ring.

"Are you single?" I asked, my heart hammering in my chest.

He held my gaze. "I am now."

My smile slipped away and my ovaries, which had already decided our first child's name (Hugo) shrank.

Travis leaned in to my ear, his stubble gently brushing my face, his tormenting aftershave driving my pheromones wild. "I'm joking, I'm single."

Like a balloon re-inflating, I gave him a playful dig. "Me too."

I tried to remain composed while screaming inside with delight. We leaned forward and our lips touched. Travis wrapped his arm around my waist, forcing me to fall into him. Melting in his embrace, I returned his hungry kiss. My life had merely been a rehearsal up to this point. I felt like I'd been taken to another place as our tongues began to entwine. Everything was happening in slow-motion, the background noise disappearing. In a deep embrace we kissed slowly, tenderly, my lady-garden's sprinklers beginning to activate themselves.

We pulled back, staring at each other. Everything was in real time again, background noise flooding back. Travis raised my hands and kissed them delicately.

With a cheeky smile, he said, "Was it as good for you as it was for me?"

Picking my jaw up from the floor, I nodded frantically and licked my lips. *Delicious.*

Laura materialised by my side, panting breathlessly. "Tara, this is Dougie, and he's the greatest dancer!"

"Lovely to meet you, Tara. I see you've more than met our Travis." Before I had a chance to answer, Laura grabbed Dougie's shirt collar and started dragging him outside. Over his shoulder, Dougie said, "I'd love to stay and chat, Tara, but ..."

Still on a high from my lusty encounter, I hadn't noticed that the band were packing up, the crowds dispersing and the bar emptying. Holding hands, Travis and I followed the herd outside. I couldn't help but think about my flight back to England in the morning. I'd been in Dublin for the best part of four days and now that there was something worth staying for, I had to leave. Typical!

Once outside, Travis swung me around to face him and said, "I'd like to get to know you more, Tara Ryan. Much more."

Phwarr. The sheer manliness of him. My lady-garden went into yet another spasm and I couldn't help but wonder what he was like in the bedroom department. I really wouldn't object to him tackling me, at all.

"I'd really like that, too." Unable to help myself, I tried to actually visualize the size of his tackle.

Sensing my distraction, Travis pulled me closer. We kissed again, wrapping our arms around each other.

"Get a load of *them*!" shouted Dougie.

"For the love of God!" jeered another.

"Sweet Jesus!" said Laura. "Get a room!"

We couldn't leave each other alone; I was already aching at the thought of leaving him.

"Come on then, gorgeous." Travis slid his phone from his back pocket. "Let's have your digits. I'm not letting you go back to England without knowing how to get hold of you."

I had to repeat my number several times before I got it right.

"Put in the English code!" I wasn't going to lose sight of this man now. I cursed myself for not taking my phone out with me. It was something else to carry, worry about, and my tiny bag couldn't fit it in, not with lip-gloss and perfume being my first priority.

Dougie slid a ring off his finger and handed it to Travis. "I've never seen you this way, man, you're love-struck. G'wan n' marry her now!"

In a drunken state, one of the rugby lads pulled a flower from a pot, put it in his hair (soil and all) and announced in a gravelly voice that he was going to be our bridesmaid. Dougie offered to be the priest and Laura would be best man. We all collapsed into each other, laughing, then began the pretend wedding ceremony. Travis, the groom, scooped me, the blushing bride, up in his arms and carried me through a human archway, supposedly the threshold, whispering sweet nothings in my ear. It was drink talk, but I felt so high on life, I felt as though I was touching God. Before I knew what was going on, I was being shoehorned into a taxi. Apparently, our evening was going to continue back at Dougie's house.

I don't remember much of the journey, as mine and Travis's tongues were doing most of the talking - I was just elated that my night out hadn't ended yet.

We arrived at Dougie's house and headed straight for the kitchen. Six of the other players had arrived back at the house too. Drinks in hand, Travis made it very clear he wanted us to be alone, but as drunk as I was there was no way I was going upstairs. As much as I wanted to rip his clothes off and ride him like a cruise ship, I certainly wasn't going to fall over with my legs in the air just yet.

I checked that Laura was okay, but as ever, when drunk, she was as happy as a pig in shit, especially when surrounded by gorgeous men and bountiful amounts of booze.

Travis led me into the living room. As I looked round for the best place to get cosy, I noticed he had his phone out again and appeared to be texting someone.

How rude! Annoyed, I folded my arms.

"I've sent you a text. You can read it when you get back to your mum's." He smiled wickedly and sat down on the large sofa, patting the seat beside him.

With a sigh of relief and the saucy temptress within me back in play, I joined him. He turned to me with a sexy smile. "What a great night." He rubbed his big-man hand along my quivering thigh. "You're special."

Then, out of nowhere, his mood darkened. I could feel him withdrawing, the atmosphere changing. My heart began to beat faster as I wondered why.

Cautiously, Travis said, "I'm afraid to tell you everything about me, in case it puts you off." He lowered his head, cupping his hands around his beautiful bronzed neck.

I slid off the sofa onto my knees and faced him. (Meanwhile, that infernal bastard thong had sliced my arse into two arses – it was so numb, it was a relief to get up off it.) I lifted up Travis's chiselled jaw and looked deep into his magnetic eyes.

Jokingly, I asked, "Have you murdered someone?"

He shook his head with half a smile. "My job ..." He shrugged his huge shoulders. "It's left me with a complicated life."

Aren't we all complicated? I thought. *Just wait till you meet the rest of my crazy family!*

I could manage complicated. His physical presence was so distracting. God, he was *so* shaggable. While comforting him, I couldn't help but rub the top of his thigh and drift off into thoughts of him in a rugby kit - all dirty, sweaty and powerful.

"I'm so glad I met you." Travis leaned forward, pulled my face to his and we kissed again. "I know it sounds corny, but do you believe in love at first sight?"

Sweet Jesus, I thought, I've hit the jackpot here. Not only is he a gorgeous northern ride, he's also in touch with his feelings. *Stay cool, Tara, stay cool and do not fuck this up! I repeat, don't fuck this up! Regardless of what he just said, do not scare him off!* As carefully as I could, I said, "I believe we can feel a deep connection –"

"We fit," he said. "End of."

Bingo!

He guided me up from my knees and sat me on the

sofa, snaking his arm around me. "We're a bit long in the tooth to play games, don't you think?"

The cheek of him! I didn't like hearing that. Long in the tooth indeed!

"I'd like to see you whenever I can ..."

That was more like it!

" ... but as I mentioned earlier, it's complicated and won't be easy for you. You in?"

If there was a time to jump straight in at the deep end, it was now. Before I knew what I was doing, with my flight home pending, I was nodding. "I'm in."

"Good, because when you know, you know," he added, teasing my jumper so it slipped lower off my shoulder. With my lacy bra strap showing, he kissed the fabric, nudging it lower, softly kissing my goosebumped skin. "I can't be seen out drunk and partying." Groaning sexily, he butterfly-kissed my collarbone. "I'm in a responsible position. Tonight was an exception because we were celebrating a win and it's Christmas." I could feel the heat from his breath on my skin, a hand slowly making its way between my thighs, gently prising them apart. "I have to keep a low profile with my personal life."

I smiled to myself. *So, this is a role of a WAG* (Wives And Girlfriends). Keep quiet, always look sexy, and always, *always* have the latest, largest designer handbag (just in case the paparazzi are out).

I'd trained for this job my whole life.

The time was ticking by too fast. It was 4 a.m., my flight home was in six hours, and I hadn't packed. My heart and all of my anatomy wanted to stay, but my head was telling me to leave. The room next door had gone too quiet. I stood up, adjusting my clothing with the intention of grabbing Laura, but before I knew it Travis pulled me down on top of him. With my legs straddled either side of those firm thighs, I could feel his throbbing manhood pushing hard against me through my jeans. I gripped his huge biceps. He slowly but firmly began thrusting his rock-hard cock against my crotch. I gasped as he buried his face in my chest and started biting my nipples through my jumper. Oh God, I was so turned on. Running my fingers through his dark silky hair, I pulled him closer. Was I really about to have a sexual encounter with a man I barely knew? Unwanted images of my childhood skittered across my mind. I shook my head to clear it. Unable to get back in the moment, I leapt up. It was perfect timing: Laura just then poked her head around the door.

"*Umm* ... Travis, some of your players have passed out on the floor while showing me how to do a scrum ... One of them is at the bottom of the pile and appears to have forgotten how to breathe. Of course I'd be happy to oblige with mouth to mouth resuscitation, but I can't get to him," she hiccupped.

Travis cleared his throat and tried to hide the huge bulge overwhelming his jeans. "The lads aren't used to alcohol. Don't worry, they'll be fine."

Dougie ordered us a taxi and proceeded to pull Laura into the living room for another snog while Travis and I stood waiting in the hallway, our arms wrapped round each other like lovesick teenagers.

He brushed some hair away from my eyes. "Can I fly over and see you soon?"

I fluttered my eyelashes so hard I nearly took off. "I'll look forward to it."

Yes! The Big Man upstairs was on my side for once. Travis and I squeezed each other's hands and sadly said our goodbyes. As Laura and made our way to the taxi, Travis shouted, "I've sent another text to you, gorgeous!"

I blew him a kiss as we spilled into the taxi.

Chapter 4

The journey back from Dougie's house seemed to take forever. My only focus was to get to my phone and read the mysterious texts from Travis. Not that Laura noticed my excitement. She herself looked like the cat that got the cream.

I had the passenger door open before the taxi had fully stopped outside Mum's. I threw the euros I'd been clutching in my hand at Laura and ran to the front door. Laura was oblivious to my torment, chatting away to the driver.

"C'mon! C'mon!!" I hollered. "I need the keys to get in!"

Laura staggered out of the taxi and fumbled in her tiny red bag. After drawing out her keys with a triumphant flourish, she dropped them. She reached down unsteadily to retrieve them from the pavement and promptly dropped them again.

"For the love of God, give them to me!" I yelled, the sound reverberating in the gloomy half-light of the suburban street. Snatching the keys from her, I opened the door, slipping and sliding in my heels, dived over to my phone and, with a racing heart, checked it.

[No New messages]

Gulping hard, I shook the phone impatiently. I switched it off and then back on. Nothing.

"BASTARD!" I didn't care who I woke up. "I can't believe it!"

With a mounting sense of desperation, I switched my phone off again. This time, I left it off for a good minute before switching it back on again. *Still nothing. THE LOUSY FECKER!* By now, Laura and the rest of Dublin could hear me screeching.

I felt like I'd taken a blow to the stomach. I flew into the kitchen to find Laura munching on crackers and cheese.

"Maybe his texts are delayed for some reason?" she said, trying to console me.

"Really?" I asked, feeling a little more hopeful.

Shrugging, she wiped crumbs from her mouth, drank a gallon of water, then staggered towards the stairs, with me hot on her heels. "Even if Travis doesn't make contact you've had a great night, so let it go."

"*Let it go*?" I convulsed, my momentary good feeling vanishing. "You mean, as in – let-it-go – just *forget about him?* Are you out of your feckin' mind?!"

Silence.

"Laura, come back downstairs!" I demanded. "What about you and Dougie – have *you* two exchanged numbers?"

No answer. *The lickarse*, I huffed to myself. "To think

she has letters after her name and has the cheek to call herself a psychotherapist!"

Standing at the bottom of the stairs, to bring some much needed attention to myself, I forced out whimpering tears, hoping someone, *anyone*, would come down and sit with me.

Nothing.

Frustrated, I plonked myself on the bottom step, resting my head against the wall, but the heavily patterned pink and purple wallpaper began moving, the flowers rotating and switching places. It made me feel nauseous. Getting to my feet, I held on to the banister and braced myself before I released a long, whiney whimper and waited for any signs of life.

Okay, so that didn't work either.

Incandescent with rage I thought back to *just an hour ago* – the rawness and hunger Travis had had for me – then I raised the decibels up to as high as I could muster, gathering pace, momentum and let out a huge, long, ear-aching shrill.

Apart from the singing Santa I'd just set off in the lounge, the house remained silent.

"Selective-hearing gobshites!" I shouted.

I didn't know whose face I wanted to punch the most; the singing Santa's, Travis's or Laura's.

I certainly wasn't about to share the makeshift double bed with Laura. I was far too annoyed. How could she be so casual about everything? She was far too blasé for my liking. I stomped loudly up stairs to get my things, flicking on the bedroom light, hoping to annoy her as much as she had annoyed me. I mean, I *needed* her. I wanted to talk through the entire 'if, but and maybe' scenarios. But *no*. I just got ignored by *everyone*.

By now, Laura was comatose and didn't even flinch during my continuing hissy fit. With my temper getting the better of me, I searched round the bedroom for something – *anything* – to destroy. My eyes fell upon a book nestling in her handbag. *How to Help Others*. The irony! I picked it up and deviously doodled multiple willies inside it. Fed up, I grabbed my clothes from off the back of the bedroom chair, humped my suitcase down the stairs, flopped on the sofa and glared at the flashing Christmas tree lights. I felt so miserable.

The throbbing pain in my arse from that bloody thong was now being diverted directly to my heart. I threw my skyscraper shoes at the wall, pulled off my skin-tight jeans and released the offending thong. Then, in a fit of petulance, I proceeded to jump up and down on the pathetic pile of clothes like a lunatic. All the while, I recited every obscenity I could think of. That didn't make me feel better either. For the want of any better way to react to what was clearly the ruin of my *whole* life, I pulled on my inside-out back-to-front PJs, thought of a few more obscenities, and started ranting again.

I collected up my strewn clothes and shoved them in my case, cursing myself for not taking Travis's number. I wanted to give him a piece of my mind! Who did he think he was? The sanctimonious bastard!

Exhausted, I lay on the sofa, tried to get some shut-eye, my phone in my hand, just in case.

It felt like I'd only been asleep a minute when it was time to get up. Of course, the first thing I did was to check my phone. Nothing. I felt like such a fool. Thank God I hadn't slept with him!

As I threw on some creased, mismatched clothes, dreading my miserable journey home, I kept having flashbacks from the night before. Retrieving my scattered outfit after last night's episode, I couldn't stop myself thinking how these clothes had been up against that gorgeous hunk last night.

What a wanker!

As I finished throwing the rest of my belongings into my case, Mum spun round to face me. "Ah sure, are you really goin' to leave this house lookin' like that?" She fussed about, tucking extra stuff into my hand luggage (including what looked like a full packed lunch). "You look like you've been dragged trew a hedge arse-ways. Will you not even run a comb trew your hair, child? And you've still got your disco make-up on – let me get that for you, pet."

She advanced on me, her thumb dripping with saliva.

I squealed and backed up in horror. "Oh God, Mum – don't! I couldn't give two shites how I look!"

Mum looked offended, but luckily, before she could reproach me any further, Laura barged past. She was running out the door and shouting over her shoulder as she made determinedly to her car, "Tara, you're going to have to shift that arse of yours if I'm dropping you at the airport, I'll be late for work otherwise."

I could barely conceal my temper as I yelled back, "Look, I can't find my Jimmy Choo trainers. Mum, have you seen them? – *KATIE*! Have you *had* them?!"

I wouldn't have put it past that little sister of mine to have them on eBay as quick as a flash to raise cash to feed her nasal hobby.

Mum wagged her finger at me. "Now, don't you be

blaming the child. Lord knows you'd blame her if it were raining!"

I looked out, and strangely enough it was raining.

Katie, leaning against the door frame, looking smug, seemed to be enjoying my discomfort. I didn't want to give her the satisfaction of saying anything, so I became determined to leave immediately, missing Jimmy's or no missing Jimmy's.

I was fuming. "Right – I have to go!" I grabbed stuff right and left and shoved it in my handbag.

"Go on with yourself and hurry over to the car," said Mum, trying to stuff a satsuma in my pocket. "God only knows what the neighbours will think with you leaving the house looking like that."

I gave Mum a big hug and Katie a half-hearted one, grabbed the first pair of shoes I could find and hobbled to the car with my case in tow. I threw my luggage into the boot and slumped into the passenger seat.

"Are you really going to the airport looking like that?" enquired Laura, with her well-practiced *have-you-lost-the-plot?* look. I decided that any answer I gave would be way too foul-mouthed, so I didn't answer her at all.

I pulled down the sun-visor to look in the mirror. They were right. I looked rough as a badger's arse. Maybe I should've brushed my hair, or at least wiped away the make-up from underneath my eyes.

I flipped the sun-visor back up and looked down at myself. I really was a mess. My open-toed, diamante-encrusted, silver, four-inch heels really didn't look good with socks on underneath. To make matters worse, the socks didn't even match. One was a rainbow-inspired stripy sock, the other a novelty Christmas sock with a reindeer's face on it. Adding to my *bag lady* look was a mismatched, creased, velour tracksuit, which had something sticky on it, more than likely a dribble of rum from those god-awful, out of date liqueur chocolates that I'd found at the back of a cupboard. Finally, completing the tramp-like ensemble was my knee-length cream faux fur coat. If James could see me now, I thought, he'd have a touch of the vapours and resign on the spot. But actually – for the first time in my life, *I really didn't care.* My thoughts were already creeping back to last night again. Travis seemed so sincere, and above all, so honest. I thought about what he'd said: 'You in?' Clearly he'd changed his mind and I was very much out!

Before I knew it, we were at the airport. As I was readying myself to say my goodbyes to Laura, she saw the sadness in my face.

"Tara, today's a new day. Embrace it. Now, go and sort yourself out in the toilets. Your hair looks like something that's just been emptied out of a vacuum cleaner."

"I don't care." I half smiled, then threw my arm around her in an attempt to be sisterly.

"Sorry, sis, I have to get going. I have to return a book I borrowed from my boss before I start work." We both stared down into her handbag. "I'll call you later."

Oh fuck!

I had flashbacks of a drunk, immature me doodling random willies on that book! Right then, right there, I didn't have the courage to own up. I'd text her straight *after* I'd put my case through – that way, at least I'd be out of punching distance and she'd know not to hand it back. Casting the thought to one side, I got out of Laura's car, collected my belongings, waved her away, then limped with my flapping, short ankle-bashers, revealing my interesting choice of socks and four-inch stripper stilettos and dragged my weary, hung-over head (closely followed by my hung-over body) across the packed Departures hall to check myself in.

"Good morning, madam." The check-in lady had crispy skin (way too much foundation!), a crispy smile and matching crispy bun.

It most certainly was not a good morning. Checking my phone for the millionth time, I placed my passport on the desk with a big sigh. Travis was nothing but a devious, silver-tongued bastard!

"Thank you. Could anyone have tampered with your luggage?"

"Everybody tampers with my things." I bet if I looked on eBay my beloved Jimmy Choo trainers would be on there right now!

"*Madam,* are you saying someone has tampered with your luggage?"

Check-in lady's eyes had widened. And, I'd become aware that I'd said something really stupid. I wiped the beads of sweat that had formed on my brow and tried to start again, but didn't get a chance.

"Madam, I distinctly heard you say your things had been tampered with."

My stupid loose tongue had taken over before my foggy, hung-over brain was able filter its content.

"Sorry. I'll start again."

I watched her hand inching towards a security phone, so, drawing myself up straight, I attempted to explain myself, quickly.

"I've had a bad night – went out with my sister – not my youngest sister – she's got drug problems and is on release from rehab – she didn't mean to kill Moses, *that's my Mum's budgie*, but I do know she stole my Jimmy Choo trainers! I was out with my eldest sister Laura, *who I think has a drink problem*, much like my dad – but she's a psychotherapist so no one questions her. *Anyway*, I met the man of my dreams – only he wasn't the man of my dreams at all because he's a nothing, only a lying bastard! A famous one at that. Not that I'm trying to bribe you with name-dropping ..."

I was greeted with narrowed eyes and, to my horror, crispy check-in lady then went to the greatest lengths to lean forward, look me up and down and sniff me as though I was some kind of animal.

"We have strict guidelines that must be followed," said her scornful bright red lips. "Passenger safety is paramount and I believe you are unsure whether your belongings have been tampered with or not. You are also intoxicated and therefore *unfit* to fly. I have to call security."

Alarmed, I watched her perfectly manicured hand pick up the phone.

The enormity of the situation hit home. "Oh come on, there's no need for that!" I said, blood thumping in my ears.

She rapidly spoke into the receiver, while never taking her eyes off me. "We have a code yellow situation. I can smell alcohol and the passenger is ..." she turned her back and whispered into the phone "... confused ... and abusive."

I looked around in disbelief. After she'd finished her call, with a dismissive hand gesture, she said, "Please move to one side, madam. There are *sober* passengers waiting."

Cheeky bitch, I thought as I scrabbled in my handbag for chewing gum to disguise the smell of alcohol. With my heart pounding (my hangover now in full swing), I broke out into a cold sweat and started shaking.

A large and unhappy queue had formed behind me. I could feel the stares burning into my back and could hear the huffs, puffs and loud clicking of tongues. A woman directly behind me loud-whispering that by the look of me I was from the travelling community.

I didn't know what to do, so pulled on my oversized Bvlgari sunglasses in an effort to hide my identity as best as possible. Heads were poking out from the back of the queue, like a Mexican wave trying to nosey what was going on up ahead.

I pulled out my phone to call Laura to come and vouch for me, but before I could, security had arrived. Two guards linked both of my arms, hustling me away, while a third walked behind, dragging my case. I tried to distract myself from the embarrassing walk of shame by imagining how I'd tell this story to my friends. It would have to be something like: Who would have thought it, three burley men ushering little old me! But I wasn't ready to laugh, so I decided to cry instead.

I was repeatedly questioned, but I was more than relieved that security decided not to body-search me: my arse was sore enough, thank you very much! In fact, they decided not to take the matter any further. After nursing umpteen coffees and regaling them with my woes from the night before – and actually delighted to have a shoulder or three to cry on - they shoved me out of the room and sent me on my way. Maybe, just maybe, the security guards realised there was no further indignity that could be heaped upon me. I was a broken woman.

Despite feeling completely demoralised after being released, I still managed to catch my original flight after rushing through security. I was still in shock when I boarded the plane, and with everyone whispering and finger-pointing I put my coat over my head and sat in mopey silence.

As soon as we touched down, I switched my phone back on. I had a new message – *please let it be Travis!*

[Text from Laura]

Tried to call you. My boss is not happy with me. Why did you desecrate the book he'd lent me? Penises all over it! Honestly, Tara, sometimes you are so childish!

With all the drama at the airport, pre-warning Laura about the book had gone clean out of my head!

[Text to Laura]

I'd never do that! I bet it was Katie. She was pissed off that we went out without her. You need to have a serious word with her! Still haven't heard from Travis by the way :-(x

[Text from Laura]

You signed each penis, Tara. I know it was you!

Oh fuck.

[Text to Laura]

Sorry, I was drunk and upset. I'll send you the money to replace it.

I collected my luggage and grabbed a taxi home. I felt exhausted, and, frankly, quite depressed. I'd returned to London with a hangover from hell, a case full of dirty washing and a thong-induced, red-raw arse that wasn't even the result of having amazing sexy times. I was sick of the festive season.

Intending to sleep the whole sorry nightmare away, I switched my phone to silent, dumped my case in the hallway, got into bed, fully clothed, and pulled the comfort of the duvet around me.

I woke up four hours later to find my phone had been busy.

[Text from (Unrecognised)]

Hi Tara, I didn't hear back from you so presumed I had your number down incorrectly, so I tracked Laura down. I miss you already. How're you feeling today? Travis xx

I screamed with excitement and jumped up and down on the bed like a frantic child, and read the text over and over again.

I couldn't believe I'd called Travis a wanker!

Lesson learnt – I was too quick to jump to the wrong conclusion and way too judgmental!

The other texts and missed calls were from Laura explaining that Travis had tracked her down at her workplace (she'd told Dougie which hospital she worked at, in the hope of a 'visit' one day), and all of a sudden my trip to Dublin was the best trip ever!

[Text to Travis]

Hi Travis, so good to hear from you! I'm glad you went out of your way to get my number. Really enjoyed your company. I hope to see you again very soon. Actually, when will that be? hahah xxx

I heard the ping of another text come through.

[Text from Siobhan]

Boo hoo ... I have a sore tummy. I think me SIM card is on its way :-(x

I woke early on the morning of New Year's Eve and immediately checked my phone. In the late hours of the night, Travis had messaged me again.

[Text from Travis]

Hi babe, hope you're ok. I'm flying to Manchester to see my parents. xxxxxxxxxxxxxxxxxxxxxxxxxxxxxxxxxxxxxxxxxx xxxxxxxxxxxxxxxxxxxxxxxxxxxxxxxxxxxxxxxxxx xxxxxxxxxxxxxxxxxxxxxxxxxxxx

A smile plastered over my smug little face and my heart leaping in excitement, I got straight on the phone to Laura, yelling the second she picked up.

"Laura! Laura! Guess what?"

"What?" she mumbled in a grumpy *I've-just-woken-up* voice.

"Guess!"

"Whaaaaaat?"

"Guess! Guess! Guess!" I implored.

She groaned heavily. "You've won the Lotto?"

"No, it's better than that!"

She continued groaning, obviously not in the mood for guessing games.

"Okay!" I said, feeling impatient. "Travis text me last night –"

"Tara, it's 7.00 a.m. on my day off. I thought you wanted to discuss something important."

"It is important. Sorry ... I'll call back later." I stopped jabbering and held my breath, waiting for Laura to cave in. She always did.

"Well, I'm awake now so you may as well tell me."

Getting the green light, I raced ahead.

"While Travis is in the country, should I invite him to Siobhan's New Year's Eve party? What do you think?"

"What's with all this texting? Don't you two speak on the phone?"

"No one makes calls anymore, Laura. Everyone communicates via text."

"Well, you know my feelings on that subject ..."

I zoned out while she droned on and on about the art of conversation, blurred lines and words being taken out of context.

She was *so* old-fashioned at times.

"Just call him and ask him."

My stomach lurched. "*Call him*? But that will look like I'm chasing him!" I didn't want to tell her that I had already asked Travis when we were going to see each other and he hadn't acknowledged it.

"It's a simple question. You're a grown woman. An adult."

Oh yes, I was a grown woman. An adult. But, since meeting Travis I felt like a teenager. Jittery, unsure and perhaps even a little neurotic.

I'd never met a man that I'd fancied more. Never met a man so upfront about what he wanted. Never met a man more husband and children material. And he was a celebrity! I was scared of getting it wrong. And even though I probably wasn't, I wanted to come across as well balanced.

I could hear Laura yawing and I felt bad. She listened to people's problems day in and day out. No wonder she drank the way she did!

She yawned again. "Tara, sometimes you just have to take a leap of faith."

Never a truer word spoken!

Feeling queasy, and after composing a zillion different texts and deleting them, I finally plucked up some courage.

[Text to Travis]

Sorry for the delay in getting back to you! I was asleep. I'm sure your parents will be delighted to see you. One of my crazy friends is having a New Year's Eve party. Fancy coming to it? It would be great to see you! Xxx

Like a lunatic, and desperate to impress Travis I cleaned the house top to bottom. Then, changing my mind, I got on the phone and booked us a hotel suite, upgrading us to as much as my purse could afford. I justified it by telling myself I was investing in my future. After that, I was running out the door heading for Glamma-Puss. I was having a blow-dry ahead of the party. It was bound to be a mad one, Siobhan's parties always were. I also needed to pick up my fancy-dress costume from James.

Hours slipped by without Travis responding. I quickly checked my phone for the millionth time before entering the salon.

"Hi, James!" I said, masking my lovelorn anxiety.

"Tara, darling." He kissed both my cheeks. "As requested, I've picked up your fancy dress costume and it's just *fabulous!* I'm so jealous. I've always wanted to wear a Miss Santa tutu in public. It's hanging up in the staffroom." He studied my face intensely. "What have *you* been up to in the Emerald Isle, because I'm detecting a glint in your eyes!"

I was grinning from ear to ear. "I'll tell you another time."

"Oh no! You are *not* doing this to me." James practically broke into a run to cut me off before I could get to the staffroom. "I have to know. *Pweeeaaase!* Is it juicy? As in *really* juicy? Have you finally had some action?"

"Well, no, not yet," I purred coquettishly, "but watch this space!"

James looked deflated. "So no sex then?"

I shook my head.

"Not even a little lick of a lollipop?"

I battled out of my coat. "No, there was no licking of

any lollipops." Although hopefully there would be tonight!

"Hmm. Well, anyway ..." Losing interest, James mimed an extravagant yawn. "... I have to finish my nails for the party."

I inspected my costume. It was just what I wanted. Miss Sexy Claus would be wearing a short, frilly tutu, and a cape edged with white fluffy fur. I'd match it with a low-cut top, some stockings and bright red heels.

"Jayde!" I could hear James screeching across the salon. "Stop stuffing pork pies down your hole and do Tara's hair!"

I watched Jayde walk past James, middle finger raised. "It ain't a pork pie, it's a carrot! I'm on diet."

"Another diet?" James howled with laughter. His bitchy diva personality was out in full swing.

Jayde looked good, her hair and make-up perfect. Indeed, she looked like she'd lost weight since I last saw her. A sparkle in her step, she popped her head around the staffroom door. "Come on then, Tara," she said, "let's get you looking even more gorgeous."

"Jayde, I saw that finger gesture to James, and if *I* could see that, with the amount of mirrors in the salon, the clients would see it too."

"Sorry, you know what he's like –"

"Yes," I interrupted before I could be drawn into a long discussion, "I do, but stop taking his bait, Jayde. And don't worry, I'll be having a word with James too."

With my hair half up and half down, tousled curls cascading down my shoulders, I bade farewell to Jackie, James and Jayde, informing them that I'd see them all later at the party, and with my silent phone sitting in between my legs, I drove home.

Chapter 5

After a two-minute walk, I arrived at Siobhan's house. I could hear the music blasting and saw hordes of people dancing, through the kitchen window. Ringing the doorbell, I was greeted by James.

I took a step back in shock. "Oh my God! What *are* you wearing?"

"I know there's not much to it -" he gave me a suggestive twirl "- but I love it! Don't you just love it, Spencer?" James turned the full spotlight of his attention on a young man who had appeared from nowhere, also waiting to be admitted to the party. Poor Spencer looked mortified. It was *very* clear he didn't bat for the same team as James, nor did he intend to.

"Do the angel wings do it for you?" continued the irrepressible James, turning around and pouting back at Spencer over his shoulder. In his view, any heterosexual man could be turned.

"Hmmm? What about these skimpy, silky shorts then? They don't leave much to the imagination, do they,

Spencer? I've got a spare pair if you'd like to try them. Or maybe you'd like to get into *my* shorts, sweetie? Anyway, come in, come in." He stood back with a flourish and looked disappointed as Spencer put his head down and darted through the doorway without giving him a second glance. "*Gay is the way*, sweetheart. You'll find that out sooner or later!" James called out to the rapidly retreating figure. "Call me when you're ready!"

Recovering his composure, he turned to me. "Oh well, plenty more fish in the sea. Everyone's well on their way to getting leathered."

While James had been tormenting Spencer, I'd been busy sending Travis another text. This one was a guaranteed showstopper because it had a selfie of me in my Miss Sexy Claus outfit, with a few suggestive words. Then I composed another, asking him if he was coming to the party or not, that he'd need to step on it if he wanted to get here before midnight, and that I'd booked us a fancy hotel suite.

"Where's the lady of the house, James?" I asked as I clicked *send,* hoping against hope my messages would stir Travis into action.

"Last time I spotted Siobhan she was trying to hump the Christmas tree."

"Oh, okay, sounds about right," I laughed, despite my desperate mood. "Thanks, James. Nice wand by the way," I added, nodding at his nether-regions as I began to weave my way through the crowd.

"Thanks, honey. I get that a lot," he shouted. "If only the right bloody people noticed it!"

Even in my distracted state, I noticed some fabulous costumes - everyone had gone to a great deal of effort, from cute animal onesies to Power Rangers to human-sized avocados. Some outfits were, I might even go so far as to say, shocking. I mean, a green glitter mankini? *Really?* Strangely, it was impossible not to gawp.

I could hear Siobhan bellowing long before I could see her. She was singing along to Wham's "Last Christmas". Entering the lounge, I spotted her just in time to witness her humping session with the Christmas tree go horribly wrong. In some sort of grotesque finale, she took a tumble backwards, pulling the tree down on top of her with a huge crash. Baubles and bits of tinsel flew into the air and the tree was plunged into darkness as the fairy lights gave up against her relentless assault.

For a few moments, the room descended into silence. Everyone stopped what they were doing and looked over. Everyone *except* James, that is. He'd abandoned his door duty and was now up on a chair wiggling his toosh and waving his magic wand (the plastic one) in the air. I'm not sure he'd even registered our friend's predicament.

I hurried over to see if Siobhan was okay. From what I could see, she was comatose as she lay trapped under the tree, her legs wrapped around it. One of her hands was sticking out from between the branches, still grasping an empty wine bottle.

"Siobhan!" I pushed the tinsel aside and plunged my hand into the foliage so I could force open one of her eyelids. "It's only 9.30 p.m.! Have you been on the sauce all day?"

"Feck – what?" she registered it was me. "I wuv you, Tara - I wuv *everyone.*"

I yelled across the lounge, "James, get down from your stage and get some water for her, will you?" Most people had already decided that the Siobhan Show was over and had carried on regardless, cranking Lady Gaga up full blast.

"But 'Poker Face' is *my song!*" whined James. "Can I get the water in a minute? Actually, where's that lard-arse of a donkey, Jayde? She can get it."

"I don't care who gets it – just please hurry up," I said in my best I'm-in-no-mood-for-messing-about voice.

"Ugh! Fine!" James minced off to the kitchen and returned with a glass of water. But it was hopeless; I couldn't get near Siobhan's mouth. We needed another strategy, so I began barking instructions.

"James, go and find me some strong men to help get this Christmas tree up and then we can get madam onto the sofa."

Gawd, I am so wasted on this lot, I thought. *I'd make a bloody brilliant parent. Look how effortlessly I take charge in a crisis. If it wasn't for me Siobhan would be trapped until morning!*

Then I had an awful thought. *What if something dreadful had happened to Travis? What if he'd been in a car accident, veered off the road and no one had noticed? Or worse, what if he had been kidnapped and held for ransom? Maybe I should call the police or something? Mind you – and say what? "My boyfriend - possibly my potential husband - seems to have disappeared and is not responding to my text messages?"* I'd be arrested for wasting police time.

James was shouting above the din of a Spice Girls track, forcing me to tear my thoughts back to the here and now. "There aren't any decent men - believe-me - I've already checked. I'll go find Jayde. She's the closest thing we have to a strong bloke."

Jayde couldn't be found anywhere. Luckily, while James was looking for her, he managed to gather a group of willing bodies, and together we managed to heave the Christmas tree off Siobhan. I moved swiftly to get the baubles out from her bra. She looked a terrible state. Her *St. Trinian's* outfit was a complete mess, her stockings full of ladders, her skirt tucked into her knickers. Hauling her onto the sofa, I told James to give her the water.

"Open wide, Siobhan," James yanked her head up by one of her pigtails and poured a glug of water down her throat. "There's a good girl."

"That tastes as good as feckin' vodka!" Siobhan sputtered, her tongue lapping up the remaining liquid around her mouth.

James sheepishly whiffed the few drops left in the glass. "Oops, my mistake. I could have sworn it was water."

"James!" I said in horror. "She's had far too much already! She's gonna be as sick as a pig!"

As if to prove my point, Siobhan immediately pulled *that* face. It was the ashen *oh-my-god-I'm-going-to-puke* face.

"Are you going to be sick?" I asked.

Silence.

"Everybody move – she's gunna blow!"

With that, I heard my phone go off. I'd left it on the side table in all the excitement (but I reckon I'd have heard a message drop if it was two miles away). Ecstatic, I promptly dropped Siobhan's cradled head. It landed with a sickening thud.

"Sorry!" I shouted over my shoulder as I dived over to read the message. "Hang on, Siobhan – don't be sick yet. I think Travis has texted me!"

Lots of delayed texts had come through at once. Beaming with excitement, I quickly scrolled through them. They were all *before the sun sets happy clappy New Year's wishes* and all that nonsense. Honestly, right then, I couldn't give a flying feck about the sun setting!

Nothing from Travis!

I turned back to my patient, only to discover she'd clambered off the sofa and was standing, green-faced, with the unsteadiness of a one-year-old learning to walk. That wasn't the real problem, though. Looking on, I could see Siobhan's face contorting as she began to retch, her eyes widening. I grabbed the nearest thing to me - a Christmas stocking - and held it out for her. Of course, she missed it. Sadly, I couldn't say the same for my outfit, which bore the full brunt of Siobhan's projected stomach contents.

"I feel feckin' great now!" she announced. She'd somehow miraculously recovered. "Where's the feckin' party gone? I need a drink!"

However, after taking one wobbly step forward, her eyes rolled to the back of her head and she collapsed, face-planting the floor. I stood there with my mouth open and held my arms out in disbelief.

"Great, just bloody great!" Covered in vomit and with my face looking like a slapped arse, I put Siobhan into recovery position (old habits die hard) and tiptoed out to the kitchen. I poked my head around the door to find that James was now on the kitchen table doing the YMCA.

"James, I'm having a nightmare." I tried not to breathe in as I talked, the stench of Siobhan's unwanted gift making me feel nauseous. "Can you go watch her? And *do not* give her any more alcohol. I need to get changed."

I stomped up stairs into the bathroom, peeled off my *not so sexy* hired outfit, showered, and thundered into Siobhan's bedroom. Flinging open the wardrobe door, I flicked morosely through its contents and eventually opted for a tracksuit. Checking my hair and make-up in the mirror, I couldn't stop thinking about Travis. He still hadn't texted me. The tosspot!

Meanwhile, the party was back in full swing. I could hear the commotion as I descended into the madness again. Fed up with watching everyone else having a ball, I burst into the kitchen in search of disinfectant and rubber gloves. As I was rummaging around the cupboards, I heard what sounded like Siobhan shouting: "Jam it up her arse!"

I looked round to find Jayde, who'd returned from wherever she'd been, running round in a homemade donkey outfit. Her costume, a set of fluffy, wonky ears on a headband, a grey cropped T-shirt accompanied by leggings, left nothing to the imagination – and she was being chased around the room by James and Siobhan. *Siobhan!? She'd puked all over me not even half an hour ago and now she was running around with another bottle of wine in her hand!*

"Come on, everybody," shouted James. "Pin the tail on the wobbling donkey! There's enough arse for everyone to have a go, you can't miss."

All the men lined up to have a go and Jayde seemed to love every minute of it. She'd come such a long way. I couldn't help but feel a glow of pride at her growth in her new confidence. James being a bitch had backfired, and it served him right. I looked at Jayde's arse and it wasn't wobbling at all. In fact, it was very peachy. Hence the queue!

"Don't worry, you all just carry on playing and I'll

clean up the mess!" I stopped scrubbing the carpet and, in a fit of temper, peeled off my gloves. Unable to contain myself, I took Laura's advice: withheld my number and called Travis's phone.

It was switched off. I quickly called the hotel, desperate for a refund. But it was too late.

After I'd finished cleaning, I did my best to join in, mingling with other guests, but my heart just wasn't in it.

Where was he?

What was he doing?

Why was he ignoring me?

I knew in my miserable, discontented mood, I was half-heartedly joining in conversations, just to kill time; but I wasn't kidding anyone, least of all myself.

At 11.58 p.m., we congregated to see in the New Year. In a fit of desperation, I quickly rang Travis again. His phone was still switched off.

"I'm doing the countdown, everyone, so shut up!" said James. "Make sure you have some champers at the ready because I've got a surprise once the clock strikes midnight! Spencer, darling! I *so* caught you looking at me just then. My eyes are up *here*, sunshine!"

Siobhan, who seemed well on her way once more, wasn't having any of it. "James, I'm gettin' in there first with Spencer, you jammie fecker! You can have sloppy seconds. Isn't that right, Spencer?"

Poor Spencer. He looked like he was at the wrong party.

"Ten, nine, eight, seven, six, five, four, three, two, one ... *Happy New Year*, bitches!" James cheered, throwing glittering fairy dust everywhere.

Feeling incredibly sorry for myself, I faked the smiles,

the kisses and the hugs. Just a simple text from Travis saying, *I'm on my way! Sorry, can't make the party, too short notice,* would've softened the blow. He hadn't even bothered wishing me a Happy New Year! *Am I really that forgettable?* Clearly I was, because here I was, yet again, my silent phone in my hand, on New Year's Eve, all alone.

I swept my tired eyes across the smoke-filled room and brushed away the *happy* glitter. I'd noticed everyone had paired up in some form for the evening. That is, everyone but *me* and, oddly for once, Siobhan. Emboldened by too much drink, she'd told both Dannys to feck off because she couldn't give a shite about either of them. She was curled up on the sofa surrounded by empty bottles and wineglasses, sleeping like a baby. Even Jayde had gone off to another party to meet a fella.

In the corner, unaware that he was being watched, James was making friends with Siobhan's much loved human-sized Blow-Up Barry. He was cupping his gentleman's area. *I must buy James the Inflatable Ben,* I thought, as I overheard him ask Barry if he'd like his fingernails painted.

New Year's Day I felt even more despondent. Not a great way to start a New Year at all! I couldn't even keep a man for more than a night. And, worse still, I hadn't *even* slept with him and he'd still done a runner!

But I couldn't get Travis out of my head. It was as though he'd hypnotised me. Then I played a few mind games with myself. What if he hadn't received my texts? I checked my sent messages for the twentieth time. *I was being ridiculous!*

Where was my pride? Too far away, it seemed, to stop my brain from formulating yet another attempt at contacting him. I scolded myself for coming across desperate. *But I was desperate!*

[Draft message to Travis]

How did you bring in the New Year?

[Delete]

[Draft message to Travis]

Hi gorgeous, what you up to?

[Delete]

[Draft message to Travis]

You WANKER! Why haven't you contacted me!!!

[Delete]

[Text to Travis]

How's the family? Wish them all a Happy New Year from me. Look forward to meeting them all one day! Xxxx

Fuck it. [Send]

Regretfully, I spent most of New Year's Day with my phone fused to my hip. *I needed to get a grip! Travis was probably in bed with a hangover.*

But oh, how I wished I was with him!

I pictured him lying in bed. Imagining his body, I could see him naked, a white sheet *just* covering his manhood, me lying next to him, running my hands down his ripped six-pack, carrying on down to his ... *Ahh, for feck's sake. I need to pull myself together. Big time!*

But then my thoughts started to change. Bad hurty thoughts, each trying to jockey for first position in my already fragile head. *The fecker better be alone. What if he went out last night and met someone? What if he's in bed with her right now? Oh my God. The WHORE, sleeping with him on the first night! I bet she's blonde and skinny, with huge boobs. Bastard, I hate him!* Right, I was going to text him a piece of my mind!

[Draft message to Travis]

Forgotten about me already!!? You're with a whore I take it? Let me guess her name ... CHLAMYDIA???!!!!!

[Delete]

[Draft message to Travis]

Wherever you've gone, please come back ...

[Delete]

Demented, I called Siobhan for advice.

"Ah c'mon now, if he doesn't get to see his parents often, they'll have loads to catch up on," she said. Siobhan could be quite sensible when sober.

"Really? Do you really think it's that?" I prayed she was right.

"I'm sure he'll be in touch," she said, reassuringly. Then she ruined the effect by adding: "But if he isn't, I'll get on the next flight to Dublin and deck the bastard!"

I laughed. "Thanks. So, how's your head, this morning?"

"I'm in top form! But you'll not feckin' believe this, right, but, I wakes up this morning with two guys in me bed, all three of us stark bollock naked – not a clue who they are. Then, I went downstairs to find some eejit had knocked over me feckin' Christmas tree – and James fast asleep on top of me Blow-Up Barry!"

"Do you remember anything from your party at all?" I asked.

"Well, I know I had a great time, that's all that matters, *right*?" she laughed. "I'm just in the middle of dragging one of those guys out of me bed – he needs to help me get the Christmas-tree spines out of me fanjita, cos fook knows how they got there."

"Okay, well, I'm glad someone's having a good time." I felt a cloud of despair descend on me again, reminding me of how lonely I felt. "I'll let you go then."

I felt like I was going to cry. Maybe Laura could be of some comfort? I filled her in.

"And you've still not heard from him? That doesn't sound right."

I instantly regretted making this call.

"Siobhan said if he's with his parents there're prob –"

"Hmm … "

I could hear her sighing, the not so gentle waft of judgement, the cogs of her brain whirring. Weighing it all up, information shifting from one side to the other. I rolled my eyes impatiently.

"Laura, I rang you to make me feel *better* not *worse!*" I hated it when she treated me like I was one of her mental patients. *I needed her to stroke my ego. Tell me I was being irrational.*

"Doesn't sound right to me."

Not what I wanted to hear!

"Forget about him. He seems unreliable. Move on, you'll find someone better."

"But I don't want to move on and find someone better!"

"Why not?"

"Because I want *him!*"

"But he doesn't seem to want you."

"Too harsh, Laura!"

"You're not in a Disney movie. The truth hurts."

Was that the best she could come up with? I thought she was supposed to be trained to deal with these situations. She was rubbish. What were all those years in university for? Angry, I ended the call.

As the days of silence ticked by, I returned to work. With a heavy heart and to stop me making even an even bigger fool of myself, I deleted Travis's number. After enjoying the brief moment of control, I swiftly deleted every in and out text message and felt momentarily liberated.

So life went back to normal. Except it hadn't. Not quite. I felt a hole. A great big gaping hole - which no amount of distractions could fill. I felt as though I'd been on a roller-coaster ride that had only one peak. Travis had made me feel something I hadn't felt before, like it was finally possible for me to unfold for the first time in my life.

I found it hard to concentrate at work - even the usual

madcap banter didn't distract me from my thoughts. I kept flashing back to that night I'd met him, dearly wishing I hadn't.

"Earth calling Tara," said James as I moped round the deathly quiet salon. "You've broken a nail. Let me fix it for you."

"Not today, thanks, James. Tomorrow, maybe. But not today."

"You're not yourself," he said. "Has that rugby guy got to you that badly?" Siobhan had obviously filled him in. "I hate to see you so sad."

I kept quiet, fighting tears back. Was I the loneliest woman on the planet? Right now, it felt like it.

"Have you noticed that Jayde and I aren't bickering?"

I hadn't noticed.

"We're trying to make you happy." Jayde appeared beside us.

I gave them a half smile as a tear trickled down my cheek. James gathered me into a tight hug, then arm in arm they led me into the staffroom. "Shall I pop the kettle on?" said Jayde, rubbing my shoulder.

I shook my head. I was all tea'd out.

"Then let me take you out for a boozy lunch and we can do a bit of shopping?" suggested James. "That's always fun. The first day back at work after a Christmas break is way too depressing. Should only be a half day really. I don't know why schools don't do it - the half day, that is, without the boozy lunch, of course."

"Thanks, James, I'm not up to it."

"Tell Uncle James everything. Let me see if I can help. A problem shared is a problem halved and all that." He glared at Jayde. "Off you go. Tara and I need to talk, *in private*; be like a mushroom and go somewhere dark, there's a good girl."

"James, don't speak to Jayde like that!" I knew those two getting on wouldn't last.

"It's alright, Tara," said Jayde, "I'd rather have rectal surgery with no aesthetic than look at his ugly mutt anyway." She turned her back, busied herself cleaning the staffroom that didn't need cleaning.

"Are you going to give up on him that easily?" whispered James. "Never had you down as a quitter."

"I didn't quit. He did."

We sat in silence, James rubbing my arm.

"I've never had a successful relationship. I'm fundamentally flawed," I said, my lungs deflating. "One minute my life is going in one direction, the next – *boom!* – it's not going anywhere at all."

James sympathised, told me how gorgeous I was – that any man would be lucky to have me in his life, etc., but I didn't want to hear that Travis and I *weren't meant to be.* That I'd meet someone else. That what was for me wouldn't go past me. I gave this spiel to clients all the time.

Ready to start howling again, I darted to the toilets to have a good talk to myself. I was bordering on pathetic. I splashed my face and lectured myself accordingly. Just as I was making my way back to the staffroom, I witnessed James and Jayde having a cat fight, Jackie in the middle trying to separate them.

"Tara, your phone's buzzing." Jayde had my phone cupped under her chin, the other hand shoving a red-faced James away.

"Give me that!" growled James. He snatched my phone clean out of Jayde's hand, adjusted his hair, smoothed down his shirt and proceeded to put on his telephone voice. "Good afternoon, Tara's phone - *James speaking*, how may I help you?"

I shook my head, indicating I didn't want to speak with anyone. It would be someone trying to sell me something or inform me of a car accident I hadn't had.

"I'm afraid Tara isn't available at the moment, can I take a message ...? Okay ... okay, and who shall I say is calling ...?"

The next thing I knew, James was pointing frantically at the phone, mouthing, *T-R-A-V-I-S*.

Not believing a word of it, I swatted him away.

Shrugging his shoulders, he gave me a *you're-going-to-be-sorry face*. "Thank you for calling, Travis," he purred. "I'll pass the message on to Tara personally. Enjoy the rest of your day." He hung up, handing me the phone. "Tara, look ... it's an Irish number. It *was* him!"

James was telling the truth. Shaking and sweating, I grabbed my phone, and ran to the toilets again, calling Travis straight back.

"Travis?" My throat was bone dry with nerves. "It's me, Tara, Tara Ryan, from England."

"Hey gorgeous, yes, I know it's you," he laughed softly. "I'm lying on the bed reading *all* your text messages. Miss Naughty Santa outfit, eh? Very nice indeed. And those stockings ... wow, how am I supposed to concentrate on work now?"

I nearly fainted.

After we'd finished our conversation, I flung the toilet door open. Earwigging, Jackie, James and Jayde all fell through. Clambering back up, they waited patiently for me to say something.

"He'd only gone and accidentally left his phone in Dublin! He flew back from Manchester this morning and has only just received all of my forty-something text messages. Or maybe he said fifty? Ahh well - who's counting? I feel *soooo* stupid! But guess what? He's flying over to see me next week. I'm so excited, I feel sick! James," I said, with a beaming smile, "fancy fixing my nails now?"

Chapter 6

I'd been planning what to wear for the best part of three days, trying on *everything* in my wardrobe in various combinations. Nothing seemed right. There was nothing else for it. I had to call in my local fashionista: James.

The next day, we headed to the West End of London, armed and dangerous with my credit card. For hours, we went from shop to shop, hunting down the perfect outfit. I liked almost everything, but James insisted I needed to make a huge impact by looking sexy and fierce. We both agreed on one thing - there was no room for error. Nothing other than *complete* perfection was acceptable.

James had been pitching *fur coat no knickers* from the moment we'd met at the train station. I resisted, but eventually, fuelled by Dutch courage (thanks to a liquid lunch), I agreed to meet him halfway. I would get a new *faux* fur coat, but there would *have* to be underwear underneath, very *sexy* underwear. So, after we left the noisy Italian restaurant, which was tucked away in the corner of

Shepherds Market, we set off with renewed vigour. The next stop was Agent Provocateur for some saucy pieces.

"It's got to be all black," ordered James as we weaved our way down Brewer Street. Then, after pausing to wave at a couple of pretty young men who caught his eye, he added, "Apart from the diamond earrings and the soles on your Christian Louboutins, of course."

The shop in Broadwick Street was buzzing with pretty young things. James and I did our best to look like we shopped there all the time, and picked out some lace hold-ups with a forties-style black line running up the back. Then we added a pair of hipster French knickers and a matching bra that gave me a cleavage you could park a bike in.

"Right! Next stop: Harvey Nicks!" said James, while the assistant wrapped my precious lingerie. "Let's grab a cab."

"I'm not a bank," I protested weakly.

"Oh come on! This is *Travis*, the man you thought you'd lost. We've already agreed every detail *has* to be none other than perfect."

He's right, I thought to myself. *I visualised a fast track future. Marriage, children. As Travis had said, when you know, you know.* I prepared myself to give my plastic another bashing and followed James out of Agent Provocateur and into a taxi. He told the driver where we wanted to go and proceeded to flirt with the poor man all the way to Knightsbridge.

As soon as we got there, James instantly forgot about the driver and headed purposefully towards the store. Once inside he went straight for the furs.

"You know I don't do real fur!" Nervously, I looked around for an animal lib fanatic.

"But it's already dead!" James exclaimed. With a puzzled face he smoothed down a coat. "It's not going to mind. Besides, someone has gone to the trouble of skinning all these fluffy animals. We can't let them go to waste."

Shamefully, despite my reluctance, a coat caught my eye. A long, black, luxurious Dolce & Gabbana mink. Carefully avoiding looking at the price tag, I gingerly put it on. With a theatrical gasp, James collapsed into the chair behind him.

"Tara, it's got your name written all over it! It was made for you." He fanned his face as though to prevent a full swoon. "You *have* to get it!"

"Come look at the price tag for me, I daren't." I felt a pang of guilt as I stroked the gorgeous mink. It felt so dreamy to the touch, falling in smooth sleek lines as I ran my fingers through it as if I was stroking a Persian cat.

"Fate has stepped in, it's in the sale!" he whooped. "It's only £3,000. That's a sign for sure!"

Gulping hard, I began a fierce mental argument with myself. *Can I justify this? Of course I bloody can't! But it fits so perfectly.* I swirled around, hugging the fur, and stood on my tiptoes adding to the effect. I imagined Travis looking at me in this black, raunchy, luxurious fur, savouring the mental image of his beautiful mouth curling into an appreciative grin. Game over. I peered over my shoulder, took one last glance at myself in the mirror. I *had* to have it.

I winced as I handed over my credit card to the stony-faced shop assistant.

James clapped his hands excitedly. "Isn't it just *fan-fucking-tastic?*"

"I love it," I breathed, "can't you tell?"

"Not really, you've paralysed your face in that sort of vacant look. Perhaps you should've waited for those first two vials of Botox to kick in before having the other three vials injected?"

I gave James friendly shove as we both fell about laughing. "I'm pleased to hear the Botox has worked." I sidestepped to a mirror, tried to raise my eyebrows. They were frozen solid. Lovely! Shelia, the aesthetic nurse practitioner had come to Glamma-Puss especially for me. I'd had my lips enhanced, too. And a little more sculpting on my cheeks.

With a snap of his fingers, oblivious to the looks the sales assistant was giving us as he rapidly wrapped the fur, James was ready for the next purchase.

"Right – shoes! Let's stop buggering about – pun *definitely* intended - and get on with it!"

"That's enough," I said, accepting the enormous Harvey Nichols bag from the assistant. "I have a beautiful pair of Louboutins at home. No more spending. I'll be living on beans on toast for a year."

James wasn't taking no for an answer. "Come with me, you only have the five-inch heel. We are going to get you the full six-inches because, as we both know from experience, anything less than six inches *really* doesn't register, sweetheart. And anyway, there's nothing quite like the unspoiled sole of a Louboutin."

"But, I could've bought a car with the money I've spent on that coat," I groaned. I was beginning to panic.

"Shoes, Tara. Come along. This way." James linked his arm around mine and marched me over to the escalator. Just as we reached them, I heard a text come through and eagerly fumbled for my phone.

[Text from Travis]

Just booked us a room @ The Sanderson. Only the best for you. Can't wait to see you! Xxxxx

I jumped up and down like a crazed schoolgirl and waved the phone in James's face. "Read that!"

We both squealed, and in unison said, "Bring on the six-inch Louboutins!"

The second we reached the shoe section James theatrically pointed, "And there they are, Tara ... your *new* shoes."

"Oh my God," I said, once I'd clocked them. "They're not shoes – they're stilts! There's no way I could stand in those let alone walk in them. I'll break my neck."

James looked bemused. "What on earth are you talking about? Of course you can! Let me show you how it's done."

I sat down and watched with embarrassed fascination as James did his Cinderella act, squeezing his perfectly pedicured (but wide) foot into this slender, four-sizes-too-small stiletto. I looked on in disbelief as he proceeded to strut provocatively around with ease and grace.

You had to hand it to him. If a man could walk like that in a six-inch pair of heels, then so could I (even if I did have to be lifted and lowered into them). They were beautiful stilettos, clad in black silk, complete with matching bow cascading from the top of the heel almost to the floor. They were extremely raunchy, yet classically elegant. Sure, they were practically identical to the ones I had at home, but still ... in for a penny, in for a pound.

While the cashier delicately wrapped the shoes, I tapped out a reply to Travis. After showing it to James, we both grinned as I pressed the send button.

[Text to Travis]

How does fur coat, 6 inch heels & naughty knickers grab you? Xxx

I'd never recalled feeling such a rush responding to Travis's text, but it was short-lived once I began totting up all the spending in my head. By the time I picked up my gift-wrapped shoes from the counter, I felt more than a twang of guilt. Bang goes the new sunbed I was saving up for in the salon!

In an attempt not to spend any more money, I made a desperate effort to drag James out of Harvey Nichols. But as we headed for the exit, I spotted my last, potentially fatal, purchase.

James cocked an eyebrow. "Don't think I didn't see you looking at that handbag!"

I began protesting weakly, "No ... I shouldn't. I *really* shouldn't, I probably *couldn't* anyhow. I think the card is already maxed."

James propelled me closer. "Let's go and find out."

I picked up the black fur Versace handbag and right on cue another text from Travis came through.

[Text from Travis]

The thought of you in fur coat & naughty knickers has made me rock hard! Xxxxxx

"Okay – he obviously likes fur." I showed James the text. "Let's do it. I'm going to try and buy this handbag, and if I can't pay on my credit card it's not meant to be."

I held my breath as I handed my card over. Amazingly, the purchase went through. With my bank account nearly £5,000 lighter, we left Harvey Nichols and headed in the direction of the tube station. "James," I said, "I'm glad we went with fur coat and naughty knickers, as there's no way I'd be able to afford a dress as well."

The next few days and nights crawled by. But come the day in question, I raced to the salon where I was having the works done. I pleaded and pleaded with Jackie to give me another Hollywood – to remove what little fluff there was (although I had to stoically block my ears to her stern advice against it).

"I don't care if it looks like a plucked chicken as long as it's smooth," I said, stubbornly. "Vajazzle it after to cover the sins."

Next, Jayde did my hair while James fixed diamantes to my long, glossy, black acrylic nails and matching pedicured feet. This was followed by a session with Jackie *and* James jointly applying my make-up. Everyone agreed that smoky eyes suited me the best, adding false lashes to finish off that sultry look.

Frankly, I'd have gone through anything to look my best. Travis and I were only to be together for such a short space of time (one night and the following morning before he had to head back to Dublin for an early morning meeting) and I needed to make a huge impact. I already knew that with my outfit (or lack of) I was well on my way to doing so. Therefore, I had to make sure the rest of me was up to scratch. I wanted him to walk out of the Arrival gates of Heathrow airport and think proudly: *She is mine.* To achieve that *wow factor*, I needed every millimetre of my body to exude sex appeal.

After hours being poked, prodded and tweaked into shape, I was finally ready. Fearful of traffic, I left the salon way ahead of time and, draped in my new finery, began my journey to the airport to meet Travis. Internally I was squealing with frenzied thoughts but knew I had to try and stay calm - because calm equals sexy. That's not easy when you feel like there are a million gymnasts somersaulting in your tummy!

... And breathe.

I must not talk incessantly.

And breathe ...

I must not try too hard.

And breathe ...

I wonder how big his cock is?

And breathe ...

Not long after I'd set off, my mobile rang. I ignored it. From the ringtone, I knew it was Laura. She rang again. Then again. With a sigh, I turned my music down and switched my phone to speaker mode.

"I thought I'd try catch you before you set off for the airport," she said.

"Don't try and talk me out of meeting Travis, Laura. I've already explained he'd left his phone in Dublin." I was also peed off that she'd interrupted my singing along to Michael Bublé!

"I'm not trying to talk you out of anything. I'm happy for you. But have you seen or heard the news?"

"No. Why? What's wrong?"

"It's just been announced that most flights in and out of Ireland have been cancelled," she said.

I felt like I'd taken bullet to the stomach. "*What?* No! ... Why?"

"We've got fog here like pea soup. Planes can't get off the runways. Apparently it's chaos."

After a long pause, I said, "I don't feckin' believe it!"

"I suggest you call Travis and find out whether his flight is going ahead."

I pulled in at the next service station. *Call Travis?* Actually call and speak with him? I didn't have time for his dilly-dally responses! A bag of nerves, finger hovering, I called him and, surprised he answered, filled him in.

In his sexy, gravelly voice he said, "We should've boarded by now, but we haven't been told the flight is cancelled. "Hold the line, babe, I'll go find someone and ask."

I could just make out what he was saying in his delicious accent: "I've got the love of my life on her way to Heathrow - is this flight going ahead?"

I couldn't quite focus on the reply he was given because I was dazed by what he'd just said about me.

He was back. "Okay, babe, they've said the fog is lifting so the flight *will* go ahead."

"Thank God! Oh Travis, I can't believe I'm on my way to see you!" I checked myself, heat rushing to my face. I was meant to be playing it cool.

I sounded pathetic!

And breathe ...

"I can't wait to wrap my arms around you," he said, just as gushy. "See you soon, babe."

At Heathrow I parked up in the short-stay zone. I didn't want to walk too far in these stilts. Flipping down the sun visor, I checked my make-up, reapplied lip-gloss, fluffed my hair, and doused myself in more perfume. Nervous anticipation about making love with Travis filled my mind. I held my stomach and tried to stop the butterflies jumping around. I had tingling sensations all over me. The thought of touching him, stroking him, smelling him, made my lady-garden moist. Very moist. I'd have to try and resist launching myself at him, but I knew the minute I clapped eyes on him I'd want to tear his clothes off and have rip-roaring sex. I'd never experienced a lust like this ever, ever, ever. But my raunchy thoughts were brought to a grinding halt when I received text.

[Text from Travis]

Babe, I still haven't boarded, there was another delay, but should be boarding in 5 mins xx

I thought he'd be mid-air by now! I knew it wasn't his fault we were losing precious time together, but still, the disappointment was crippling.

Having even *more* time to kill, I made the decision to stay put in the car. I put some music on and chain-smoked a few cigarettes. Soon, though, I started to feel cold, very cold. Nice one, Tara. Only I could come out in January with just a fur coat and naughty knickers.

[Text from Travis]

Babe, the flight has been delayed again! This time by 2 hours! What do you want me to do? Xxxx

Two hours! I could develop varicose veins in less time that that! And a poxy phone call would've been nice! What if that text had been delayed? I could've been sat here none the wiser. *What did I want him to do*, indeed! I wanted him to get his arse over here and shag me, that's what I wanted. In a temper, I called him.

"Travis, I wish you'd *call* instead of texting all the time!"

"Sorry, it's just so noisy here with announcements and so on. Tara?"

"Yes?" I was angry.

"Do you think someone is trying to tell us something?"

"Maybe," I answered, sulkily.

"Babe, I hate the thought of you waiting around. Why don't you get yourself to the hotel and I'll get a taxi over to you when I land."

Go to the hotel without him, *indeed! Was he out of his mind?*

But his voice and concern melted me. I was *so* ready for this, to be part of a couple, to have a man. My Mr Right, worrying about me for a change, making sure that I was okay, that I was safe.

"I'll go into the airport, grab a coffee and wait for you there, as I'd prefer we arrive at the hotel together."

"Okay, if you're sure."

"I'm sure."

"I'll let you know the minute I board, but with such little time left we won't be getting much sleep."

We both laughed and ended the conversation. Travis and I were destined to be together and a delayed flight was *not* going to ruin that for me. With a face full of determination, I climbed out of the car, locked it and strode purposefully towards the main terminal building.

The second I walked in, my resolve vanished. Standing in my fur coat and stripper heels, I stood out a mile amongst the crowds of backpackers, holidaymakers and banker wankers. Overdressed was an understatement. It didn't help that there were bodies lolling around everywhere. Lying across seats, even sleeping on the floor! It was surreal, like something out of a disaster movie.

Precariously, I made my way over to Starbucks, stepping gingerly around the prone figures. I couldn't believe what I was witnessing. Doing my best balancing act in my stilts, I eventually carved a path through the crowds. There was no coffee, no seats ... no anything! Apart from perverts. There were plenty of those. I don't think I've ever been gawped at by so many men - their beady eyes following me round the airport.

I was like a circus act. Over-the-top hair and over-the-top shoes. The amount of make-up I had on would rival that of any clown. My head spun with the embarrassment of it all. And the lighting?! The fluorescent bulbs were so cruel. *And why are the floors so damn slippery? Surely not everyone has to wear hiking boots for a flight? Victoria Beckham herself said she couldn't concentrate in flats! Only a man would choose tiled, slippery flooring. I'd love to get the designer to try and walk on it - in six-inch heels, while carrying a ton in a suitcase.* The fact that I didn't have a case was irrelevant. I had my brand-new handbag with me, which was, in my opinion, the same weight as the average weekend case, if not heavier. I had everything with me: make-up, hair irons, hairbrushes, perfume, phone, tissues, *protection* (and lots of it), keys, nail file, nail buffer, purse, chewing gum, baby wipes, spare knickers and two pairs of sunglasses – one Versace and one Bvlgari.

I traipsed round desperately trying to find somewhere to sit so I could kick off my crippling, killer heels, but to no avail.

Airport staff began handing out sleeping bags. What on earth was going on? It looked like the world was coming to an end!

It didn't take a genius to work out it was going to be a long night, so I headed for the ladies. I needed to sit down, even if it was on a public loo. And I was desperate to scratch my lady-garden. *(Why, oh why didn't I listen to Jackie? I should never have had another Hollywood.)* When I got to the ladies there was a massive queue, snaking almost back round to where I'd started. Dozens of poor mums trying to calm down their screaming toddlers and babies. *Honestly, could this situation get any worse?*

As I walked back onto the concourse to seek out another loo, a group of drunken men caught my eye and beckoned me over. I lowered my head and tried to make out that I hadn't heard or seen them.

"Oi, blondie," one persisted, "yeah, you in the black fur coat, c'mon over and share my sleeping bag. There's room for one more!" The group of men he was sitting with began howling with laughter.

The cheeky feckers! Ignoring them, I carried on walking round in circles. Suddenly, I spotted a family ready to leave their table. The trouble was, so had everyone else. There were many predators dotted around, poised and ready to pounce on the almost-free table. Everyone's eyes - mine included - were darting around, assessing the competition for the great race. As soon as the last family member raised their arse off their seat, that was it – the flag was down and we were off! The whole world and his screaming child made a dive for it, but as I started to run I felt my left hold-up come loose and slip down my leg.

I cursed under my breath as I clapped a hand over the trailing end of the hold-up. *A chair ...? Or dignity ...? Feck dignity - I want to park my arse!* The chair was within my reach, but I'd have to let go of my hold-up if I was to make a grab for it. So I reached out, releasing my hold-up; the chair - almost mine - *was so close*, but I could sense someone just as close as me, and without looking up I gave them an almighty shove and told them to feck off. Looking up, I realised the *someone* I'd assaulted (after winning the chair, of course) was a priest.

Hardly surprisingly, he looked none too happy with me.

I was mortified.

"Oh ... Father, I'm *so* sorry!" I got to my feet, unable to look him in the eye, my face flaming red with shame. "Please, take the chair."

The portly priest nodded in approval at my quick volte-face. "Ah bless you, my child, sure it's like a game of musical chairs, is it not?"

As I watched him sit down on *my* hard-earned chair, I felt my hold-up hit my ankle. The priest didn't say a word as his eyes travelled down and looked at the offending object. All I can say is the look on his face was one of utter bemusement. The memory would stay with me for life.

I didn't want a man of the cloth to see me trying to recover my hold-up from around my ankle. Surely I had suffered enough? I swung my big fur handbag off my shoulder and draped it in front of my leg as I shamefully backed away with an uncomfortable smile.

"No problem, Father, no problem."

I could hear some clever dick shouting behind me, "Hey, Nora Batty! Need some help pulling your tights up?"

Tights indeed! I shuffled backwards, retrieving my dangling hold-up. With the priest out of earshot, I cursed back, ready to punch something. "They're hold-ups, you thick arse. You wouldn't know your arse from your elbow!"

[Text from Travis]

Just been an announcement over the Tannoy: Would the man meeting Tara Ryan please make himself known, we want to tell him he's one lucky bastard! Xxx xxxxxxxxxxxxxx

Travis was definitely worth the wait (and the embarrassment). To compound the good feeling, as I began to type a reply I spied a nearby café opening its shutters. They had coffee! *Thank God!*

[Text to Travis]

I'll wait all night for you if I have to Xxxxx

The two-hour delay was now a three-hour delay, but Travis was assured that the flight was still going ahead. At this rate we'd only have time for a quickie in the airport loos and I'd be waving him goodbye!

While I waited, I discreetly put my fingers into my coffee to add moisture to the top seam of my hold-ups. The last thing I needed was another collapse. My bum was numb, but I didn't dare move off my chair. Indeed, I had just witnessed a guy asking someone to mind his chair but as soon as his back was turned, the chair-thief ran off with it. I wasn't going to be fooled. Numb bum suited me fine. I switched the pressure on my bum cheeks every ten minutes or so.

After an hour, I managed to shimmy the chair (albeit rather noisily) to the other side of the café to have a flick through an abandoned magazine. *Ugh! People could look up hopefully all they liked - the chair was mine for the foreseeable. I'd drag it with me - even if I needed a wee!*

After what seemed like an eternity, my phone rang. Travis must be boarding at last!

"Babe, I'm sorry, they've just announced the flight has been cancelled."

"Tell me you're joking?" I begged.

"I'm not joking."

I had no words.

"I know you're upset. I am, too."

I held my breath in despair.

"Get yourself home, call me when you're back."

I stared into oblivion, my feet nailed to the ground. I couldn't move. The Big Man upstairs had thrown me a double-whammy. *First my hold-ups - and now this? All that pruning! All this bloody itching!* That was it. *I'm not scratching myself through the pocket lining of my coat any more.* I wrenched my coat back in a temper and gave my lady-garden a much-needed scratch. The relief was almost orgasmic. Everything was throbbing: my head, my feet, my arse cheeks; everything was pulsating, but for all the wrong reasons!

I began rummaging around in my bag, found my car parking ticket under the pile of beauty products, and despondently headed to the kiosk to pay.

"That'll be eighty-five pounds, please, miss," said Mr Bored-looking Kiosk Man from behind the Perspex.

"Hang on ... what do you mean, *eighty-five pounds?!*" I said incredulously. "I've blown five grand on a date that didn't happen ... " I paused to draw breath, doing my utmost not to start bawling.

"Miss, there's nothing I –"

I continued my rant. "The flight was cancelled and you're suggesting I pay *eighty-five pounds* for the pleasure of waiting round *all night* to find that shite out?"

"As I was saying ... there's nothing I can do," he began, with the patience of one who is used to being yelled at by furious customers. "You should've parked in the long-stay car park, miss. The short-stay is just that – *short-stay*. If you wish to dispute the charge I'll give you the address, but if you wish to leave the premises *with your vehicle* you'll have to pay first."

With my feet throbbing to the point where I wanted to throw up thanks to James and his bright ideas, I took off my stilts and threw them on the ground in protest.

"For feck's sake!" Reluctantly I handed over my credit card and watched in mounting fury as he punched in the details.

"Your card has been declined. Do you wish to try again?"

Oh feck! "Right, give it back. I'll just give you all the cash I have in the whole world, shall I?"

"Thank you, miss," Mr Bored-looking Kiosk Man's face was impassive as he took the wad of notes.

I stropped off to the car park in my stockinged feet, with the killer heels dangling from my fingers. And sure enough the next crisis hit. *Where was my car? I was sure I'd parked it on the third floor, hadn't I?* For the love of

God, I mouthed up to the sky, *can't you be on my side? Just for once? Please?!*

Maybe the Big Man Upstairs had heard me this time because, after walking further, I eventually spotted my vehicle sandwiched in between two vans. Relieved and infuriated, I dashed over and swung the driver's door open. I stepped in a puddle. *Ewww*. Jumping in, I gunned the engine, putting the heater on full blast to warm my frozen, wet feet, and headed for the exit. As my feet defrosted, I noticed an overwhelming stench ... *Is that ...* I sniffed and sniffed until I discovered the source.

I banged the steering wheel in a temper. I'd stepped in urine! Some *grotty little wanker* had pissed next to my car. *My car!*

At boiling point, I evaluated my pathetic little life. *I've spent five thousand pounds on a date, (so, was significantly poorer) and I've come away without a man. My lady-garden will probably look like I've got an STD with all the scratching, and I have blistered, pulsating feet that smell of piss ...*

Chapter 7

The following day I was like the Antichrist. I rang Laura and explained the nightmare episode, even though I knew there was nothing she could say that could make me feel better. Sure enough, her *why-on-earth-would-you-wait-that-long-at-an-airport* attitude got on my nerves, so I ended the call quickly.

I'd navigated my way home slowly last night. Very slowly. The bastard blanket fog that had ruined my date, delaying flights left, right and centre had descended on London. With severely reduced visibility (not even able to see the bonnet of my car) I'd pulled in to a petrol station and, scared out of my wits, texted Travis for comfort. He didn't respond. I rang him. He didn't answer. And I hadn't heard from him since.

I hated Sundays; the clock never seemed to move forward quickly enough.

There *was* plenty to do to keep myself busy of course, apart from chain-smoking, tearing my hair out and shaking my phone, but I didn't feel like doing sensible, adult things, like catching up with the washing, ironing, housework, etc. or any of that crap: I wanted *Travis*. I wanted to be sore from having sexy times!

God, I was so hungry for him!

Dejected, restless and unable to let go of my self-pity, I sat with my hand in a box of Rice Krispies, mechanically shovelling them into my mouth, and at one point sighed so hard that most of them came flying back out. I didn't care. I had every right to be feeling this way. I was determined to feel sorry for myself and that was that.

A text came through and I instantly snapped out of my misery mind-set. Spitting and choking out the remains of the cereal, I fumbled my phone out of my dressing-gown pocket.

[Text from Siobhan]

I've had the worst night of my life. R u home yet from your shag fest? x

[Text to Siobhan]

His flight was cancelled. What happened to you? X

[Text from Siobhan]

Oh no! I'll b round in 5! xx

I handed Siobhan a cuppa. Her hair was up in a messy bun, her cheeks flushed, her eyes wild. She looked like she'd been up to no good. "You okay, you look a bit –"

"Am I feck alright. I spent the night in the cop shop!"

"What? Why?"

"Well, I was mindin' me own business, driving to Luke's, when I realised I needed some petrol," she began with gusto.

We got comfortable at the kitchen table. I was already smiling; Siobhan was like chicken soup for the soul.

"So there I was with a lit fag when me mobile rang. Thing is, it was sitting in my jeans back pocket – so I undid me seat belt and answered. I'll be honest with you now, Tara, I did use me elbow just a little to steer me car into the petrol station – I was in deep conversation with me mammy, filling the tank – and you know it's hard to smoke, hold a phone *and* fill up at the same time."

I gasped, my eyes widening in horror. Shocked by her story, I momentarily forgot about my own trauma.

"You didn't?!"

Siobhan looked thoughtful. "I coulda done with three hands, really. But the next thing I know, the fuzz was there havin' a go at me! Well, this eejit *thought* he was the fuzz, but I told him to feck off with himself. 'You're no policeman,' I sez to him, 'you're one of those community support officers.' Then he only went and rang the real fuzz!"

I winced.

"I got fed up of this *arse* telling me that he *could* arrest me, so I sez to me mammy, 'I'll have to let you go, but I'll call you back in a bit.' I shoved me phone in me pocket and threw me fag on the forecourt, cus I meant business now, right?"

I cupped my face in horror.

"Siobhan!"

"Tell me about it!" She slapped the table hard with

her hand. "Some fuck-nugget pretending to be the fuzz! Someone had to sort him out. I decided I'd do one of those citizen's arrest thingies for impersonating the law. So there's me, right, trying to shove this loser into the back of me wheels, when three gorgeous policemen turn up. And what do they do? They feckin' cuff *me* and put *me* in the van! They only released me an hour ago!" Her eyes were ablaze with devilment. "But I ended up having a right laugh - spent the night playing the *would you rather* game with a gorgeous police officer. I sez to him, 'Would you rather lick your boss's arse after he's had a curry and run for the bus, or gargle the collected sweat from an athlete's armpits after he's been marathon training across the desert for six days without washing?' After much deliberation, he chose the athlete's armpits – but they're still pressing charges and takin' me to court! I don't even know what for. I don't see their problem," she concluded, shaking her head in genuine bewilderment.

"I ... I don't know what to say, apart from cigarettes and mobiles don't go with petrol stations," I lectured.

"I hope I don't go to prison, but if I do, I hope by then I can go to one that's mixed," she said. Then she grinned: "Imagine the wall-to-wall cock!"

"*Jesus* ... that's not funny." But her crazy antics got the better of me once again and as usual I started laughing.

"So what happened with you last night?" Siobhan asked.

I waved the question away.

"I'd rather not go through it again but let's just say the only part of me that got wet was my foot."

"So the drought continues." Siobhan shook her head in wonder and got up to leave.

I felt the loneliness creep straight back in. My brain

scrambling to find a reason for her to stay. "I could make us dinner?"

Siobhan slurped the last dregs of her tea, "Thanks for the drink and I'd love to stay, but I've to go see a man about a dog." She winked at me, "The gorgeous police officer's dog." I'll call you later to make sure you haven't hung yourself from the curtain rail. Look on the bright side, at least you have a real fur coat I can borrow."

After she'd gone, I noticed that my mood *had* lifted a little. I called Mum for a chinwag, but she wasn't able to chat because she was visiting Katie at the rehab centre. And I'd already spoken with Laura. My thoughts drifted to Travis, my anger that he hadn't contacted me softening a little. He'd said life with him wouldn't be easy. And it wasn't his fault the flight was cancelled. He was a busy man - organising a rugby team, injured players (broken bones, cauliflower ears, teeth smashed out, etc.), and would have meetings and what have you. I needed to be more understanding and learn that when I clicked my fingers he wouldn't always be able to jump.

The day was nearly over and the house was a mess. Just I was crunching my way through a sea of dropped Rice Krispies in an effort to start clearing up, a text came through.

[Text from Travis]

Hi babe, sorry for the delay. I want to see you ASAP Xxxxx

Oh the relief!

[Text to Travis]

I want to see you ASAP too! Don't worry, I know you're busy - I'm just pleased to hear from you Xxx

[Text from Travis]

Okay gorgeous, well my work schedule is hectic. I have some free time, but not enough to get out of the country. Any chance you could come over to Ireland? Please? Xxxxxx

I was ecstatic, but had one big problem: *money*. I was borassic! I'd been so stupid spending all that money on a fur coat, shoes and handbag I couldn't afford! If this date was going to happen, I'd have no choice but to try to figure a way of persuading Travis to pay. Yet my pride would never allow me to admit I had a severe cash flow problem. I bit my nails and began to compose a message.

[Text to Travis]

Are you going to be a gentleman and pay for me?

[Delete]

[Text to Travis]

Spent all my money on a fur coat and naughty knickers!

[Delete]

[Text to Travis]

I would love to, but the salon has hit a quiet spot

[Delete]

My phone vibrated suddenly.

[Text from Travis]

Let me know if you're okay to go ahead, I'll book the flight for you, babe xxx

YES! I ran to get my diary. *He must be keen,* sending two messages that quickly!

[Text to Travis]

Tomorrow's good for me Xxxx

[Text from Travis]

Haha, you're funny, babe! I like a sense of humour in a woman. How about 10th of Feb? I'll pick you up from the airport. I have a meeting early the next morning though Xxx

"10th of February!?" *How am I supposed to wait that long?* That was a whole feckin' two weeks away! *Stay calm, Tara, stay calm.*

[Text to Travis]

Can't wait! Book away! Xxxxxx

The next couple of weeks building up to my trip were gruelling. I worked non-stop in the salon, placing an advert in a magazine offering discounted prices on both hair and beauty treatments, desperate to claw in cash to make up for my stupidity. My mood made for a very uneasy atmosphere.

It probably didn't help that I had my phone practically fused to my hip on constant text alert. I mean, how long does it take to book poxy flights? I'd given Travis my details two weeks ago! We'd managed to have text sex – well, kind of. But I wanted to actually see him!

I couldn't help but get frustrated with Travis's snail-like responses and stomped moodily round the salon, hot and cold with anxiety.

"It's easy!" I said in temper to the staff and customers, my eyes almost popping out of my head as they looked back at me nonplussed. "You just press some buttons on a computer, tick a couple of boxes and *voilà*, flight booked!"

Of course, my meltdown dispersed with immediate effect the moment the text landed with the flight details. I was euphoric. The staff breathed a huge sigh of relief, as did my clients.

"Sorry," I said to all concerned, "I haven't been that bad, have I?"

My question was greeted by silence.

The day finally arrived. I woke early in the morning like a five-year-old at Christmas. The only thing to dampen that overwhelming feeling of excitement was the vile smell of the fake-tan wafting up my nose. I couldn't wait to shower it off. I wished companies would come up with a perfumed fake-tan, one that didn't leave evidence on the bedsheets. I dived in the shower and gently washed myself while trying my best not to rub it all off - watching the water run orange around my feet.

Whilst packing for the trip I received a text:

[Text from Travis]

I have a permanent grin on my face, so excited. Can't wait to see you! xxx

I grinned too. Within a few minutes, I received another text.

[Text from Travis]

Are you okay??? Xx

Huh! He makes me wait days for a response and because I haven't responded immediately he's panicking. Good: it shows he too has a vulnerable side. I will respond when I'm ready, so he can just wait!

God, I felt unusually powerful. Perhaps it was because I knew he was waiting around for me for a change.

I set myself a target: *I'm going to make him wait at least an hour before I respond. Maybe even two. In fact I might not even text him till I land.*

Sad to say, I only managed about fifteen seconds before I responded, just in case he got put off. I was never very good at meeting targets.

[Text to Travis]

Hello gorgeous. Will set off to airport in 10 mins. Can't wait to be with you Xxxxxxxx

This time around I was going less extreme in my choice of outfit. I opted to wear a simple, figure-hugging nude woollen dress that draped off one shoulder. Hoping the Big Man Upstairs wouldn't notice, I decided not to wear any underwear. I accessorised with a leopard-print belt that pulled me in at the waist, a matching bag, and brown boots complete with leopard-print heels. All courtesy of the fabulous Mr Jimmy Choo. Even though these were from last year's collection, they were timeless classics. I completed the effect by applying soft gold tones of make-up and lashings of lip-gloss. Stepping back, I pulled a few poses in the mirror and left for Heathrow.

I arrived in plenty of time, making a note of where I parked the car this time. (In the long-stay car park). I also listened very carefully to the attendant who checked me in. I wasn't going to risk anything, given my recent experience.

It was unusually warm for February, yet the airport heating seemed to be on full blast. I began to regret wearing the woollen dress and could feel beads of sweat appearing on my forehead and squelching under my armpits. Nonetheless, I teetered through to the departure lounge and waited to be called. *So far, so good.*

With time to spare, I decided to take my obligatory walk around the Duty Free section. As I idly wandered around, a flamboyant male make-up artist caught my eye. I was intrigued and I couldn't help over hear him - in a French accent - *bitching*, quite distinctly, in a repulsed tone - to what appeared to be his assistant.

"... he was likea Monet, incredibelle from a distonce, but *revolting* op close!"

Fascinated by his mystique and conversation, I lingered. Glancing through the corner of his eye at me, in an exaggerated, *I'm busy* fashion, he sighed and turned back to his assistant, carrying on his conversation.

I coughed to let them know I'd like to be served.

They both ignored me.

"Excuse me." Without even acknowledging my presence, the male make-up artist raised his voice along with his hand, right up to my face. It was a deliberate attempt to cut me off, the cheeky fecker! Then, once he'd decided he'd finished his conversation, he lowered his hand, swivelled on his heels and with a snooty expression, sighed heavily at me.

"How can I 'elp, *monsieur*?" He turned his eyes away from mine to inspect his well-manicured fingernails.

"Pardon?" Horrified, I looked around for this *man* he'd addressed. Nope, he was most definitely addressing me!

"Err, *pardon ... madame*?" he said, his face deadpan.

"I'm ... I'm looking for some perfume." Did he think I was a lady-boy? A transvestite?

His nostrils flared. "Okey." He couldn't have looked less interested if he'd tried. "Daytime-Evening-Floral-Musky-Woody-Light-Spicy, or ... *Sexy*?"

With my confidence severely knocked, I ploughed on, ignoring the lump in my throat.

"Well, *umm* ... a sexy one? Something a little ... *provocative*?"

He tutted as he proceeded to make his way over to me from behind the counter.

"Right, *madame*, I am presuming you are referring to a fragrance?"

"Yes," I replied gingerly. I took a step back in confusion and weighed up in my mind whether this guy was on something. What the feck else would I be referring to?

With an increasingly disgusted look on his face, his eyes darted over to his assistant.

"*Sacré bleu* ..." he muttered. Then, glaring back at me, he gave it to me with both barrels while shaking his head vigorously. "*Non-non-non. Madame*, surely we need to sort *this* –" waving his hand around my face "– before we can deal with your –" whiffing through his flared nostrils "– *odour*. But it's okey, I understand *that* time in a voman's life – those 'ot-flushes – it must be ... difficult – *non?*"

Is this man Satan's very own PR? I took a deep breath, tried to square my shoulders and verbally attack him back, but the words stuck in my mouth. Instead, I found myself reaching round for the shoulder strap of my handbag, and with a tight grasp, like it was armour, pulled it closer to me. The make-up on my face had obviously melted with the heat.

I was panic-stricken. The first time Travis and I met was night-time – and he would have had his beer goggles on. He might see me coming through Arrivals, take one look and run for the hills. I needed all the help I could get.

"Can you fix me, like, *now*?" I begged.

Silent once more, his eyes zoomed in on my last-season's boots.

"Well, I cannot work miracles, *madame*. But I am *ze* best, so I will do vot I can."

Empowered by his own self-righteousness, I watched him flick his perfect mane to one side as he turned to walk off. His exaggerated steps and thrusting of the hips made for a magnificent stride that any catwalk model would've been proud of.

He summoned his assistants with a fierce snap of his fingers. "Chantelle. Candice. Come," he demanded.

Two young women came hurrying across. "Yes, Franc." (Pronounced *Fronc.*)

"You!" he ferociously commanded one of the girls. "Pallet. Now. And get me *ze* latest collection, we will surely need it!" With a sharp clap of his hands he propelled me into a chair.

As he and the assistants busied about removing my melted make-up, I took some time to analyse my ridiculer. Despite the fact that he was a *complete* bitch, I was curious about him.

He was beautiful, with amazingly high cheekbones and a raven-black Vogue-ish haircut that complemented his chiselled features. He was tall, and super-slim. There was no doubt about it, he had the ultimate size-zero waist, from which he had draped a shimmering studded black leather belt complete with a pouch overflowing with make-up brushes. His all-black outfit left nothing to the imagination; it consisted of skinny leather jeans (through which I couldn't help noticing that his manly-hood was parked to the left) and a very tight-fitting deep V-neck T-shirt. Of course, Fronc was more than aware of his superiority. We were mere mortals compared with this god-like creature. His presence was intimidating, to say the least.

While I was acutely aware that I severely disliked him, I also knew I wanted to be just like him. He was everything I was not. Commanding. Confident. Compelling. I was the woman, yet he was infinitely more feminine and sexy.

Why is life so cruel? How is it fair that I work so hard trying to look normal – to fit in – and still hate what I see?

Over the years this thought process had eaten away at what little self-confidence I had left, so I'd put on a mask, raised an emotional shield and buried my painful thoughts deep as a crater, along with all the other emotional rot and baggage I had, where it couldn't be accessed.

I'd always known I looked different to everyone else – school had taught me that. I'd spent most of my days in class worrying and unable to concentrate. But in a way it was my own fault I'd been singled out, that the spotlight was shone on me.

One particular occasion stood out. Dad was drunk. Angry drunk. Pick a fight drunk. Late home for dinner, he sat with a tray of food in front of the TV and before I knew it, and for no apparent reason, he hurled it. The tray hit the ceiling with an almighty crash. Cutlery flying through the air like weapons – gravy and Guinness splattering and dripping down the walls. The plate and glass in pieces on the carpet.

Settling Dad down, (him passing out fully clothed in bed) Mum and I cleaned long into the night. We carried the smashed glass coffee table out to the back garden. We took down the curtains and put them in the wash along with cushion covers. We scrubbed the carpet, the rug, the splattered photo frames, and binned the unsalvageable hessian ceiling shade.

That night I didn't sleep a wink in fear of Dad kicking off again. The following morning, over-sleeping, unwashed and hungry, I arrived late for my English lesson. To my horror, my classmates were taking it in turns to stand up and read aloud. Not able to read that well, my heart thumping in my chest, red-faced, sweating, on trembling legs, when my turn came I began – and immediately floundered. I broke down in tears and the class laughed uproariously *at me*, which earned everyone, myself included, a detention. And that was it, that was the moment all eyes were on me. The whispers. The daggers. The secretive notes being passed round. The minute the bell rang, I was up like a shot and making a run for it. But the bullies were fast - faster than me. I never asked why they wanted to inflict so much pain and misery on me. I just took it.

"You look like the runt of the litter," they'd laugh, kicking and punching the back of my head the whole way home from school. Then, using various terms of abuse, they'd go on to tell me how un-cool I was, with my carrot-coloured frizzy hair, pale skin, unfashionable clothes, and, of course, crazy, alcoholic dad.

I'd lie in bed, a hot water bottle soothing the bruises and cuts. *Why don't the bullies taunt Laura? Why don't they kick and punch her? Why don't they rip her coat and throw it in the river?* We both had the same dad. The answer was simple: Laura was beautiful and I was not.

Then I had an epiphany: I was going to physically change everything about myself that was humanly possible. I'd recreate myself to fit into society. I've spent the last twenty or so years doing just that, even though I've never truly managed to get rid of that gawky teenager underneath my recreated self.

Willing myself to appear confident, I cleared my throat.

"I need to look as good as possible," I said.

Without acknowledgement, Fronc began pulling my face (now bare of any make-up) into different lights. He took a step back. "These lights, *madame* - zey do you no favours."

My eyes pricked with tears.

"You should invest in some of ze Botox."

"I've had some," I replied. The penny dropped. My face was as frozen as an iceberg! Fronc was going to try and sell me some miracle cream that would promise the world and not deliver. Commission. It was all about commission. I may have been low on confidence, but I wasn't stupid!

"Ask for ze Botox refund!" he said, wearing a haughty expression. "It 'as obviously not vorked."

I bit my lip and dug my nails into the palms of my hands, deeply regretting coming to the counter.

"'Owever, *madame*, I can make you look *magnifique* with this new collection," he added, in a slightly more humane tone. "It 'as just arrived from Paris."

I checked my watch. "Maybe it's not good idea. I don't have long before I board," I lied. I had nearly an hour, but wanted to get away from this mad Frenchman and his egotistical abuse as soon as possible. In fact, I wanted to report him. He was *so* rude! Better still, I wanted to deck him with a breezeblock or two. *Then* I'd report him!

Fronc tutted away my concerns. "*Madame*, you are in *ze* best hands, I will create a work of art from you. You will look and feel *fantastique,* do not vorry." With that, he pinched his fingers together and kissed them: "*Mmwah!*"

His spiel worked. I did want to look and feel *fantastique.* Maybe I wouldn't report him. Not yet, anyway.

Strangely, the moment I gave the nod, Fronc became nicer. As I mused over how much commission he'd get if I purchased the new Parisian collection he'd been raving about, my beautifully blow-dried hair was pulled back to within an inch of its life. Not the best start!

The makeover seemed to go on and on as he blended in this and rubbed in that. I flicked a nervous glance at my watch. I didn't have long till boarding.

A Duty Free shopper tripped over her suitcase staring at me. A gang of young teenage girls stood watching, giving the occasional *wow*, chewing gum and nodding to each other in approval. My stomach butterflied and flipped with excitement.

Finally, Franc stepped back and his assistants *ooh'd* and *ahhh'd* at his masterpiece.

"I am a *god* – and now you are a *goddess,*" he gloated. Without a trace of irony he flipped open his Prada wallet and flicked a business card at me. "Candice! Get ze mirror for ze gorgeous *madame.*"

Mirror handed over, I surveyed my face. I moved the mirror to arm's length, then up close.

"Holy-Mary-Mother-Of-God, what have you done!?" I flung the mirror down. "I look like a corpse bride!" I couldn't catch my breath. "Oh my God ... you said you'd ... I've got a date and I look like I've head-butted a make-up counter!"

Fronc had given me a white, ghost-like face, contoured charcoal blusher, with sunken scary eyes and black glitter lipstick.

I covered my mouth to stop the screams and tried to look up to tackle Fronc eyeball to eyeball. But thanks to the super-heavy peacock eyelashes he'd welded on, it wasn't possible.

Fronc raised his pencilled brows, dropped his jaw and glared at me with wide mascara eyes. Flabbergasted by my reaction, the earlier traces of niceness had well and truly vanished. He knew he wasn't getting a sale, let alone a tip!

"Well, my dear," he scowled with a razor-sharp tongue, "I cannot polish a *turd!*" Giving me one last death stare with his devil-like eyes, he pursed his lips, snatched his card out of my hand, turned on his Gucci loafers and minced off muttering French obscenities.

"I'm being taught a lesson, Candice. I'm being punished for acting like a wild, wanton hussy – you see, I'm on my way to have *sex with a gorgeous man* and I'm not wearing a bra or knickers!" I sobbed hysterically.

Silent, Candice stared at the ground.

"My dad told me the Big Man Upstairs always knows." I wiped the snot from my nose on my sleeve. "God is always watching – do you always wear underwear, Candice, or do you have the odd day off and go commando?"

I picked up the mirror and took another look at Fronc's *artwork,* not taking a blind bit of notice of Candice's response. I did, however, hear a call to board my flight.

"This is the final call for flight number WWFR12Z to Dublin. Would all remaining passengers please make their way to gate number 12," boomed the Tannoy.

Shit! I shot up out of the chair. "That's my flight!"

Almost hysterical again, I scooped up my bag and ran out of Duty Free. Once outside, I spun around six times looking for the ladies.

"Where are the feckin' toilets?" I wasn't directing the question at anyone in particular, I was directing it at the whole airport.

Finally, spotting the *stick lady* sign, I put the door firmly in my sights and shielding my face as best I could, went on a one-woman stampede for the entrance. Sweating profusely, I flung the door open. I must have looked like an unhinged mental patient. I scrambled over to the mirror and winced. *Arghhhh!*

Even though my flight was boarding, there was no way I was getting on that plane looking like this. I whimpered as I ripped off the peacock lashes. I held my hair back with one hand, squirted soap into the other and flicked the tap on. Yet the more I tried to wash the nightmare away, the more the dark eye shadow, lashings of eyeliner and black glitter lipstick smudged.

I began grieving at the thought of my glorious array of make-up in my case, buried somewhere in the airport baggage system, completely unreachable.

"Would a Miss Tara Ryan make her way to gate number 12 immediately," announced the Tannoy. **"This is your final call for flight WWFR12Z to Dublin."**

"Oh God! Feck-arse-shit-bastard-bollocks!" My heart was pounding. *I can do this, I can do this!*

Using both hands and *much* more soap, I scrubbed again. After a frantic minute, with my face raw and my eyes stinging, I took another look in the mirror. An uncanny resemblance to a heroin addict stared back at me. But feck it, I really wanted to see Travis!

I grabbed my bag, and a wad of toilet roll to dry my face, and began my sprint to the gate. I gasped for air as I reached it and, apologising, handed over my passport and boarding pass. I was fully aware of the pieces of toilet roll stuck to my face and the small trail attached to my heel, but I was beyond caring.

Ground staff waved me through the gate.

Like I was on an assault course, I ran down the concrete stairs two at a time, made my way out to the runway, and, holding my knockers for dear life, ran up the steps to the plane *just* as the flight attendant was closing the doors.

"Sorry ... sorry ... sorry ..." As I made my way towards the back of the stuffy plane, I was aware of serious eyeballing. *I know how much everyone hates the last person to board.* But they could all feck off with themselves! I hadn't made us that late! I pulled out my compact and checked my face. It was red and blotchy. I closed my stinging eyes, took some deep breaths and promised myself I'd be able to sort myself out at the other side.

As the plane descended into Dublin, I readied myself to run. I know I was the last person to get on the plane but I was going to make damn sure I was the first off. I legged it through passport control and shimmied between the crowds at the baggage reclaim, managing to get myself a prime position in front of the carousel. I was like a woman possessed. Right now, I needed my make-up like I needed air.

[Text from Travis]

Hi babe, have landed in Dublin too. I'm in baggage reclaim xxx

A flash of heat whooshed up my body.

What the hell was Travis doing in baggage reclaim! I didn't know he was flying into Dublin; I'd presumed he was already here! I immediately dropped to the floor, left my case on the carousel and made a dash for the toilets on all fours, my bum sticking up in the air as if on another assault course. My eyes darted around. *Any one of those pairs of legs could be his!*

Relieved to be in the safety of the ladies' toilets, I took a few moments to compose myself. Exhausted, I walked warily over to the mirror to survey the damage. My trendy symmetrical fringe was now in a kiss-curl after getting it wet whilst removing Fronc's so-called *magnifique artwork*. Deciding not to linger too long on my face, my eyes travelled down. Confused, I stepped closer.

No ... No! Sweet Mother of God. So that's why everyone was eyeballing me on the plane! There, for all to see, were two *perfect* circles - one on each breast. I stepped closer for a better look. All the sweating had made my fake tan seep through the wool of my dress, leaving me with two perfect sweaty brown circles on my enhanced boobs, complete with sweaty brown dots in the middle.

No jacket to cover my sins. No make-up to fix my face. No straighteners for my kiss-curled fringe. Meanwhile, the man of my dreams was mere feet away the other side of this toilet wall.

I couldn't have looked more like a pig if I had tried. I turned on my heel, slid down by the washbasins, lifted my knees and bowed my head. Startled, I felt something hard hit my arm then clank to the floor. It was a euro. The well-dressed woman rapidly leaving the ladies had mistaken me for a homeless person.

This had to be one of the lowest points of my life.

Startling me, my phone sprang to life. It was Travis. Typical. He never phones and the *one and only time* I don't want to speak to him, he calls. I let it ring off. If I was having a nervous breakdown, I wanted to do it in private.

I threw my hands in the air, shouting at the heavens. "I've paid my price, can we please call it quits now?"

[Text from Travis]

Got my bag. Will wait outside arrivals for you. Hope you're okay? xx

I let out a huge sigh of relief. Now it was possible to run out, get my case, fix my face, fix my hair and get my jacket to cover the fake-tan disaster. *Or should I get the next flight home?*

I peeked out of the ladies. Travis wasn't there. I could see my case going round the carousel, and with hope climbing back up inside me, I made a run for it.

I grabbed my case and darted back to the safety of the ladies. *Okay,* I thought, standing in front of the mirror. *If I can fix this mess, I'll see Travis. If not, I'm booking the next flight home.*

But more horror was to come as I pulled out my one and only other outfit. My crisp white shirt and bright red skinny jeans were now in the colour of *Warm Beige*. The lid of my foundation had opened and the contents had exploded.

After ten minutes of wailing and shrieking like a banshee - "*So we're still not quits?*" - and kicking over three sanitary bins, I calmed down. But only slightly.

This isn't how a WAG acts, I scolded myself, clouting myself around the head a couple of times. Grabbing a toilet roll, I began rinsing and wiping each item that could be salvaged. I smeared my face with my white shirt, collecting as much foundation as possible, and blended in some concealer, then more concealer, then more concealer on top of that. In the end, I decided it wouldn't take as much of an overhaul as I'd feared. My breathing returned to normal.

[Text to Travis]

Just waiting for my case. Be with you in 10 mins xxx

A shaky hand applied soft golds and smoky browns, nude lip-gloss, lashings of mascara and a ton of cream blush, all while rehearsing a pout to help me get back into the moment.

With no power socket for my straighteners, I had no choice but to pin my fringe back with a diamante clip. As much as I hated my hair off my face, needs must. After agonising for a few moments, I sadly tossed my now unsalvageable *Warm Beige* shirt and jeans in the bin.

I elected to put my dress on back to front. There was one disadvantage to this strategy - as the dress was woollen, the fabric wasn't what you'd call *forgiving*. In fact, there was now an arse-shaped bulge flapping in front of my lady-garden. Still, it was better than before. I threw on my jacket, gathered my things and headed out.

Exhausted, I dragged myself towards Customs. *Please ... please, God,* I prayed, *please don't let them pull me over.* A female security guard darted towards me. *For the love of God ... not again*, I thought as I prepared myself to break down in tears. I was so close to touching Travis, I thought I might actually kill *anyone* who stood in my way. Luckily, the guard walked straight past me and began questioning a shifty-looking man behind me.

Trying to emulate Fronc's catwalk strut, I held my head high, pulled my shoulders back and began my hip-swirling, lip-pouting walk out of Arrivals.

And there he was.

Chapter 8

All six foot of my muscle-bound hunk of burning love was standing at the entrance waiting for me. Travis picked me up and hugged me so hard it hurt. With my feet back firmly on the ground, he held me at arm's length, searching me from head to toe.

Please don't look too close!

His mouth curved into a devastating, wicked grin. "God, I want you – but first, let's get us some champers."

As cool as a cucumber, Travis adjusted his Ray-Bans and led us purposefully through the airport crowds towards the bar. "How was your flight, gorgeous?" he asked.

"Perfect." I smiled sweetly. Holding on to him for dear life, I checked out his gorgeous arse. Sweet Holy Mary Mother of God, it was so perfect it looked like it belonged in the Louvre Museum. Here I was, at last - able to see, touch and smell him. I wanted to pinch myself!

He looked smoking-hot, wearing a dark blue Ralph Lauren shirt, the collar popped, sexy Levi's and tan hiking boots. *All* man. Why on earth had I ever fantasised about marrying a pot-throwing temperamental chef like Gordon Ramsay when I could have a high-flying rugged rugby coach like Travis? I checked his arse again. Travis was so much better.

Stopping dead in his tracks, he swung round to face me. "You're even more beautiful than I remember." Just as I was about to return the compliment, he was on the off again, picking up the pace - we were almost sprinting. "Sorry about the rush," he said over his huge shoulder, "but I'm desperate to have you alone with me. After we reached the bar, he said, "We'll have a quick drink in here, and then …" he grinned and bit the side of his lip "… then I'm going to eat you alive."

I was soooooo ready to be eaten!

He signalled to the barman, but not before delicately kissing me on the lips. "Two glasses of your finest champagne, please, mate."

I couldn't help but get turned on by his authority.

Travis tenderly caressed my cheek. The second he made contact with my skin I felt a zillion volts pass through me. Guiding my jaw with his finger, he pulled me closer.

"So you've just flown in to Dublin too? I thought you were already here. Where were you?"

He groaned. "Meetings. I don't want to talk about work. Let's talk about us."

He got close, so close I could feel his warm breath on my face. Smell his intoxicating aftershave. Teasing me, he pulled back, cocked his head to one side, removed his Ray-Bans and studied me intently. We were silent. Despite the fact we were standing in a packed, noisy bar, the atmosphere between us was charged. His pupils were dilated. I could almost feel the air around us sparking. I would've dropped my knickers right there, *if I were wearing any.*

Travis slid his big-man hand down to my waist. I bit my lip to stop myself convulsing as it travelled further down the small of my back. With a deft movement, he locked our nether regions together. Transfixed, I felt intense desire as his hand dropped further, touching my bum cheek, sending shivers down my spine.

Was I really about to make love for the first time in my life? And with this beautiful man? *Hell, yes!* I mean, I wasn't a virgin or anything, but I'd never actually *made love,* because I'd never actually *been* in love.

Not up until now, anyway.

This was completely different.

So fine me for speeding?

We were in the fast lane.

When you know, you know.

Travis widened his eyes excitedly. "You've got no knickers on." Whispering in my ear he grabbed a handful of butt cheek. "This *delectable* derriere is all mine."

With his swoon-making comment, I eagerly responded, nuzzling my lips down the side of his neck. Breathing him in at such close quarters nearly made me convulse on the spot.

To emphasise his point, he pushed his groin even harder into me. He was rock hard, a fact I couldn't help but greet with moan of tantalising pleasure.

The barman placed flutes of champagne in front of us, interrupting the intensity of the moment. Handing over notes, Travis indicated with a wave to keep the change.

Excellent manners!

Drinks in hand, we headed for a quiet table in the corner. We slipped onto a bench, getting as close as it was possible to get without me actually sitting on his lap. "God, I've missed you," he said.

"I thought this day would never come," I said back.

"*And* I really did forget how beautiful you are."

I was melting.

He rubbed my leg seductively, easing my dress up a few inches. I smiled, with what I hoped was a naughty, *that's-for-later* expression, and emphasised my point by smoothing my dress back down.

"Patience. Anticipation is the strongest aphrodisiac," I laughed, gulping my champers.

"And you're just so *natural*." He drew me even closer. "I love natural beauty."

I had to use every ounce of strength I had not to choke. There was very little left of my face or body that hadn't been tampered with in one way or another. I recovered well and even managed a polite – and, *dare I say it,* demure - thank you. Well, who was I to burst his bubble? And Sheila had done the most fabulous job of ironing my face out, so Fronc could go feck himself!

We kissed again, this time a little harder. I felt so alive the second his full lips touched mine, my fingers tenderly trailing the outline of his tapered jaw-line. He wrapped his hands in and around my hair, pulling me ever closer. Suddenly, remembering my extensions, I panicked. *What if he feels my glued-in bonds?* But he clearly wasn't thinking about such minor details. Either way, he never said a word.

I'd noticed an old fella sat at the bar, his beady eye watching our every move. He swung round on the bar stool, directly facing us. "Are you that rugby fella off the TV?"

Travis smiled at me.

"G'wan der, my son!" he shouted.

Travis straightened himself up. "Let's go." Knocking back his drink, he pulled his Ray-Bans on, so I fumbled into my bag, producing my huge Victoria Beckham pair, and did the same. *He must want to avoid being seen by the paparazzi,* I thought excitedly. *That's something I'll have to get used to.* (Note to self: carry a wig, or possibly a large hat, at all times! However, this may depend on size of handbag being used at the time as I might not be able to fit it all in!)

Travis gave me an amused grin. "Ready?"

I downed the rest of my champagne, straightened my sunglasses and grabbed my case. "Ready."

Taking my hand, Travis determinedly led us out of the crowded Arrivals hall. *This is how a WAG must feel,* I thought, proudly keeping a tight grip of my man. Before I knew it, we were in a taxi – back to snogging each other's faces off. We were oblivious to the nosy glances of the driver, who seemed to be doing his utmost not to get caught looking at us.

After a short while, I became aware of the luxurious sound of crispy gravel crunching under the wheels, then the taxi came to a halt. Prising myself away from Travis's mouth and removing his wandering hands from up inside my dress, I surveyed the surroundings through the steamed-up windows.

Travis, already out of the taxi, was gathering up our belongings. Ruffling my hair back into place, I smoothed my dress down and stepped onto the gravel.

"My Princess, your castle awaits." Travis took a bow.

"Castle Clontarf?!" I cupped my face in astonishment.

I'd read reviews of the boutique hotel after Siobhan attended her posh cousin's wedding there. *Wait till I tell her!*

"I want to look after you, always."

He wants to look after me, always? Where had this man been all my life?

I swung round to face him. "It's beautiful!" Tears climbed into my eyes as Travis threw an arm around me. Blowing my snotty nose and sniffing like a two-year-old was *most* unattractive and very un-WAG-like indeed. *I mean, for God's sake, what if the paparazzi got a picture of me like this? Now that really would be something to cry about!*

I stood facing the picturesque castle, reached up and squeezed Travis's hand tightly, savouring every detail.

A bedazzling array of spotlights in whites, blues and pinks bounced off the trailing ivy leaves covering the soaring castle walls and turrets. The picture was topped off by a pair of giant, moss-laden stone lions sitting at the entrance, guarding their fortress. Like a Hollywood film set.

"It's *the* most romantic setting I've ever seen," I said.

"It's the best hotel in town." Travis swooped up our luggage. "Come on, gorgeous, let's get you inside - you'll freeze out here."

I felt weak as I walked into the vast, richly decorated lobby. Probably a combination of over-excitement, lack of food and the glass of bubbly at the airport. I took the opportunity to sit on one of the entrance-hall thrones, which were covered in plush scarlet velvet. The one I chose was in front of a large, ornate stone fireplace. I took great pleasure from the intense heat radiating from the roaring fire. As Travis checked us in, my eyes traced the lavishly carpeted stairs and the exquisitely engraved granite stairway. I instinctively knew these were the stairs that would take me to heaven.

In the distance, I could hear the tinkling of a piano playing soft jazz, together with murmuring voices. I closed my eyes, savouring this precious moment. I had never felt this special, *ever.*

I shivered nervously at the thought of what lay ahead, and turned my attention to the grand reception desk where, I realised with a start, Travis had been watching me. Mentally, I was already undressing him, my mind spinning with possibilities. I fluttered my lashes back at him, my gaze slowly roaming over his luscious body: his solid legs, narrow waist, strapping chest and magnificent arms, not forgetting his perfect come-to-bed smile. I had to be the luckiest girl in the whole wide world.

All those days and nights of the wanting; the waiting, the text-sex. Finally, it was moments away from happening.

Travis strode over. “We’re on the top floor, so we’ll take the lift.”

Leaving the soft sounds of the piano behind us, I remained silent and swallowed nervously. The sexual tension between us was mounting by the second. We entered the lift, gazing into each other’s eyes as the brass doors shut.

The moment we were away from watchful eyes, Travis exercised full, hot-blooded assertiveness. He whipped me up into his arms and separated my legs to straddle him. I felt a rush of adrenaline as he slammed me against the wall, making the lift judder. He bit my neck lustfully, sending orgasmic pulsations straight through me, his hips grinding against me. I moved in sync with the rumble of the elevator, panting and ready for more. Alas, our lusty encounter was over too soon and the brass doors subsided, letting in some much needed oxygen.

Travis put me down and winked. "... And that's just the warm-up."

Offfttt! I was already fully stimulated and we hadn't even got in the room yet!

Steadying myself, I felt the thick, plush red carpet beneath my boots as we glided down the softly lit corridor.

Taking the lead, Travis eased open the large wooden door, revealing a suite fit for royalty. My eyes zoomed straight towards the magnificent, heavily carved, mahogany four-poster bed, then all around the majestic room.

I was speechless.

His gaze was smouldering. "You approve?"

I nodded, still taking in all the finery. This was the lifestyle I'd always craved.

"Perfect. The champagne is still chilling." Travis rattled the ice around the bucket. I had it sent up earlier today." He picked the bottle of Dom Perignon 2003 out of the ice bucket and showed me.

I didn't know much about vintage plonk, but I knew I needed Dutch courage. Travis found some glasses and tore the metal wrapper off the top of the bottle. I felt yet another rush of adrenalin as he popped the cork with masterful ease.

"I could've got a bottle from Room Service, but it wouldn't have been as good as *this,*" he smiled.

I searched him head to beautiful toe. He was the most

perfect, most beautiful looking creature I'd ever clapped eyes on - like something you'd see in a magazine adverting expensive designer aftershave.

"To ... *us*," I toasted, my heart racing. We chinked our glasses and sat on the bed. "Feel the spring on this mattress!" I bounced up and down with childlike exuberance, spilling some of the extortionate champers down my already stained dress.

Travis smiled, ignoring my clumsiness.

I quickly wiped my dress down. *Anyway, I'm ready! Take me. Take me! Ravish me!*

"Sorry, babe, I have to make a quick work call ... I don't want anyone to interrupt us later." He was up off the bed heading for the door. "I'll take it in the corridor."

Oh.

I tried to disguise the annoyance in my voice. "No problem. Take your time," I said, lying through my porcelain veneers. "I've got calls I need to make myself." I pulled out my phone to make myself look important, but the minute the door clicked closed, I lobbed it at the bed.

The tosspot!

I've waited all this time to see him and he fecks off to make a call – in private! Who could possibly be more important than me at this precise moment? Whoever they are, they're a wanker, and so is he. Don't they understand how little time we have? I may not even have sex with him if he's not careful. No ... that's a lie, of course I'm going to have sex with him. But still!

It's a shame Travis wasn't this reliable with calls to me. Well, two can (and will!) play that game. In the future, that is, not now. I'm gagging for it way too much to be playing games at this precise moment.

Taking advantage of the interlude, I darted over to the huge mirror and checked my make-up. I reapplied cream blush, lashings of lip-gloss, and doused myself head to toe in perfume (not forgetting a quick spray of the lady-garden, of course).

Despite topping up my own glass of champagne, and with Travis *still not back*, I became increasingly self-conscious as I waited in the huge suite alone.

Fidgeting, I decided to soften the lighting, so dashed around the suite like a madwoman, drawing the heavy red curtains, switching off the main light and turning on the table lamps. Once I was happy with the ambience, I hurriedly took my *relaxed* position back on the bed and waited.

And waited.

And waited!

Travis strode back in a whole feckin' thirty minutes later. Not looking the least bit sorry! *Wanker!* He eased himself down on the bed beside me. "Now, where were we?"

Where were we indeed!

I'd have loved to give him a swipe for leaving me for so long! Instead, I raised my glass to my lips, forgetting that I'd already emptied it, then held it out for a refill.

He hurled the glass behind him, gave me one of his killer smiles, and straddled me. "*Finally* together."

The boy who cried wolf came to mind. I wanted *it*. I wanted *him*. But now the moment was here, I was scared.

"You going to undress, or am I going to do for you?" His searching eyes stopped at my boots and darkened. "Leave those on?"

Nodding, I cleared my throat. "I'll leave the boots on

if that's what you want." I would've covered them in feckin' Marmite and eaten them if it meant he would make love to me!

He unbuttoned his shirt, loosened his belt, and in a single, strong move, picked me up and placed me at the top of the bed. If he'd been any faster, I would've got travel-sick.

His Herculean torso was staring me in the face. My eyes went straight to his bulge. Nervous, I looked away.

"Fuck, I want you so bad. That dress is coming off." My belt was off, my dress up over my head, and then flung in the air.

I pawed and squeezed his muscle-bound flesh and frantically undid the buttons on his jeans. I wrenched them down and his massive throbbing manhood burst over the top of them. Panting with lust, I yanked down his boxers to release him fully; he grabbed my wrists and pinned them to the bed.

Easing himself further towards the end of the bed, he bent down over my lower regions. Inch by inch he kissed my thighs, working his way slowly, inexorably, towards my lady-garden. I arched my back in ecstasy, closing my eyes as he gently bit and licked and firmly guided my legs apart with his hands. I reached down and felt his pulsating, wet tip. With an uncharacteristic flash of steel, I pushed him off and climbed on top of him, sitting astride his knees. Sliding myself down his body I took his rock-hard member in my mouth and sucked and licked it like a woman possessed. Repeating my name, Travis groaned like a wild animal, tearing his fingers in and out of my hair.

I never wanted the moment to end.

"Stop, Tara. Stop … it's too soon," he panted. To emphasise the point, he forced himself out of my mouth. As I licked my lips, our eyes locked. "You dirty bitch," he growled.

I preferred the term *Princess*, but dirty bitch would do for now.

He flipped me over so he was on top, and to my complete and utter shock, spat on my face.

Horrified, I pushed him away. This wasn't what I'd expected at all! I wiped my cheek with my forearm and instinctively spat back, slapping him clean across the face.

His eyes twinkled. "You're fucking amazing," he said.

"So the fuck are you," I said back.

"Turn round." I didn't have a chance to complete the request before he'd flipped me over and I was on all fours, my curved backside offered, my face squashed into the headboard. He used one hand to pin both my hands, his free hand gathering my hair up in a vice-like grip. He pushed forward, penetrating me in one masterful movement. Writhing hard against my backside, he moved powerfully back and forward, crashing in and out of me with wicked skill. *So I guess this is what they call doggie style?*

"You are on the pill, aren't you?" he asked breathlessly.

"*Umm* … no." My hands were fisting the bed sheets. "I'm not. You have anything?"

"No. I'll be careful. I'll pull out. I'm not stopping now, not for *anything*." He slowed his pace down. "Unless you want me to?"

I shook my head, dizzy with pleasure.

He slapped my backside hard in approval, then pulled out.

"Ladies first." He flipped me back round to face him,

then disappeared down my body, devouring me, his tongue circling, going ever lower, groaning as he inhaled my feminine scent.

I was quivering in ecstasy, my breathing erratic as he licked and teased, alternating his fingers as he rubbed and manipulated me in every conceivable direction.

"Baby, you're so wet!"

As I headed towards orbit, moaning and groaning with pure, unadulterated pleasure, I allowed myself to fully let go. As in, really let go.

"That's it, that's my girl." Travis's voice was horse. "Cum for me. Cum for your man." His nimble fingers continued to push hard and fast inside me. The sensation was exquisite.

I was overwhelmed by a tsunami of emotions and sex liquid, gathering at a phenomenal pace, a force so strong I wasn't sure if I was dying. Then, in a fantastic release, out it poured onto the bed.

I froze in horror.

"Holy Mary Mother of God!" Had I just pissed myself ? O-M-G ... *like a baby?* I shot off the bed, fluid dripping down my legs onto my boots.

Travis, on his haunches, looked at me with unbridled gratification. Mortified, I used my hands to cup my lady-garden in embarrassment, confusion and panic. I didn't want any more to come out.

"I love a squirter," he said, with evident satisfaction. "I want you to cum again, just like that."

"You do?!" I asked, my face the shade of a ripe tomato. I was too embarrassed to look at him, so I kept my eyes fixed to the ground. "I've never ... *ever* ... ever had that happen before."

"Don't go shy on me now, baby, we have unfinished business." We both glanced at his rock-hard cock. Luring me back to bed, he scooped my legs up high across his broad shoulders and entered me. His eyes never left mine as he began to thrust in and out. He groaned as he gathered his pace. "Tara, I'm in love with you."

I had to close my eyes because I was on the point of reaching another orgasm.

Hearing him say those words, *he loved me,* I wholeheartedly surrendered, mind, body and soul. No man had ever said that to me, *ever*. Not a sober one, anyway. I was vaguely aware of tears of joy snaking down my cheeks as I climaxed again. I opened my eyes to drink in the wonder of him enjoying my body. "I love you too, Travis."

By now, he too had been forced to close his eyes. His slightly open mouth and blank expression told me he was on another planet. Nothing else mattered. Nothing else existed as he shot himself into me and promptly collapsed.

It was the most erotic experience of my life.

Chapter 9

I had mixed feelings when Travis began to unwind himself from our sweaty, post-coital embrace early the next morning.

I knew he had to go to a meeting here in the hotel, in one of the conference suites. That was, in part, why we were at this incredible hotel. But I'd have given anything for him to say: *Sod it! I'm with the most amazing woman in the world, let them get on with it without me for once.*

Even though part of me wanted a breather for a few minutes, to mentally relive every detail of our night of passion, I would have said "Yes, yes, yes!" in a nanosecond to a repeat performance.

Instead, I felt Travis tenderly brushing the hair to the side of my face and kissing me gently on the lips.

He looked intently into my eyes. "I'm sorry, babe," he breathed. "Leaving you here ... looking like *this* ... after what we've experienced ... is the hardest thing I've ever had to do. You are the sexiest woman I've ever seen.

Could you imagine what beautiful babies we'd make?"

I floated back down from heaven.

As he stood up, his hands slowly trailed down the length of my body. I did my best to arrange myself in a coquettish pose to tempt him back to bed. We had beautiful babies to make!

"Stop it," he grinned. "You know what that'll do to me."

Without a word, he dived back on top of me, kissing long and hard, his tongue searching deep in my mouth. His hand roughly grabbed my breast as he began to work his way down my body.

I was in ecstasy. I could barely wait until he reached my lady-garden, and stretched out my legs in eager anticipation.

Then, I heard the sound of his phone.

I didn't know if I could physically cope if he stopped right now. "Leave it," I begged.

It was too late. With one movement and a hint of a growl, he was off the bed, answering it.

"Hi, yeah, sorry, I got a little held up," he said, in a completely matter-of-fact tone which showed no hint of what he'd just been doing not ten seconds earlier. In fact, if he wasn't standing there with a massive, glorious erection, I'd never have believed he was the same man! *He's clearly a very accomplished actor,* I thought with a glow of pride at his endless talents.

He began to busy himself around the room, picking up his scattered clothes and pulling them on as he spoke, his mobile cupped under his chin. "Yeah. No problem, if you have the contract ready. Okay. See you downstairs in a few minutes."

Snapping his phone shut, he looked over at me as he continued to dress. Standing there with his fists clenched, he let out a groan.

"Sometimes work *really* sucks," he said. "Will you wait for me? Order yourself a champagne breakfast. I'll be back as soon as I can – sooner, if possible." He leant over me, his mouth close to my ear. "Don't bother to get dressed, you'll only have to take it all off again," he whispered. "I've got plans for you, Tara Ryan."

Before I could respond, he'd walked out the door.

Lying back in the crumpled bed, I revelled in what had happened. *We've just had countless unprotected baby-making sexy times - that's what happened!* And, best of all, he didn't seem the least bit fazed; in fact, he'd commented on what beautiful babies we'd make!

I shivered with excitement, pushed my tummy out, and gently rubbed it. I didn't want to disturb his supercharged sperm after they had just left their testicular boot camp. I shoved a pillow under the small of my back to keep my oven at the correct tilt and lay still. *Swim, my little ones, swim,* I thought, encouraging them on their long journey to my "petit pois". I visualised the sporty ones in Nike tracksuits with cool Ray-Bans, others in Speedo trunks wearing swimming goggles. Some will get lost and just give up, some will be confused and idly shoot the breeze with each other, probably go cross-eyed from swimming around in circles, pissed after our champagne-fuelled binge.

On the other hand, there would be those who would be swimming down a *No Entry Zone*. They'd be swimming past my tonsils and down into my stomach, wondering where the hell they were meant to be going.

I began mentally commentating, like an over-excited

sports presenter. "Overtaking the lot of them with supercharged stamina comes the super-duper sperm whale. His Olympic medals are shining brightly – this dude is so relaxed, he's even wolf whistling and winking at the receptive petit pois. Oh no, she's barricaded the doors and appears to be throwing heels, handbags and lipsticks at him! Ah, no, it's a poor defence. But old super-duper sperm whale has flashed his muscles and medals and she's creaked open the door ... Will she let him in? Yes! And in he goes! What a performance, ladies and gentlemen!"

I don't know how long I lay there going over it all in my head, but I was brought back to reality by the arrival of a text. Bursting with excitement, I dashed across to the side table to retrieve it and was rewarded with a message from the Love God himself.

[Text from Travis]

That was outstanding sex! Never experienced anything like it. Can't concentrate on meeting Xxx

[Text from Travis]

Hoping to break for lunch at 12 x

[Text from Laura]

Well, come on! How did it go!? X

Eager to share details, I immediately texted back.

[Text to Laura]

Faked a few orgasms; I even had my legs shaking ten to the dozen and a soprano vocal range to match! I deserve an award for my acting skills! (Google wet-the-bed orgasms!) But the real ones were off the scale! Get saving for a hat because I'm in love. Call you later xxx

I smiled smugly as I watched the text whisk away to – Travis. *Travis!*

No!

No!!

NOOOOO!!!

That text was meant for Laura!

My body whooshed up like a furnace.

What a stupid, stupid, stupid cow!

I wanted to smash my hand into the phone and pull that dump-able text back. But off it had flown, around the swanky corridors of this five-star hotel, straight to the phone of my gorgeous Mr Right, who would now most certainly think I was his Miss Wrong.

Frantically, I read the text back. Then I read the text back again, and again a third time. It got worse each time I read it.

Dizzy with sweat, dropping the phone like it was a hand grenade, spinning round in hopeless, nail-biting circles, I locked myself in the bathroom and stared at myself in the mirror. After cursing myself and screaming like a banshee, I unlocked the door, scampered back to the bedroom, grabbed my phone and read that awful message again. I switched the phone off (hoping the message would miraculously unsend itself) and then back on again. Of course it was still there, in my sent messages.

"Pull yourself together, Tara!" *You can't fall apart now.*

You have to think - and think quickly. Quite frankly, and under immense pressure, that wasn't something I was very good at. Trembling head to toe, I began to compose a text.

[Text to Travis]

Hi, sent you a text by accident. Really sorry ...

[Delete]

Legs like jelly, I sank down onto the loo, my head shamefully bowed between my knees.

[Text to Travis]

A text was sent to me from a friend. I meant to forward it to Laura, sent to you by mistake! lol xxx

I clicked send, accompanying my text with a silent prayer: *"Please, God, don't let him think I was referring to him!"*

I placed my phone on the side of the bath, feeling helpless. Obviously, I'd need to leave the hotel right away. That was a given. There was no way I'd ever be able to face him again.

Lightning speed, I turned the heavy shower lever to one side and jumped in, tilting my lady-garden forward, desperately trying to scrub his sperm away. I jumped up and down, willing it to drop out. No way I was going to be a single parent from day dot!

I poured the entire bottle of Molton Brown Black Peppercorn body over my body and soaped myself. Every time I thought about what I'd written in that text, I cringed. For lack of any other options, I let out a huge, dramatic sob. Since it felt a little soothing, I did a few more for good measure, frequently pausing to peer across at my phone. It lay deadly silent.

Maybe he hasn't read the testosterone-destroying text yet? I brightened. *After all, he is stuck in that meeting, so at this moment, I could still be the woman he wants to be with.* I smiled faintly, feeling an optimistic sliver of calm.

But it won't stay that way, will it, Tara?

Feckin' texting!

Whoever came up with that stupid idea needed a breezeblock round their head. I'd have done anything to turn the clock back. Bloody Laura and her need to know everything!

Nosy cow!

This was all her fault!

I'd called Travis a Sex God only a few hours ago! I'd managed to insult him and made out he was a crap lay. To make matters worse, Travis was amazing in that department. Most men needed a satnav to find their way round lady-gardens, but this one knew exactly where he was going. He didn't think that my nipples were for tuning a 1970s-style radio, either.

I'll probably never hear from him again!

Just as I stepped out of the shower and reached for a towel, a text came through. Legs unable to keep me upright, I shakily sat on the loo, and plucking up the courage held the phone at arm's length.

[Text from Travis]

Lol. She needs to find herself a real man if she needs to

fake. Meeting's running over, babe, not sure when I can get back. Miss you Xxx

My body crumpled, almost collapsing in on itself. "There is a God. There is a God. Thank you, thank you!" Reading his text again I took some deep stabilising breaths. Then I screamed like a banshee as I thought about all the little super-duper-charged sperm swimming through the hotel pipes I'd scrubbed away. Hopefully one had swum to the finish line in time.

After all that stress, I had to pull myself together.

I was back on full shag alert!

Dying for a cigarette, I pulled on a dressing robe and, ignoring the NO SMOKING MAXIMUM PENALTY €120 sign, hung out the window. Puffing away, I counted my blessings. *Perhaps I am a quick thinker after all.*

Now I knew I was in the clear, I hoped Travis's meeting wasn't going to run on for too much longer. My flight home was at 4.00 p.m., so we were already cutting it fine.

Waving as much cigarette smoke out of the window as I could, I slammed it shut. *What am I going to do now?* I ambled aimlessly around the suite, listlessly opening drawers and cupboards and peering inside. For the want of anything better to do, I took out my phone and began recording a video diary of the plush suite. I'd been begged by James and Siobhan to record the dirty details. I decided to begin where it all began, so I laid my crumpled dress flat on the bed and started with a shot of those awful fake-tan stains. After verbally pointing out the two brown titty circles, I began the tour. I started in the bathroom, filming the huge Victorian free-standing bath, the his and hers sinks, and the sparkling shower unit.

"Plenty of fluff, very high-quality white towels - right up your street, James," I commented while filming myself in one of the large mirrors. "Oh, and look at this beautiful dressing robe." I zoomed in on the embroidered castle logo.

"Moving swiftly on, this is the lounge area." I trailed my fingers over the dark red leather Chesterfields strewn with raw silk scatter cushions laid out in perfect formation.

I stopped filming for a minute while I fiddled around with the TV remote. I was trying to locate the music channel on the huge plasma screen. I had to scroll through hundreds of channels before I got to it, but when I did, I was rewarded with my favourite song in the whole wide world: "Je T'aime". "*Je T'aime*"*!* Serge Gainsbourg and Jane Birkin bought the world to their knees when they released it in 1969.

I vaguely remember Mum years later boasting to all our neighbours that Dad, being in the music industry, had managed to get her an illegal seven-inch vinyl. She was red-faced and sweating profusely, clutching a "Learn French" manual.

"It was banned in England and Ireland years ago and now it's been re-released," she said in a smug tone to her nonplussed neighbour Mrs Murphy.

Mrs Murphy folded her arms under her large breasts and raised her eyes skywards in mock disgust. "Those Frenchmen, dirty little feckers so they are, sticking their tongues in your mouth when they kiss. Disgusting really, when you think of those slimy snails and frogs they eat. Couldn't be very hygienic, now, could it?"

Mum sighed longingly, a huge smile on her face, "But

sure isn't that the French for you, so bloody sexy."

I turned the volume up as my thoughts plunged back to the past. I remembered when I first clapped eyes on the most beautiful, most perfect woman I had ever seen, Brigitte Bardot. I could vividly recall Dad actually salivating watching a TV documentary about her, and "Je T'aime" was the backing track. She was the epitome of sexiness and beauty. She had it all. I wanted to be her. It wasn't that I fancied her (well actually, if I ever was to become a lezzer, she'd be my type); I was just in awe of her stunning beauty *and* she was idolised by all.

Seeing Brigitte Bardot on the TV when I was a schoolgirl meant that I decided not to throw myself in front of the number 10 bus after all. Instead, I decided to change everything about myself. I would start with my carrot hair. I'd been dragged to enough salons to witness Mum having her tightly wound perm and mile-high bangs to know anything was possible. I would turn *myself* into a blonde bombshell.

I waited till the house was empty and gathered my makeshift tools carefully. My attempt to create a homemade highlighting cap involved: one Woolworth's carrier bag (to place over my head), one strip of thick Sellotape (to tape the bag to my forehead), and one sharp, rust-free screwdriver (to prise areas of hair through that I wanted to be baby-blonde). Oh, and not forgetting one extra-large bottle of Co-op economy toilet bleach.

Sadly, instead of Bardoesque blonde curls (perhaps predictably) I ended up with a head of hair that represented every colour of the Irish flag: orange, green and white. When I saw what I'd done, I was hysterical.

"What in God's name has the child done to her hair?" Dad asked horrified.

"Lord have mercy," gasped Mum. She slapped one hand across her mouth and used the other to shield Laura's eyes.

No matter, I thought, breaking my heart in the salon chair as the hairdresser clipped my mass of smoking, burnt hair away. Once back home - with my hair scuttered into a disastrous Sinead O'Conner (unlike her, I didn't have the stunning face to carry this look off), and unable to find my winter hat, I shoved a knitted tea cosy over my head. *It will grow back*, I thought, *and there's always a number 10 bus that I could throw myself in front of tomorrow.* With Mum losing pay from being off work looking after me in my fake illness, I had to brace myself and get back to school. The bullies had a field day for weeks after.

As the song faded away, I snapped back to the present. Pressing the video icon on my phone, I resumed my diary.

"And this is the feckin' empty bed!" I pulled back the sheets in frustration. "Travis and I should be Fifty Shading in this four-poster right now!"

Desperate to keep myself occupied, I started to pack my things. At least that way, when Travis did return, we could use the time usefully.

Thinking about it, I realised that part of the reason I was so on edge (apart from the fact my lover had shagged me and gone off to a meeting) was that I knew I was on the precipice of something big with him. I didn't want things to go back to the way it had been, where I spent my life waiting for text messages and us barely speaking. Everything was different now. We had exchanged bodily fluids. *I mean, we could be pregnant!*

"Is that the sound of wedding bells?" I laughed to

myself. Imagine being *Mrs* Travis Coleman!

My stomach flipped, my imagination racing, as I hared off through our wedding day. I knew the exact wedding gown I'd have. Baby pink, sparkly – a corset clinching me in at the waist, a fairytale puffball, with layer upon layer of organza, a bustle on the back. Just like Cinderella.

Oh, and a towering tiara and cathedral-length veil with a huge bling bouquet. The wedding cake will be in the shape of ... a castle! Covered in mechanical butterflies - all tastefully done, of course. There'll be nothing tacky allowed at my wedding, no siree. We could marry here at Castle Clonarf!

I visualised myself standing next to Travis at the altar, him wearing an all-white long-tailed tux, looking like my knight in shiny armour. White horses, carriages ... I wondered how Travis would propose. Would we give *Hello* magazine the contract, or *OK*?

[Text from Travis]

Babe, won't get back till 2. They've laid on lunch and I can't get away. I'm so sorry. I'll call you ASAP Xx

In an instant, my fluffy world fell apart.

Bastard!

I'd pictured us going to the airport hand in hand, both sobbing uncontrollably and having to be prised apart. Surely he'd remembered I was leaving for the airport at 1.30? He'd booked the feckin' flight, after all! I despondently put on my tit-stained woollen dress, then my belt, then zipped up my boots.

[Draft message to Travis]

Can't you sneak out for 10 mins? Xx

[Delete]

[Draft message to Travis]

I want to puke, maybe morning sickness? Xxx

[Delete]

[Text to Travis]

So I won't get to see you before I leave? :-(Have to get a taxi by 1:30 latest. Please come say goodbye properly? X

I stared longingly at the blank screen. Funny how one minute I was dreaming about wedding gowns, wedding cakes and venues, and haggling vast amounts for our wedding pictures, and the next ... I felt so let down.

With no time to spare, I dialled zero and asked the annoyingly cheerful receptionist to order me a taxi to the airport. After one last glance around our love nest, I picked up the Castle Contarf dressing robe Travis had been wearing, inhaled his scent, shoved it in my case and walked out the door. Part of me hoped I'd see Travis running down the corridor in a desperate bid to see me before I left. But no, the corridor was eerily quiet. I could hear other guests chatting in the far distance and the low sound of the lift rumbling, but that was it.

Walking back into the vast lobby I realised I was a completely different person from the one who had been sitting in that chair the night before, bristling with anticipation. I had experienced everything I had expected and more, but at the same time it hadn't turned out anything like I had imagined. Here I was, slinking out of the hotel *alone*, like some guilty hooker.

The smartly dressed doorman opened the door for me and gave me a kindly smile as he showed me to the waiting taxi. It was all I could do to hold back the tears.

"Airport, please." *Come on, Tara,* I said to myself, in a vain bid to gee myself up. *You hate goodbyes anyway.*

[Text to Travis]

I'm sad that we didn't get to see each other before I left. About to board, hope your meeting is going well. Call when you can? xxx

Right up until the moment I boarded the plane I honestly believed Travis would call. But he didn't. I flicked my phone back on after we landed – there were still no messages.

By the time I arrived back home and put my key in the door, I'd managed to get myself into a better place emotionally. I was exhausted, every inch of my body aching from the sexual gymnastics, but it was worth it – Travis was worth it. After a few stretches to straighten my back out, I convinced myself that he would be been suffering as much as I was. And he had to work. There I was, cursing him while he was stuck in a boring meeting, desperate to see me and hating himself for letting me down like this.

What was it he said? *Leaving me was the hardest thing he had ever had to do.*

I placed my phone on the bath mat and eased myself into the hot, bubbly water for a long soak. I looked down at my body where he had laid his, just a few blissful hours ago and closed my eyes. I smiled and drew in a deep breath. I wanted him in my life, now more than ever.

After my long bath, I wrapped my Castle Clontarf robe around me, stuffed my face with all things sugar, and lay on the sofa, ignoring all calls from friends and family. Eventually, bone tired, I drifted off.

[Text from Travis]

Hi babe, sorry it's so late, had a mad busy day. I hope you got home safely Xxx

It was midnight! He'd certainly taken his time getting back to me. *The cheek of him,* I thought. *The bloody cheek of him! I've a good mind to tell him to feck off with himself.*

[Text to Travis]

Thanks so much for such a lovely time. I'm home safe and sound. I'm awake if you want to call? xxx

Chapter 10

In the following three days I received one solitary message from Travis.

It was an angry, brief text complaining that the hotel had charged him for a bathrobe he *hadn't* bought. There was no way I could admit to him that I'd taken it. I quickly called the hotel and paid for it on my (already dented) credit card, begging the receptionist to tell Travis there'd been some sort of admin mix-up. *How do you tell a man that you stole his bathrobe so you could retain his scent?*

I didn't dare tell a soul that Travis and I hadn't spoken since the morning he'd climbed out of the hotel bed.

My phone never left my side. In a desperate bid to be strong, I refused to be the first to give in and contact him, but it was killing me.

"Tara, darling," said James. He was about to try yet another tactic to cheer me up after I'd spent another day moping about the salon. "You know that New Year's resolution we all made? About getting fit? Well, I've found the perfect class for us all. It's street dancing. Siobhan, Jackie and *she who shall not be named* – who invited herself by the way – you and I are all going – so go and fetch your gym kit and we'll all meet back here after work?"

"I'm not in the mood," I said, full of self-pity. I'd had enough of yesterday, enough of today, and I was already dreading tomorrow. After work, I'd planned to go home, wee on my hundredth pregnancy stick (the other ninety-nine had come up negative), put my head under the duvet and eat my way through multiple tubs of ice cream.

James waved away my objections. "Of course you're in the mood. You want to keep yourself fit for Travis, don't you? He'll be constantly surrounded by rugby groupies looking to sample what he has on offer. You've got to keep in shape, okay? *Fabulous*. See you there."

Just as I was about to tell James to bugger off, my phone received a text message. It was all I could do to stop myself shrieking.

[Text from Travis]

Hi babe, miss you so much. Sky Sports tomorrow. Live match. Watch it. I'll scratch my nose to say hi. Love you xx

[Text to Travis]

Love you too! Of course I'll watch the match. When and where can we see each other next?
Xxxxxxxx

[Text from Travis]

How about me popping by after the match, gorgeous? It's not far from your salon and we've got some unfinished business ... :-)) xx

[Text to Travis]

What??? Yes, yes, yes!! Are you serious?
Xxxxxx

[Text from Travis]

Yes, I'm serious. We fly to London tonight ready for match tomorrow xxx

[Text to Travis]

OMG! What time do you think you'll be here? Shall we go for dinner? What type of food do you like? Soooo excited! xxxxxx

[Text to Travis]

Did you get my text? Xxxxx

[Text to Travis]

Tried to call you 100 times, you're not answering! Can you please let me know what time you'll be here, OR I

WON'T BE THERE, DRESSED UP SEXILY WAITING FOR YOU! XXX

[Text from Travis]

Sorry, it's mad busy. It'll be early evening. WHAT SEXY CLOTHES ARE YOU GOING TO WEAR? XX

Huh! I'll let him know what I'm going to wear when I know myself. Funny when I mentioned not being there he magically responded. Clearly I needed to sharpen my *treat 'em mean, keep 'em keen* tactics.

Feeling like a completely different person now that Travis had not only made contact but had also told me he loved me, *again*, I turned round to my staff with a beaming smile.

"Right, everybody! Who wants to see rugby players getting all hot and sweaty?" For once, I immediately had James's attention, and the girls weren't far behind.

"We're all going to watch my hunk of burning love on Sky Sports tomorrow," I grinned. "We can watch the game here, in the salon, but afterwards you've all got to feck off, because Travis is coming here to whisk me off then have rampant sex with me."

With that, I grabbed my stuff and marched out of the salon, leaving everyone speechless at my transformation. I didn't care. I had less than twenty-four hours to get into shape. Sod the dance class. I didn't have weeks to hone my body. I needed to fast-track my glamour. Heading towards the shopping mall, I called Travis to ask his preference for food again so I could book a restaurant, but his phone kept going to voicemail.

[Text to Travis]

Good luck tomorrow, darling. Can't wait to see you on TV. (And in the flesh) :-) Xx

Arriving at the mall, I headed straight for Ann Summers. I wasn't messing about. Walking purposefully around, I surveyed the lingerie on the rails with deep intent. As I headed through the shop, I couldn't help but notice the merchandise grew more intriguing the further back I went. A black leather whip caught my eye. *Hmm,* I mused, my imagination boggling for a moment. Alongside the whip was a PVC catsuit, also in black. Strategically placed beside it was a matching pair of leather handcuffs. A whoosh of domineering thoughts overcame me.

I should whip and tease that gorgeous fecker into place. Dominate him for a change. My mind flashed to images of Travis tied to a bed, unable to move. This was somewhat appealing on more levels than one.

That's what you get for being a gorgeous, inconsistent pig, I laughed to myself. *On second thoughts, he'd probably love that.* So far, that was the favourite scenario for tomorrow night. I made a mental note of the scene, but couldn't stop myself wondering what repercussions the Big Man Upstairs would have in store for me.

As my eyes traced the next section, my softer, more feminine side came out. I dreamily gazed upon a row of soft, feathery boas in a spectrum of pale pinks and whites, laid out beside matching frilly bras and lacy knickers. I ran my hand across the array of fluffy fabrics, imagining what they'd feel like on.

What to choose? I'd become awful at making decisions.

Far too loved-up for my own good! Baffled, I stood back, feeling dizzy with the choices. *Do I go hardcore with a few Hail Mary's for my sins? Or girly?*

I sighed deeply as I tried to organise my muddled thoughts. Just as I'd decided the only thing for it was to try everything on that I thought Travis might swoon over, a male customer caught my eye.

"Well," said the tall, tanned, blondish, tattooed, late-thirties hunk, "she's kind of …" Without a trace of embarrassment the Bradley Cooper lookalike cupped his hands on his chest in an effort to show his girlfriend/wife's breast size to the assistant, which was, apparently, considerable. "… *this* big," he said. "What do you mean, her *back* size?" he looked confused. "Not a clue. Does it matter? She's … well, *umm* … *her* size, over there." Smiling, he pointed at me.

Red-faced, I accidentally grabbed a dildo.

"Is the underwear for your wife?" asked a woman standing in the queue behind him. "Because if it is, you *really* don't want to get that wrong." She finished by raising her eyebrows.

I quickly put the dildo back on the shelf. *Men don't have a clue!* Shaking my head, I began my search again. *But bless him* (I turned back round for another sneaky look), *at least he was trying.*

Right, time to focus. Time is of the essence. Let's see. To give myself some momentum, I grabbed a couple of items and tried the colour next to my skin. Black balconette bra, or red? Side-tied, bowed or crotchless undies?

My eyes kept darting back towards the PVC catsuit. It was winking at me. Telling me to come buy it. It was so raunchy! Once it had lured me over, I took it by the hanger and held it up to eye level. While I was tussling with my inner demons, an assistant popped up, causing me to jump.

"Gorgeous, isn't it? Would you like to try it on?" she asked.

My face flamed red.

"Due to its rubbery nature we recommend a sprinkling of talc on the inside. There's some in the changing room."

I shook my head, mortified. I felt like I was advertising to the world I was about to have a steamy session of S&M sex. "I'll just hold it up against myself in the mirror." Along with a pile of sexy underwear, I clutched the catsuit closer to me and, like a crab trying to find a hiding place, scuttled off.

Apart from the fact I really didn't want to admit liking such an outrageously raunchy outfit, I was afraid the talc would have an adverse effect on my newly applied spray tan. I only had a few hours to get body-perfect. I couldn't afford any fuck-ups!

I disappeared into the tiny changing room and wrestled my way out of my clothes. I'd hung the catsuit on the hook behind the door and did my best to ignore it as I tried on the other, safer garments. After trying on endless pieces, the devil knocked at my door. I turned to look at the sexy, slinky catsuit and swore quietly to myself. *Lord, I'll seek forgiveness after I've worn it.* Taking it off its hanger, I bit my lip hard and blessed myself.

It felt surprisingly cold and slippery as I slipped a foot in each leg hole and heaved and pulled. *She certainly wasn't kidding about the talc,* I thought, as I yanked the catsuit up just past my hips. I paused briefly to see what it looked like so far. *Hmmm ... not bad. Not bad at all!* I swivelled round to a look at the back view. I'd have to see the *whole* thing on to be sure.

The further I pulled the catsuit up my body, the more complicated it seemed to be. I couldn't figure it out. There were no zips or buttons; meanwhile, there was a large opening around the chest, yet a small neck collar. Completely thrown, I lifted up one component after the other as it flopped around my waist.

Determined not to be beaten, I pulled it back down to waist level and put my arms through the only two holes I could find - which then automatically pulled the back of the outfit up. I winced as the crotch piece nearly fractured my lady-garden. Straightening up and surveying myself in the mirror, I could see the neckpiece was still flapping. *What the ...?*

Scratching my head, I wondered how the hell I would ever get the rest of it on. I pulled it back down to waist level and started again. Okay, this time I would put my arms and head in at the same time. *It's about coordination,* I told myself. With another supreme effort, I tugged the suit so hard that for a moment I thought I'd dislocated my arm. The collar was now stuck around my nose. I was seriously losing my temper.

"There must be a fault on this one," I cursed, sweating profusely. But with one final yank, the bastard was on. *Haha, no one messes with Tara Ryan!*

Like a lump of jelly in a vice, I stood back and squinted at my reflection. I forced myself to visualise the *sexy* me, bright red glossy lipstick and brooding come-to-bed eyes. To complete the effect I stood on my tippy toes, ruffled my hair and roared like a tigress.

I wasn't sure. In fact, if I was honest, I looked like a she-devil gone wrong. This catsuit would look better on a twenty-year-old. Feeling turned off, it slowly dawned on me that it was probably even more difficult to get off than it was to get on. Good job I didn't need the loo. Sod's law, the moment the thought entered my head, I realised I was busting.

Oh God. How on earth am I going to get out of it? I'd probably have to be cut out. *Oh, the shame of it!* My bladder was now feckin' bursting. Crossing my legs, I grabbed hold of my lady-garden and mumbled at my poor, constricted bladder to *hold on, hold on. HOLD ON!*

Pulling at any loose fabric I could find, I jumped up and down, frantically wriggling this way and that. But every time I attempted to pull the collar over my head, the body of the catsuit shortened, pulling itself even tighter. No matter how much I tensed my butt cheeks and pulled my stomach in, it wouldn't stretch.

I began flapping.

"Pull yourself together, Tara, for feck's sake!" *Think!* After a moment's deliberation, I tried catch the catsuit off guard. To surprise it, I closed my eyes and meditated briefly while I planned a sneak attack. *This was war!* However, as I quickly found, fighting a battle with my eyes closed against the rubbery predator was probably the worst idea I'd ever had. My assault was immediately repelled as it threw me back against the changing room door. Defeated, I slid to the ground in a panting mess.

I was too ashamed to ask the assistant for help: I'd been warned about the talc. A thought hit me. Maybe I could rip it off? Damn it! That should've been Travis's job! I hunted for a good place to start, picking at a seam with my tweezers.

Then, like a godsend, a voice from heaven filled my ears. It was James. I'd know that voice *anywhere*! I hissed over the top of the changing room door. "James? Is that you?"

Easing the door open, I tiptoed out just enough to pop my head round the corner and saw the back of his blond hair.

"James!" I hissed. "Come here!"

Looking confused, he leaned away from a shelf of sex toys, his eyes and head darting in every direction before he finally spotted my torso-less head.

"Come in here, I'm stuck." I scrambled back into the changing room and slammed the door closed, my head peeking above.

He sauntered towards me - lips on full pout. "Tara!? *Oh*. So this is where you dashed off to? We abandoned the dance class because *you* wouldn't come with us. Never mind, we can go next week." He gasped excitedly. "But actually, now that you're here, you can meet my new boyfriend! I'll go get him!"

"No! Listen to me." Ashamed, I opened the door, my arms dropping to my sides in exhaustion. "I can't get out of *this*, I'm stuck." I watched his eyes light up and his mouth open wide. God, he was a bitch at times.

"But *oh my*, you look fabulous! Christian, sweetie," he hollered over his shoulder, the sound echoing throughout the entire shop, "come quick! Come see what my boss is wearing. We have *soooo got* to get us one of these!"

"*Please, James,* I've been like this for fifteen minutes. Just come in and help me out of it."

Much to my humiliation, Christian arrived. He was James's usual type: about nineteen-years old, athletic and achingly good-looking.

"Christian, be a love and hold this butt plug, Tara

needs me." Melodramatically, James swept in, slamming the door behind him. He gasped, scanning me head to toe. "Wow, it looks like it's been sprayed on. It's magnificent! I hope you're going to buy it? If not, *I* certainly will. Does it feel good? Do you think it would fit me?"

I was almost hysterical. "Shut up and get me out of it!"

Of course James was immediately distracted by the wall-to-wall mirrors. "Oh, Tara, look at me - I look like boiled shit. All this wind is doing no favours for my hair and ... *oh-my-God*, my arse is so massive in this mirror!"

He yelled over the top of the door. "Hey, Christian ... *Christian!* Does my arse look big today? Looks like I'll need an extra large butt plug after all," he laughed.

"James, please stop poncing around!"

"Sorry." He tilted his head to one side. "It doesn't leave much to the imagination, does it? I can see all the weeds in your lady-garden."

I gave James the evil eye. "I'm going to bloody wet myself in a second! Now please just hold the collar and stretch it apart as far you can."

I spun around to give him better access and waited for him to help release me from the clutches of the evil black suit. I tried to ignore the feeling of his fingertips vibrating as he held back shudders of laughter.

"Christian," said James, snorting heavily with the effort of it all. "We need all hands on deck here. There is a big black rubber to deal with. Come in and help." He turned to me, smiling. "It's okay. He's got me out of far worse."

I didn't care anymore. I'd gone past that point. Christian hurried in, and after the briefest of introductions the gay brigade set to, pulling and pushing me this way and that. It seemed to take forever. Meanwhile, my eyes were rolling into the back of my head with the pain of it all - I had to constantly bite my lip to prevent myself from peeing everywhere.

"Tara, have you tried undoing the Velcro on the back of the collar?" asked Christian.

I swung round to face him. "What?"

"You mean you got that rubber on with the VELCRO done up?" said James. "Wow, get *you*. I bet you're a *right* minx in the bedroom!"

Both he and Christian collapsed into each other, snorting with laughter, mascaraed tears running down their pretty orange faces.

"James, I implore you – *DO NOT* mention this to *anyone*!" I instructed as he finally began releasing me from my bonds. I rolled the hot PVC prison off each leg. "I'll give you a bonus at the end of the week. And Christian, you can come to the salon and have a couple of complimentary sunbeds – but both of you, please, keep shtoom!"

James placed his right hand on his chest (around about where his heart would be, if he had one). "I swear on my *huge* bonus and Christian's twenty free tanning sessions, we won't tell a soul."

I flopped down on the chair as both James and Christian held the catsuit by the ankles and pulled and heaved. To help ease things along I peeled the rest away from my now chafed, sweaty skin. *Voilà,* it was off!

Cupping my lady-garden, jumping desperately from one foot to the other, I shoved both my saviours out of the changing room, got dressed at lightning speed, raced out of Anne Summers and got to the toilets just in time. While having the longest, most gratifying wee of my life, a text came through. *It'll be Travis, making last minute arrangements, I'm sure.*

[Text from Jayde]

Just fort I'd let you know, James has sent everyone a picture of you in a sex shop, trapped in a gimp outfit. Is it true or is it photoshopped?

The following day, I decided to close the salon earlier than I should've - but hey, it's not every day you get to see your man live on TV! Siobhan offered to get nibbles and alcoholic provisions to make it extra special. No doubt she'd end up crashed out somewhere completely arse-faced, but the deal was that we'd all watch the match together and once the game was over she'd be in charge of getting everyone out, so I would be alone when Travis arrived. In a brief text exchange that morning, Travis had said he expected to be away from the stadium by 7.00 p.m. and would meet me at the salon. I'd bombarded him with questions about where we'd go once he got there, but as always his text messages dried up. I didn't throw my usual hissy fit. In fact, I'd go as far to say that I was beginning to understand my role as his supportive girlfriend. He was busy - mentoring his players, building them up - working out strategic positions, etc. A huge responsibility!

James walked - or should I say limped - into the salon, making his usual dramatic entrance thirty minutes before kick-off, a frozen bag of peas over his crown jewels.

"I've only gone and pulled my groin! I've spent my whole day off in Accident & Emergency! I sat there for five hours! But worse than that, the only *Vogue* magazine they had was three years out of date. All they did in the end was tell me to go home and take some paracetamol. Well, I said to them, 'Only if you can give me a suppository.' I don't think the doctor had any idea how much danger my money-maker was in. Mind you, I did get him to have a cup of the plums before I left – just to make sure I hadn't pulled them as well."

I eyeballed him sarcastically. "Oh *poor* James. Could that have happened to you because of karma? As a result of gossiping? Sending pictures of *me*, *a* helpless victim, trapped in a catsuit?"

Jayde interrupted. "Don't ya be worryin' about Screamin' Queenie over there, Tara, he just wants even more attention than usual." She looked at me sincerely. "Me and me mates fink that photo of you in that gimp outfit was tampered with anyway. You can stick a face on anything these days. Anyway, she was much fatter than you are. Shocking funder-fighs."

Straightening my posture and pulling my core tight, I went for James (to give him another ear-bashing), but just as I caught hold of his collar there was an almighty crash at the salon door. It was flung open by Siobhan - accompanied by her usual manic grin.

"Sorry, Tara. It's this feckin' trolley. Got a mind of its own, especially now it's only got three wheels. By the way, if the neighbouring shop says anything about their car being scratched; it wasn't me, *right?* It's a coincidence. Me fourth trolley wheel is stuck underneath his car, along with me right shoe – *which proves nothing*."

I wasn't going to ruin the evening by informing her that there was CCTV outside.

"So you alright, then?" she asked, hobbling through the door, dragging the wobbly Tesco trolley filled to the brim with nibbles and wine boxes.

"I'm good. Really good." I rubbed my hands together excitedly. "Siobhan, what's with the trolley?" Sometimes I despaired.

"Well, I was going through Tesco looking for something for tonight, right. I see these boxes of wine on offer. *That'll do nicely,* I thought. So I pile them into me trolley and you know how it is, you try a little tipple on your way to the till. *Who doesn't?* But I took a little detour and didn't realise I'd been through nearly a whole box. Anyways, I get outside and I can't remember where I'd parked me wheels! Plus, I'd be over the limit, and you know me, have to stay on the right side of the law and all that, so I walked here, trolley and all. I've paid a pound for it anyway, which reminds me, I'll be needing that pound back. Have you a fork I can jemmy it out with?"

"Oh, Siobhan ... help yourself, but leave the trolley outside, please. Now, come on – the match is about to start."

We all crowded into the staffroom, finding space as best we could around the tiny TV. As I took a seat, I began to gloat to myself: *Not only am I going to watch my lover at work, I'm going to tape it so I can watch it as many times as I like.* The thought of seeing Travis in his shorts made my pulse quicken. As an added bonus, I'd be surrounded by my girlfriends and gay best friend. At last they'd be able to see what had brought me to my knees.

The match got off to a cracking start. For what felt like eternity, I was glued to the TV but hadn't caught a single glimpse of Travis. The camera was on *everyone but* him. I kept scanning the team and mistakenly shouting "There he is, there he is!" before correcting myself and beginning my search afresh. Luckily, after a few minutes of this, Jackie informed me I was looking at the wrong team entirely.

After a quarter of an hour of pointlessly scanning the TV, and with a player getting injured, the game broke for a few minutes. In the distance I could see a man, legs of steel, running onto the pitch to his aid. *Is it Travis? Please, God, let the camera do a close-up.* With that, my prayers were answered.

There he was! I turned to everyone, hands clasped to my face in joy, screaming, "Is he not the most beautiful creature you've ever seen?" Glowing with pride, torn between serenely watching his every move and jumping up and down like a child, I saw him reach a hand up, smile and scratch his nose, just as he'd promised. That was it for me. Game over.

I was hysterical.

All hopes of playing the calm Goddess of Love were gone. There was *my man*, standing on a pitch, wearing the sexiest hoodie, shorts and trainers I'd ever seen. And he was sending a signal to me! Unable to help myself I leapt up and kissed the screen. *I, Tara Ryan, had made love with that man!*

As play resumed, the heavens opened. The mud, the sweat, the ear-pulling (they really shouldn't do that), the diving, the skidding and scrumming – the whole rugby match experience left us all *oohing* and *ahhing*. Everyone in the staffroom was caught up in the excitement. We chanted and squealed so much we drowned out the commentary. Some time in the second half I caught another glimpse of Travis, soaking wet and running his hands through his hair.

My God, but I loved that man so much it hurt.

By the time the match was over and Travis's team had won, we were all frenzied, laughing, crying and screeching at the top of our lungs while swigging Siobhan's supermarket wine. I watched with pride as Travis and the subs poured onto the pitch, embracing and congratulating each other.

James sighed wistfully. "Tara, darling, does one know if the gorgeous Mr Travis Coleman is into spandex at all? That's what the good Lord invented it for, sexuo-erotic gods like him. He's just so … so … *so* … dick-matising! Pwweeeese can we stay to meet him, just for a nanosecond?"

Siobhan shot a look at James and shook her head. "I've made a promise to Tara that we'll vacate the salon without a fuss."

[Text to Travis]

Well done! I'm so proud of you and your team! You looked smoking hot in your kit Xx

James tugged at my shirt. "But I want to meet him! Can't we just stay here for an incy-wincy bit, just so I can checkout his cuticles? He might want a manicure or something. I'd be perfectly happy to give him a quick soak and a hand job."

[Text from Travis]

Thanks, babe. See you in 30 mins or so. I'm rock hard just thinking about you xxx

"Sorry, James, what were you saying?"

Siobhan had dragged James to the corner of the salon and was whispering urgently in his ear. I could tell she was bribing him with something, because he was jumping up and down like a schoolboy.

I raised my hand to calm everyone.

"Sorry to be a party pooper, guys, but I'm throwing you all out." I tried to stop the grin that was spreading across my face. "I'm about to do some intense scrumming of my own – and sorry, but this isn't a team game."

Jayde already had her coat on and was rushing out the door, quickly followed by Jackie. And surprisingly, James and Siobhan were also compliant, heading off without a murmur of complaint or even a ribald comment. *They really are great friends,* I thought. Very understanding and supportive indeed.

Chapter 11

I squealed like a child, excitedly sprinting round the salon checking everything was perfectly in its place. *Finally,* here was my opportunity to show off Glamma-Puss to Travis. It was, after all, the one thing I'd got right in my life. It was nothing but a shell when I had first viewed it, but with blood, sweat, tears and sheer determination I had achieved my dream of creating a successful top-class Hair and Beauty salon with a reputation to match.

Dashing over to the staffroom, I placed my all-time favourite Bambuddha Grove CD into the stereo. Hearing the hedonistic and erotic pulses flood through the salon sent me wild with thoughts of Travis and I having an all-night steamy sex session. *I must remember to take the CD home with me*, I thought. I'd scrubbed the house top to bottom. Changed the bedsheets, got in every type of healthy breakfast I could think of. Four types of herbal tea and coffee. Purchased new cups and saucers, then thought about his big sexy man hands, so bought new mugs, too.

I walked back into the salon and switched off the main overhead lighting, preferring the soft, seductive glow from the Bourgie table lamps either side of the chaise longue. The salon looked perfect: towels stacked and rolled, colour coordinated in minks and creams, ornate mirrors gleaming and workstations neat and tidy. I was desperate to impress him. I'd show off my entrepreneurial flair then planned to taxi us to the fancy, romantic restaurant I'd booked. After that, I'd whisk him back to mine. Travis had set the bar so high on our last date, it was the least I could do for the man I wanted to spend the rest of my life with.

Pacing nervously over to the mirror, I did a quick check of my efforts to pull off the perfect WAG look.

Hair, ruffled and humongous, *check*.

Acrylic nude nails, still attached, *check*.

Lashes glued securely, *check*.

Lips lined and dripping with nude lip-gloss, *check*.

Black sheer shirt, daringly transparent, *check*.

Lacy black bra, visible, *check*.

I popped open another button.

Cleavage on display, very visible, *check*.

Startled, I swung round to face the door. "Travis ... is that you?" I totted over and peered through the blinds. I couldn't see a soul. I could've sworn I'd heard someone.

Right, back to the preparations. After witnessing countless men dropping their jaws over Laura's Christmas outfit, I'd decided to copy it for my date. Of course, my version *had* to be more expensive. This wasn't deliberate one-upmanship; the sales were over, which forced me to spend considerably more than I'd wanted. I smoothed down my horrendously uncomfortable black leather skirt and heaved the thick black waist-emphasizing belt-buckle in by one more notch. I'd teamed it with an elegant Yves Saint Laurent sheer black shirt with diamante fastenings and statement satin cuffs.

I quickly shoved on my skyscraper Louboutins and fussed about my stockings. No more hold-ups for me - I'd certainly learnt my lesson. This time I was wearing an extortionately priced silk and lace suspender belt. I'd hoped they wouldn't *just* be more reliable, but more comfortable, too. So far, that wasn't the case. When I'd attached my stockings to the clips of the belt, I'd almost put my back out. How the feck are you meant to clip the damn things on behind you and keep the stocking seam straight? Thankfully, Siobhan had helped line them up earlier.

I glanced up at the clock. I felt nervous. Giddy. Travis would be here any minute, flashing me one of his killer smiles.

I wanted to appear busy. I paced round doing various nonchalant poses. Eventually, I decided the best impression would be if I were on the phone taking a booking. It drove me insane waiting for him at the hotel when he did that to me!

Just as I picked up the phone in readiness for my charade, I spotted him trying the door handle. My heart leapt.

"Push the door harder." I busied myself with my fake conversation but lost the thread the minute I saw him. My gaze was riveted by his presence.

"Hey, you," he smiled.

I blew him a kiss, pointed at the phone, swung myself round in my chair, pen in mouth suggestively, keeping him in my line of sight.

He tapped his watch impatiently. "Come on, come on," he said, eyes wild with excitement.

Indicating with an elaborate mime that I wouldn't be long, to raise the stakes in my game I provocatively sauntered to the front of the reception desk. Now he was only inches away.

I hadn't seen Travis in his kit before. I had to pinch myself that this was really happening to me. One minute he's on the TV in front of thousands of supporters, and the next, he's *here,* with *me,* in the flesh. The fact that he had mud all over that flesh just added to my longing to touch him.

Forgetting that I was supposed to be in an intense client conversation, I exhaled in a rush. I became acutely aware that my breathing was now quite audible. In fact, I may even have been panting. Anticipation ran through me as I watched him casually stride back to the salon door. He nonchalantly leaned back against it, propping his muddy trainer up against the once-spotless sill. Without looking at me, he whipped out his phone and diverted all attention to seemingly more pressing matters.

"Sorry," I said, "won't be long." He didn't look up.

A lump appeared in my throat. I wanted to kick myself for not throwing my arms round him the second he arrived, but not me, *oh no,* I have to plan a stupid staged greeting and he's bored shitless already.

"I'm gonna fuck you hard when you've finished your call." Still not meeting my eyes, he continued tapping on his phone.

I slammed the phone back in its cradle. "Not in your dirty kit, surely?" I laughed.

He tossed his phone onto the chaise longue then peeled off his hoodie, pausing to wipe his brow with it.

"Tara, you look so fucking hot in that outfit." His eyes glinted. "I want you – and I want you *now.*"

I gestured down at myself nonchalantly, tutting and fluttering my lashes. "This old outfit? I haven't even had time to get changed from work yet, what must you think of me?"

He stepped closer. "Right here, right now, I want to rip it off and fuck your brains out."

I was taken aback. This didn't seem like my Travis at all. He didn't have any of his usual charm. He seemed focused on one thing and one thing only. It wasn't that I was complaining, because, to be fair, I was thinking the same thing. I'd just expected ... well, I don't know what I expected. Perhaps a yielding mattress would have been a good start. *It must be the adrenaline still pumping round him from the match. I must be understanding. It's very important that I support him at a time like this.* I'd been reading all about this in my research on all the dos and dont's of a WAG.

"Let me show you round the salon first?" I simpered.

He glanced round, his face impassive.

"Or we could go straight back to mine, freshen up, then go out for dinner. I've booked a fabulous restaurant."

"Babe, I've already eaten, I grabbed a quick bite after the match and had a protein shake; but I haven't had dessert ... yet."

His voice was laced with unfamiliar tones of urgency. I swallowed hard, picked up my glass of wine from earlier and gulped some down.

"Okay, perhaps you might eat later." I smiled, doing my utmost to sound accommodating. "Where's your overnight bag?" I noticed he had nothing with him.

Travis didn't respond; instead, he cleared the reception desk with one fell swoop, sending everything smashing to the ground, and lifted me on top of it, his lips pushing hard against mine. I released an involuntary moan, almost dissolving on the spot.

"I need you, Tara." Breathing in my sweet perfume, he groaned, nuzzling his stubbly jawline over my chest; skilfully teasing, he descended lower with his tongue. I felt wild with passion, encouraging him, my legs hooked round his waist, pulling him tighter into me, my fingers weaving in and out of his sweaty hair while his mouth sucked in desperate search of my erect nipples; finding them through the lace of my bra, he teased them until one breast burst over the cup.

He abruptly stopped, then yanked his shorts and boxers down over his trainers before kicking them away. Frantic, he hitched up my skirt, steering me into position. I watched his eyes widen as he caught sight of my stockings and suspenders. The sight seemed to encourage even more crazed behaviour. He worked his way down my body, plunging his tongue through the lace of my scanty knickers, tracing my lady-line folds, panting like an animal.

"Travis, please, not here ... we can't!" I said. "Anyone could walk in. The door isn't locked."

"I don't mind, if you don't mind." He pulled his T-shirt over his head, and with wild abandon flung it in the air.

"I mind," I said, weakly. I was both disgusted and turned on. "Travis, stop!" I slapped his hands away as he started again.

He groaned, "I can't stop, I don't want to." He nuzzled his nose against my temple.

"Please, not like this. Slow down." I clutched his hard-set jaw at arm's length and stared into his brooding dark eyes before kissing him tenderly. "I need to lock the door, okay? There's no rush, we've got all night."

I popped my boobs back into their lacy cups, shimmied my skirt back down into place and headed over to lock the door. Travis was butt-naked apart from his trainers. Christ, he was a sight for sore eyes. He looked like Action Man, with perfectly formed muscles, his hard glory-crown glistening and ready.

I hardly had a second to dwell on the vision as he stepped forward, took my hand and guided me over to a mirrored workstation. He stood behind me, nibbling my ear, his arms wrapped round my waist, rocking me side to side.

"How fucking sexy does this look?"

I purred back at him, sticking my bum out further to greet his hardness while trying to absorb the madness of it all. "We make the perfect hot couple."

"No, *this* is hot." With that, he pushed himself into the back of me. "Do you feel that, baby? We're going to fuck in front of this mirror."

I gasped.

"Tell me how much you want me," he murmured.

"I want you more than anything."

"I have a panoramic view." Undoing the buttons, he peeled my shirt off my shoulders. I shuddered in delight as we watched it float, then pool on the ground.

I seized the opportunity to turn round and face him, but without ceremony he turned me back to face the mirror.

Shocked, I placed my hands tenderly on top of his;

desperately trying to follow his erratic lead as his hands travelled all over me.

I was finding it hard to keep up with him in any sense. I swung between being paralysed and confused by his playboy mood and then turned on by it. He ripped down both straps of my bra, whipping my arms free.

"You're a naughty girl, aren't you?"

Am I? I didn't think so, but nodded anyway.

"Look at me squeezing your tits, Tara."

I watched his hands moving at a crazy pace. He pulled my hair back, rocking wildly behind me.

Desperate to get this new turn of events right, I kneaded his tightly toned butt, my fingernails digging into his skin. I did my best to follow his crazy rhythm as his hands descended with lightning speed, aggressively hitching up my skirt to waist level.

I was dizzy. Alarmed. Turned on.

"Those fucking stockings and suspenders are driving me wild." He weaved his fingers in and around the lace knowledgeably, pinging one of my stockings free from its clip.

I smiled wickedly and ran my hands down his hot naked flesh, reeling with pleasure. Just as I felt I was getting to grips with the moment, he was urging me to bend over.

I gripped the salon chair as he yanked my knickers to one side, mounting me like a bull from behind. Ready to accommodate him, I yelped in pleasurable pain.

"Feel that, baby." He writhed into me harder, kicking the salon chair away, which turned over, its wheels mid-air. My heart pounded hard in my chest as I fell forward, my hands catching the floor just in time. I was encased by Travis and his muscle-bound strength. The sounds of his body slapping hard behind mine, enjoying me, made me feel suddenly powerful, brazen almost.

"I love how much you want me," he groaned.

"I want more," I moaned shamelessly. "I want it all."

A life together, marriage, children – the works!

With just a view of the salon floor and his trainers (due to me being folded over), I cocked my head round to the side. I could see the rear of him in another mirror. His perfectly formed butt muscles were working at a phenomenal pace, fucking me hard. His muscular back flexed and dripped with sweat, while his huge arms held my waist in place as he thrashed in and out of me.

"I can see us in all the mirrors. It's like I'm fucking ten women. Fuck. I'm in heaven!"

Wait ... What?

I was just about to reach up and grab a pair of thinning scissors and stab him in the ankle when he quickly added, "I meant ten of *you.*"

That comment stung. Viewing him in another mirror, I caught a glimpse of his stormy expression.

"We look so hot, so horny." His voice was wicked with enthusiasm.

I'd had enough and wished he would hurry up already.

I was just about to take a bite-sized chunk out of his calf in protest when I felt awash with *the* most erotic, leg-trembling sensation. Zillions of volts flooded through me and a kaleidoscope of colour misted my vision.

"*T-rrraa-vvvv-i-sss! Oh – my – Godddd!*" I pitched at a soprano level, my legs going to jelly. "Whatever you're doing ... *Oh my God!* I ... can't ... I ... can't-catch-my-breath ... don't stop. I beg you, don't stop!"

"I knew you'd love a finger up the bum ... I knew it!"

"WHAT THE FUCK!" I punched his hand away. "Get out of my allotment!"

I would do anything for him, but not that! Nobody goes up my back garden! "That's sacred, holy ground!" I blessed myself and began reciting a Hail Mary alongside asking the Big Man Upstairs to forgive for Travis taking my bum-ginity without my permission.

Distracted, I heard sounds in the distance, just like the ones I'd heard before Travis arrived.

"Did you hear that? Travis? ... Did you hear that noise? I can hear voices!" I slapped the back of his leg to still his marathon shagathon. He grunted loudly, carried on. Puffing my sweat-soaked hair from my face, I cocked my head round to get his attention.

"*Travis!* Please stop, or just cum, for God's sake, I can't take anymore!"

In a world of his own, he plunged harder and faster. He kept one hand strategically around my waist, the other over my forehead, his fingers grossly dropping over my eyelids, into my mouth. I heaved at the thought that one of those *polluted* fingers had been fiddling where it was forbidden to be. I held my breath, my eyes crossing in repulsion.

Finally, giving an almighty Tarzan like yell, Travis shot himself into me. Folding over, he buried his sweat-soaked face in my back, his body juddering behind me, both of us panting breathlessly in an otherwise silent salon.

Within seconds he retracted himself, staggered over to the chaise longue, retrieved his phone and collected his strewn clothes along the way.

"Damn it. I've got to go, there's a crisis with one of the players." He shrugged his shoulders and rattled through his phone.

"Oh no, what's happened? Do you want me to come with you?" Standing in just my stockings, suspenders, shoes and with my leather skirt twisted up and around my waist, I grabbed a cutting apron to cover my modesty.

"No. I don't have time to wait." He paced eagerly over to a backwash, splashed soapy water over his face, manhood and hands, before grabbing a towel to wipe himself dry. As soon as he was done, he tossed the towel to the floor.

"Will you come back to my place *after*?"

He didn't look up from his phone. "Doubt it."

The blood drained from my face at his snap decision. I stood, leaning my hip against the washbasin, folding my arms tightly around myself. My gaze narrowed as he pulled his clothes on and strode towards the door.

Involuntarily, I paced over to him. "I can be ready to come with you in minutes."

"Gotta go. Sorry." He barely turned round before unlocking the door.

"Please don't go." My hand pulled his hoodie.

Travis turned, glared at me. "I've learnt a lot about you tonight, Tara."

An awkward silence hung in the air.

"I don't do needy. The team come first."

I hung my burning face in shame. "Sorry." I raised a hand – my lash strip had attached itself to the side of his neck. Before I could get it, he pulled away.

"I'll call you." He flung the door open and without a backward glance scampered off into the darkness.

I stood, shivering in shock, pressing my forehead despondently against the door. My quivering hands clasped the keys for support as I locked it. I slid into a crumpled heap on the floor, a block of pain lodged beneath my chest.

Eventually, I attempted to piece together what had just happened. Time seemed to have stood still. I glanced at the clock. *Can it really be only 7.30 p.m? Did the man I'd been building my world around actually just come and go in less than half an hour?* I'd spent longer applying my lip-liner!

I double-checked the time on my phone to see if either the salon clock or my watch had stopped. Nope - he'd been here for a matter of minutes. The reality of what just happened dawned on me, like a drawn-out punch in the face.

He said I was needy! His words painfully bounced round my head. Was I? I didn't know, my internal compass was out.

Shivering, I shoved my arms through the cutting apron and on my hands and knees I crawled towards the reception desk through the chaotic paraphernalia of my clothes and desk debris.

Something glimmering in the low light caught my eye. My dad's pen. He'd written his love song with it. The one and only thing I had left of him. I picked up the broken pieces and held them against my heart as a flurry of emotions overcame me: guilt, anger, shame, longing and loneliness. A torrent of tears uncontrollably followed.

A muffled sound interrupted my misery. Voices again! The same as earlier. Had I become a schizophrenic like my dad? I mean, I always thought Laura had the potential – and definitely Katie, but *me*?

The voices were louder, moving closer. My vision blurred by tears, I shot up from the floor, alarmed.

"Travis?" I cried, my heart banging.

I rubbed my make-up-smeared face to see James and Siobhan striding towards me.

My jaw dropped. "What the ...?"

"No need to say anything, we saw the whole thing." James took me in his arms and held me tight. "What an arse-wipe-of-a-bastard!" He rubbed my back. "There, there."

"Oh, James," I howled, trembling in his tight grip. "Travis has gone and he was only here half an hour!" I wiped my tears with the back of my hand. "He said I was needy!"

Siobhan was bellowing furiously into the phone. "... Right, he's wearing a grey hoodie and black shorts. Shoot the fecker on sight – but don't kill him ... cos me fag mate wants to ram a rusty nail file up his jacksy ..."

"*And then* I'm going cut off his oversized dong and feed it to Jayde," said James, finishing Siobhan's orders.

"Stop." I pleaded breathlessly. "Don't make this any worse by getting him done over."

Siobhan was still shouting profanities down the phone. "In fact ..." she turned to me, covering the phone so not to be heard "... we could ruin his reputation with a vicious rumour or two. After this call, I'm gettin' straight on to the paparazzi!"

"Tell the paps Travis's dong is bent." James looked at me for approval, his eyebrows raised in hope.

I whipped the phone clean out of Siobhan's hand, ending the call. "I've been through enough this evening." If these two spilled the beans to the press, there'd be no going back.

I could be pregnant! I didn't want our baby being bullied in the playground with our family name tarnished by this. I needed to play it down.

As my mind spun, something else troubled me. It occurred to me that the response time from my life-saving emergency team was suspiciously short. In James's own words: "We saw the whole thing."

"You two," I broke in, as the pair argued about a strategy to destroy Travis. "How *did* you get in here so quickly?"

"Ah, yes, well, err ... *umm* ... you see - we were, *umm* ... doing a stock count upstairs," mumbled James. He looked over to Siobhan for support. "Weren't we?"

She nodded enthusiastically but it was easy to see this was a blatant fabrication.

"There's nothing up there but cobwebs and sawdust, you fibbing, spying toe-rags!"

"Don't go on about it, woman," said Siobhan, waving away my protest. "We wanted to make sure you were okay, isn't that right, James? Which reminds me, it's all on your CCTV if you want to go to the press with a sex tape. We could blur your face out and everything. You'd make a fortune!"

James looked thoughtful. Oblivious to my baleful look, he leaned in. "Would now be the wrong time to say *I told you so* about your back garden? *Any hole is a goal,* you know. Your expression was most peculiar ... it did that to me the first time, but I've never looked back since."

I cupped my face in shame. "Oh God, you both saw that? Is *nothing* sacred?"

"Hmm ... no." They shrugged in turn. "Not now we have CCTV and the internet. It could go viral with that kinda footage," said Siobhan. They both nodded in agreement.

Siobhan turned to James. "Carry on, tell us more about *your* first time."

Not one to turn down a request for a personal story, James sighed dramatically. "Well, if you insist. I knew I wasn't a diner for vagina after my first and *only* hetero encounter. The lady in question tasted like a nine-volt battery. I had to gargle white spirit for weeks to get rid of the taste!"

"Fook off," said Siobhan. "We taste like batteries?"

"I've never so much as had a suppository up there," I said, my words falling on deaf ears. James's story was far more entertaining. "Travis committed one of the worst sins possible under the eyes of the Heavenly Father, and worst of all," I sobbed, "I didn't exactly *hate* it either!"

Neither James nor Siobhan batted an eyelid.

"He's a gobshite for taking my bum-ginity *without my permission* ..." I carried on, largely to myself, "... an outrageous invasion of the worst kind ..."

The word "bum-ginity" seemed to have caught their attention as they both swung round to face me.

"Here," James passed me the glass of warm, flat wine that I'd left earlier, "knock this back. It'll calm you down. Siobhan and I will clean this up. Rest assured, we've got everything under control." Sitting me down, he wrapped his coat around me and Siobhan stroked my head.

I felt dirty, used, everything spinning around my head in a twisted mess. I was overcome with the discrepancy of my strong commitment versus Travis's lack of respect. I loved him and loathed him in equal measure.

James picked up the overturned chair. "That Travis is

a complete shambles of a very well-endowed beast!"

"The stamina that man had would give you an early heart attack." Siobhan bent over and picked up the appointment book.

I began wailing like a banshee. "But I love him," I cried, "I'll never meet anyone as gorgeous as that *ever again*!"

"Course you will – listen to me, you'll meet someone that's right for you. Any man would be lucky to have you," said James.

"But I don't want just *anyone*. Travis was my last hope!"

"Oh, darling," hushed James. "Whilst he's a celebrity, which under normal circumstances would be top of *my* wish list – delicious-looking, built like a human tripod ... cash to splash ..." I could see that James had gone off into a wistful place in his head, then he remembered he was meant to be comforting me. " ... he's also a total shit! I mean, shagging you senseless and just abandoning you like that. What a dastardly man-whore!"

Siobhan was nodding. "I hate to say it, but I think Travis planned it that way."

"So do I," said James. He rubbed my arm tenderly. "Tara, never see that poor excuse for a man *ever* again."

"Shall we have a group hug?" said Siobhan.

The thought of which made me sob uncontrollably again.

Chapter 12

I didn't hear from Travis.

I had resumed texting him two weeks later – apologising profusely for my behaviour. How much regret could I put into one moment? A lot, it seemed, as I recalled my behaviour that night (reciting a Hail Mary alongside asking the Big Man Upstairs to forgive for Travis taking my bumginity. For coming across as needy). As much as I had begged for his forgiveness and explained that of course I understood the team came first, Travis hadn't answered.

So here I was, yet again, hiding away from the world in Glamma-Puss's staffroom. A week ago I woke up motivated and passionate, filled with hope that Travis would contact me, but as time went on, as another week went by, and then almost another, I despondently spent hours staring into space with no idea of what the hell to do and no hope at all. The inane bid by staff to cheer me up all but dried up. Even the indefatigable Siobhan was out of ideas.

Apart from my broken heart, I wasn't myself at all.

Something was off.

With my monthly cycle all over the place I wondered if I was experiencing early signs of pregnancy. I'd done a hundred tests after spending my first intimate night with Travis – each one negative. But as the weeks had gone on, something had changed. I was weepy. Moody. My breasts were tender. And I was eating for England.

Desperate to be pregnant, I'd called the doctor's surgery and was booked in for blood and urine tests later that day.

A baby might be all that's needed to tame Travis. Ground him. At this stage in both our lives, it could be the perfect solution to bring us together.

Travis was like a rubber band: he'd bounce back eventually. He always did, if his past actions were anything to go by.

I closed my eyes tight and muttered yet another silent prayer to the Big Man Upstairs.

Dear God, if Travis makes contact and I'm pregnant, I'll be so good.

I'll go to church every Sunday …

I'll give to every homeless person I see …

In fact, I'll raise thousands of pounds by running a marathon. I thought about that one long and hard. I think I'd gone a tad too far … *If it's all the same, God, I'll retract the marathon running one? I'll do a bake sale instead.*

I waited with bated breath and like a miracle my phone sprang into life. My eyes flew open, my heart hammering in my chest.

It was Laura.

"Got a minute for a chat?" Her tone was far too official for my liking.

"No."

"Make time. You're worrying everyone."

"There's nothing to worry about."

"That's not what I've heard."

I paused, braced myself for impact. "Go on."

"Lets start with Travis's latest booty call."

Siobhan and James had grassed on me. Bitches, the pair of them.

As if on cue, one of those bitches minced into the staffroom. Casting James a venomous look, I shoved him out, slamming the door closed.

I was fuming but switched my tone to nonchalant. Laura and everyone else needed to butt out of my life.

"For your information, it wasn't a booty call. There was a crisis and Travis had to go."

"But you haven't heard from him since?" Laura interrogated.

"Travis contacted me last night, actually. Told me how much I meant to him," I lied airily. "We had text sex!"

This happened weeks before. At 2.00 a.m., the night before I met him in Dublin, *out of the blue* he sent a series of suggestive text messages. We went on to have steamy orgasm-inducing text sex.

But I wasn't about to disclose to Laura that the minute his manlyhood had cum, he'd gone - left me playing with my lady-garden while staring at an unresponsive phone. While I'd been texting *"I'm nearly there, I'm nearly there"* (by the time I'd typed the text, I wasn't there at all), Travis had disappeared off the face of the earth. For all I knew, he'd switched his phone off and gone to sleep!

Laura sighed hard. "Text sex? So still doesn't bother calling?"

I skirted round her questions.

"It's the way we do things. Texting works for us."

"You mean it works for him."

That stung.

"He's playing you. Using you."

"Travis wouldn't spend all that money on flights, a fancy-pants hotel and extortionately priced champagne if he wasn't into me. He warned me it wouldn't be easy, that things could get complicated ..."

Laura remained silent. *It was her thing.* It was something they taught her at *Shrink School.*

I began to stammer, drying up almost immediately because I couldn't think of how else to defend him. "He's under an immense pressure –"

"You sound desperate. Delusional even."

How dare she! "I'm neither desperate nor delusional! Travis and I may not have the most conventional relationship but that doesn't mean we don't love each other."

"*Love?*" Her voice was high-pitched. "Isn't it a bit early to be talking about love? You two barely know each other, and *love* ..." she added primly "... is an *action* word. If Travis *loved* you, he'd show you. Running off every time he gets his end away isn't very loving, *is it?*"

I didn't dare tell Laura I might be pregnant!

"*So what* if Travis puts his actions in a text and can't see me often. We're in a long-distance relationship. He has work commitments, and you're making out like he doesn't care about me at all!" I said, recovering my poise.

"But your so-called relationship is *purely* virtual. At

best, it's a fantasy pantomime played out over a plastic handset."

I bit my tongue to refrain from telling Laura to fuck off.

"Look, I'm sure he does care about you – *in his own strange way* – but do you really want to share your life someone that inconsistent? Doesn't have time for you?" she poked. "It must be exhausting."

I was exhausted. But I didn't care. I wanted Travis and that was that!

"You're worth more than this, Tara." Laura switched to her *soothing shrink* routine.

I steadied my quivering voice. "You've got to fight for what you want in life. You've always said that."

"Yes, I have said that. Still say that. But fight for something that's worth fighting for. Fight with your heart – but keep your head."

"He is worth fighting for. Our relationship is worth fighting for. Travis needs a bit of taming, that's all. We have loads in common." I was about to reel it all off, but on the spot couldn't think of anything, so kept my mouth shut. And judging by the sounds of Laura's *hmmm-ing* I thought she was thawing, so it didn't matter anyway.

I'd have be careful what I told people in future. I needed everyone to love Travis. I couldn't bear the thought of my family and friends not approving. Particularly Laura. Nicknames notwithstanding, I admired my sister so much. Nothing fazed her. She always came up smelling of roses. After she'd ended her marriage, she dusted herself down, and even though a single parent, she furthered her career in psychology. Now she had an amazing, high-flying job. If I had a drop of her drive and confidence,

I'm sure I wouldn't have been in the situation I was that day: hurtling towards forty, childless and in a (now clinically diagnosed) dysfunctional on-off – but mainly off – relationship with the world's most elusive man.

"It may appear to *you* that you and Travis have *some things* in common, but these commonalities are circumstantial – they don't mean anything. You're not looking at the relationship itself ..."

She was moving in for the kill. I could feel it.

"You're not *in* a relationship. The *conversations* you've had are hollow words typed on a plastic handset. Your *dates* with Travis have been nothing more than meaningless shagathons. You know each other more orally than emotionally. I bet you've had more conversations with his balls than his face ..."

Each sentence was a like gunshot wound and she wouldn't stop. My head was ready to explode.

"How can you base a loving relationship on *that* alone? Where's the effort there? Have you two even been out for a meal?"

I wasn't answering those questions without a lawyer present.

I'd had enough listing to her assassinating Travis's character, so I emotionally checked out. As Laura continued her attack, I dug in my handbag for my diary, double-checking my appointment time for the doctor's surgery. I was cutting it fine.

My hand fell upon the Perspex vial that I'd picked up earlier. Heading for the loo, I put Laura on loudspeaker, placed her on top of the cistern and flushed it (not the short flush, the long flush), drowning out her lecture, *literally*.

Did people really pay for this kind of demoralising bullshit?

I yanked my tights and knickers down and placed the vial under me. Even though I could feel it was in the correct place, I tucked my head down in between my legs to make sure enough urine was being collected.

It wasn't. Instead, my wee was shooting out in every conceivable direction, and dribbling down my hand.

For the love of God! I stopped mid-flow, adjusting my stance.

My lady-garden used to pee out in the most beautiful, reliable, straight and gentle stream. Now it resembled a broken showerhead, leaking and pissing all over the place. I peered between my legs, concentrated, tried again. Managing to catch the some of the spraying splutters shooting to the left, I screwed the lid on the vial and popped the sample beside my phone. I dried myself, pulled up my underwear, washed my hands, only to find Laura was *still* talking ...

"... don't want to see you get hurt. How about doing some work on yourself?"

"What do you mean?" I snapped out of my reverie about my peeing ability.

"I'd suggest some emotional-personal development. Fill your life with things that don't involve *him*, some structure of your own that fulfils and nourishes *you*."

"Structure? Actually, that's not such a bad idea. Sheila's been raving about a new nourishing filler that plumps your face out like a pillow, I might give that a go!"

Laura sounded exasperated. "Not *that* type of structure, I meant in the *emotional* sense."

"You're right." I tried to sound enthusiastic as I stuck

two fingers up at the phone. "Clever, Laura. Thanks so much. I have to go now, and I swear I'll do some of that personal stuff. Call you later." I stabbed the hang-up button so hard I chipped a nail.

Personal feckin' development? She hasn't got a clue how I'm feeling. In fact, I really don't like her attitude! But yes, I sighed to myself, maybe Laura did have a minor point about Travis's inconsistencies.

"Pop your specimen in that box. You'll be called for your bloods. You've got a bit of a wait." The receptionist barely looked up.

As I sat in the packed waiting room, I slid my phone out of my handbag and stared at the blank screen. The aching for Travis to contact me was never-ending. The limbo of not knowing where he was or what he was doing was like a physical pain. His silence was eating me up from the inside out. Was he thinking about me? I thought about him every minute of every day.

It had been nineteen days, nine hours and twenty-three minutes since Travis had run out the salon door. This was the longest he'd ever gone without contacting me. Nearly three weeks of crippling uncertainty. Nearly three weeks of wine-indulging, nail-biting, comfort-eating, uncontrollably sobbing, *bastard-I-hate-him! Fuck-it-I-love-him* days of hell.

Clutching my phone to my heart, I decided to have another go at bargaining with the Big Man Upstairs.

Please let him contact me today and I promise - *in fact* I swear on everything I own - as well as doing all the things I promised earlier I'll say a decade of the Rosary and I'll go to your house and light a candle for St. Jude, the Patron Saint of Lost Causes," I muttered. *This has surely got to work, hasn't it?* Mum always said that if we did this, we would have our request granted.

"Now, your Holiness, I know it seems that I only talk to you when I want something – and I know you're busy with at least a zillion other requests from all your real fans who actually attend mass every week – but to hear from Travis right now would mean the world to me. I won't ask for a call – *that's a little unrealistic* – just a text with an 'x' is all I ask for?"

I drew a quivering breath. Moments passed ... Maybe I wouldn't see the results right away, or my request could be waiting in line, go through shortly. Mind you, the Big-Man hadn't got to my prayer from this morning yet; he might need a few angels to sort his admin out. I counted to three, then to ten, then to thirty, very slowly. Nothing. I stared at my phone pleading with it to stir into life. Giving it a shake, I performed my now obsessive switch-off/switch-on routine. This had become a fully-fledged compulsive disorder. *Okay, your Holiness, when you're ready ... but can it please be today?*

A thought occurred: my phone had been quiet. I'd had calls, but no texts. Was there something wrong with my network? Hope soared within me. Craving a form of acknowledgment, I gave it a test.

[Text to Siobhan]

I'm testing my phone, I think it's broken, did you get this? And if you did, can you text me back ASAP? Thanks Xx

[Text from Siobhan]

Testing testing! I like 2 b wined dined & 69nd. Did u get this?? xxxx

Disgusted, I threw my phone into my handbag and headed off to the ladies. I shouldn't have had that coffee en route, it was going right through me.

"Oh God!" A flash look in the well-lit mirror made me jump. My peroxide-blonde hair, recently extended by ten inches, had climbed up my head and nested, resembling a cat's arse.

Mortified, I patted it down.

I'd also noticed the growth of my leg hair had slowed down in recent weeks, which was *excellent,* but as I discovered as I stepped closer to the mirror, said leg hair had migrated to my upper lip.

I began my routine facial inspection, pulling the skin by my hairline tightly upwards, momentarily taking away ten years' worth of the effects of gravity. Of course, this only ever lasts about a nanosecond: as I let go, ten years came flopping back.

I gasped. "I don't remember *that* line on my face!" *It certainly wasn't there yesterday.* I tried smoothing it away with the tips of my fingers, hoping it might have been caused by ill applied make-up. No such luck, it was definitely a new wrinkle. Plus, I wasn't wearing any make-up. *"You, little bastard, are going to get filled tomorrow!"* I pulled my face this way and that, lifted my brows with my fingertips and tilted my head at different angles. God, I looked rough. I needed a face-lift. As I continued scanning the rest of my ageing body in the cruellest of mirrors, I staggered back.

No. It can't be. It's not possible. WHEN DID THIS HAPPEN? I could actually see my own arse without turning round. Just as I was gathering momentum to hyperventilate - scream the roof clean off the building - something occurred to me.

I looked pregnant.

Definitely pregnant!

I turned to the side, pulled my jumper tight. My tummy was swollen!

Nearly weeing myself with excitement, hovering as far from the porcelain as was physically possible without peeing on my shoes (which wasn't easy now I could apparently no longer pee straight), I heard an exasperated voice shouting my name.

"Tara Ryan? *Tara Ryan?*"

"That's me!" Quickly washing my hands, I flew out of the ladies.

Tutting, the sour-faced phlebotomist motioned me to follow her into brightly lit room, everything about her demeanour screaming she didn't want any small talk. *That's fine by me. The miserable old camel. She should be nice to me.* I was pregnant! I had a good mind to start crying to make her feel bad but I made a decision there and then not to tell a soul. Travis would be the first to know the good news, not some random stranger. I took off my coat. How would I tell him he was about to become a father?

I'd wear a white, virginal diaphanous flowing gown and cook a candlelit dinner for two (okay, actually I couldn't cook, but I could certainly order food in that would look like I had).

Then I would make my announcement:

We are with child.

No.

We are pregnant.

No.

You've scored.

Hmm ... I might need to work on that line.

I'm so not letting myself go while pregnant either. No way!

Lost in my dreams, I rolled up my sleeve and stuck out my arm. The phlebotomist tapped on my veins till she announced she'd found a juicy one.

MENTAL NOTE TO PREGNANT SELF:

No puking - it's very unflattering. Morning sickness, if applicable, must wait till Travis has left the house.

No leggings, no anoraks and absolutely NO lesbian haircuts.

No stretch marks. I will bathe in Bio-Oil for at least two hours every day.

Buy a sexy Agent Provocateur Babydoll nightie to give birth in; with fully matching mules - piped in their classic colours with the initials 'T.C.' (Tara Coleman) on them.

No screaming or howling during labour. I will breathe like a Buddha; controlled and in a peaceful manner.

Must schedule tightening of lady-garden immediately after birth of our perfect baby.

Breast is best. Hmm ... not sure I want to have my silicones removed. I will definitely have to think about that one. I will miss my chin-hitting friends.

Caressing of breast area will only resume once re-inflated with new 'sticky-up bosoms'.

Book a tummy tuck. And throw in a sneaky facelift for good measure (they might do buy one, get one free!).

Must ask Travis to give me a list of his celebrity buddies; need to choose suitable godparents.

Satisfied with my to-do list, I pictured what I'd wear whilst pregnant. Sexy skin-tight dresses to show off my long-awaited event. Louboutin heels. I'd look every part the radiant mummy-to-be.

Meanwhile, we would keep up a strict regime of mind-blowing sex daily, maybe even three times a day, or for as long as is possible.

"Nearly done." The phlebotomist grabbed another vial to fill and before I knew it the crook of my arm was being pressed, a plaster applied. "Right, that's it. Call your doctor in a week's time for the results."

"*A week?*" My voice came out strangulated. "Can the results be any faster?"

Her face, unfriendly, gave me my answer.

I walked to my car, an invisible protective shield around me, and drove home in a trance, my hand circling my tummy delicately.

I thought about who the baby would look like, Travis or me? Then I thought about all the work I'd done to myself over the years. The nosejob. The teeth. The breast implants. Not to mention the other tweaks. I hoped for that reason it was a boy and that he'd take after his father. A girl wouldn't look a dot like either of us!

I was home and desperate to share this build-up with Travis. I know books on relationships advise not to chase a man (I'd cleared the shelves in bookshops in the past few weeks in a bid to understand him better). And I get that you're supposed to leave them alone once they've disappeared into their cave, and if you pull them out too soon you'll face the dragon burning you (getting dumped). (Thank you, *Men are from Mars and Women are from Venus*). But Travis had been in his cave way too long. And surely, if he was padding round in said cave, he'd at least have boy toys in with him? Like his phone, for example? Plus, I was having his baby!

Pride could cost me everything and leave me with nothing.

Time to be an adult.

Time to break the silence and make contact.

[Text to Travis]

Hey stranger, how are you? x

Heart pounding, I settled down to wait.

As the hours passed, a rage within me ballooned. It was a feeling unlike anything I'd ever felt.

Burning.

Corrosive.

Fury.

Unable to take any more, I withheld my number and called the bastard's phone. To my astonishment, the line clicked. My heart banged as he answered.

"Hello."

"Travis."

The moment he heard my voice he hung up.

I could barely breathe.

My phone startled me in my shaking hand.

[Text from Travis]

Tara, it's over. Never contact me again.

The world tipped like I was drunk.

As I read and re-read the devastating message my insides collapsed with such force that a wave of nausea swiftly followed. I threw up over the sofa.

My face contorted into the ugliest expression imaginable as I tried to catch my breath. Pacing the floor, I hysterically phoned anyone who would listen.

"The relationship books said *not* to go into his cave, but I *did,* and the dragon has burnt me!" I said, blubbering an incomprehensible language that no one understood.

Call after call, I repeated my verbal diarrhoea like a mantra. I bemoaned my absolute failure in life, love and everything in between before clicking the red button and phoning the next number. Siobhan was call number four. Actually, she'd been call number one, but I hadn't given her a moment to pick up.

"Calm down and breathe," she said, the second I got through. "Who burnt you? *A dragon?* Tara, are you hallucinating? You haven't had a party without inviting me, *have you?*"

I wiped the dribbling snotty mess from my face onto my sleeve and forcibly lobbed my phone. Regretfully, I watched the object of my addiction hit the wall and explode.

What if Travis changed his mind? Decided he had made a mistake? If my phone wasn't working he wouldn't be able to contact me! On my hands and knees, I searched for its scattered remains, struggling to piece the various parts back together.

I curled up in a ball on the floor and cried like a wounded animal. After what felt like hours, I forced myself onto my knees and finally to my feet, and wiping my face with grim determination, screamed at the top of my lungs what Laura had said only a few hours ago: "I am worth more than this!"

Engulfed in toxic rage and waves of intense despair, I raced upstairs to the bathroom mirror and searched my twisted face.

Come on, Tara. You're not going to lie down and take this! I was going to win that bastard back if it killed me! I knew he still loved me. I just needed to remind him of that fact.

"I have to fight for him," I told my distorted, tear-stained reflection. "I have to fight for *us*. For our unborn baby."

I have no idea how I made it to the bottom of the stairs, or how I planned to win him back. The last thing I remember was booking the first available flight to Dublin.

Chapter 13

First thing the following morning, I launched myself into the shower like a woman possessed. I was on a mission and there was a hell of a lot of work to do.

Once I had towelled myself down, I looked at my swollen and blotchy face with grim purpose. *Feck.* I was gonna need a lot of work. A face-lift at the very least. But there wasn't time.

My initial attempts at vajazzling myself were thwarted by trembling hands. That, and I kept pausing to wail loudly. I plastered on layers of make-up and smeared on some slutty red lipstick. Looking at my reflection, I promptly burst into tears. Big black stains of mascara streamed down my face. *Feck. Feck. Feck.* I reached into the cupboard for the Clarins make-up remover, wiped it all off and started again. *Just don't feckin' cry, Tara,* I warned myself. *I'm not sure I have enough mascara left to do all this again.*

Flipping my hair 360 degrees, I pushed through

diamanté earrings - stabbing myself in the neck in the process. The shock nearly made me start blubbing again, so I dug my fingernails into the back of my hand to distract myself. *There. Floodgates closed.*

I walked purposefully from the bathroom to my bedroom, swinging open my wardrobe door, where my eyes fell upon my prize. My beautiful black fur coat. Travis hadn't yet seen it on me. I fanned myself frantically, my head zipping back to the euphoric high that had spurred me on to max out my credit card and purchase it.

I thudded my head hard against the wardrobe door, remembering the highly suggestive texts that had sizzled back and forth between Travis and me that afternoon. One particular text he'd sent was burnt into my mind:

"The thought of you in fur coat and no knickers has made me rock hard."

Laying the bag carefully on the bed, I unzipped the coat from its pristine holder, and paused. This coat defined my mission to ensnare his heart and win him back. I stood back and stared at it. It was a lot to expect from a coat.

'Travis Coleman - I'm coming to get you - in a fur coat and no knickers!'

My eyes caught sight of the clock beside the bed. *Shit! Look at the time.* If I didn't leave now, I wouldn't be able to get another flight till tomorrow. Without a moment's hesitation, I took the fur coat out of the bag and slung it on. Then I floundered for my passport in the cabinet drawer, wrestled on my tatty slippers, shoved my Louboutins underarm, and ran out of the house.

As I raced along the motorway to Heathrow, I tried to reflect on what I was doing and why. *This is lunacy! Travis told me never to contact him again.* I had screwed things up good and proper and managed to alienate the man of my dreams. I needed to tell him to his face that I knew the team would come first. That I *got it*. That I wasn't asking him to choose between me and the team.

I felt heavy with failure, shifting around uncomfortably in my car, my thoughts flashing back to the rip-roaring (albeit very agitated and somewhat unusual) sex we'd had that night in the salon.

I shook my head, thumped the steering wheel in temper. "Damn it!"

This was all *my* fault. I hadn't responded in the most grown-up manner to his mischievous wandering finger. I mean, there he was taking our sex life to a whole new level - and what did I do? I could feel my bum twitching, at the very thought. "No bloody point in sweating now!" I yelled at my arse.

Among other things, I'd also been extremely close to stabbing him in the ankle with a pair of thinning scissors! *No wonder he's buggered off and never wants to see me again.*

I cringed as I reflected further on my appalling behaviour. I'd pleaded with him not to leave. And I had inadvertently asked him to put me before the team.

I *was* needy.

I'd totally embarrassed myself, and worst still ... I'd embarrassed him to the point where he'd felt compelled to end us.

Gulping back the sob that was growing in my throat, I

tried to look on the bright side. I *had* to, or I'd be howling and smudging my feckin' make-up all over again!

Stomach clenched with anxiety, I arrived at the airport. As I sat in the queue outside the Short Stay car park, I checked my make-up again. God, I looked a mess. I shook my head. *Come on, Tara, be positive.* What would Lickarse Laura say? Probably some psychobabble about positive thinking and making things come right; I was gonna need a barrel-load of that babble, that was for sure.

After I had nosed my car into one of the parking bays, I yanked off my warm slippers and slipped on my cold skyscraper Louboutins. The second I opened the door, a whoosh of cold air cut through me.

Clutching my bag, I heard my phone go. Checking the cracked screen, I could see Laura was calling. Then Mum. James. Siobhan. Jackie. Even Katie. Ignoring the string of calls, I walked purposefully towards the main terminal; except I couldn't get my feet in rhythm with each other. Something was wrong. I was totally off balance. Looking down at my feet, I immediately saw the problem. I cursed James and his bright ideas. Thanks to him, I was wearing nearly identical odd shoes! One a five-inch Louboutin, the other a six-inch. *Argh! JAMES!*

I couldn't stop now. I had no choice. Setting my course firmly in the direction of the main terminal, I continued hobbling. I had a driving force of passion and love and nothing was going to stop me; *not even you – yes, you, Big Man upstairs. I don't care if it's a sign, or if you think I'm doing the wrong thing. I'm going to ignore you the way you've ignored me.*

Once I'd struggled through the interminable queue at security, I threw what little possessions I was travelling with into a tray, pushed it along the conveyer belt.

"Remove your coat please, miss," said a security guard, barely acknowledging me. "And your shoes."

I froze in horror, my face flaming red. "I-I-I ... *umm*, I can't take my coat off."

The guard abruptly stopped stacking trays. "Remove your coat please, miss, or you're not coming through." He stared at me, his brows knitting in annoyance. I stepped to the side, beckoned him over. I watched him visibly tense in apprehension, his hand twitching by his side, a truncheon fixed to his belt.

I looked pleadingly into his eyes and whispered, "Sir, Mr Security Man, I *really* can't take my coat off." *And now the humiliating confession.* "I'm not wearing anything underneath." Jaw clenched, my eyes dropped to the floor in shame.

"I've heard them all now," he said, in disbelief.

May God forgive me!

I swallowed my pride, inhaled a deep, nostril-widening breath, undid the buttons, opened my fur coat for a nanosecond and revealed my entire naked body (well, naked apart from my vajazzle). His eyes widened in shock, his face breaking out into a grin.

"*Ahem*! ... Okay ... please remove your shoes, miss." Shaking his head, he called over a female security guard.

"Boyfriend problems," I said, trying to keep my voice as casual as possible. With raised eyebrows, the two guards exchanged glances. "Pregnant and trying to win him back." I looked up at the ceiling, arms outstretched whilst being patted.

Once through the torture of security, I dashed towards my gate. I couldn't tear myself away from the paranoid state of thinking ahead of what I was actually going to do, or say, on the other side, when I saw him?

I couldn't think straight.

It didn't help that my eyes were irritated from a combination of tiredness, excessive howling and sloppily applied mascara. But I was on a mission.

The first thing I'd have to do was actually find Travis. I hadn't thought properly about how I would do that.

He could be in one of three possible places. I'd grab a taxi to the training ground first, and then swing past the local coffee haunt. Failing that, it was Dougie's house. If Travis wasn't there, then I'd have to wait it out till he was.

I struggled past the cramped flight deck, down the aisle, eventually spotting my seat near the back and squeezed my way into it. As soon as I'd fastened my seatbelt, I closed my watery eyes, sending my best, do-not-try-to-talk-to-me signals to the young girl sitting next to me.

My nerves were shot to bits. I still hadn't thought of what I'd say when (or if) I found him. Maybe I wouldn't say anything at all. Perhaps I'd strut up to him like a wild wanton hussy, allow my fur coat to seductively slip off my shoulders, then dramatically drop it to the ground and that would say everything for me.

I visualised his stern face breaking into a smile as my coat floated down. He'd step forward quickly, cover me up and take me in his arms and it would be just like it was in that fairytale hotel where he'd professed his love to me. We'd go for a walk, where I would go on to tell him I was having a baby. *His baby.* Travis would go into shock at first then pick me up and tell me it was the best news he'd ever heard. That we would make it work.

The vibrations of take-off shuddered me back to the real world. I didn't know what to do with myself. As soon as the seatbelt sign flicked off, I pressed the call button for a flight attendant. I needed a stiff drink. A warm glow of being pregnant suddenly swept through me. The maternal instinct to protect was so overwhelming that I ordered herbal tea. I didn't even like herbal tea, it tastes like piss water!

The girl sitting next to me began retching. I fumbled in the seat pocket for a sick bag for her (or, more accurately, for me). *Please don't get any vomit on my fur coat!*

"Nervous passenger?" I enquired, handing the bag over.

She shook her head and pointed at her tummy, spluttering between retches. "I'm sorry."

I looked at her properly – overcome with a wave of empathy. She was pregnant.

"Five months gone, still being sick," she said, with a tiny embarrassed smile.

The words were out of my mouth before I could stop them. "I'm pregnant, too." I was annoyed at myself. I wanted Travis to be the first to know.

I looked for her reaction – she didn't hear me, she was way too busy throwing up.

She looked way too young to be having a baby. Young enough to be my daughter. Nineteen? *Twenty at a push?* Her pretty face was small and pale with neat little features. Despite my sympathy to her plight, I couldn't help but think her boring, brown shoulder-length hair blended in seamlessly with her boring, brown polo-neck jumper. Being pregnant was certainly not an excuse to wear that colour. She should wear something far more fetching! That's dangerous territory letting yourself go like that. I pulled tissues out of my bag and passed them to her. Heaving again, pregnant girl left her seat. She'd obviously gone to finish her puking in the loos. Good, because my pissy herbal tea had arrived, although it was typical: we were now descending into Dublin.

With adrenaline rushing around my body, I deplaned. I had the sensation that I was watching myself from above, like this drama was happening to someone else. Like I was a spectator. But the intense longing to seduce Travis was more powerful than anything I'd ever felt.

I had to win him back.

But then the doubts begun to creep in thick and fast. *What if he rejects you? What if he laughs in your face? What if he really doesn't want you? Doesn't love you anymore?* I couldn't let myself think like that! I reminded myself that he had said he wanted to look after me, always.

Negative thoughts buried, I paced numbly towards the exit, swept along with other passengers. My body shook and trembled with every step. Legs on autopilot. Once through passport control, before I planted myself in a taxi, I diverted to the ladies to straighten myself out. As I walked through the large swing door, a familiar retching sound crept its way back to my ears.

I called over the cubicle where the noise was coming from. "Pregnant girl from the plane, is that you?" No answer. "I'm the lady who sat next to you. Are you okay?"

"Yep ... fine." The splattering in the toilet bowl suggested otherwise.

I rested my head on the outside of the cubicle door, unsure of what to do next. "*Umm* ... is anyone coming to get you?"

"*Eww* ... " Louder splatters and splashes. "I'm fine. I'm being picked up. Thanks for being so kind."

"Okay - well, good luck. Bye!" With relief, I detached myself from the situation.

I touched up my slutty red lipstick, took one long, lingering look at myself then swung the door open to leave.

My footsteps echoing eerily in the now-empty corridor. As I proceeded through the doors of Arrivals, my eyes spotted someone familiar.

I did a double take. "Travis?" my scalp pricked.

There he was. Right in front of me, casually leaning against a pillar, waiting. I saw him glance up in surprise, his body rigid as he spotted me.

The colour drained from his face and was replaced with an expression of wide-eyed horror.

I stopped in my tracks: happy, shocked, confused.

All my plans and elaborate scenarios disappeared from my mind. The only sound I was aware of was the thumping of my heart, which seemed to be trying to break through my chest.

Then two things happened very quickly. I heard footsteps close behind me and saw Travis's expression change. It softened, but still looked full of panic. He was looking at the source of the footsteps behind me.

I turned my head just as the person drew up beside me. *Pregnant girl from the plane.* She wasn't looking at me; she was staring straight ahead at Travis with a huge, sloppy smile.

She placed her hand on my shoulder as she walked past. "Thanks again." She picked up speed, walking straight towards Travis, calling out to him. "This kind lady has been like a mum to me looking after me and your baby on the flight!"

I was frozen to the spot, my head spinning, unable to take it all in. I could see Travis's pleading eyes burning into mine, begging me not to say anything as she enveloped herself in him.

And I didn't. I *couldn't.* I was paralysed.

Pregnant girl turned and gave me one last cheery wave as she buried herself under the protective cloak of Travis's arm.

Tearing his eyes away from mine, he bent down, kissing her tenderly on the forehead. For a final kick, he rubbed her tummy and whispered something in her ear. I caught sight of her giggling. As I watched them go off hand in hand, I felt compelled to scream out that I was pregnant too, but the words stayed trapped in my mouth.

As they reached the sliding doors of the exit, Travis briefly looked over his shoulder. Our eyes met, for what I knew would be the last time. The expression within Travis's was unlike anything I'd seen before. My love god - the man who had made me feel like no one had ever done before - looked at me with complete chilly disdain. With that, he nestled pregnant girl closer and disappeared outside.

I don't know how long I stood there, unable to move or speak. My mobile began to ring.

Wiping tears on my sleeve, I fumbled in my bag.

"Miss Tara Ryan?" said the caller. The brisk voice didn't sound familiar.

"Yes, uh ... yes?"

"It's the doctor's surgery. Your test results are through – there's a note here that you wanted to be contacted as soon as possible?"

I placed my hand on my heart. I still wanted this baby, with or without Travis.

"Nothing serious to worry about ... you're entering the menopause."

"Wait! *What?* So I'm *not* pregnant?"

"No, you're definitely not pregnant."

My legs buckled and my body, unable to keep itself upright collapsed to the ground.

Chapter 14

I hadn't been anywhere near the Glamma-Puss salon in two weeks. I'd texted family and friends informing them all I had a bug and they were all to stay away as it was highly contagious. Also that Jackie was acting manager, and if James and Jayde had any issues they were to go to her.

[Text from Mum]

I think that Botox you're always sticking in yourself has made you go a bit funny. Get to the doctors! Ask them to check it hasn't leaked into your brain. Love you xx

[Text to Mum]

Mum, Botox can't leak into your head! I've got a bug. X

[Text from Mum]

You're such a beautiful looking girl. You really don't need all that cementy stuff in your face. Please leave yourself alone Xxx

I pulled up to the doctor's surgery in a daze, not quite remembering the drive. My breathing was shallow and I couldn't stop my hands shaking.

I needed my head to shut up! To stop tormenting me – regardless, it chatted incessantly, morning, noon and night, adding colour to my nightmares – like a seal had broken and rot was surfacing.

Just getting out of the car felt like an impossible task. World-weary, I counted to three, held my breath and made a weak attempt to run for it.

I prayed I wouldn't bump into someone I knew in the waiting room. It wasn't just that I was wearing dirty pyjamas, hastily covered by an overcoat – I was unable to make small talk and was desperate get back to the sanctity of my bed.

I was due to see Doctor Angus Lancelot. A no-nonsense, hardy Scot. Large in stature. Big mop of untamed frizzy hair. The type to go ice-swimming, shear a sheep and knit himself an Aran jumper, all before starting work. He most certainly would not be my first choice of doctor - because he was a shit! Always wanting microscopic details. Always trying to find natural remedies. Always following up and checking in with patients. I'd heard of plenty of my neighbours whining that he wasn't fond of prescribing chemicals. A stingy bollox! We'd soon see about that!

Eyes nailed to the blue, office-like carpet for thirty unbearable minutes, I was finally called in.

"Come in, Tara, sit down. How are you?" His voice

projected so loudly from his diaphragm, I swear I felt the building shake.

"Not great." As the words tumbled out, so did a torrent of tears. That wasn't meant to happen. I needed to hold it together!

He handed me a box of tissues, his clear blue eyes holding mine.

"Sorry." I blew my nose then sat on my hands to stop them shaking. "I'm not getting much sleep. Feeling a tad low in myself."

"Have there been any life-changing events to make you feel this way?" asked his booming voice.

I nodded, afraid to speak because I didn't want it all spewing out of me. I needed to proceed with caution.

He tapped on his computer, reading my notes. My new early-onset menopause label would catch his attention. I studied his room for a distraction – there was a framed photo of him in a white vest and kilt, tossing a caber. Another of him playing the bagpipes, his pretty wife and brood of children standing proudly beside him.

He had a lot to get up for in the morning.

He swung back to face me. "Disturbed sleep during menopause is very common. Are you having night sweats?"

More like night terrors.

"No."

"Are you feeling super-sensitive? Defensive?"

"No."

"Are you crying a lot for no good reason?"

"No."

I burst into tears again.

He weighed me and took my blood pressure. "I could

offer you HRT?"

I stiffened. I wasn't here for feckin' HRT! HRT wasn't going to bring Travis back. *Prevent me from visualising him with his young, pregnant girlfriend. Stop my ovaries shrivelling up. Give me a baby to love.* I needed a buffet of mind-numbing prescriptions! Still, I suppose I should be a little grateful he offered me something, albeit not quite what I was looking for.

"I'm looking for *something* to take the edge off."

"Is there anything else worrying you? Anything else you'd like to talk about?"

"Isn't early-onset menopause enough?" The tears made another appearance. I was not going down that rabbit hole with him!

"Do you get much exercise? It'll help raise your serotonin levels."

Not everything could be fixed with feckin' exercise! "I can't seem to muster up the energy," I said with a hint of sarcasm. This wasn't going as I'd expected. I'd have to be more specific.

Like ordering off a restaurant menu, I got straight to the point, reeling off what I came in here for. "I'd like triple-strength sleeping pills and high-dose Valium, please."

Doctor Angus Lancelot's head jerked up, his gaze narrowing. "Are you having suicidal thoughts?"

"I'm not brave enough for that *just yet*." I fake-laughed, brushing tears away with the back of my hand.

I checked myself. I needed to stop the word-vomit. I carefully I backtracked, "I'd never commit such a sin."

I wasn't about to admit that I'd been praying to the Big Man upstairs - *every single night* - to take me away in my sleep. Needless to say, as yet, my prayers, just like the rest, had gone unanswered.

"Medication of that kind is not always the right solution, it's a last resort. Indeed, there are other more natural –"

My voice was high in alarm. "I've tried meditating, lavender spray, guzzled a zillion bottles of high-strength CBD oil –"

"It's important to *resolve – talk through* what's making you feel this way, not cover it up with medication."

I squirmed in my seat, not listening to a word of it. There was no amount of time, money or comforting conversation that could undo the past. Fix the future. It was pointless discussing it. I needed instant numbing! Peace between my ears!

"Can I have just have *double*-strength sleeping pills and high-dose Valium then?" Maybe I'd been a little greedy asking for triple-strength sleeping pills.

He leant forward, elbows on desk, and steepled his fingers together. "Looks and sounds like you have other emotional issues that need to be worked through. Would you like to talk with a professional? We have an in-house counsellor. Bit of a wait I'm afraid –"

I was already shaking my head, anger flaming through me. My heart was banging hard in my chest. Armpits wet in fury. I wanted to crawl over his desk and swing from his stupid stupid fuzzy beard. Pull his neat little tartan tie round his neck and choke him into submission. If I'd had a set of bagpipes handy, I'd shove them right up his arse.

"I don't need to see a counsellor." I had Lickarse Laura to talk to if I wanted, but she wouldn't be able to take the heartache away either. Nobody could. It was futile. I needed medication and lots of it! Feeling beyond desperate, I blurted it out. "I want to be numb so I can't feel anything."

"You need to feel something, Tara. I'll get that referral for you."

"But that could take weeks - months," I said, my hysteria rising. I tried another shot in the dark. "Can the in-house counsellor prescribe me numbing tablets?"

"No." He was busy tapping on his computer. "They can be highly addictive, add to the problem."

I couldn't take in what he was saying. My nerve endings were screaming: *Please, God, not another minute like this!*

Beyond desperate, I changed tactics.

"Look, you're a busy man ..." I made a point of looking at my watch " ... running behind – the surgery *inundated* with patients in need of help with physical and mental health issues – *and it's really kind of you to offer*, but I'm not one of them. So if you'd kindly write me a prescription, I'll get out of your way." My hands, shaking, had come loose. I quickly shoved them back under my legs.

Eyeing me steadily, he returned to his computer. "I'm booking a referral now, get the ball rolling."

"I'm *not* happy!"

"I can see that."

How dare he play God with my life! I was not leaving these premises until he prescribed medication. Most of my clients were on something (not from this doctor, obviously), and don't even get me started on what celebrities took ...

I wanted to tie myself to the chair in protest, or lie on the floor like a tantrumy child and not get up, but before I knew it I was on my feet, pacing the floor. "You're supposed to *help* me! I'm demented from not being able to sleep. It's driven me cuckoo! You men have not an ounce of an idea what it's like to go through early menopause!" Then I said the line that every doctor must dread. "If you don't give me *something* and something happens to me, I'll make sure my family hold you personally responsible!"

Like music to my ears, his printer kicked into life. Immensely satisfied with my performance, I calmed down.

"I'll give you a four-week supply of sleeping tablets to help get you in a routine – *by which time* your referral should be through." He went to hand over the precious prescription but hesitated. "Please remember, Tara, this is short-term only."

I snatched it out of his hand, held the piece of paper to my chest and stroked it. "Are they nice and strong?"

"They'll help you sleep. Make an appointment to come and see me in two weeks' time."

Will I feck come and see you in two weeks, I thought as I dashed out of the door. *I'll be in La-La Land!*

I raced to the chemist to pick up my goodies.

Come on, come on, I thought, as I stood behind an elderly couple in the queue. I wasn't sure who smelled worse - them or me. *I'll shower tomorrow ... maybe.*

I finally got my hands on my precious numbing pills and promptly shoved two in my mouth. I know the packet said take one just before bed, but I figured they'd take a while to kick in.

[Text from Siobhan]

Me and James called round to see you, no one in. Hope you're feeling better? We're worried about you xxx

[Text from Laura]

Me, Mum and Katie are concerned about you. Stop ignoring our calls and pick up your phone!

The following morning I woke up freezing, still in my week-old pyjamas. At last I had something that knocked me out. Twelve hours of blissful nothingness where I wasn't obsessing about Travis, life, and how pointless it all was.

Parched, I stumbled into the kitchen, collapsed on a chair and stared into space. Soon enough, images, faint at first, but increasing in intensity, and chatter-chatter conversations were on the off again, rampaging through my head like wildfire.

Swallowing another two pills, I shut out all daylight, went back to bed and buried myself under the duvet. I lay there shivering, waiting for the medication to take effect. I shook my head, flipped myself round in the bed. Memories of Dad drinking, Mum, Laura and Katie packing up, leaving the family home, me trying to finish my apprenticeship, trying to make ends meet, trying to keeping a roof over mine and Dad's head wouldn't go away. The worst: me selfishly going out to celebrate my birthday.

Dad lying dead in my arms.

I pulled my pillow over my face, adding pressure, desperate for it all to go away.

Sleep, sleep, blissful sleep.

I tossed and turned, but to my despair, an hour later I was still wide awake.

Convinced the pills weren't working, I took another.

Then another.

But still I merely drifted.

I swallowed another two pills for good measure.

I repeated this pattern over the next week, popping pills like sweets. In one week I'd all but taken the whole month's supply. I needed more.

With my heart pounding, I called the doctor's and was put on telephone surgery. I clutched my phone all day waiting for Doctor Lancelot to call. And just as I'd given up ...

"How are you, Tara?" he asked in a cheery voice.

I nearly cried with relief.

"Much better, thank you." Then cautiously added, "But I've a small problem. I've returned from Dublin – I went to stay with my sister for a few days ... for company and you know, get fresh air and exercise – *she's a psychologist, by the way*, but being a family I don't like to burden her too much ... Anyway ... she has these two mischievous dogs and, well, one of them ate my sleeping pills – *straight out of my bag!* The whole packet, *even the foil!* He had to have his little doggy tummy pumped. Such a naughty pup! He was very sick, slept for three days straight ..."

I listened hard for a reaction.

"Are you still there, Doctor?"

"I'm still here. Tara, I can't give you –"

"My sister is so angry with me." I threw in a few sniffs. I had to do something. I could feel I was losing. Then I added very quickly, "And I was feeling so much better – all thanks to you; but without the sleeping pills I can't get into a routine at all and if I could just sleep a few more hours a night, I'm sure I'd cope better ..."

Silence.

" ... I've decided to embrace the counselling thing. In fact, after chatting a few things through with my sister, I can't wait to get started. No matter what others say about you, I think you're an amazing doctor and –"

"Have you booked an appointment to come in and see me?"

"I have, yes. It's next week ... *Ummm* – I don't have my diary to hand –"

"I'll leave a prescription for you at reception," he said. "We'll hopefully have an appointment for you to see a counsellor soon. And Tara, please be more careful this time."

Breathing a huge sigh of relief at my potentially Oscar-winning performance, I ended the call.

A week later, a letter arrived from the surgery with the date of my counselling appointment. I had no intention of going! What was the point? I cancelled it, saying I'd come down with flu, promising I'd re-book as soon as I felt well enough.

Once again, my pills became depleted fast. Terror gripped me at the thought of having to ask for more. Even though I felt more unwell as time went on, I'd at least achieved what I wanted: to feel numb; to feel nothing.

I nervously rang the surgery to make a dreaded appointment.

"I'm afraid Doctor Lancelot is away on holiday, Miss Ryan," said the receptionist. "Will you see Doctor Griffin instead?"

"Of course, no problem!" Relief flooded through me.

When the time came, with the surgery full of patients

and Doctor Griffin running forty-five minutes behind, I easily pulled the wool over his eyes by rambling through my "dog ate all my sleeping pills" story.

I'm getting good at this, I thought. *I should've taken a career on stage!*

Doctor Griffin barely lifted his head to acknowledge me, but that suited me fine. He didn't care and neither did I as he printed off my prescription, adding some glorious Valium into the mix.

It was only a matter of time before I'd be in the same situation again, but for now I could breathe again. Or sleep more, rather, and that was all that mattered.

Meanwhile, I continued to fob off friends and family with tales of flu or a contagious stomach bug, whatever I could get away with. I became a convincing liar.

All too quickly I needed another prescription. With a note on my records that Doctor Lancelot had asked to see me in person, I had no choice but to make an appearance. I couldn't recall when I'd last washed. I looked bad, smelt bad and felt bad. In an effort to look a bit more *together*, I dragged myself under the shower. The water hurt as it pounded my body. Looking in the mirror at my wasteland eyes, I convinced myself that I really had come down with flu. I had no clean clothes so picked the least creased ones off the floor, pulled them on and, like a zombie, set off for the surgery.

As I was called to go through, I kept telling myself to stay calm and in just a few short minutes I would have what I needed.

"Hello, Tara, how are you?" he said.

I gulped hard. "I'm good, thank you. I just need a repeat prescription please."

He consulted his computer. "I see you cancelled the counsellor?"

My face flamed red. "Umm ... yes, I did. I had flu and a stomach bug, nasty business. Forgot to re-book. But I'll do it on my way out."

He clearly wasn't impressed with the bullshit I was spewing. He could see straight through me. He knew that I knew that he knew I was bullshitting. He turned back to his screen then back to me.

"Tara, I'm not prescribing you any more medication."

"But I need it! It takes the pain away. Stops me thinking!"

"With the amount you've been taking, it'll stop you living. Please remove your coat so I can take your blood pressure."

"I haven't taken *all* those pills, you know," I began to protest. "I told you, my sister's cat – *umm* – I mean *dog* – demolished a whole packet. And, and –"

"Medication of that kind is highly addictive. By the looks of things you've been taking enough to knock out a horse."

"I hope you're not implying that *I'm* addicted," I said, doing my best to sound indignant, "or the size of a horse?" And he called himself a doctor? Anyone would think I was asking for cocaine or heroin!

"On the scales, please."

Petulantly, I removed my coat with a few huffs and puffs and stomped on the scales, hands on hips.

"Hmm ... just as I suspected. You've lost nine kilos since I weighed you last."

I secretly wished he'd told me what that was in stones and pounds (I'd never been able work it out in kilos).

"*Nine* kilos in a matter of weeks *is* quite a concern."

"I did say I'd had a stomach bug." I was getting more irritated by the second.

"Nearly a stone and a half in such a short space of time is *not* healthy."

"A stone and a half?" What a shame I didn't have these pills when it mattered! I was quite stunned, quite excited; but then I remembered what had happened, how shit life was, and everything felt pointless again.

Goody Two-Shoes doctor Lancelot continued his checks. My blood pressure was through the roof, I was underweight, didn't look well, *blah, blah, blah.*

I put my coat back on. "I'm *not* addicted," I said desperately. "And surely I can't just *stop* taking these pills? Don't I need to come off them slowly?"

"As I said, I won't be prescribing any more. Besides, if you're telling me that you're not addicted, then you won't miss them, will you?"

The cheeky gobshite! Addiction is Katie's department! She's the druggie of the family - not me. Why do I have to have a doctor who does everything by the book?

"You'll have to go cold turkey. By the end of the week your sleep pattern should start to go back to normal."

Ignoring my rants, he picked up his phone. With my mind racing, I picked up the tail-end of his conversation.

"Ah, she's still here," he said into the receiver. "Can she see a patient now?" He glared at me. "Yes, I consider it an emergency. Thank you, I'll send her through."

He straightened his tartan tie. "Right, then, let's get you back to a good state of mental health. The counsellor is here and is willing to see you now."

"But I don't want to talk to anyone! I'm not mental! I

just want to sleep –"

Unable to finish my sentence, I broke down. Doctor Lancelot's hand was on my shoulder, gently escorting me into another room, where there was a lady waiting for me.

Amongst a mass of wild grey curly hair, yards of floral floaty fabric and jangly silver jewellery, sat a kind-faced lady. "Hello, Tara, come, sit down, my name is Dawn."

My brain had split off in another direction. I didn't want to be in this room! I wanted to be at home in my bed, off my face!

"How are you feeling right now?"

If I told her the truth, she'd have me in a straitjacket! Drained, I almost fell into the chair.

"I'm fine," I sniffed, unable to make eye contact. I wanted to be anywhere but here. I wanted to be anyone but me.

Apart from my sniffling, the room fell silent. But my head wasn't silent. The incessant chattering was back, and the images ... and to add to it all, I was going home empty-handed. I felt like my life support had been switched off.

"If the doctor gave me numbing pills I'd feel better. Please can you go speak to him?" I ran a hand through my matted hair. "I'm begging you."

"That's an interesting name you've called your medication," said Dawn. "Can you tell me how you are feeling right now?" she repeated. "Try and use a *feeling* word if you can?"

"Broken." I sobbed into a tissue. "Broken."

"Broken," she repeated softly, nodding her head in a sympathetic manner. "Tell me about *broken*."

"I hate myself. I hate what I've become; and *this* ..." I said bitterly, pointing at my heart " ... this has had enough. No more hurt. No more hurt. No. More. Hurt."

"So, what I am hearing is ... you hate yourself and you hate what you've become?"

"I've lost everyone I've ever loved." I could taste the grief in my mouth. "We love, we lose love ... and it cuts so deep." I let the words hang in the air. "So deep."

Dawn nodded, indicating for me to continue.

"What's the point of anything? We live, get hurt, then die." I broke down again.

"Okay, Tara, it's okay to cry." Dawn let me cry for a full ten minutes without saying another word.

Eventually I was able to piece some words together. "I feel alone. It's dark. I can't see a way out. When you need people the most, they leave you."

"So you're in darkness and you're feeling alone?"

"But you get fooled because they are there in *body*, but not there in *mind*." I thought about Dad. Physically present, emotionally dead.

"Someone is there with you in body but not in the mind?"

"And you end up trying everything – *anything* – to get that person back." Travis was never coming back.

"It's okay, Tara. It's okay. Stay with those feelings."

"But I don't want to stay with these fucking feelings!"

After the initial sting of saying it out loud, more came out. "Everyone has left me, Dad, Mum, my sisters, Travis ..." It was like earth had been disturbed in the graveyard of my mind.

"Everyone's left you, your dad, your mum, your sisters, Travis?" repeated Dawn, in a calming voice.

"My dad went and died on me - *while in my care!* He never even said goodbye!" I gasped between sobs, buried my hands in my face. "I looked after him as best I could – kept a roof over our heads, but he still left me after everything I did for him!"

My stomach, burning, tied itself in knots.

"You think it was your fault your dad died while you were looking after him?"

I nodded. "Of course it was my fault. I couldn't stop him drinking. I should've been there minding him, but I'd selfishly gone out for my birthday – I didn't check in on him when I came home."

"So you couldn't stop your dad drinking? So it's the child's job to look after the adult, is it? How does that make you feel?"

"Guilty," I whispered. Tears rolled down my cheeks.

"You feel guilty for putting a roof over your dad's head and for doing your best as a daughter?" Dawn pressed.

"A good daughter wouldn't have gone out! He was an alcoholic, diagnosed with schizophrenia - I didn't know that he'd stopped taking his medication. His death *was* my fault."

"Your father *chose* not to take his medication and he *chose* to continue drinking – and this makes it your fault?"

I nodded, tears running like a river down my burning face and onto my lap, leaving wet dots on my tracksuit bottoms.

"How does that make you feel?"

"Like a failure," I whispered.

Dawn glanced at her watch. "Tara, we've made great

progress today but our time has come to an end."

"*What!*" I stammered. "But I haven't even started on the other fecker who abandoned me! He's gone for a child as a lover! *And* I'm in the *menopause – me* – in the menopause! I'm only in my feckin' thirties!"

Dawn got her diary out. "This is good."

"What's *good* about that? All you've done is repeat everything I've said! Please go tell Doctor Stingy-Bollox I need a prescription for my numbing pills." I stubbornly folded my arms.

Dawn smiled and shook her head. "Another appointment would be far more beneficial."

We walked out to reception, where I made another stupid, pointless appointment. The minute Dawn was out of sight, I cancelled it.

I arrived home distraught and empty-handed. The slightest noise drove me insane. I ripped the phone and TV out of their sockets and pulled down the blinds in every room of the house, and, jumpy as a cat, began pacing the floors. How was I going to get more pills? Reluctantly, I switched my mobile back on and in pure desperation called Siobhan.

"Siobhan, it's Tara. I need a favour."

"Well, feck me! I've been knocking at your door, phoning, texting - I started to think you'd been abducted by aliens!"

"Very funny." I wasn't in the mood for her humour.

"How've you been? Where've you been? Are you alright? Feeling better?" She sounded genuinely serious for once. "We need to catch up, there's been so much goin' on –"

I wasn't in the mood for one of her stories, so I cut through her ramblings. "I need a favour: can you to go to the doctor's for me?"

"Oh ... okay."

"Can you make an emergency appointment at the doctor's *today* and get me some sleeping pills and Valium, please?"

"Okay ... You know I'd do anything for you. We're all missing you, woman! Jackie –"

"Do not get booked in with Doctor Lancelot – he's a right stingy bollox. Think's he's God. Want's to know the ins and outs of everything. Ask for Doctor Griffin. He's newish. Weak-willed. A patient-pleaser.

"Okay."

"Tell whoever you see you can't sleep. Say you've got a stressful job and it's causing insomnia. Tell whoever that you've tried all natural and over-the-counter remedies, because they'll try and palm you off with a load of nonsense – so be ready and get your story straight."

"I was born ready."

"Pop round when you've picked the prescription up?"

"No problem, I'll get on the blower right now. I'll be with you as soon as I can and we'll have a good catch-up. Call me if you need anythin' else."

It was late evening when Siobhan turned up. She flung the back door open, grinning from ear to ear, wearing a protective face mask, Blow-Up Barry (also wearing a face mask) tucked under her arm. I'd forgotten I'd been fobbing them off with a contagious bug.

"Well?" I said, wide-eyed, with my hands out ready to snatch the booty from her.

"You're not gonna feckin' believe this, right –"

"Did you get my pills?" I asked impatiently.

"Well, I goes in and it's a new doctor - and he's only feckin' gorgeous. I thought, right, I'm not missing out on this, so I says to him, 'Me fanjita's feeling a bit funny, like, can you gimmie a once-over? Y'know, get right in there and make sure everything's hunky-dory.' So he goes, 'That's fine, lie on the couch and I'll get a nurse.' I wasn't sure about that at first, but then I thought, the more the merrier, you know. Anyway, nurse walks through the door and her face is like a bag of boiled shite and she's built like a brick shithouse. I thought, *There's no way she's fiddling with me flaps!*"

I massaged my temples irritably. "Siobhan, stop! Did you get my prescription?!"

"Wait, wait, wait," she says, doubled up in hysterics. "I threw me thong to the floor and spread me legs, guiding him in like. It was fookin' great. I was lying there, me legs wrapped round his neck, pretending it was me first time and that I was frightened. Meanwhile, while his head was in me crotch, I was waving me middle finger at the sour old dinosaur in the corner. It was fookin' great."

I eyed Siobhan suspiciously, folding my arms.

"Then it went out of me head to ask for your prescription."

"You didn't go to the doctor's for me, did you?"

"Ah, lookit, I'm sorry. I was runnin' late at work and kinda got distracted and by the time I did remember, the surgery was closed."

"For fuck's sake!" I banged my fist hard against the kitchen cupboard. "What the hell am I going to do now? I asked you to do one simple thing for me. That was it."

"Oh right, well, sorry for havin' a laugh." Siobhan

looked hurt by my outburst. "I can pop down to the offie and get some brandy for you. Few of those will knock you right out. In fact you might need a stiff drink when I tell you –"

"Alcohol keeps me awake. You don't understand. I needed those pills like you wouldn't believe." I felt like punching her.

Siobhan fixed me with a steely expression. "You're not addicted to these pills, are you, Tara?"

I squeezed my eyes tight and gritted my teeth in frustration. "Don't be daft. I just need a good night's sleep, that's all."

"Are you sure now? Because you don't look *or* sound so good."

"That bug, it's disrupted my sleep pattern. I'm fine." With that, I made my excuses and abruptly shoved her and Blow-Up Barry out the door and locked it. If my doctor and friend couldn't help me, then surely the internet could.

After days spent glued to my bed in my own private hell, my supply of internet-sourced numbness arrived. *Hallelujah.*

Catching up on my dosage, I drifted in and out of sleep, dizzy spells and restless, foggy thoughts. Everything became grossly distorted. My brain was spiralling and I couldn't put the brakes on. The more I took, the more I needed.

On and on I plunged, further down within myself, on a one-way ticket to the bottom of the deepest, darkest ocean. Every time I opened my eyes, the ceiling, floor and walls felt like they were closing in on me.

I tried to get out of bed, get downstairs, retrieve more medication - but my legs gave way. As I tumbled, I reached out, taking the bedroom curtain and rail with me.

I lay in the foetal position for what felt like hours, gasping for air. Somehow, eventually I crawled out through a mass of crap on my bedroom floor and made my way to the top of the landing. I placed my hands over my ears and begged the ringing to stop. Blood was seeping from my head.

Unable to catch my breath or hold myself steady, I began bum-shuffling downstairs. My mind was in fast-forward, flashing images of the past, present and future: Dad falling over drunk; Mum holding rosary beads, sobbing. Going to church to repent our sins, priests up on their altars, images of the crucifix. The bullies at school. Katie on Mum's hip, screaming. Laura laughing while reading a book. Travis cradling his newborn baby. All of it flashed before my eyes.

Reaching the bottom of the stairs, clutching my chest, I crawled over and propped myself against the kitchen door. I cradled myself tight and repeatedly banged the back of my head. *Please, please, God, help me. Make this stop!*

I slapped my hands over various parts of my body to still it. To stop my jaw chattering, to stop my eyes twitching. It was as though I was wandering off the edge of the world, stepping closer to the edge. I could hear myself screaming.

Out of nowhere, a blanket of calm washed over me. The thought of not being here anymore became ever more seductive. I realised with absolute certainty that death was the only escape.

I hauled myself upright, grabbed a pen and began scribbling a desperate message on the kitchen wall. Then

I emptied the remaining supply of the internet-sourced pills down my throat.

Reasons to live: none.

Everything went dark.

Chapter 15

I'm shivering. I assess myself further. Everything is pulsating. My throat, neck and shoulders are throbbing, but I lie still. Paralysed with fear.

Scared of what I might see/not see, I keep my eyes clamped shut - terrifying thoughts race through me. Have I been buried alive? I dare not move a millimetre in fear of feeling a coffin around me. There's a drum, it's banging violently – it's *my heart* – so loud I fear my chest wall will blow open. My ears are ringing, too, the pitch excruciatingly high.

I hear a whimper in the distance. I realise with a start, it's *me*. Another involuntary sob escapes my throat.

"Hello, you," says a voice.

I recognize it immediately - Laura.

I became aware of a soft light being turned on beside me. Even though it generates barely a glow, it hurts my eyes. I raise my hand to shield them.

"Back with us?" Her tone is gentle. "Did you mean it?"

I don't answer. I'm swamped in intense confusion.

"Tara, do you want to die from terminal disappointment?" Laura's voice is firmer now.

I gulp hard as the tears stream uncontrollably from me. I turn away, pulling my knees up to my chest, and scream so loud I even shock myself ...

"Good girl, let it all out." Laura pulled me into her with force. "I can't imagine life without you in it." She burst into tears.

I don't think I'd *ever* seen her cry before. *Maybe she is human after all?*

I clung to her like a baby. "Please don't let go of me," I begged clinging tighter still. "Don't let go – "

"I'm not going *anywhere*. I'm here. We're all here for you. After getting a distraught call from Siobhan, me, Mum and Katie got the first flight out." She stroked my head. "Mum and Katie were here all night, they've not long gone back to yours."

"I'm sorry ... I'm so sorry."

Cradling me, Laura hushed my sobs.

"What's happened to me, have I gone mad?"

"You've had a breakdown, overdosed."

I sobbed harder.

Laura cupped my face. I could feel her hands shaking. "You'll get better, promise. There's a limit for us all and you've reached yours. You're not mad, just at the end of your tether."

I gripped her shoulders.

"Can I be fixed?" I promptly broke into floods of tears again.

"Hey, listen, my reputation's at stake here. We'll work through this, slowly and together." She thumbed away my tears. "If I can't help my own sister, then I'm not much of a psychotherapist, am I?"

I flopped backwards, my head hitting the pillow.

"I'm so tired."

Laura opened the curtains, filling the room with blinding light. She looked smart, professional. Her navy-blue trouser suit and crisp white shirt were well fitted, her dark hair in a bob, all neat and tidy. "Of course you're tired, you were hooked up to monitors, your stomach pumped. Doctors had to fight to save your life – do you understand?"

I nodded, wishing they hadn't.

She took a deep breath, placed her hands in her trouser pockets and stared out the window. "It was touch and go at one point."

My hand flew to my throat. It felt like I'd been eating shards of glass. I flashed back to the rubber tube going into my mouth and down into my stomach.

Laura settled herself back on the bed. "Do you remember being taken in the ambulance – coming here, to the hospital?"

I shivered. "Bit of a blank."

She unfolded a blanket at the foot of the bed, covered me. "Siobhan and James found you on the kitchen floor."

"I –"

"They thought you were dead. Siobhan said she'd upset you?"

I shrugged, thought about how mean I'd been to her for not getting my pills. I pictured myself shoving her out the door while she was mid-conversation, and cringed.

"She called round for days after, there was no sign of life … curtains and blinds were closed. Siobhan called

James in the end and the pair of them broke in."

I couldn't look Laura in the eye.

"Anyway, if they hadn't found you, God knows where we'd be now."

I'd be in feckin' peace! Then I felt bad for thinking that.

"Are James and Siobhan okay?"

"There're okay. Shocked, of course. As we all are." Laura's pallor was ashen.

I covered my face with my hands.

She peeled my fingers away and eyed me sternly. "Mum's only been at yours an hour and she's already signed for two packages this morning. You could open a pharmacy with the amount of medication you've bought on the dark web. What were you thinking?"

My hands were back over my burning face. I really wanted Laura to fuck off.

"Deadly concoctions, the lot of them." She smoothed the sheets on my bed. "But I guess you knew that."

I hung my head, my mouth completely dry.

"I've been chatting with Doctor Lancelot; he said you'd failed to turn up for your counselling. Why didn't you go?"

"They couldn't fix me." I shrugged helplessly.

"I'm your sister, why didn't you call me? Tell me how bad things had got?" Tears streamed down Laura's cheeks; she quickly brushed them away.

"Because you're not God, Laura, that's why. I can't be fixed!"

Animated, Laura paced up and down my room. "You *are* fixable, but only if you *want* to be."

To keep the peace I nodded my head.

"Since meeting Travis –" she said.

I shot her a venomous look. Just hearing his name made my insides burn, my heart pound, my hands shake.

"I know there's more to this. There are conversations that you and I need to have. They're long overdue." Her lips formed a thin line. "Now, it's not normally recommended, but I've convinced the hospital psychiatrist and Doctor Lancelot to allow me to counsel you. They've expressed concerns that, as I'm your sister, I won't know when to pull back and when to push forward."

A voice in my head was screaming *God help me!* But there was a silver lining: Laura would never be able to take that much time off work.

"My boss has kindly agreed I can work from home – your home – *remotely*, so I can speak with my patients via video link." Smiling, she walked over and patted my hand. "So I'll be by your side for as long as it takes."

I groaned, wishing I'd never woken up. Ignoring my reaction, she carried on: "I have assured everyone – Mum, Katie – *given my word* that I will get you back on track."

My life was over.

"You'll have to promise you won't take *anything* without me knowing what it is. In fact, when we get you back home, you'll notice that anything you could harm yourself with has been removed."

I wrenched my head back, let out a wail to the skies (or, more precisely, the asbestos hospital ceiling). *No more sleeping tablets? No more Valium? They might as well lock me up and throw away the key!*

I couldn't promise that.

"Tara, the hospital were about to admit you into a

psychiatric unit – do you understand what that means?"

I eyed her coldly. "Yes – I do. Okay. You've made your point – lecture over."

Her voice went up an octave. "I'm not lecturing, I trying to help!"

My hand flew to my pounding head. "Can you please lower your voice?"

Laura searched my face. "I don't mean to be hard on you. We nearly lost you." She burst into tears again.

I felt bad then.

"I'm sorry." Our hands locked tighter. "I'll try as hard as I can."

"Good girl. You're a Ryan, we're made of strong stuff. "

"Could you get me a painkiller? My head is banging."

"No! For God's sake, you're unbelievable!" she flicked my hands away. "You can't have *anything*. Your body is still full of toxins."

Laura straightened her jacket. "I'm waiting for the hospital psychiatrist to come see you – chat a few things through, then hopefully he'll sign you off. He'll put you on antidepressants – that *I* will administer. Then we'll get you back home."

I didn't argue. I couldn't be bothered. Part of me wanted to launch into a full "mind-your-own-fucking-business" verbal attack, but whatever I was feeling stayed trapped inside. I had nothing left to give. *Surely it would be easier to be dead than alive*, I thought, as I slowly turned to face the wall.

God, I am such a screw-up. I was and always will be a failure on so many levels. I couldn't even manage the simple task of suicide.

* * *

We came home late afternoon. I was ushered straight to bed while Laura began tackling the devastation I'd left. Although Mum and Katie had made a start, the house still looked like it had been burgled.

I came to with Laura picking up debris from my bedroom floor. After I'd shared *some* of the tragic circumstances with her. Travis dumping me by text. Flying to Dublin to try and win him back. Me like a prize eejit in fur coat no knickers, sitting next to his *young* pregnant girlfriend, helping her. The *final nail in the coffin* – that I thought I was pregnant, and wasn't.

"Today is the first day of the rest of your life," she said smiling. "Mum and Katie will be back soon. They're still out getting provisions in. Now you've had some rest, there are some things – *minor things* – we need to talk through." She patted my hand. "Nothing to be alarmed about." She settled herself gingerly on the edge of the bed. "Were you aware that Glamma-Puss has closed till further notice?"

I stuck my fingers in my ears. I didn't want to know.

With a barely discernible tut, Laura was up off the bed and was heading for the door. "I'm putting the kettle on."

I slouched down the bed, pulling the duvet around me. I wasn't quite sure how I was feeling, but the words *unbearable* and *miserable* came to mind.

Hearing the kettle boiling felt strangely comforting. It was nice to know someone was here with me, even if it was Laura. To be fair, I knew deep down she was the best person to have by my side. Well, that was if I did really want to live. The trouble was, one minute I did, and the next I didn't.

My eyes searched my bedroom. Everything felt strange. Memories jumbling together - impossible to make sense of. Bad things and bad feelings had taken place in this room. I'd spent so much time in here alone, counting cobwebs, looking at the cracks in the ceiling, the peeling paint on the windowsill.

I caught my breath as my eyes settled on the fur coat lying redundant, half on and half off my chair. Its sleeve pointing at me. I hated that coat. I despised the very sight of it. Heart pounding, I turned away.

I could hear Laura chatting on the phone downstairs. I needed the toilet badly. As weak as I was, I'd have to try to get up. As I pushed the duvet away, the stench of the bedding hit me. I inched the duvet back. As well as fake-tan stains, I found empty crisp packets, biscuits, tissues, make-up brushes, pens, self-help books, and, worst of all, a pair of scissors and ... blonde hair. My blonde hair. My hand flew to my head. I had no recollection of cutting my hair. As I peeled the duvet back further, I gasped, discovering the snapped heels of my precious Louboutins. Four of them! Seizing the scissors, the clumps of hair and needle-thin heels, I quickly tucked them under my pillow. I didn't have a clue where the rest of the shoes were.

I didn't want Laura to see this, or anyone else for that matter so eased my legs round to the side of bed, desperate to find the rest of the shoes before anyone else did.

My search was interrupted by the sound of Laura coming up the stairs. I tried to move faster, but light-headedness engulfed me. I swayed towards the chest of drawers and clung to it to keep me upright. Not a butchered shoe in sight, slowly I began to make my way to the bathroom, using the walls as support, my eyes still searching the floor as I went. Reaching the toilet, I flopped down, trembling.

"Cuppa here for you," said Laura. "I was going to make you some toast but your bread is growing the next best antibiotic known to man."

I sobbed quietly to myself, unable to move.

"Tara?"

"Can you give me a minute?" I couldn't disguise the despair in my voice. I wasn't sure if I was about to have a panic attack.

Before I knew it, Laura was in the bathroom, crouched down, her arm wrapped tightly around me.

"Come on. Back to bed, you need rest."

"My bed smells awful, I can't get back in there." I raised a small smile as she walked me back, my breathing slowly returning to a reasonable pace.

"Hmm, *that* I agree with." Laura wrinkled her nose, easing me down onto the chair, having dropped the fur coat unceremoniously to the floor.

"There should be some clean covers in the airing cupboard," I said. I watched her begin to efficiently strip my fake-tan-covered bedding. Before I knew it, she'd thrown the bastard fur coat over me. I pushed it away as though it was poison.

"I see you've been giving that coat a haircut," she said as she struggled with the duvet. "One of the sleeves is downstairs."

"Oh God." I had no memory of cutting a sleeve off.

I watched as Laura tossed the scissors, hair and Louboutin heels out from under my pillow. She said nothing, just turned and stared at me. *I wish she wouldn't do that!* Within a few seconds she was back perfecting her hospital corners.

"In!" she commanded.

It felt so nice to be looked after.

"Laura, Tra ... Tra ... *he who shall not be named* is having a baby." Tears leaked from my eyes as I climbed back into bed. "And the girl he's having a baby with is only a baby herself! And I've gone into the menopause!" I could feel the hysteria rising again.

Laura tutted. "I went into the menopause years ago."

"What? *Really?*" She'd never mentioned this before. I patted the bed, indicating for her to sit with me.

"Yes, *really*. It's part of life. Menopause happens to every woman in the world. Some earlier than others. Some later. Just think, no more periods. I'd just embrace it if I were you. Get a bit of HRT in you and you'll be a new woman."

"So you don't feel like a redundant, dried-up old prune?" I fumbled with the corner of the duvet, wiped my tears with it.

"No. And children *aren't* everything."

"That's easy to say when you have one."

"Jemi is all grown up now – living her life – travelling the world, doing what she wants to do, so it's allowed to be about *me*."

"I've always wanted a baby. I'll never feel complete without one. I would've made sure my baby and me would be close ... like best friends. I would've gone travelling with them when they were old enough. Posh travelling, mind."

Laura rubbed my shoulder. "I can guarantee they wouldn't allow you cramp their style. And anyway, children are *borrowed*. They eventually leave the nest and make their own way in life."

"But I wanted to dress a baby up in designer clothes, cute trainers, trendy jeans, cool sunglasses, take it to Harrods for lunch ... New York for shopping. Sightseeing in Paris. I've got so much love to give, and now I've got nowhere to put it!" I pulled the duvet over my face, hiding my tears.

"When you're ready and feeling stronger, get a pooch. You can stick it in one of your designer handbags."

"It's not the same and you know it!" I muttered through the duvet.

"No, granted, it's not the same. It's cheaper. No tantrums, no arguments, and they're *always* pleased to see you. Bliss, if you ask me." Laura eased the duvet off my face. "My friend Kath recently rescued a Bichon Frise; it's the cutest thing I've *ever* seen. A ball of white fluff - she's even put a diamante collar round her neck."

I pulled the duvet back over my face. "I don't want a bloody dog! I want a baby and I want Travis. You get a bloody dog if you want one!"

Ignoring my outburst, Laura peeled the duvet back down. "Kath called her dog Gucci; she hadn't been treated very well, poor little thing."

Miss Treated? I couldn't bear the thought of a defenceless animal being mistreated. I sniffed, "If I had a white fluffy doggie I would've called her Miss Dior."

Laura beamed. "That name is *so* you!"

My ice-cold heart warmed slightly.

"As for that Easter egg you were supposedly *dating*, well what can I say? Gorgeous on the outside, but very disappointing on the inside. When you took the foil and ribbons off, Travis was – *and is* – empty, Tara."

I shrugged helplessly. "I miss him. I know it's wrong, but I *do*." Anger began surging through me. "I hope when he's fucking his boring-brown-shoulder-length-haired-brown-polo-neck-jumpered *young girlfriend*, he accidently calls my name instead of hers!"

"Tara. You don't mean that."

"I do." I took a deep breath. Then I thought about that poor baby being caught up in this mess. "I know it's not *her* fault, it's *his*."

"You've got to stop chasing every shiny thing you see."

I hung my head again.

I could hear keys in the door, Mum coming in, Katie bounding up the stairs. "Is she awake?"

I wanted to hide under the duvet. I felt ashamed that Katie and Mum were going to see me like this.

I quickly patted my hair down, tucked the sides behind my ears, and braced myself.

"Hey, Tara!" Katie said brightly. "You look ... *umm* ... interesting. Jesus, I forgot how good-looking the fellas were in England. Even Mammy was chatted up by the shop assistant. At her age, too – *can you believe that?*"

"I'm sorry you have to see me this way," I said, with a wry smile.

Katie planted a kiss on my forehead. "No worries at all. Lickarse Laura will get you sorted good and proper, won't you, sis ... and if not, can I have first dibs on your clothes?" Katie grabbed my hand and winked at me.

I cracked a faint smile.

"Mammy was just telling me when you were younger you took a metal nail-file and tried to file down your big rabbit teeth, is that right?"

"Not now, Katie," said Laura, throwing her a look.

"Hey, pet." It was Mum, out of breath from climbing the stairs. She threw her arms round me and gave Katie a stern look. "Don't be tellin' fibs, Katie, I never said no such thing about her having big rabbit teeth."

"You did so, Mammy. You said Tara had enormous rabbit teeth and when she took the file to them you said in hindsight it was probably the start of her body dysmorphia."

I shot glances at everyone. Body dysmorphia? I no more had body dysmorphia than the man in the moon! Utter nonsense!

Rightly so, Mum gave Katie a clip round the ear. "I merely said that her head took a little while to catch up with the size of her teeth, that's all." Mum turned to me. "Don't be taking any notice of your sister. Will I run you a nice bubble bath, pet?"

Katie again: "I think Mammy's trying to be polite ... You *do* smell bad, real bad. But I bought you a nice body spray if you wanna use it after your bath?"

I nodded. "Thanks. I might just do that later." I ran my tongue over my porcelain veneers. Just because I'd had my teeth done (and admittedly, *did* once try to file them down) didn't mean I had body dysmorphia!

"No bother, can I go through your wardrobe?"

I smiled, despite myself. Even a near suicide didn't deter my little sis.

"Boiled bacon and cabbage for dinner." Mum theatrically licked her lips in my direction as though I was three years old.

"Katie!" I barked, sitting bolt upright. "Are they my Jimmy Choo trainers you're wearing?"

"No. They're mine! Sweet Jesus, you gave them to me." Katie stuck her earphones in. Little bitch.

I was annoyed. Katie was lucky I didn't have it in me to pin her to the ground and wrestle them off her feet. Still, at least she hadn't sold them on eBay.

I turned to Mum. "I'm sorry to put you through this – especially, well, you know ... after what ..." I eyed Katie, who was now knee-deep in my wardrobe.

"It's okay, pet. Just promise me one thing," said Mum, pointedly ignoring my reference to Katie's errant past. "Please stop puttin' that poisony cement and Botox nonsense in yourself. It's leaked into your brain. I had the fright of my life earlier when I found a sleeve of a fur coat downstairs. I thought you'd killed a cat or something! Anyway, you don't need all that stuff because you're beautiful just as you are."

I looked straight at Mum. I have to confess I was beginning to enjoy the attention.

"I just want my girls to be happy. Saints preserve us. That's not too much to ask for, is it?"

Laura was in there like a shot. "Fillers and Botox wouldn't do that to you, Mum. Leak, I mean, into your brain. Although, studies have shown that people who have excessive aesthetic work or plastic surgery often suffer with low self-esteem."

I vaguely remembered Sheila refusing me more Botox and fillers, questioning my mental state. From deep in my wardrobe Katie popped her head out, her earphones dangling. "What a gobshite that Jackie's husband was, *eh?* And that Jayde! Who would have thought? The dirty bitch." Katie held up a heel-less Louboutin, squinted at it, and thankfully, without drawing attention to it, lobbed it over her shoulder.

"Katie, not now," Laura snapped, "I haven't discussed any of that with Tara yet."

I was suddenly alert, my hands shot up to my face. "*What*? What's happened with Jackie's husband and Jayde? Oh my God. Don't tell me ... don't tell me they're together?"

"Yep – Pete's a perv, he's at least thirty years older than her!" said Katie.

I was already calling Jackie. It went straight to voicemail. Leaving a message, I told her how shocked I was, and how sorry I was for not being there for her, and to please call me. I then sent a text in case she didn't pick up my voicemail. In the midst of it all, I couldn't help but notice Katie had my good cashmere jumper out, sizing it up against herself.

"Get out of my wardrobe," I said.

Laura glared at Katie, her expression softening when she turned to me. "I didn't think you were ready to hear about Jackie – *just yet*."

"I can't believe it! Poor Jackie. How could Jayde, sweet little Jayde, do that? How long have they been carrying on? Does anyone know?"

Katie had my leopard-print Louis Vuitton scarf draped round her shoulders. "Months, apparently. That business with the text Jackie got on Christmas Eve – *the underwear* – was meant for Jayde all along."

I went hot and sweaty. Poor Jackie!

Laura opened the window, letting much needed air into the stuffy bedroom. "I know the news is upsetting – Siobhan did try to tell you ... This means you have no staff at Glamma-Puss. Hence, the salon closed. James did try to manage the place in your absence, and Siobhan even tried to pass herself off as a beautician in the evenings, after she'd finished her work - God help us. But don't worry, it's nothing that can't be fixed." Laura's face glazed over. "Granted, it may require a lawyer or two –"

Katie cut Laura off. "Siobhan did an online tutorial and tried to learn how to wax backs, sacks and cracks and couldn't get any models to practise on, and obvs James wouldn't allow her near his crown jewels, so she practised on Blow-Up Barry and melted his bollocks!"

I cringed and sank further down the bed. My salon's reputation would surely be in shreds.

"She tried to patch Barry up, but he was too far gone – not a scrap of air left in the poor fella," said Katie, feigning deep shock. "His memorial service was the other day. I wanted to fly over for it but Mammy wouldn't let me." She stuck her earphones back in, her head bopping to the beat.

Mum solemnly shook her head and blessed herself. "I lit a candle at mass for him, poor old Barry."

"It was a blow-up doll. He's not real!" I wished I'd never purchased that bloody Blow-Up Barry in the first place.

"Siobhan threw caution to the wind, booked in some hairy blokes and went for it, and even though she managed to burn every one of their idiot arses, I still think she rocks," said Katie, way too loudly.

"And now Siobhan could be facing a lawsuit and that's not funny at all," Laura said even louder. She was glaring fixedly at the wardrobe door, trying to get Katie's attention.

"Jeez, I mean, I like a man to be a *man*," Katie said, as she found another heel-less Louboutin. "I mean, what's the point of your man acting like a pussy? I have a perfect pussy of my own, thanks very much, I don't need another one."

"Language, young lady! Lord bless us and save us," said Mum, crossing herself again.

"What am I going to do?" I asked. While I was horrified with the news from the salon, I was also shamefully distracted by Katie: she was holding up another heel-less Louboutin, examining it. I was waiting for her to question the state they were in. *Oh God. The next thing I know, this will be all over Facebook!*

"Now is *certainly* not the right time to talk about any of this," said Laura, studying me. "It's all sortable."

I burst into floods of tears. "It's not sortable. It's all a mess. A great big mess; my life, my salon, everything!"

Mum inched up the bed and stroked my arm. "Ah, c'mon now, pet, don't be cryin' otherwise you'll be settin' me off."

"Sis, can I borrow this?" Katie came out the wardrobe holding up my silk Yves Saint Laurent shirt.

"Yes ... umm, no. Katie – please, not now!" Memories flooded back of that night - me wearing that very shirt for Travis. "I can't breathe ... I can't breathe." A panic attack was looming.

"Katie, get out of Tara's wardrobe now," said Laura. Katie, unable to hear, carried on until Laura walked over and yanked the plugs out of her ears. "Go downstairs." She turned to Mum. "Mum ... *Mum*, your boiled bacon is burning."

Mum looked upset, confused. "But, I've no boiled bacon on yet, pet."

"Then go and put some on!" Laura snapped.

Laura was back by my side. "Take deep breaths, Tara

... it's okay. It's okay. In for four, out for four."

Mum gave me a weepy smile. "Right so." She grabbed Katie's arm and marched her out of my room.

I closed my eyes and focused on my breathing. "Will I ever get better?" I asked in a wobbly voice.

Nodding her head and smiling gently, Laura passed me my tea. It was stone cold, so I spat it out. "Fancy a cigarette?" she asked.

"I'd love one."

Just as I was sticking my head out the window, Katie came through with mugs of steaming fresh tea.

"I love you, Tara. Anything you need, give me a shout, okay?"

I was taken aback. "I love you too." With that, she slipped out of the room.

Laura closed the bedroom door. "When was the last time you had a good laugh?"

I sipped my hot tea and thought about it. I couldn't remember.

Laura grinned. "Mum's reading *Fifty Shades of Grey*."

We both threw back our heads and began laughing. And it felt good. Really good.

We talked for a while about nothing in particular. I know it was *what Laura did* but I had to admit she was good at it. I felt calmer. Felt comforted by her presence. It was as though a thick mist was beginning to clear from my head.

After a few more cups of tea and a pause for dinner, Laura said I needed to rest: tomorrow was going to be a big day for me.

***

The following morning, the next stage of my recovery began.

"Do you miss Dad?" Laura asked, joining me at the kitchen table.

I always got a burning pain in the pit of my stomach whenever I thought of Dad.

"Terribly." I closed my eyes and pictured his face. I eyed Laura head on, anchoring her down – feeling a volcanic rage erupt within me; I had a sudden urge to slap her. "Why didn't you help me with him?"

Laura was about to talk – no doubt her *shrink spiel* would be at the ready – but I quickly put my hand up to silence her. What I had to say had been a long time coming.

"Before buggering off to Dublin, *you* did nothing! *Nothing!* Had your nose stuck in books, ignoring the fact that our dad was sick. You three left and I was left to deal with him *on my own*! I know I told you all to go – that I could manage – but evidently I couldn't because he went and died on me!"

"Dad was an alcoholic, Tara."

"Why didn't *you* do something?" I had a bitter taste in my mouth.

"Did you notice the genre of books I was reading?"

I glared at her, my face burning in fury. "No. I was too busy looking after Dad! While you were reading *nonsense,* he was losing his mind!"

Laura looked horrified.

"I was ..." her voice was shaking, "I was researching alcoholism and schizophrenia. I'd convinced myself that if I kept studying I'd find a cure. Be able to help him." Her hands flew to her face and she began to cry. "I was hurting too."

I was frozen in shock. Undiluted silence sat between us. It hung in the air and hovered awkwardly until I let out a pain-filled breath.

All these years I had considered Laura to be a cold, heartless bitch. I had no idea that she had also been suffering.

How could I have got it so wrong?

She pulled a string of tissues out of her pocket, the sunlight catching the dust motes in the air. "We all have our own way of dealing with trauma – reading up on it was *my* nerdy way of coping." She dabbed her tears with the crumpled tissue. "I went to the library – borrowed every book I could get my hands – read till my head hurt – till my eyes burned. *I didn't understand most of it* – but I kept studying in the hope of finding a cure. It's also why I went on to become a psychologist. I wanted to wave a magic wand and make our family okay again."

With my heart feeling as though it was about to break into two, and tears running rivers down my cheeks, I quickly grabbed Laura's hand. "I can see now it wasn't easy for any of us."

"We had a different upbringing from most. None of us able to bring school friends home - to develop vital social skills - because we never knew if Dad was going to be drunk or not."

I closed my eyes, nodding in agreement.

"You know Tara, we were *so* young – we weren't expected to know what to do." She placed her hand on top of mine.

I nodded again. She was right.

I felt something shift inside me. I felt lighter. Like my

soul was drifting back inside my body. I'd carried that heavy resentment towards Laura for years.

"*We* were the children, *he* was the parent," she said. A flicker of pain darted across her face. "Mum was so frightened of Dad; the more unpredictable he became the more she feared for her safety. Can you imagine: the man you've been in love with all your life hearing voices? Voices telling him that he was the *chosen one*? And he had an evil sinner for a wife?"

I gulped hard and gripped Laura's hand tighter.

"Poor Mum, and she had to deal with Katie – she was still a baby."

I rolled my eyes. "A nightmare of a baby, always attached to Mum's hip, howling. You and I didn't get a look in."

Laura searched my face. "Why do you think that was?"

"She was spoilt!"

Laura smiled pitifully at me.

"Let me put it another way. Do you think Katie was terrified of Dad starting on Mum? Her tears and tantrums were the words she couldn't express. We were at school when the worst was going on. Katie witnessed it. Every. Single. Day."

As I absorbed what Laura had said, I got a pain in my chest. "I've never thought about it like that. Oh God, poor Katie." I felt ashamed and had an urge to go get her, and wrap her in my arms, make her feel safe.

"Mum had to spread herself thin to try and keep us three going. *Imagine.* Having to put on a brave face every minute of every day. Her morning starting with Dad forcing her to get on her hands and knees to pray – *pray for forgiveness* when she hadn't done anything wrong.

Can you imagine?"

I couldn't. The hairs on the back of my neck stood on end.

"Mum is a remarkable woman." Laura's eye's filled with tears again. "Did you know Dad accused her of having affairs? He made out he had detectives following her. He even maintained that Katie wasn't his."

I was speechless. The pain in my chest gripped me further.

"Mum had to leave, Tara. You didn't want to come, even though we begged you. You wanted to stay and finish your apprenticeship. Leaving you behind broke our hearts. Mum wept for months."

My sisters were heartbroken and Mum wept for months?

So they did love me?

Laura looked me dead in the eye. "Remember the night we left?"

My stomach knotted. "I'll never forget it."

"You and I made a pact. You'd watch Dad and I'd watch Mum and Katie. It wasn't fair, I know, but the family was divided by a terrible situation – not because we didn't love each other."

They did love me!

I leant over the kitchen table, threw my arms round Laura's neck, and united as sisters we sobbed together for the very first time. Our entire family had been caught in the crossfire of living a life with an alcoholic.

"I know you didn't understand this at the time and neither did I, but I understand it now, and it's so important you understand it too. Alcoholism is an illness. A terrible, terrible disease. None of us got away without being damaged. I got pregnant *way too young* – tried to build a nest of my own because our nest was broken, and my marriage inevitably failed. You're suffering abandonment issues, separation anxiety, low self-esteem –"

"Am I?"

Laura nodded.

"And Katie, well, she went on to became an addict herself."

Now that Laura had pointed it out, I could see the pattern. The impact of having a parent as an addict. The dysfunctional environment we'd lived in – the emotional wrestling we'd each endured.

The damaged net had cast itself far and wide.

I thought about Mum and how long she'd held it together.

She really was the bravest woman I'd ever known.

Laura and I continued speaking of our childhood on deeper levels, leaving out none of the pain, sadness or guilt. From me blaming myself for going out on my birthday, not checking in on Dad, not knowing he'd decided to no longer take his medication, to him dying in my arms, to me finally accepting his death *wasn't* my fault. And, that I wasn't constantly being watched and punished by the Big Man Upstairs.

Together, as sisters, we bonded tightly for the first time. It was excruciatingly painful for us both, yet we helped each other, as Laura too found herself revealing issues that had lain unresolved for so long.

Chapter 16

Over the following weeks, with Mum and Katie back in Dublin, Laura continued her mission of piecing me back together. In her professional opinion, the key to my recovery – *from negative beliefs* - was to change how I perceived myself. One of Laura's biggest bugbears was the fixation I had on my appearance.

"Let's start with your breast implants," she said.

"Let's not."

"Botox?"

I shook my head.

"Teeth?"

I scowled at her.

"Nose-job?"

"I'll go make us some tea."

"Lips like a duck? Cheeks like a hamster?" she followed me out to the kitchen.

"I'm not listening! *Lalalalalala.*"

"You have beautiful red hair, yet you bleach it platinum-blonde, glue false hair on your head - *why*?" Laura cocked her nose up.

I shrugged, slamming mugs down. "I like it!" I flicked the kettle on, my arms folded tightly around myself.

"Okay, think about that one for a moment. Why do you cover your skin in orange muck that quite frankly makes you look silly?"

Sometimes Laura was so annoying. "There's nothing wrong with a little enhancement," I said defensively. "I'm in the Hair and Beauty business – it goes with the territory. And anyway, you're meant to be helping me. Not making me feel worse!"

"I see nothing wrong with a little enhancement either – it's when boundaries get broken, when it becomes excessive, obsessive, destructive ..."

Was I obsessive?

Excessive?

Destructive?

I was just about to gear up and defend myself again, but a tired voice inside my head interjected.

Perhaps I was all of those things.

I thought about my credit card bill and the extortionately priced five-starred hotel suite I'd booked for Travis and me, on New Year's Eve. Among a whole host of other stuff bulging out of my wardrobe was the fur coat. The designer shoes. The new handbag. I couldn't afford them.

"I'm peeling back the layers. I'm trying to get to *you*, the *real you*. The real *you* is hidden, covered up. You're beautiful inside and out – "

My head shot up. Laura said I was beautiful? *Me, beautiful, inside and out?*

"I know you can't see it. You never have."

I'd spent my entire life trying to fit in. Hearing her compliment me like that sent a warm glow through my body. My posture straightened. I was two inches taller.

"Travis played a large part in this recent episode, but we know he wasn't the *sole* trigger for where you ended up."

Hearing his name still stung; my body deflated, my height shortened again.

"I'd say Travis might even have been a blessing in disguise. Revealing what needed to be revealed."

"I wouldn't go that far." I handed Laura her tea.

"If you want to fully recover, we need to dig deeper to a greater understanding. You don't need mind-numbing pills, or a brood of perfect children, or some phoney love god to make you complete. You are already *the* most incredible woman. It's time you learnt to love your crazy, funny self."

And so the process went on. With twice-weekly cognitive behavioural therapy, and Laura helping me focus on changing my distortions, patterns, behaviour, and guiding me through copying strategies, I could feel my mental health improving. There were days where I took two steps forward and three back, but it had taken years to develop this unhealthy way of thinking and getting better wasn't going to happen overnight. Learning to love yourself, *really* love yourself, with all the imperfections, warts and all, was hard.

After Laura decided we'd made sufficient progress, she allowed Siobhan and James to come back into my life - and not a moment too soon: the pair of them had been endlessly bugging her to spend time with me. I think she finally relented as much for herself as for me.

I felt a glimmer of excitement as I heard them bounding up the stairs together.

Laura shouted up, "Hey, you guys, try and keep it as calm and as light as possible, eh? She's still …" Earwigging, I heard her whispering the word *fragile*. "I'll be downstairs if you need anything."

"No problem!" they shouted back. Flinging the bedroom door open, wearing matching fluffy fuchsia onesies, they bombed on top of my bed like a pair of naughty school kids.

I hugged them tearfully. "It's so good to see you both!"

They smothered me in hugs and kisses. "*Mmmwha, mmmwha, mmmwha!* We're so glad you're back with us!"

In unison, they shot off the bed and turned their backs on me. Their bright pink onesies were emblazoned with the words *Team Tara* in day-glo yellow.

"Team Tara!" they both yelled.

"We've had these printed in your honour," said James, blowing me a kiss.

Siobhan jumped up and down and shook a brown paper bag in my direction. "We've got you one, too!"

"And black sequined UGG slippers," said James. He did a few ballerina-style pirouettes across the bedroom floor to demonstrate. "Look how sparkly they are!"

Then, before I knew what was happening, the pair of them were stripping me out of my old pyjamas and were shimmying me into my Team Tara onesie along with the sequined slippers.

I felt instantly lifted.

After they'd finished bouncing all over me, and the

three of us had done a quick ring-a-ring-a-rosy, I put my arms around the pair of them and flopped breathlessly back down onto the bed.

"Thank you, guys." Tears sprouting, I pulled them both closer. Our three heads resting on each other's.

"For what?" asked Siobhan.

"For everything." I shrugged. "For caring enough, for breaking in and finding me. For saving my life."

"Nonsense," said James with a dismissive hand gesture. "Anyway, you're back from ... *wherever you've been*, and getting better. That's all that matters. We love you, we miss you. Glamma-Puss misses you, too!" He kicked off his UGG slippers and snuggled in closer.

Siobhan stroked my head then bolted off the bed. "We come bearing more gifts." She dug around in her tote bag. "Ta-dah! Wine. We bring red wine!"

"*Shhh* ... don't let Laura hear you," I whispered urgently.

Good old Siobhan, she even managed to produce three wineglasses from her bag. She removed the cork. "It needs to breathe for a while, so I'll just leave it for a bit." She placed the bottle and glasses on the chest of drawers and flung herself back on the bed.

"So, come on, you guys, what's been happening out there in your crazy worlds?" I asked. "Anyone heard from Jackie?" They both shook their heads.

I'd left countless messages with her but still hadn't heard back. I'd even made Laura drive round to her house, pop a note through the door telling her to contact me.

"She'll make contact when she's ready," said James. "I won't say I told you so – but I *warned* you about Jayde, the man-eating super-slut."

"I knew from the moment Jackie got that text on Christmas Eve that Pete had fooked her over. I have a nose for such debauchery. No smoke without fire," said Siobhan.

We all sighed.

I'd really believed in Jayde, invested a lot of time and money training her up.

"I've been head-hunted," said Siobhan, picking up the low mood. She flicked her messy ponytail.

"I'm always getting head-hunted," said James, adjusting his crown jewels. "It's no big deal."

"Not that sort of head-hunted, ya big gobshite!"

I laughed. I'd missed their antics.

Siobhan continued. "I've been chatting with this guy online, he's an environmental fundraiser; he's all beard, snow goggles and icicles." She rubbed her hands together excitedly.

James flapped his hands impatiently. "I-wanna-tell-Tara-*my*-story first," he whined.

I patted his head. "You'll have you turn in a minute."

"Soon I'll be packing me rucksack with a hot water bottle, a box of porridge and thermal socks and setting off for the Arctic." Siobhan raised her hand up, indicating faraway shores. "I've adopted a baby polar bear and may go and see it."

James squealed. "Oh! I've always wanted to adopt a chimpanzee. We'd have matching diamante sunglasses and a vest top saying *we like monkey business*. I just never got around to it."

"Okay." I could sense where this conversation was heading. Even though the thought of never being able to have a baby broke the surface of my conscience a million times a day, I didn't think I'd ever be allowed to adopt a baby, with my mental health and medical history. I looked at the pair of them. They were good friends. Good, dear friends. I knew their hearts were in the right places, but I needed to steer the conversation in another direction.

"Any other news?"

James clutched his heart dramatically. "Well, Christian has just landed the job of his dreams. The *'tea, coffee or me'* job."

"The *'tea, coffee or me'* job?"

"He's in training to become cabin crew!" Spitting feathers, James was up off the bed, hands on hips, staring out the bedroom window. He swung round. "I was the one who told him about the openings for the airline! We both went for an interview. I didn't get the job. *He did.* And that's not fair!"

"But James, you're *my* nail technician. You can't leave Glamma-Puss."

"Well, hurry up and open it back up, then!"

"I will. I promise, soon." For the first time in weeks, instead of feeling a lump of dread, I felt a flicker of inner resolve. My thoughts raced. Could I really get the place back up and running? I'd done it before; maybe I could do it again.

"James, what the feck are you doing?" said Siobhan.

"Checking the wine is breathing, darling. It's not, so I'm giving it mouth to mouth resuscitation." He took another swig from the bottle.

"Feck off with yourself and give it here!" Siobhan dived across the bed.

"It's delightful and plummy!" James took another swig before handing the bottle over.

I was howling with laughter. Actually, really belly-laughing. It was something I never thought I'd do again. It felt wonderful.

Siobhan clutched her chest till she caught her breath. "Tara, I've a letter for you. It's from Katie; she came to see me before she went back to Dublin."

I was puzzled. Taking the letter from her, I opened it and read it out loud:

To my sister, Tara (AKA head nutcase) ☺

I hope you're well on the way to feeling better. If you wanna do drugs in the future, come to me and I'll get them sorted for you, but you have to share them. (Only joking.)

Mammy and Laura have told me that your baby oven has blown its fuse and over-heated itself and can't be repaired.

I'd like you to know, my oven is your oven. I've already discussed this situation with James and he has offered to have a party in his designer pants, so, between the pair of us, we can make you a sprog.

Siobhan (!!) wants to be the birthing partner.

Think about it. Love you.

Katie x

I held the letter to my heart, and for a while said nothing, letting its contents run through my head. The words were like cool water for a migraine.

James and Siobhan were staring at me, then back at each other. "You okay?" Their voices were gentle, comforting.

My throat was constricted. Nodding, I grabbed both their hands in gratitude, injecting love into them.

Siobhan handed brimming glasses of wine to James and me and raised her own. "To absent friends."

Tears were threatening again. "To Katie." I was shocked by her thoughtfulness and surprise offer of becoming a surrogate mother for me.

"To Barry," toasted Siobhan, "may God forgive me for singeing his bollocks. May he be resting in plastic heaven."

"To Katie and Barry," we cheered tearfully.

Between Laura aiding my recovery and my best friends back by my side, it was time to make a decision about Glamma-Puss. As I thought about various options, I realised how strongly I felt about the place. I was proud of it. I didn't want to give it up, but with both Jackie and Jayde gone, I didn't know where to start.

The following day, me, Laura, James and Siobhan sat round the kitchen table brainstorming. And, as if Laura hadn't already taken on enough, she decided to take charge of getting the salon back up and running, too. That also meant taking charge of Siobhan and James, who were both eager to get involved, but taking charge of those two wasn't for the faint-hearted. Laura was amazing, holding court with the two of them, pointing out random facts and figures, and preaching about synergising. Neither Siobhan nor James questioned her or dared to refuse her suggestions.

Laura said the priority was to get money coming in again, as quickly as possible. I hadn't managed to pay my mortgage, let alone the rent on the salon or staff wages.

It didn't help that financially I was deep in the red, broke. I needed to raise cash, and fast.

With Laura excusing herself for a work call, James made his first suggestion. "Open a high-class brothel. Tara, you be the Madam - actually, on second thoughts, Laura should be the Madam. No one would dare mess with her. She could whip anyone into place with that tongue of hers. I can see her as a dominatrix, tying a man-slave to a bed and whipping his poor ass, standing on his chest with her stiletto heels. Scary thought." James shivered.

Siobhan slapped her thigh with excitement. "I've got it! You can still sell your story; it's not too late! Do a kiss-and-tell on that gobshite Travis?" She looked at me expectantly.

"I can't do that, I wouldn't lower myself. Plus, I'd have to relive the ordeal all over again. No, that's definitely not the answer."

"Don't be a wuss, he deserves it! The world needs to know what he did to you. Give him his comeuppance."

"But I don't want the world to know that he broke my heart and got a girl half my age pregnant."

"I'm not talkin' about that part." She leaned closer, whispering. "I'm talkin' about when Travis slipped his finger in your tea-towel holder."

James shrieked with laughter.

"*NO WAY!* Jesus," I said, heat rushing to my face. "I'd never be able to look anyone in the eye ever again."

In the end, I turned down most of their wackier ideas. I did, however, relent to Laura's more sensible idea to sell off some of my designer pieces - even that poisonous fur coat. Mum had done a fantastic invisible mend on the sleeve before she'd gone back to Dublin. I let Siobhan and James open me up a new eBay account and do the listings for me:

Seller: Gay-bay69

For sale

<u>Dolce & Gabbana Mink Fur Coat</u>

As new, apart from left sleeve that's been sewn back into place, (easily unpicked if you wish to cut other sleeve off - using this fine fur as a long, trendy gilet instead). Could also be used as a rug for shagging on in front of a cosy fire.

Has been nearly touched by high-profile celeb, who will remain anonymous for now.

All offers considered.

After that, Siobhan and James rummaged through my wardrobe, sourcing other pieces to sell. In no time they'd amassed an impressive pile of my once prized handbags, designer clothes and jewellery. Everything was slapped on eBay. I didn't care one bit.

Laura placed an advert online asking for experienced staff to replace Jayde and Jackie. When I thought about the pair of them, I felt so sad. I missed Jackie and I missed the Jayde I once knew. I still found it shocking that Jayde stole another woman's husband. I was even more dumfounded that Pete would leave someone as wonderful and wholesome as Jackie.

Poor Jackie. We'd gone through similar situations in recent times. Both our men going off with younger women. The thought sent shivers down my spine. Jackie had been with her husband since they were teenagers.

My mind drifted to thoughts of Travis and his young, pregnant girlfriend. Their baby was due soon. My mouth filled with acid. *Stop thinking like that, Tara,* I chided myself. *It's over! You're better off without him. You've got lots of good things to look forward to!*

When the dreaded day of the interviews came, I didn't feel positive at all. Apart from nature walks with Laura, I hadn't set foot outside, let alone inside Glamma-Puss. Two positions needed filling, one to run and manage the hairdressing, the other to manage the beauty side.

As I tried to work out what I should wear, I realised the days when I obsessed about what I looked like were long gone. I managed to get myself dressed in something other than a tracksuit to appease Laura, throwing on some skinny jeans, a dark blue sweater and some comfy old brown boots. I scraped what was left of my hair into a ponytail, applied a little mascara and brushed bronzer on my cheeks.

Arriving at the salon was like greeting a ghost. Memories flashed as I stood hesitating outside the entrance. Eventually, after waiting respectfully for a few moments, Laura took the keys out of my hand and opened the door. She held it wide and motioned that I should go in. Taking a deep breath, I stepped inside. Trembling from head to toe, my eyes flooding with tears. Laura held out her hand, encouraging me further in.

"It's okay. You're experiencing association," she said reassuringly. "It's to be expected."

Slowly letting go of her hand, I walked round, remembering flashes of laughter, scenes of sadness - and there, right there, was spot I'd allowed Travis to have his wicked way with me.

My eyes travelled over to the staffroom. I'd spent hours in there, on edge, staring at the walls waiting for him to make contact.

It felt like a lifetime ago.

The place was cold and lifeless. I ran my fingers across the workstations, the mirrors. They were dusty. It was as though someone had died in there.

James came bounding in, provisions in hand. "Lady Laura," he curtsied. "You okay, Tara, darling? You look like you've seen a ghost. Shall I pop the kettle on?"

James arriving made everything feel better. Within moments, the music was playing, the kettle was boiling and the heating was on. It felt quite … dare I say it, okay.

The roar of a motorbike interrupted my thoughts. James almost knocked me over as he dashed to the window to take a peek.

"Oh my!" He had his nose pressed up to the window, drooling. "How utterly, slutterly gorgeous!"

"Is she?" I asked nervously, hoping our potential new member of staff wasn't *that* beautiful.

"Not *her*. *Him*. I love, love, *love* a man in black skin-tight leathers. And look how he's parked to the left! I wouldn't mind getting my hands on his helmet." Without an once of shame, James began waving.

"James, please, come away from the window, you're making me jumpy," I begged.

Ignoring me, he raced to get to the door first.

"Well … hello, gorgeous man. Come in, come in," he waved. "Oh sorry - *and* you, dear - I didn't see you there. *Where are my manners?*"

"James, it's Camilla that's come for the interview, not her boyfriend," I said.

Camilla stepped through, removed her helmet and gave me a big smile. "Hello, you must be Tara?"

I nodded, shaking her hand.

"Sorry for the entrance. My car is in for a service so my brother brought me here. Please excuse my flat helmet hair." She fluffed her wheat-coloured hair back into place.

I instantly liked her.

"Ah, so, gorgeous leathered male is your *brother,* even better," said James, his eyes practically raping the poor man. "He must come in and wait for you, I absolutely insist. I'm more than happy to keep him company. You don't mind, do you, Tara?" Before I could say, yes, I do mind, James was outside pulling Camilla's brother in.

Little bastard! That's the last thing I want! Why does he always put me in awkward situations!

"Marvellous, magnificent. That's settled, then. In you pop, come along ..."

I helplessly looked round for Laura. She was already in deep conversation with Camilla.

I turned back to James and glared at him. He'd sat Camilla's brother on the chaise longue – and *James*, in his most provocative pose, was practically sat on top of him.

For the love of God!

At a loose end, I sat myself at reception – deliberately eavesdropping on James's conversation.

"My, my," said James, "what a beautiful big thing you have parked there, Mr ... er ..."

"Lewis." He looked up and smiled at me, seeming amused by the exchange. He looked strangely familiar. He turned and looked outside. "Yep, she's a Ducati."

"How does it feel to have something so *big* and

throbbing between your legs?" asked James. "Is it as wide as it looks? I'd love to take a ride on it. By the look of it, I might be a little sore afterwards, but I'm sure I could take it."

"James, can you take Lewis into the staffroom, please?" I was fuming! I didn't want him to blow my chance of getting decent staff because of his ridiculous flirting.

Lewis turned to me apologetically. "Sorry, I can see it's inconvenient for me to stay, I'll get out of your way. How long do you think Camilla will be? An hour, two?"

Great. Now I look like a total bitch!

I laughed it off as jovially as I could. "No, no, you're welcome to stay! Hahahah. I wasn't expecting ... I'm not sure how long the interview will take, so ... *ummm* ... you're welcome to wait." I didn't know what else to say. It had been a while since I'd spoken to anyone outside my close-knit group of family and friends. Why did the first person have to be an Adonis on a motorbike? I was too scared to even make eye contact with him! As hard as I tried, I still couldn't place him.

With Laura beckoning me over, I turned back to James. "Could you make everyone a hot drink, please? Laura and I are about to start the interview." I gave Lewis another smile and James a serious eyeball. "And behave yourself."

"Don't worry, Lewis is in safe hands with me." James sounded very sensible even though his facial expression said otherwise.

Laura and I sat down with Camilla. The interview lasted much longer than I wanted it to, but Laura being Laura and a complete jobsworth, she went through every detail of Camilla's CV then insisted that she cut and blow-dry my hair. I really didn't want her to. I had patches that I'd hacked myself. My hair looked like that of an unloved doll. Meanwhile, I could hear James laughing uproariously the staffroom. It was very distracting.

As Camilla fussed around with my hair, I half-heartedly asked her what she would advise if I were a client.

Laura interrupted. "I think she should have a short, classic style. No more of that porn-star bleached mass - but of course, Tara," she back-peddled, "it's completely up to you."

"Laura!" I hissed, desperately trying to smooth my voice. "I know I'm in the bloody menopause, but does my hair *have to look* like a siren stating it?"

Camilla searched my face. "You *can't* be in the menopause, you're way too young!"

Despite myself, I smiled. "Thank you. It's a rare genetic disorder to be going through it at such a young age."

Laura's eyes widened. "Tara, no, it's not a rare genetic disorder – it's part of life, *remember*? We *don't do* denial anymore, *do we*. We embrace it, *don't we?*"

I couldn't believe my feckin' sister! She was slowly nodding her head at me like I was an imbecile.

Camilla quickly changed the subject to prevent an impending assault. "I love short, sassy hairstyles. With a beautiful face like yours, you really could take it."

Good. Camilla sounded confident. "I'd like to hide a little of my face. That's all I ask. I don't care about anything else."

Laura shook her head. "No hiding anything."

Laura and Camilla began pulling out hair magazines as I sat and waited impatiently.

Camilla pointed to a picture. "How about this one? It's perfect for your face shape, short, edgy and youthful – we'll keep the fringe heavy so you can tuck it behind your ears, or it can fall sexily over one eye."

"That's fine." I nodded briefly, giving Laura a stern look.

"We could tone down the platinum-blonde with a gold toner, soften it." Camilla passed the magazine to Laura.

She nodded in agreement. "Oh yes, very Gwyneth Paltrow from *Sliding Doors*."

Just a few months ago, if anyone had come near my hair with a pair of scissors, even suggested changing the colour, I would've had a seizure. Now she could tint it black for all I cared. I wanted it over and done with. I didn't want to give Camilla a bad impression, so plastered on a fake smile.

Camilla was perfect. She had years of experience and just the right personality. Plus, she'd managed a salon earlier in her career, before she'd taken a year out to travel.

The whole interview and styling took an hour and a half. Poor Lewis must have been desperate to escape.

I entered the staffroom to let him know the interview was over. James clapped his hands, spun me round. "Wow! You look amazing!" he said. "Short hair is so sexy on you!"

I rubbed my hand over the back of my bare neck, glanced shyly at Lewis, looked away quickly. He was staring at me.

"Tara, this gentleman sitting before me likes stroking furry things, particularly snakes, *don't you,* Lewis?"

Lewis grabbed his motorcycle helmet, laughing. "Well, I guess you could put it like that."

"Can I have a little stroke of your helmet before you go please, Lewis?" wheedled James outrageously.

Lewis pretended to knock James over the head with the bike helmet. "I've been trying to keep you away from my helmet for the last ninety minutes, I'm not giving in now."

I showed him out to the salon, held out my hand to shake Camilla's.

"Thank you so much for coming in, Camilla," said Laura. "We'll let you know in due course if you've been a successful candidate for the position."

"Camilla - you've got the job. You can start Monday." I glared at Laura, then whispered, "It's *my* salon and I want her working here."

Laura pulled me to the side. "Tara, we haven't discussed this. We need to see other applicants. Don't make rash decisions."

"Well, I think this arrangement is just perfect," said James, never once taking his eyes off Lewis's crotch. "I can't think of anyone else I'd rather be working with."

"What do you think, Camilla? You up for working here?" I asked, ignoring James, who was fast becoming the annoying local queer pet.

She was beaming. "Wow, thank you so much. I really wasn't expecting to be offered a job so quickly. I'd love to take it!" She looked at Laura, then back to me. "I promise you won't regret hiring me. Monday would be perfect."

"Monday it is." I watched Lewis and Camilla high-five each other as they left the salon.

Laura stood beside me, didn't say a word - she didn't have to, her face was etched with disapproval.

I began pleading. "Please don't be angry with me. I need to start making my own decisions – you're not going to be around forever, and I'm grateful for everything you've done ... you've been the epitome of patience – a lifeline for me ..."

Much to my surprise, she gave me a hug. "You've made a good decision. She's perfect. Your hair looks the best I've ever seen it."

"Really?" I swept a hand over it. Hearing Laura compliment me like that had made my day.

While watching Lewis mount his motorbike, James dropped to his knees and fanned himself with a magazine. "My, my, you can't help but enjoy the view, can you? That man is sooo hot. Image of Bradley Cooper."

Oh, so that was why Lewis seemed familiar! I joined James at the window, watched him run a hand through his surfer-style hair, put his helmet on. There really was an uncanny resemblance. What a shame he was gay.

Laura checked her watch. "The next candidate for the beautician's post should be here any minute."

As I rubbed my tired eyes, Siobhan's voice ricocheted through the salon. She clicked her heels and saluted Laura. "Captain, mission accomplished. I've found the missin' Caucasian!"

Laura's face lit up.

There, hiding behind Siobhan, was Jackie! I raced forward and hugged her as hard as I could before bursting into floods of tears.

"Can I have my job back, please?" She had a huge tearful grin on her face.

"Yes ... yes! I couldn't think of anyone else on this planet I'd rather hire!"

That was it. The torrent of tears started again. While Laura sat at reception cancelling the remaining applicants, the rest of us snuggled in the staffroom and caught up with Jackie.

"I had to get away. Well, until those two idiots were out of the picture at least," she said.

"I warned you *all*," said James, *again*. "That trollop was good for nothing."

Siobhan jumped in. "In fairness to James, he'd always maintained there was something dark about her."

Jackie nodded, as did I. "They've buggered off to Marbella. It was meant to have been mine and Pete's dream to get a place out there. He's done it with *her* instead." She shrugged her shoulders. "Good riddance to the pair of them."

"I'm so sorry." I shook my head, exhaling a breath of deep sadness for Jackie.

The staffroom fell silent until James began fake gagging. We all stared at him. "I'm trying to un-visualise Jayde in a bikini! Oh no, I'm never going to be able un-see that image!" More gagging. "How was [gag] that [gag] *hoe* [gag] even allowed entry to Marbella!"

Siobhan jumped on the bandwagon. "I know a man who knows a man who knows that Judge Rinder fella off the TV; we'll get their scabby little arses up in court!"

"He'll regret it, Jackie," I said, rubbing her arm. "They always do. Pete will be pleading for forgiveness before you know it."

"Thanks, you lot," said Jackie once the commotion had died down. "I'd never take Pete back. I gave him the best years of my life, three children, and that's how he repays me? No, thank you. I'm ready for the next adventure in my life."

I looked at her in awe. She looked so confident. Then I looked closer. "For all the heartache you've been through, you look fantastic. Really fantastic." There was something different about her.

James was casually filing his nails. "Jackie's had a lot of fun with a wind tunnel, haven't you, darling?"

"I might've been to Turkey," she grinned. "Might've had one or two procedures." She lifted her hairline to show minimal scars. Smoothed down her jumper to reveal perky boobs. "Sheila added Botox, fillers and a new skin care range and that *idiot ex-husband of mine* has paid for it. By the time I've finished with his bank account those cheating toe-rags will be sleeping on the beach. He hasn't even bothered contacting his children. I think he deserves to suffer for a good while yet."

James and Siobhan were squealing. "Go, Jackie!"

My jaw had hit the floor. I had my flight to Turkey booked, was lying on the operating table, the surgeon ready with his scalpel to chase the years away. Could be just the pick-me-up I needed!

I began whispering urgently into Jackie's ear, asking for the surgeon's details, when Laura popped her head into the staffroom.

"Tara," she warned. "Don't even think about it!"

Laura must have feckin' bionic hearing!

I think I was ready for her to go back to Dublin.

Jackie winked at me. "Come on, Tara, let's get the kettle on, I want to hear all about what you've been up to."

Chapter 17

Three months later

James sighed dramatically. "*Ughh*. I'm so bored! Nothing exciting ever happens around here anymore. I've even run out of horrible things to say about Jayde. Tara, come on – the salon is quiet and you've been talking about getting set up on a dating website for ages now. So let's get to it."

"I haven't been saying that, *you've* been saying it!" I'd been desperately racking my brains for another topic that might divert James from his mantra about getting me back in the saddle. "And anyway, I'm not sure if I'm ready. Apart from anything else, I still can't understand how my love life ended up like this. You know, where my so-called *friends* think it's okay to publicly discuss me having to go on a poxy website to find romance!"

"*Come on,* it's free to sign up." James ignored my protests as always. "The best way to get over a man is to get under another one! Your lady-garden must need tending by now. There's only so much a Rampant Rabbit and some AA batteries can do. Trust me on that one."

I was running out of excuses. "Well – okay," I sighed. Anything to shut him up.

"Right. We're doing it! Marvellous. Camilla, can you woman the phone? Tara and I are off to get some tending sorted for a particular garden of hers."

James hustled me towards the staffroom. He began speed-typing information into the computer like a man possessed. I think he was racing through it before I could change my mind. In a matter of seconds, he had uploaded my best (Photoshopped) picture. I began to feel a rising sense of panic.

"Right, what are you looking for?"

"Hmmm. I don't know really."

"A pretty boy? Tall? Thin? Gorgeous hair? Cute bum? Young?" James looked at me, one eyebrow raised quizzically, his face full of expectation.

"This is *supposed* to be in aid of getting a man for *me*. Not a plaything for *you*."

"Just trying to help." He looked crestfallen, and for a second I felt bad for snapping at him. Then I realised it was just an act because within a nanosecond he was back, pounding away at the keyboard again.

"Okay," I said, "I'm seeking a knight in shining Armani, with washboard abs. Must be into sports – preferably rugby, with a northern accent, six foot plus. Weaklings need not apply. In fact, if you're not remotely like –"

James swung round in his chair and glared at me.

"*What?*" I asked even though I knew.

James reached over and slapped my wrist. "Travis was

weak and broke your heart. Watching you wither like that broke all our hearts. We're going to find you someone better!"

I was touched. "Okay, let's start again. I'd like someone ... kind and gentle," I began. *Maybe if I think about Travis and then just list everything he isn't ...* "Someone with a good, kind soul. Above all, *and this part is very important,* they must have excellent communication skills and be consistent."

"Shall we put in *no pecs, no sex*?" James tapped away, ignoring my more romantic aspirations. Sighing, my mind flashed back to Travis's perfectly sculpted body.

"Actually, no, there are more important things." I pushed the image of him out of my head.

James had a puzzled face. "But, you don't want to end up with a sack of lard, do you? Just imagine Jayde with testicles. Not pretty, is it?"

"Oh, I don't know, just put what you want. I'll leave it to you." With a client due in for a cut and blow-dry, I left the staffroom.

Hold on, I thought in alarm as I inadvertently began gnawing at my hand. *I must be out of my tiny mind leaving my dating destiny in James's hands.* My mind skittered around nervously. I had a terrible feeling that I'd just made a humongous mistake.

Hours passed and James was still on the dating website. To take my mind off what he could possibly be doing to me, I started to go through a pile of receipts. Takings were down. Although I felt determined to pull the business back up to where it once was, it wasn't easy: every time we got anywhere, we were knocked back by some unexpected cost or a sudden downturn in business.

My train of thought was abruptly interrupted by a squealing noise filling the salon.

"*OH-MY-GOD. OH-MY-GOD. OH-MY-GOD!*" James was squawking, running towards me on his tiptoes, his arms flapping wildly in the air.

"Tara! You have *ten* potential gardeners looking to get their fingers in your lady-garden. How fabulous, darling!"

I blushed in shock. "Really?"

"Really!" he screamed like a schoolgirl. "Come take a look!"

I raced to the staffroom with Jackie and Camilla close behind me. With everyone looking over my shoulder, I opened the first email.

No. 1:

Hey, I'm so into older women, fancy having a toy-boy? Give me your number and I'll send you a pic of my dick.

My heart sank. I deleted him before reading the rest of his email.

No. 2:

Hi, first, you are so hot! Definitely a solid 7!
I came across your profile and thought BOOM, there she is, so dropping you a message.

I know it's forward of me, but as my mum said, live for the moment! Can I take you for dinner in town next Thursday? I can come out between the hours of 6 &10 p.m. as I need mum to drop me off and pick me up before she goes to bingo.

Unless you're heading my way? I don't mind if you wanna pick me up? How about I let you choose where we go? Or, how about we all go to bingo together? Mum would love that.

I look forward to hearing from you!

Larry

No. 3:

Hello, Neville here, I'm 45. I'm an IT Support Manager from Norwich.

I'm recently single after my wife left me for the decorator I hired to do our kitchen. He did a great job, but I don't think I'll be recommending him. I'm looking to make new friends and start dating again, so I wondered if you'd like to come to mine for dinner one evening? Now the wife has gone and taken everything (apart from our four children) money is a little limited, but I'm sure you'll love the kids when you meet them. Honestly, I could probably do with a hand at bath time anyway! Sundays are homework days, but if I had a lady to help that would ease my life considerably. If you're free, let me know? Anyway, I'll stop jabbering. Hopefully you'll reply and we can arrange a day.

I have a people carrier so could pick you but I'll have to bring kids with me.

Look forward to hearing from you.

Neville

It wasn't a good start. After that disappointment, I scanned each email quickly. If it didn't catch my eye immediately, it was deleted. Amongst them, two stood out. One from a guy called Jack, the other from a guy called Luke. We all agreed they were the only two worth a response.

Finally alone in the staffroom, I began composing my reply emails:

Dear Jack,
I hope to find you well?

[Delete]

Hey Jack,
Thank you for looking at my profile.

[Delete]

FOR FUCK'S SAKE!!!!!! I don't know what the fuck to write! I just need a shag!

[Send]

"Shit! Shit! Shit!" Instead of hitting the delete button, I'd accidentally hit the send button.

Just as I was about to put my foot through the computer, I heard a pinging sound.

Your message cannot be sent as it contains explicit content.

"Oh, thank God!" Flopping back in my chair, I tried to calm my nerves, and eventually started typing with much more care. I sent a simple, carefree email to both Luke and Jack.

My replies seemed to do the trick. After a lot of back-and-forth, I'd loosely arranged dates with both of them. Although, I was quickly put off Luke, his replies taking far longer, his responses too short, too sharp compared to his rival, Jack. I was wary of another Travis-type scenario, but Luke's good looks kept him in the game (just).

Jack was the first of the pair to ask for my mobile number. The email landed while I was with a client, and James, being James, took charge and gave Jack my number without asking me. Within a few minutes, I'd received a text and a promise of a phone call later that day. I made out that I was cross with James because I worried things were moving faster than I could cope with, but I *was* secretly pleased. If left to my own devices, I'm sure I would've dithered so much that by the time I met up with one of these guys I'd have been ready for my care home.

To prepare myself for the call, I went back through Jack's profile (after all, I didn't want to confuse him with Luke and say something stupid). Jack's picture was that of a very handsome, distinguished man. He was a few years older than me – had a bit of a George Clooney look going on. His description said he was five foot eleven, brown eyes and hair - with an athletic build. He liked fine dining and motor racing. *Maybe I could do with someone a bit older and wiser*, I thought, as I nervously paced the floor waiting for him to call.

When the call came, I scuttled off, away from the giggles and screams of my excitable employees. Jack sounded very posh. In fact, his voice sounded like royalty

- incredibly arousing, but also slightly intimidating. I chuckled to myself - watching my P's and Q's, I put on my best telephone voice. After a chat, he asked if I'd like to see him that Sunday evening. I was still emotionally fragile - some days worse than others – but I'd made good progress; in fact sometimes an hour or two would pass before Travis, his girlfriend and baby even entered my head; so I agreed.

Even though the website had advised against it, I gave Jack my home address. He was old school, had insisted on picking me up. Quite frankly, I was flattered that a man was prepared to go out of his way for me. I intended to start as I meant to go on.

For the next few days leading up to the date, my nerves were shot to bits. I couldn't concentrate on anything. On more than one occasion, I keyed a text to cancel, but at the last moment, didn't.

I didn't sleep at all the night before, and on the evening of the date itself I was no good to anyone. I don't think I'd ever been so pleased to hear my front door open and familiar banter as my two best friends charged up the stairs.

"We're here!" they shouted.

"Come on, come on," I ushered. As they tumbled into the bedroom they were greeted by the sight of me standing in odd shoes, a skirt and a chunky jumper, worn in a crumpled lump over a fitted dress, my arms laden with other garments. "I don't know what to wear and Jack is picking me up in forty minutes!"

"Right, first thing to do is calm down," James ordered. "Now, let's see." His eyes flicked me up and down. "Let's start with some make-up."

"I've already done my make-up!" In a temper, I threw the garments I'd been holding to the floor and stamped on them.

"Darling, *I'm* wearing more make-up than you. Let's just touch it up a bit. Well, a lot."

"I don't want to go, I won't be ready," I sulked. "I'm going to cancel."

Siobhan poked her head out of my wardrobe. "You will in yer arse cancel!" she said. "You're goin'! I won't hear anything different! But then – if you really, *really* don't want to go, can I take your place? I could do with a good shag."

"Now, now, Siobhan," said James, sounding cross and shaking a large blusher brush at her. "That's *not* helping."

"Ah, sure, I'm only playin' with yous." Siobhan's head was back in the wardrobe. "Don't worry, woman," said her muffled voice. "I'll find you something better to wear."

James added another layer of mascara. "I'd go sexy and classy. A long dress with a vicious slit up the side to show off some leg, and put some cleavage on display."

Siobhan snorted. "Fook that, you big fairy, we're trying to get her some cock." She stood back to observe a pile of clothes she'd dug out. "I'm thinking a mini-skirt - *no* - just a thick belt, stockings, suspenders and some nipple tassels cos it's cold out, like."

James tisked. "Remember what she's been through? If she's going to go dressed like a hooker, she's going like a high-class one. Isn't that right, Tara?"

Siobhan leapt onto the bed, gyrating her hips like a wanton hussy, a dress held up against her. "You need to wear this one, it's feckin' gorgeous!"

The dress was one of my favourites: rich, lilac satin to the knee, adorned with sequins, low-cut back and front, and fitted. It was sexy yet elegant. However, it was the sort of dress that required a lot of confidence and attitude to wear.

Unsure, I slipped it on and smoothed it down. "James, what do you think?"

"Perfect!" Just as James was spinning me round my phone rang. He dived over and answered it. "Tara Ryan's phone, how may I help you? ... Oh, good evening, Jack, she's a little busy at the moment, can I take a message?" James spun me round again, pointing out what shoes to pair with the dress. "... Ah, you're early ... and you're *outside*? Okay, I'll let Tara know."

"*What!?* Jack is outside? *He's here?* Shit! He's fifteen minutes early!" I said in a panic.

"Feck this for a game of soldiers, I'm going out for a look!" said Siobhan, making a run for it.

"Not without me you're not!" said James, bolting after her. I watched them, shoulder-to-shoulder, battling it out at the bedroom door, each trying to get down the stairs first. It would've been funny if I wasn't so sick with nerves.

"*Umm ... guys?* Well, I guess I'm wearing this dress, then," I said to the now empty room.

After smoothing down my hair, I stepped into the heels that James had suggested, grabbed my pashmina and bag and nervously headed downstairs. I cautiously went over to the window and pulled the blinds apart. Horrified, I looked out to find Siobhan straddling the bonnet of Jack's car while James, in deep conversation with Jack, was performing his trademark *highly suggestive* hair flick.

Cursing, I snapped back from the window. *The feckers! What on earth is Jack going to think of me?*

James flung the front door open, looking flushed. "Oh. My. God! He's gorgeous! He's perfect! He's driving an Aston! And I *love* him already! I've tested the waters, and fortunately he's 100 per cent straight. Now, go on – get out there before Siobhan eats him alive."

A thought flashed - I wished it was Travis who was picking me up. But I didn't have long to dwell on it because in the next second the other half of the comedy duo crashed through the door.

Siobhan was gasping, pulling her skirt down. "*Jesus Christ!* Go get him, girl! He's ripe and ready for the picking, that one. But keep off his bonnet, it chafes like a bastard." Siobhan took one last look at me. "Come here to me – your best assets need a bit of plumping and pumping." With that, she grabbed my boobs and hoisted them. "Now, remember the golden rule? If you can't be good, be good *at*!"

With that the duo shoved me out the door.

The date with Jack was very pleasant. He was a perfect gentleman and had led a very interesting life. His good looks took my breath away, and I'll admit our goodnight kiss lingered longer than it should've done, although that was as far as it went. And as much as I had tried to silence it, there was one big problem: Jack wasn't Travis.

"Laura's right, maybe I do need to wait a while." I looked at James and Siobhan as I nursed a coffee in the salon the following morning. Bless them, they were trying to be on their best behaviour but I knew all they really wanted to know was if Jack and I had shagged.

"But, you're gonna see him again, right?" wheedled James. "He is exceptionally gorgeous. Drives an Aston ..."

I shrugged. "I don't know, he's going off to Germany for a month on business." I was put off by him travelling Europe so much. I'd prefer to date someone who lived and worked in the same country as me. "Maybe I should leave the dating game for a while?"

Siobhan scoffed. "What in God's name are you talkin' about, woman? You've got to throw your arse *deeper* into the dating game. Not literally, of course, although ... I rather like a bit of back garden tending meself."

"Siobhan! Can you *please* stop bringing that up!"

"You're just out of practice; you need to get back on the saddle. And fast!"

"A shag a day will keep the weeds at bay," said James, strutting around like a peacock.

"*A-shag-with-a-stud-and-a-roll-in-the-mud*," sang Siobhan in her lowest bass voice.

I groaned. "You two! I'm not some twenty-year-old sex-starved nymph!"

"But having a few good rounds of damn fine rodgering will help," said James.

"Yeah, just get in, sit down, hold on and shut up," said Siobhan. "It's easy, I do it all the time, *yeah-baby-yeah*." *Her* accent turned American as she playfully grabbed James's hips and began gyrating into his backside.

"You need some good old sexercising – at least daily," said James, greeting Siobhan's exaggerated thrusts with a crazy howl, slapping her thigh as she pretended to mount him from behind.

Out of nowhere, I had a hot flush, the heat rising up my body like a furnace. "Hot flushes are hardly attractive," I said, fanning myself.

James was horrified. "Women don't have hot flushes. They have *power surges!*"

I gave James a hug in between his thrusting. "What a lovely way to put it. That's so sweet."

Power surges. That would be my new mantra. Very empowering indeed.

"Anyway," he said, "there's nothing wrong with looking like a menopausal Barbie."

I have no idea how James and Siobhan persuaded me, but, fed up with their constant badgering, I agreed to try dates with five other men. They gave me a month to complete the challenge. We agreed that if it didn't work out I'd either try Jack again or give up dating for a while. If I agreed to their terms, they'd agree to stop hounding me. It wasn't a brilliant deal, but I could see it was the best I was going to get.

The only problem was, even though I had a few dates lined up, setting up five in one month was chaos. In the end I got so confused with all their names and interests that I had no alternative but to set up a spreadsheet.

TARA'S DATING SPREADSHEET

Name Jack
Age: 55
Height: 5'11"
Zinger/Minger: Zinger!
Job: Race Car consultant
Overall rating: 9/10
Notes: Kissed like a dream, gave me goosebumps. A very busy man and frequently out of the country on business.

Name Charlie
Age: 39
Height: 5’1” (ish)
Zinger/Minger: Minger
Job: Financial advisor
Overall rating: 10/10 for his manor/castle, (minus 10 for him)

Notes: Despite the incredible abode, my imagination couldn’t bypass the lack of height and far-from-symmetrical face. I have to stay true to myself.

Name Steve
Age: 36
Height: 5’11”
Zinger/Minger: Zinger
Job: Unknown
Overall rating: 2/10

Notes: Gorgeous (he ordered the most expensive things on the menu, champagne, lobster, etc.; I had salad). At the end of our date, he pushed the pay terminal to me. I thought he was joking and pushed it back to him. He pushed it back to me, the waiter got confused, so did I. I paid. Bastard!

Name Zak
Age: 42 (allegedly)
Height: 6’1” (allegedly)
Zinger/Minger: Zinger (based on profile photo)
Job: “Surgeon” (I doubt it)
Overall rating: (Unknown)

Notes: Cancelled date at last minute – I gave him a gentle warning, refusing to be mucked about. Now I’m even more desperate to meet this elusive gobshite.

Name Troy
Age: 38
Height: 6'0"
Zinger/Minger: Minger (in person)
Job: In between jobs.
Overall rating: -99/10
Notes: Spent the evening discussing his 2 ex-wives and 7 children. I yawned so much I got lockjaw.

Name Omar
Age: 30
Height: 6'2"
Zinger/Minger: Zinger
Job: Claimed to be a model but later disclosed he was in fact a porn star.
Overall rating: 1/10
Notes: Arrived tanned and waxed to within an inch of his life. Was buffed and wearing the tightest pair of skinny jeans (enhancing the lunchbox he was concealing in his pants). Date consisted of him detailing the "ins" and "outs" of his schedule - by that I mean the number of people he was sexually "in" and "out" of on a daily basis. Passed his number to James.

By the end of the month I hadn't made an ounce of progress. In fact, I felt more deflated. All that effort to get ready, with high expectations every time, only to end up more disillusioned than ever.

After dating my agreed five, I informed both James and Siobhan that I was giving internet dating a wide birth.

Even though Jack kept contact while away in Germany, and really was so sweet, I made the decision he wasn't right for me. The spark just wasn't there. Rightly or wrongly, the feelings I had for him didn't compare to the feelings I'd experienced with Travis. Why is it the ones you want don't want you, and the ones you want, *don't*? Life could be a cruel mistress at times. Just as I came off the phone ending our relationship, Camilla wandered into the staffroom and sat beside me.

"You know, my brother has really got the hots for you."

"That's sweet." I smiled and tried not to sound too dismissive.

Camilla pressed on. "Lewis has been dying to ask you out on a date, but I said it was too soon. I told him to wait ... you know, after the hurt you'd experienced."

My face crumpled. How was I going to approach this subject tactfully? "It's lovely of you to try and matchmake." My face flushed. "And your brother is gorgeous ... we've become great friends ... have so much fun and get on so well ... but I want a man who likes ... *women*. Just me in particular."

Camilla looked confused. "But you think he's cute, though, right?"

Oh God, where is this going? Did Lewis want to sample me to decide which sex he preferred? Maybe he was bisexual? Whichever way round it was, it wasn't for me. I was definitely a one-woman-one-man kind of girl.

"He's not stopped talking about you since the day you hitched a ride on the back of his bike. Remember when you left your bag in the bank? He said it was like having a little angel wrapped around him."

I cast my mind back. I'd had a bad day, my head up my arse. I'd come back to the salon bag-less and panicked, and as Camilla was cutting Lewis's hair at the time he whipped his cutting gown off, grabbed her helmet, took me by the hand, stuck me on the back of his bike and came to my rescue. The journey back to the bank was quite a thrill!

"It's very sweet Lewis said that, but I think he's more suited to, *umm* ... James?"

"Why James?" Camilla looked even more baffled.

I became hot and sweaty. She didn't know her brother was gay. I didn't feel comfortable outing Lewis. It wasn't my place.

"Tara, you don't think my brother bats for the other side, *do you*?" Her mouth curled into a wide smile, which was followed by a roar of laughter. "Lewis is as straight as they come. That's hilarious. Wait till I tell him!"

"But James said ... James told me Lewis likes stroking furry things – snakes!"

Camilla was doubled up with laughter. "That's because he's a vet!"

James was busy doing a set of nails. I walked over to the nail bar, put my hand on his shoulder and squeezed it hard. Really hard, digging my fingernails in. "When you've finished with your client, can I have a word?" Turning back to Camilla, I wanted the ground to swallow me up. "I'm really sorry, please don't tell Lewis I thought that."

"Okay, I won't tell him, but only on one condition. You have to go on a date with him!"

Chapter 18

[Text from Mum]

So I hear that Lewis is a dentist, can you ask him about my denture that keeps falling out? Well done anyway. So much better than a football player. Xx

[Text from Laura]

Have fun tomorrow. Just relax and be your lovely self x

[Text from James]

Please video him in action!

[Text from Siobhan]

Don't be having sex with him on the first date, wait till he asks for a threesome and call me, pronto!!

The night before my date with Lewis, I began to get cold feet.

I called Laura.

I explained that, as gorgeous as Lewis was (perfect even), I feared that as we were going on a first official date we might spoil the friendship we'd made. I was apprehensive that conversation could dry up and then things could get awkward at work with Camilla and me. *What if, what if, what if …*

Laura listened and listened some more, pausing to make soothing sounds, then blurted it out after I'd non-stop gabbled for half an hour.

"Stop over-analysing and dissecting it all and go and have some bloody fun!"

Well, that was easy for her to say!

Then she said it sounded like it suited me to stay wallowing in the loss of Travis. That I was comfortable not walking forward and wanted to stay stuck. That I was self-sabotaging. Touching a nerve, I ended the call. Bloody cheek!

She was far too good at her job for her own good, that one.

I heard the roar of Lewis's bike approaching. *Oh.* I'd rather hoped he'd be picking me up in a car. *Come on, have some fun!* I warned myself. I straightened my T-shirt, hoisted up my skinny jeans, checked my face in the hallway mirror and, putting on a fake smile, opened the door.

Lewis removed his helmet, smoothed down his tousled hair and pecked both my cheeks. "Morning, Tara." His spicy aftershave aroused my pheromones. I didn't want to be turned on and was annoyed at myself.

"Hey, Lewis," I said, breaking into a smile. *He looked so goddamn hot, standing there clad in full biker leathers.*

"Ready for our little adventure, then?" He handed me pair of leather trousers and a biker jacket.

I eyed the bike-wear suspiciously but tried to sound enthusiastic. "Where is it we're going?"

"It's a surprise."

Panicking, I involuntarily began blurting, "Look, Lewis, I don't know how to put this – but can we *just* be friends? It's just – I don't know if I'm ready yet."

His bright green eyes sparkled against his tanned face. "Ready for what, exactly?" he asked with a cheeky grin.

I felt my face flush. *Cocky sod, he knows exactly what I mean!*

"Ready for ... well ... I don't know," I floundered. *Actually, that's a good point: what is it exactly I'm not ready for?*

"Would you like to get ready, then? Personally, I think you'll have a great time. But you're under no obligation whatsoever to enjoy it. I won't even ask for one of your beautiful smiles. Scout's honour." He held up three gloved fingers.

"Okay ... But do I *really* have to put this lot on?" I cocked my nose at the pile of leather in my arms. It was a colossal weight. *God knows if they'll fit me. And doesn't leather put at least ten pounds on your arse?*

"I didn't realise we were going out on the bike. I thought we could ..." I stopped short, seeing the spark of disappointment in Lewis's face. *God, I'm such a miserable moany-hole.*

"I have a picnic ready, with champagne. It's in a cool-box on the bike, waiting to go," he said, having recovered. "It'll be fun."

Before I could change my mind, I excused myself and ran upstairs to change into the leathers, leaving Lewis standing in the hallway. Privately, I was chiding myself. I knew I needed to make more of an effort. I'm sure part of the problem was the leathers reminded me of my shameful experience with that bastard catsuit.

I shouted down: "Umm, how easy are these leathers to get on? I mean, do I need talc or something?"

He shouted up: "Not normally, no. If they don't fit I can return them for a different size. Are they too small?"

Even if they were too small, there was no way on this earth I'd admit it. I'd get them on if it killed me! Grim-faced, I slipped off my jeans and, one foot at a time, pulled the leather trousers on. Wobbling off balance, I fell into my bedside table, sending myself and a lamp crashing to the floor.

I could hear Lewis pounding up the stairs, calling my name. "Are you okay?"

"Yes, I'm fine. Please don't come in!" I shrieked. I was horrified at the thought of Lewis seeing me like this, the trousers half on, my arse hanging out. But too late! There he was, standing in the doorway of my bedroom. I grabbed the leathers and held them tight against me, my hand held out like a policewoman in a vain bid to stop him in his tracks.

He shielded his eyes from my modesty. "Sorry – are you alright? You need a hand?"

Red-faced, I pulled the leathers on and heaved myself up from the floor, then, laughing, playfully shooed Lewis back downstairs.

Halfway down he shouted, "By the way, purple is most definitely your colour."

I laughed out loud. Slammed the door closed. *Bloody cheek. My underwear is pink.*

Underwear ... Ann Summers ... Bingo! I knew I'd seen Lewis before: he was the guy in the queue trying to buy underwear the day I'd got taken hostage in that gobbling catsuit! *What a small world! I wonder who he was buying underwear for?* Then I felt jealous.

Within moments of composing myself, we were out of the house and roaring up my street on Lewis's motorbike.

As I moulded my body around his and rested my helmet on his back, I realised I felt totally relaxed around this man. And even though I was clinging onto to him on for dear life, I felt safe.

Before I knew it, we were thundering out of the city and swishing around corners on country roads. I closed my eyes tight and screamed at the adrenaline-fuelled, heady mixture of delight and fear rolled into one. After a while, Lewis turned off the road into a picturesque green field laden with bright red poppies.

"Phew!" I exhaled as I removed my helmet. After that incredible journey, I couldn't help but smile. Then I had a proper look at the breathtaking setting and smiled even more. I shook my head, my heart a long way from its normal rhythm. Cobwebs gone and speechless, I clutched my chest.

Lewis was beaming. "It's so good to see you smiling."

Blushing, I caressed the warm leather seat of the gleaming motorbike. "I've got to get me one of these – what a rush!"

As Lewis laid food and drink out on a picnic rug, I suddenly felt weepy (not in an I'm-going-to kill-myself kind of weepy, but more like today-I'm-glad-to-be-alive weepy).

"You okay?" Lewis handed me a glass of champagne.

I nodded, breathing in the Surrey air, forcing a smile to make up for my soppiness. "I'm good. It's stunning here. I get emotional when I see things of beauty, sorry."

Lewis politely ignored my moment of weakness and held out a bottle of water for himself.

"You're not drinking champagne with me?"

Smiling he knelt down and picked a poppy from the field. "I don't drink and drive, especially when I'm carrying such precious cargo."

I chuckled. "Well, you certainly score points for that corny line."

We both laughed.

"I have to be honest, I *was* going to cancel our date, but now I'm so glad I didn't."

Lewis grinned. "I'm glad you didn't, too." He placed the poppy in the side of my hair, pecked my nose and began quoting: "*'Just living is not enough ... one must have sunshine, freedom, and a little flower.'* Hans Christian Andersen."

"Wow, that's beautiful. True and poignant." Impressed, I knocked back my bubbly.

Desperate to impress Lewis with an equally mind-blowing quote of my own, I stood, gormlessly, waiting for my brain to engage, looking up to the cloudless-sky for inspiration. *Nope. Nothing up there. Bugger. Come on brain, engage, engage.*

I linked my hands behind my back (just as I had seen Laura do so often) and began pacing up and down in deep thought.

I tapped my head with the empty champagne glass. "Sorry, it takes time to kick-start this thing. It's not that I'm not clever," I added, recalling one of Laura's sessions with me, "I'm more of creative person than an academic."

Lewis rubbed my arm tenderly. "Relax, please, this isn't a competition."

I waved a finger in the air, indicating I had an impending brain wave. "*Wait – I've got it!*" I squealed, causing Lewis to startle. *Be prepared to be impressed*, I thought, thanking God for sending me this Eureka moment.

"*'A woman carries her clothes, but it's the shoe that carries the woman.'* Christian Louboutin."

Right back at you! I thought smugly.

"Get you. See, that's what I love - *umm - like* about you, Tara. You're smart, cute and so innocent. You're wonderful."

Lewis was beaming, not in a Christ-she's-dim sort of way, but rather with a look of genuine affection. Laura may be a total lickarse, I thought, but she'd certainly done a fine job at getting my grey matter to re-engage.

I smiled bashfully, fingering the delicate flower in my hair, almost swooning.

We sat down on the blanket, our legs just touching. I felt strangely shy. "There's not another soul around for miles. Weird, for a city girl like me. Mind you, I could get used to it." A flock of birds flew overhead. "You can hear nature. The air smells cleaner. The sky looks bluer." I breathed in every drop of the freedom I felt.

Lewis nodded.

I pointed off into the distance. "Have you seen that old dilapidated building over there? It's huge! And with all this quiet land around it, could you think of a more idyllic setting for a home?"

Lewis casually chugged on his water. "You like it?"

"Who wouldn't?" I said.

"My grandparents left it to me - well, me and Camilla. She preferred to live in London, so I bought her out. We share a flat for now, more for company than anything; after our parents died we stuck together like glue."

Camilla had told me about their parents dying. It was heart-breaking.

"When I'm ready, I'll restore the place to a home – use the outbuildings to run my veterinary practice."

I swung round to face him. "Wait, you *own* all of this?" I needed to check whether he was just teasing me or not. Scanning his face, I could tell he wasn't. I was gob-smacked. "So you own those *huge* trees over there?" I pointed off into the distance, miles away. I swivelled my head in the opposite direction. "And those fields over there?"

"Sure do."

My glass slipped out of my hand. Suddenly, I eyed Lewis from a whole different viewpoint. He was indeed a man to be taken seriously, *very* seriously. *I could end up being a vet's wife*, I thought. *I wonder if he has letters after his name? Or before his name? Is he classed as a doctor? He must be, he's a vet! But would I be able to use those letters or his title with my name? Would that then make me ...*

"Lewis," I began, as casually as possible, "your surname - is it the same as Camilla's?"

"We're both Copelands, why do you ask?" He casually lay back, arms tucked behind his head, his T-shirt rising. I couldn't help but stare at his tanned midriff.

"Nothing ... just wondering."

Hmmm. Mrs Tara Copeland. Mrs Doctor Tara

Copeland. Surely if we were to marry ... I would get the doctor title?

Oh stop it! Here I go again. I mean, why bother staying grounded when I can manufacture yet another crazy dream in my mind. That's the old Tara, raising her stupid ugly head. Clearly, my grey matter was shrinking again.

I must not think this way. I must not become obsessive. I must not be delusional. I must not become destructive. Good, well done, I thought triumphantly. *I'm at least recognising the signs of unhealthy behaviour. It's all about the Zen.* I began humming to myself.

"I was wrong this morning," said Lewis, interrupting my thoughts. "I shouldn't have come upstairs whilst you were changing. I don't know what came over me; I panicked because I thought you'd hurt yourself. Commenting on your underwear was wrong. I don't want you to think I'm –"

"It's okay." I blushed. I lay down beside him, us both staring up at the blue sky.

"No. I was out of order. I'm out of practice. It's been a while since ... well, I've taken a lady out."

"You're forgiven – but don't do it again," I warned, wagging my finger playfully. Although, I didn't mean a word of it: I desperately wanted him to do that again.

"Time is most definitely a healer. I never thought I'd get over my ex-fiancée." He shuffled closer to me.

I felt another stab of jealousy come out of nowhere. "Fiancée? I didn't know you'd been engaged." Ann Summers - he must have been there that day buying *her* underwear!

Lewis shrugged his shoulders. "I thought she was *the one*, couldn't have been more wrong, though."

The mere thought of Travis and *her*, together with their baby, left a bitter taste in my mouth.

Lewis sat up, twiddled a blade of grass, threw it. He picked another, so I sat up, rubbed his lovely strong back. His dark-blond sun-kissed hair hung sexily over the collar of his leather jacket. I had to stop myself from stroking it. I picked up his delicious doctor hand and stroked that instead. I'd get to his hair later. Then I had a thought: *Maybe, just maybe,* the *Big Man Upstairs has been trying to pair Lewis and me together - even back then, in Ann Summers ...*

"I caught her in bed with my so-called best buddy."

I gasped, clutching his hand tighter. "That's awful! Losing your fiancée *and* your best friend."

He nodded. "It was tough."

"How did you get yourself through that?" I pictured myself as a gibbering mess.

His face broke out in a grin. "I got myself a new girl. The quickest way to get over someone is to get on top of someone else."

"*Oh really!?*" Fuming, I tossed his disgusting hand away and felt my emotional balance sway low. *Bastard!* I huffed under my breath, my stomach clenching in disappointment. *Men! They're all the same! And to think, just a few minutes ago I wanted to be his wife! No siree, not-in-a-million - he's a gobshite, just like all the rest.* And, quite frankly, I didn't fancy putting my hand up a horse's arse anyway, no matter how much the vets gloves could stretch!

Sensing my repulsion, Lewis quickly pointed at his motorbike. "Her name is Thumper and she's over there."

He picked my hand back up and kissed it. *And so he*

should, for scaring me like that, I thought, as relief washed over me.

"Perhaps there's no such thing as *the one*, perhaps it's all just wishful thinking." I was suddenly feeling philosophical and hoped Lewis would argue the point with me.

He remained silent. All I could hear was him taking in a deep breath as he squeezed my hand. I exhaled sharply and then dared to ask the next question.

"Do you still think about her?"

"Who?" With a sexy grin, he slid his thumb playfully round the palm of my hand.

Okay, I get it. Keep calm. He is saying his ex is history. Maybe Lewis and I have more in common than I realised.

He studied my face intently. "That was then, and this is now. And I'm rather enjoying the now." Smiling, he topped up my glass.

I fluttered my lashes and closed my eyes and pouted, giving off signals that it was okay for Lewis to kiss me.

He didn't.

Instead, he lay back on the blanket and stretched his arms up behind his head again. Dizzy from the champagne and disappointed that my signal had failed, I clumsily lay back beside him.

"Has Camilla told you what happened to me?" I was feeling emboldened by the alcohol. I was positive that James would have filled her in on every tiny, dreadful detail.

But before Lewis could answer, I blurted out the worst: "I can't have children. I left it too late." Choking on my words, my vision blurring, I gulped back the emotion.

We both turned our heads to meet, our lips inches away from each other's.

"My animals are my babies. That's plenty for me."

Before I realised what I was doing, I downed the remains of my glass, dived on top of Lewis and began kissing him. Instantly, the two of us were locked into a passionate embrace, tearing and fumbling at each other's zips and layers of thick leather that separated our quivering flesh. Around and around the grass we rolled, ripping off clothing and gasping for each other.

One moment Lewis was on top of me, then I was on top of him, fumbling and biting each other wildly as our tongues danced in each other's mouths. God, I wanted him so badly.

He breathed hoarsely in my ear. "This is all I've wanted to do since the day I met you, hold you in my arms and keep you safe."

His eyes were searching my face for clues, or perhaps permission to take me. As I nodded, he swooped in again, kissing me recklessly. Everything inside me stirred, awakening eager, wild lust. It felt so good to be with him. All the crap that life had chucked at us both seemed to be falling away.

I clambered on top of him and rocked my semi-naked body gently against his.

"Tara," he moaned, staring intently at me. "You sure you want to do this?"

I nodded. "*Shhh.*" Smiling, I placed my fingers over his full lips, feeling his strapping body beneath mine.

"You're perfect," whispered Lewis.

I gathered my hip-rocking pace and eased his throbbing love-muscle into me slowly, arching back into a yielding curve.

Lewis was groaning, his hands gliding softly down my

back, his expression desperate. "It's been a while ... I need to hold on."

I grasped his hands in mine, raised them up. "Let go, Lewis, let go." I stared at his hair, splayed around him like a halo. *Clearly, another message from the Big Man himself.*

"I want you to have pleasure first," he groaned hoarsely, desperately trying to hold on.

Not on your life, I thought to myself, holding it back. There's no way. *Not after my last nappy-requiring orgasm. No, mine can wait till we're both in the bedroom. And anyway, it would make me far too emotional.* I wasn't quite ready to go there, not yet.

Lewis was cursing, his voice husky. "I can't hold on, please let's do this together."

"I'm with you, I'm with you," I yelled, totally lost in him. And I was - maybe not in body, but certainly in mind. I cupped his stubbly square jaw, encouraging him as his body trembled and shook, draining itself into mine.

As we lay there absorbing the aftershocks, I couldn't help but think about how I felt. I was happy, yes, and satisfied, absolutely. *Yay! My days of waiting for the washing machine to vibrate on that particular cycle are over. Well, they will be later, when I get in his bedroom.* But there was something else: I felt calm, relaxed and safe. I knew instinctively this man would never hurt me.

Pulling my T-shirt on, I poured myself another glass of bubbly to celebrate.

Lewis cleared his throat, tucked himself tight beside me. "I know this is kind of sudden and I don't want to frighten you off ..."

"What?" I raised my chin to the sun, placing my hand on his stomach.

"Look, I'm just going say it. You don't have to say anything, but I've been busting a gut to say something all afternoon."

My heart jumped. I froze, everything flashing through my head like a whirlwind. *Please don't tell me that you're bisexual, or worse that you do want babies and this was all a big mistake. Or that you're going off for a year travelling on some stupid spiritual fecking journey to go find yourself. Or,* I thought, my heart pounding even harder, *he loves me!*

Panicked, I dismissed the glass and reached for the bottle and poured it down my throat.

"Tara," said Lewis, clearing his throat again.

"Yes," I hummed to myself, willing him to say whatever it was, and quickly. The latter of my thoughts would be perfect (*love*), but knowing my luck it would be the first of my thoughts (bi-sexual). Time stood still as I held my breath.

His eyes met mine. "I ... *umm* ... love your hair short."

"*What?*" I spat in horror. "You were building up to say *that?*" I felt like my lungs had been punctured. I mean, *really?* All that build-up for that crock of shite!

"Tara ..."

Doing stuff like that could give a woman of my age, with my *rare genetic disorder*, a stroke or heart attack. *What a custard-launcher!* I wouldn't look at him - why the feck should I?

"Tara ... "

"What?!" I huffed. Sulking and refusing to make eye contact, I stumbled around, pulling my leathers back on.

"I want you to remember this moment. This is *our* special place."

Not sure what's so special about it now. I stopped what I was doing, and, all contrary, folded my arms in protest.

He took my hand. "That didn't come out like I'd planned. I was joking earlier, about your hair, I mean ... I love your hair." He grunted, looked frustrated. Took a deep breath. "What I mean is, I've fallen in love with you." His face went a little pink.

"You have?" Well, that statement certainly grabbed my drunken attention!

Lewis took me in his arms. "Hearing about you going off on those dates nearly killed me. Camilla wouldn't allow me to ask you out, said you weren't ready."

"Your sister was right, I wasn't ready. But I am now," I smiled, and felt the warmth of his love exploding in my mouth as he kissed me again.

"Tell me you love me again," I begged. "Tell me *again!*"

Lewis scooped me up in his arms and swung me round. "I love you, Tara Ryan!"

And at that moment, I think I felt the stirrings of love awakening for him.

Joining Lewis, I stripped myself butt naked and like a crazy pair of kids, we held hands and ran with wild abandon through the fields and poppies, then made passionate love all over again. Only this time I didn't hold back - well, I'm sure the poppies needed a good watering anyway.

I'm not sure how long we lay there after that. It was certainly getting dark by the time we began to think about moving. I was starting to feel cold.

"I love this place," I said, breaking the silence.

"It's amazing, isn't it? I come here when I need to think - or sometimes when I *don't* want to think. I love the journey over on Thumper; I feel as though I can go as far as

I want, as fast as I want. The rush can be surreal, sliding around switchback corners with thousand-foot drops, my palms sweating, fingers clenching, muscles tightening."

I could see that Lewis had drifted off. I loved the faraway look in his eyes. I loved his free spirit and sense of adventure.

"Sorry, am I boring you?" He snapped back to the here and now.

I started pulling my leathers on. "Not at all."

Lewis grinned. "Today was special, wasn't it?"

"I've had the best day ever."

It was like a fairy tale. *Girl meets hot boy of her dreams and they live happily ever after.* Sorted.

As we walked back to the motorbike, I felt like I was walking on air. Finally, *finally,* it had all come good. I had met someone who genuinely liked me for me - after all, Lewis had seen me at my worst (well, nearly at my worst) - no fake tan, no hair extensions, no flashy clothing - and yet he loved me.

I watched him gathering up the last bits from our picnic and couldn't help grinning. *You soppy loon,* I chided myself. I picked up my bag ready to put it on the back of the bike when I heard a text come through. It was probably James or Siobhan wanting the *dirty details.*

[Text from Unrecognised]

Hi Tara, hope you're good. Turns out the baby isn't mine. I still think about you every day. I need to make things up to you. Please will you meet me?

Travis x ...

... Find out what Tara does next ...

Fur Coat Big Knickers is available now in paperback and ebook formats.

Fur Coat BIG Knickers

THERE ARE TWO SIDES TO EVERY STORY ...

OMG — Tara Ryan, hair and beauty salon owner and walking calamity, has finally got her shite together; she's bagged Mr. Right (a.k.a. Lewis) and is well on her way to Happily Ever After. However, given her track record, disaster is long overdue, and a demon from her past reappears.

The disturbingly addictive Travis Coleman has returned, with a scandalous explanation behind his brutal dumping of Tara the previous year. Consequently, her new fairytale life begins to unravel, exposing unhealed wounds and reigniting toxic temptations.

Battling to keep the lid on Pandora's box, Tara embarks on a daring mission, putting her potentially perfect life with Lewis on the line ...

Keep up to date with C. B. Martin and see what else our Tara has been up to. Visit:

facebook.com/FurCoatNoKnickersTheBook

Reviews save lives!

(Well, they could stop me from starving to death.)

If you enjoyed this book, I'd be delighted if you left your review on Amazon and Goodreads. I read all reviews there, the good, the bad and the downright ugly.

(Equally, if you didn't enjoy this book, then, "If you ain't got nothing nice to say ...")

Thanks again for your support – it really means the world to me.

Sending love your way,
Caroline
xXx

Printed in Great Britain
by Amazon

58545703R00195